Pokémon™ Journeys

1

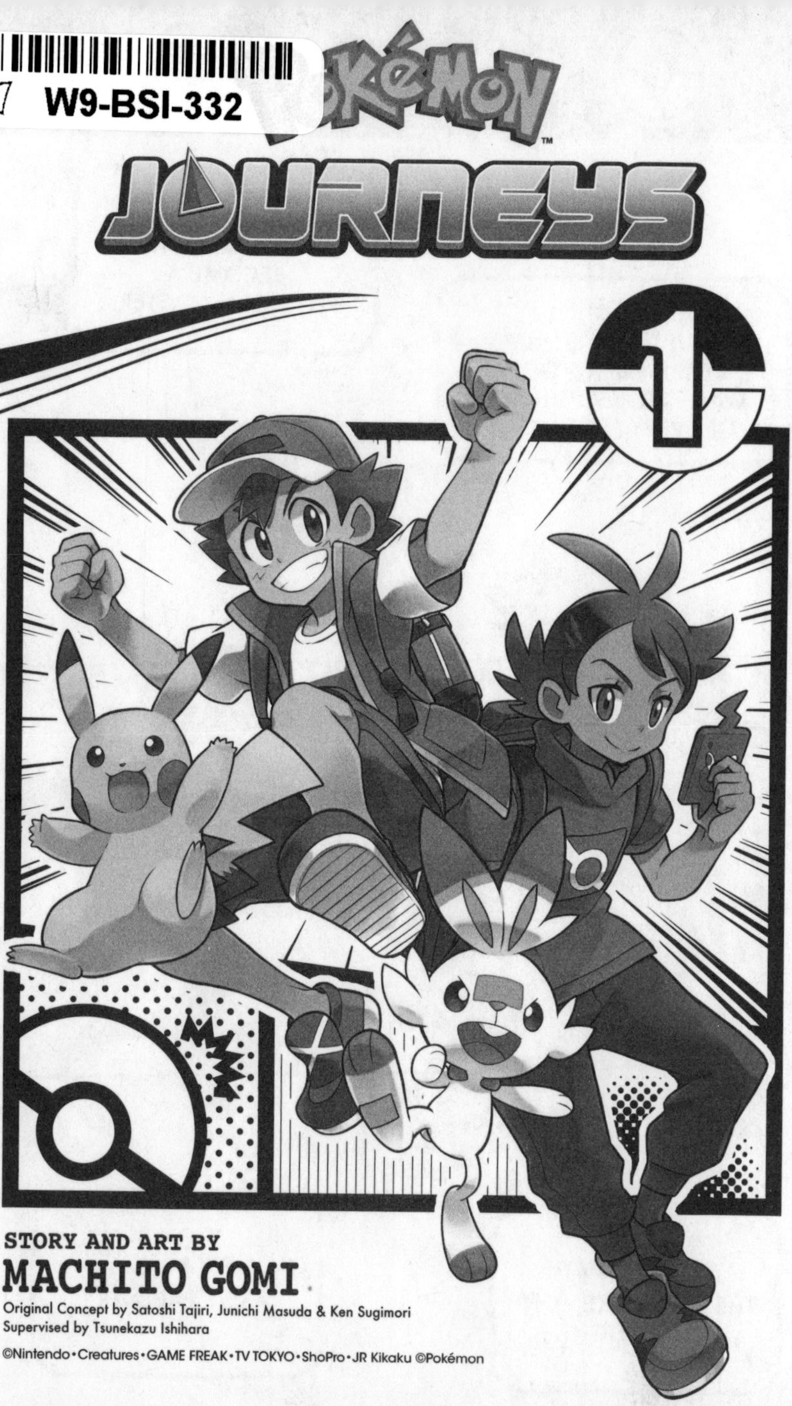

STORY AND ART BY

MACHITO GOMI

Original Concept by Satoshi Tajiri, Junichi Masuda & Ken Sugimori
Supervised by Tsunekazu Ishihara

Characters

ASH
ASH WANTS TO BECOME A POKÉMON MASTER!

GOH
ASH'S TRAVELING COMPANION. GOH WANTS TO CATCH ONE OF EVERY POKÉMON!

SCORBUNNY
THE FIRST POKÉMON GOH CAUGHT.

PIKACHU
ASH'S PARTNER.

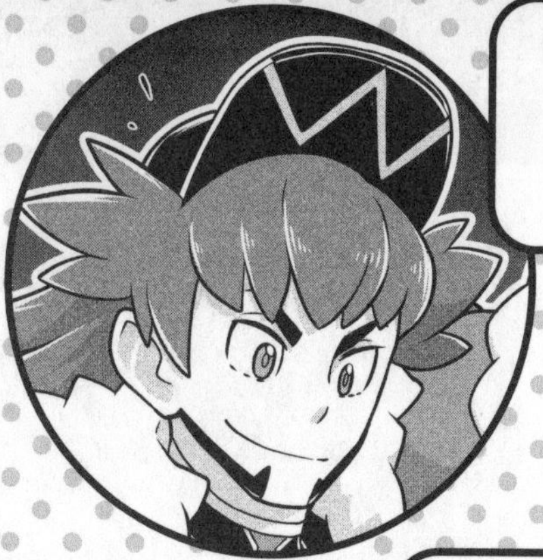

LEON

THE CHAMPION OF THE GALAR REGION'S POKÉMON LEAGUE.

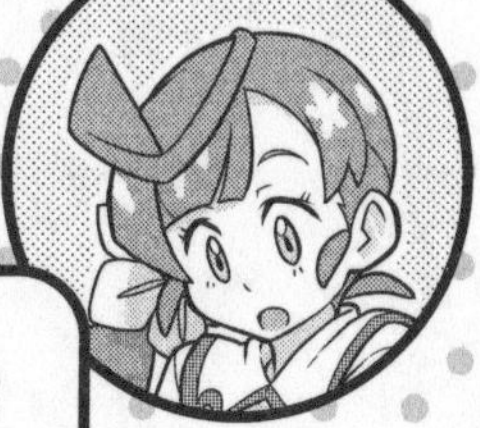

CHLOE

THE DAUGHTER OF PROFESSOR CERISE, AND ALSO GOH'S CHILDHOOD FRIEND.

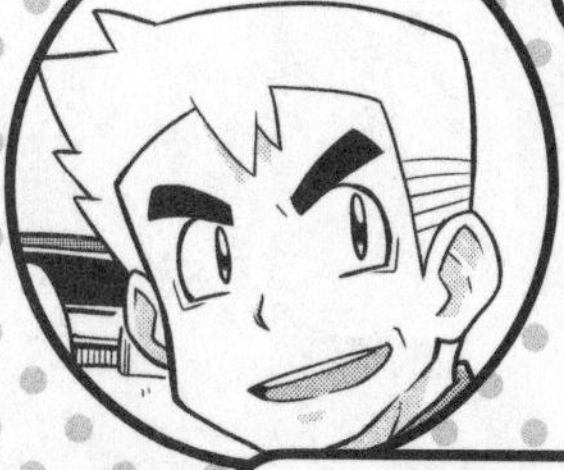

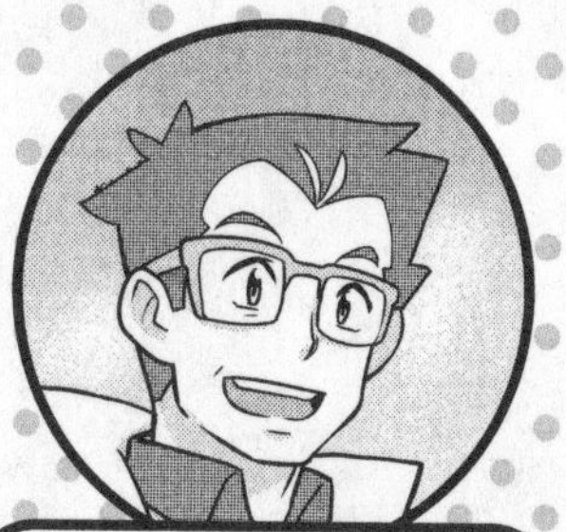

PROFESSOR OAK

A POKÉMON RESEARCHER FROM PALLET TOWN.

PROFESSOR CERISE

PROFESSOR OAK'S FORMER PUPIL WHO LIVES IN VERMILION CITY.

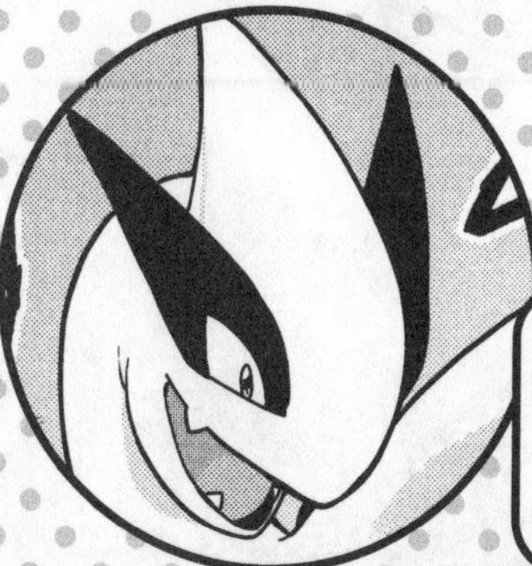

LUGIA

A LEGENDARY POKÉMON.

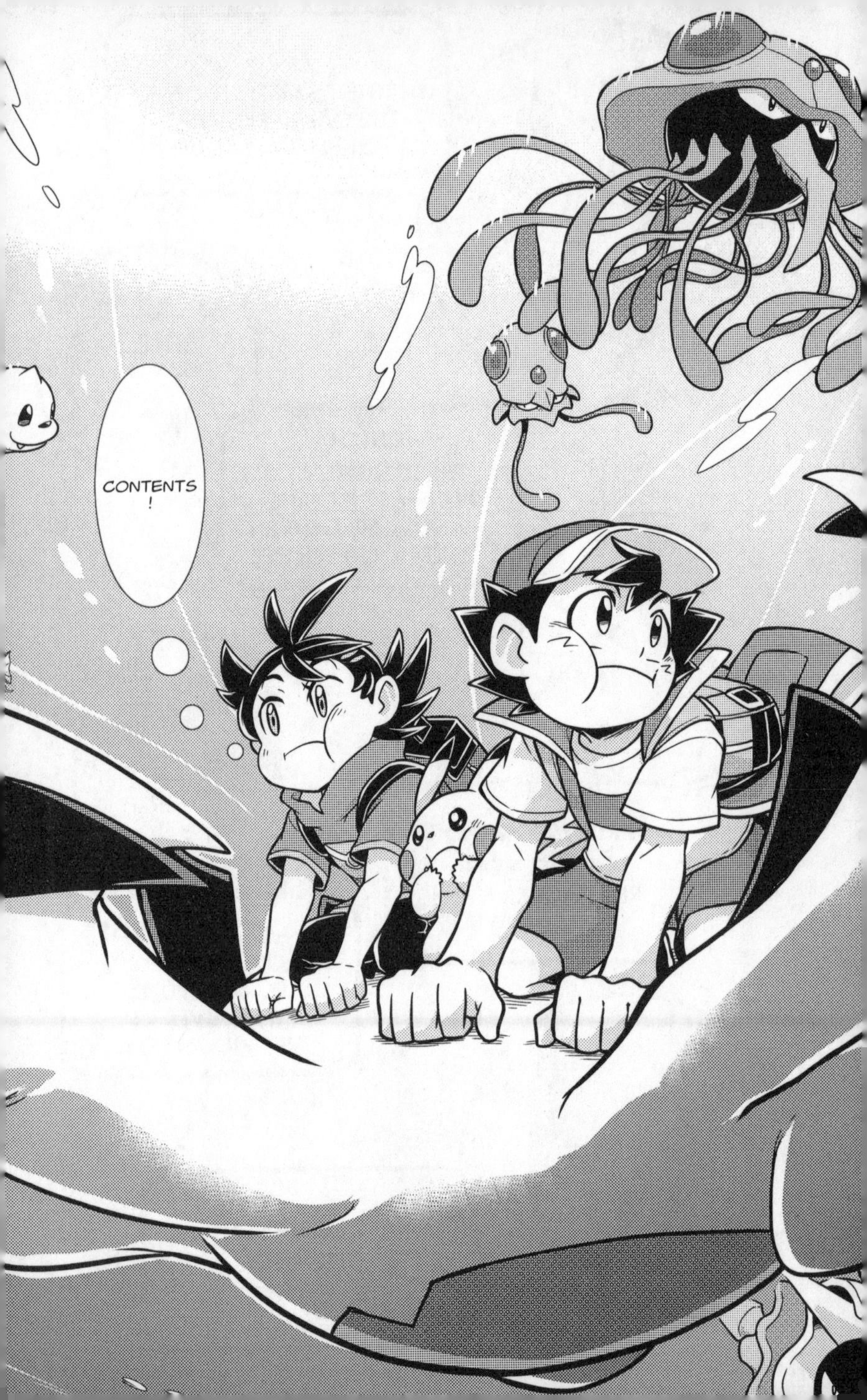
CONTENTS
!

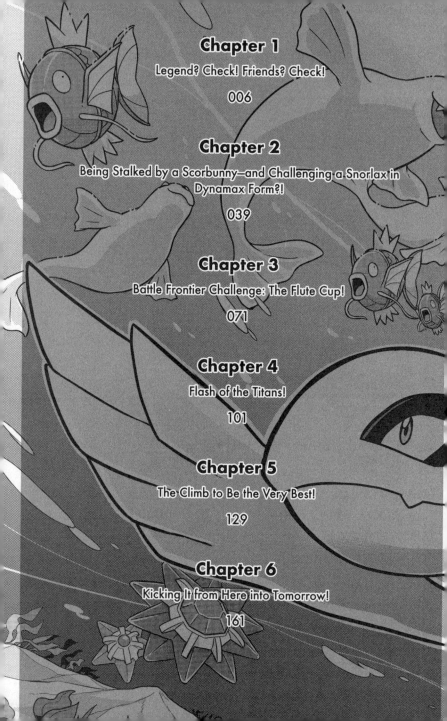

Chapter 1
Legend? Check! Friends? Check!

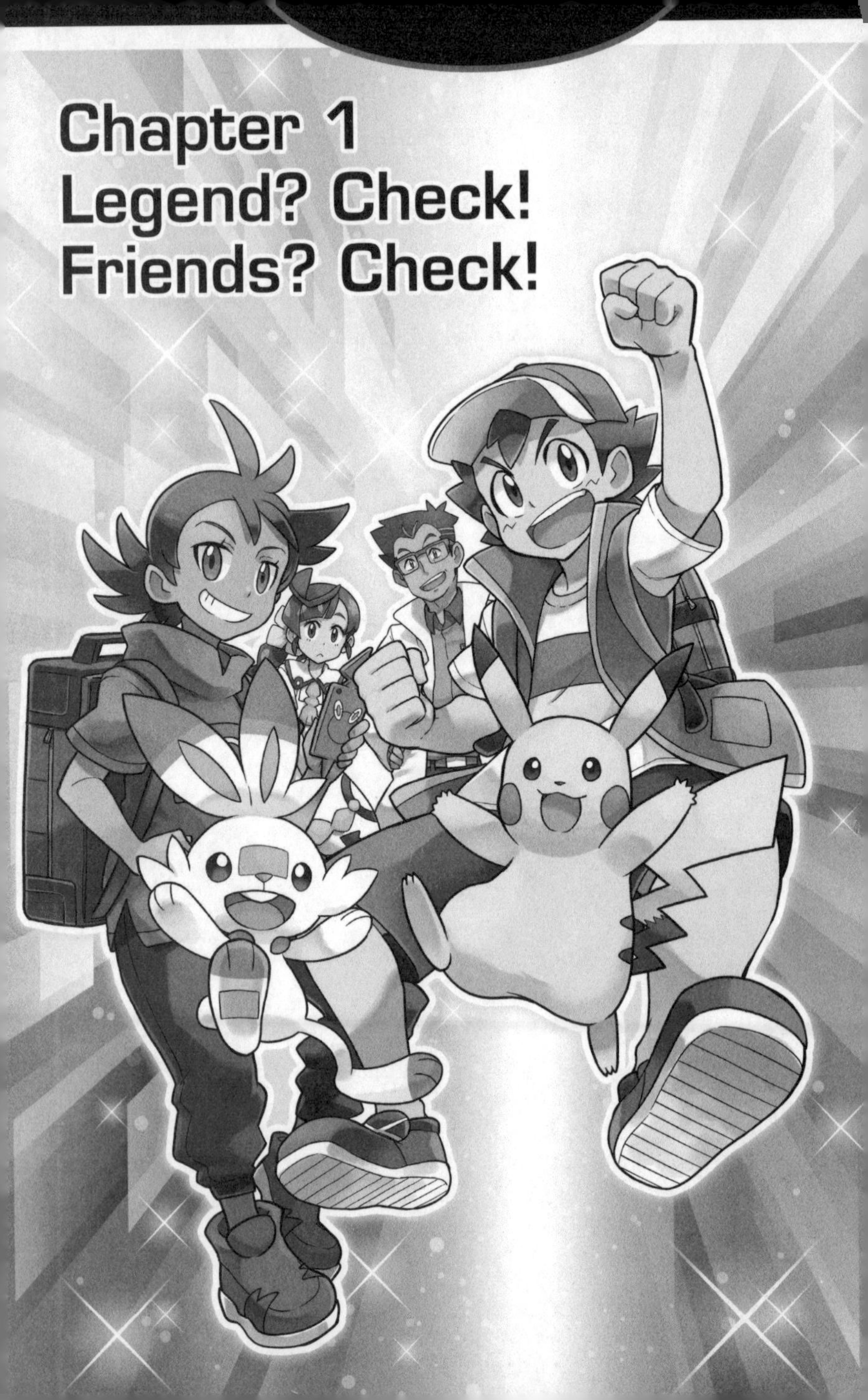

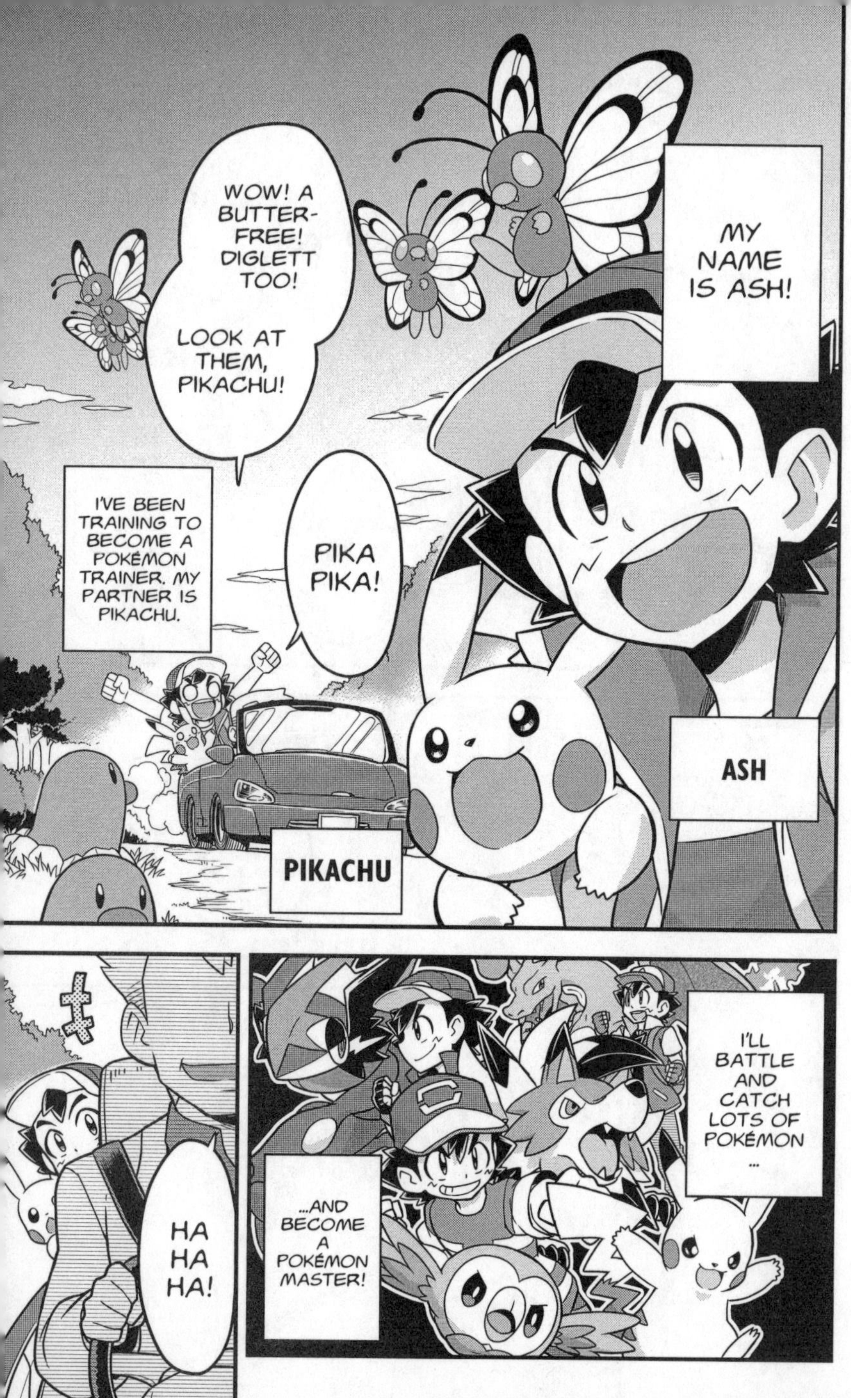

MY NAME IS ASH!
WOW! A BUTTER-FREE! DIGLETT TOO!
LOOK AT THEM, PIKACHU!
PIKA PIKA!
I'VE BEEN TRAINING TO BECOME A POKÉMON TRAINER. MY PARTNER IS PIKACHU.
ASH
PIKACHU
I'LL BATTLE AND CATCH LOTS OF POKÉMON ...
...AND BECOME A POKÉMON MASTER!
HA HA HA!

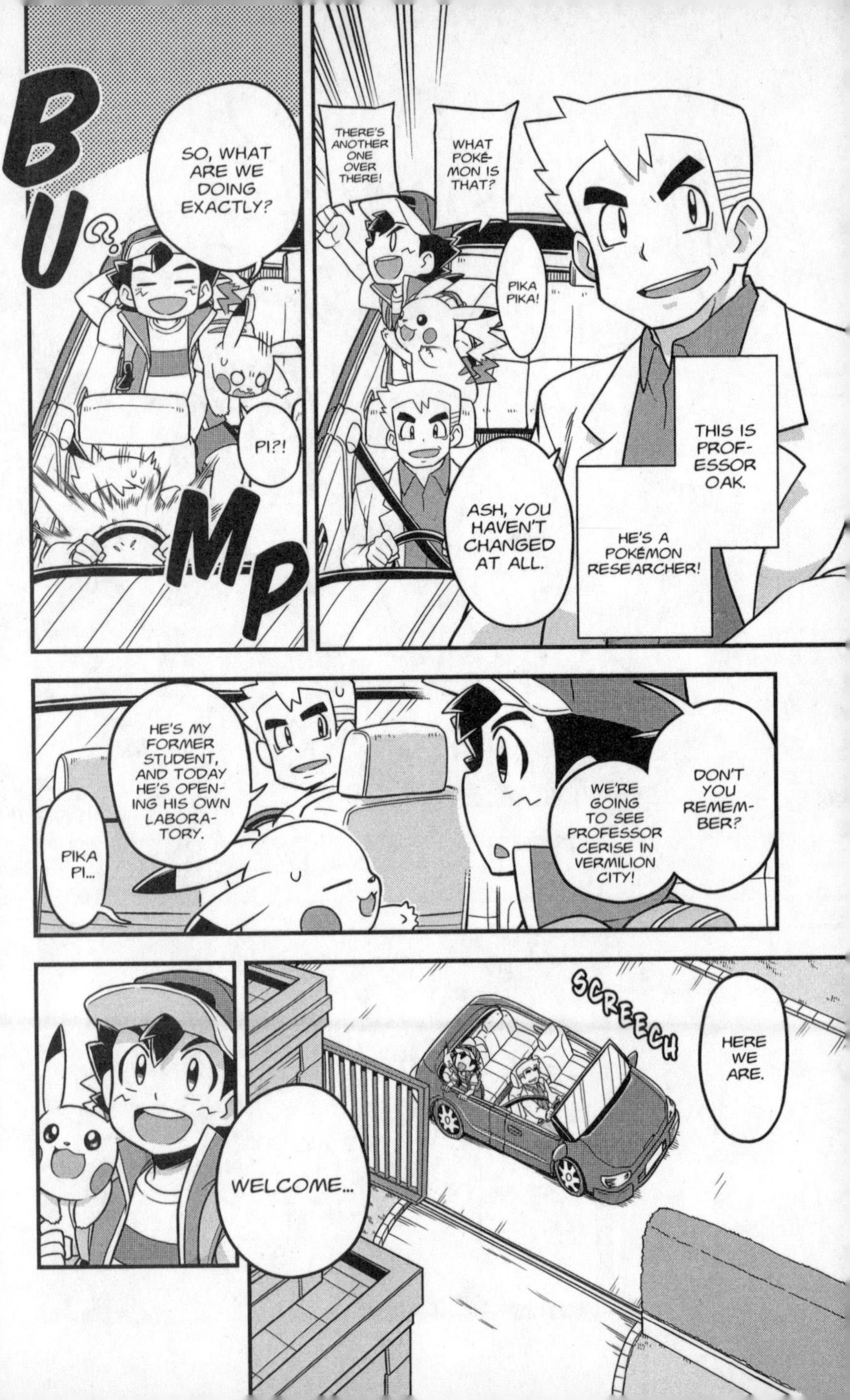
WHAT POKÉMON IS THAT?
THERE'S ANOTHER ONE OVER THERE!
PIKA PIKA!
THIS IS PROFESSOR OAK.
HE'S A POKÉMON RESEARCHER!
ASH, YOU HAVEN'T CHANGED AT ALL.
SO, WHAT ARE WE DOING EXACTLY?
BU
PI?!
MP
DON'T YOU REMEMBER?
WE'RE GOING TO SEE PROFESSOR CERISE IN VERMILION CITY!
HE'S MY FORMER STUDENT, AND TODAY HE'S OPENING HIS OWN LABORATORY.
PIKA PI...
HERE WE ARE.
SCREECH
WELCOME...

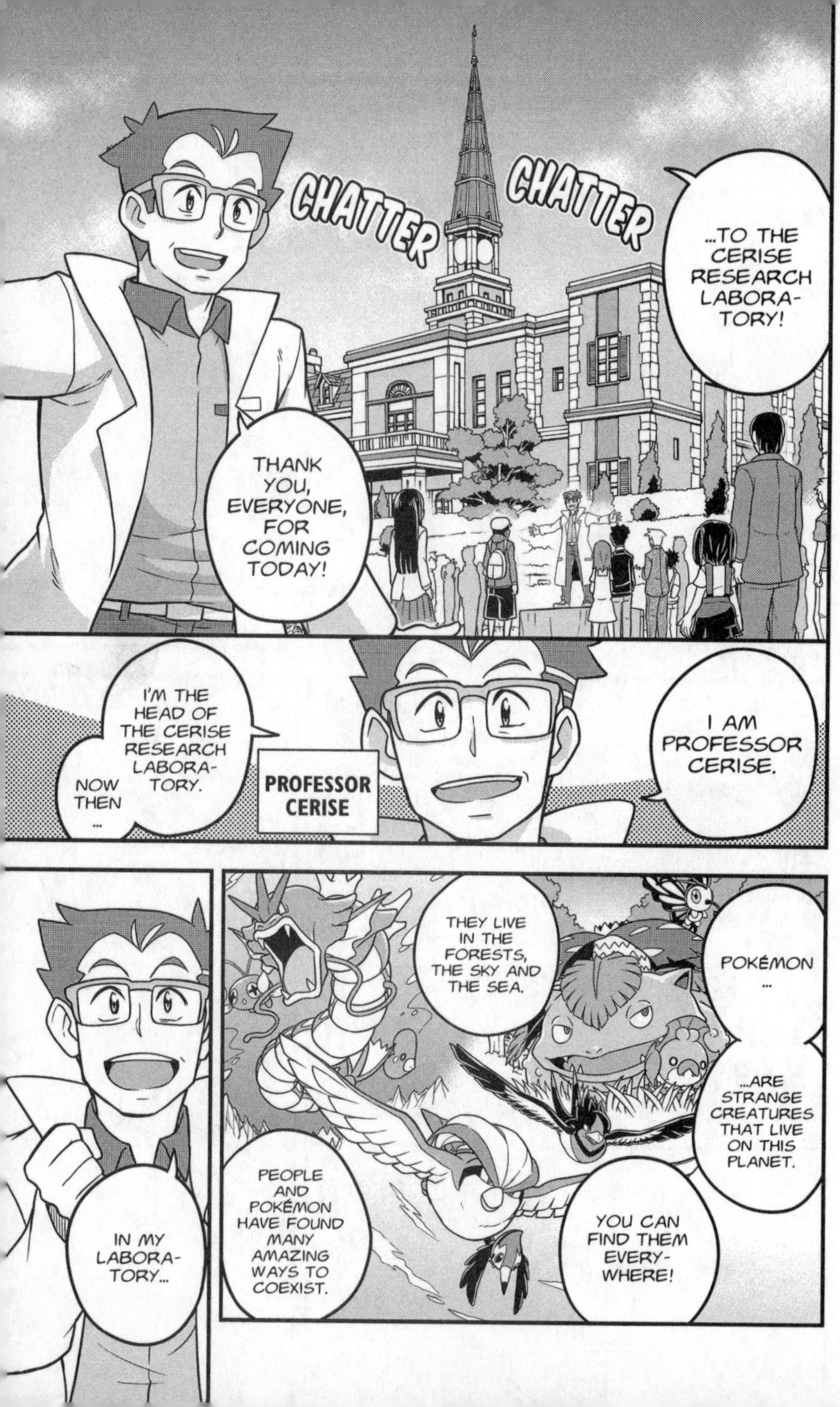
...TO THE CERISE RESEARCH LABORATORY!
CHATTER CHATTER
THANK YOU, EVERYONE, FOR COMING TODAY!
I AM PROFESSOR CERISE.
PROFESSOR CERISE
I'M THE HEAD OF THE CERISE RESEARCH LABORATORY.
NOW THEN...
POKÉMON...
...ARE STRANGE CREATURES THAT LIVE ON THIS PLANET.
THEY LIVE IN THE FORESTS, THE SKY AND THE SEA.
YOU CAN FIND THEM EVERYWHERE!
PEOPLE AND POKÉMON HAVE FOUND MANY AMAZING WAYS TO COEXIST.
IN MY LABORATORY...

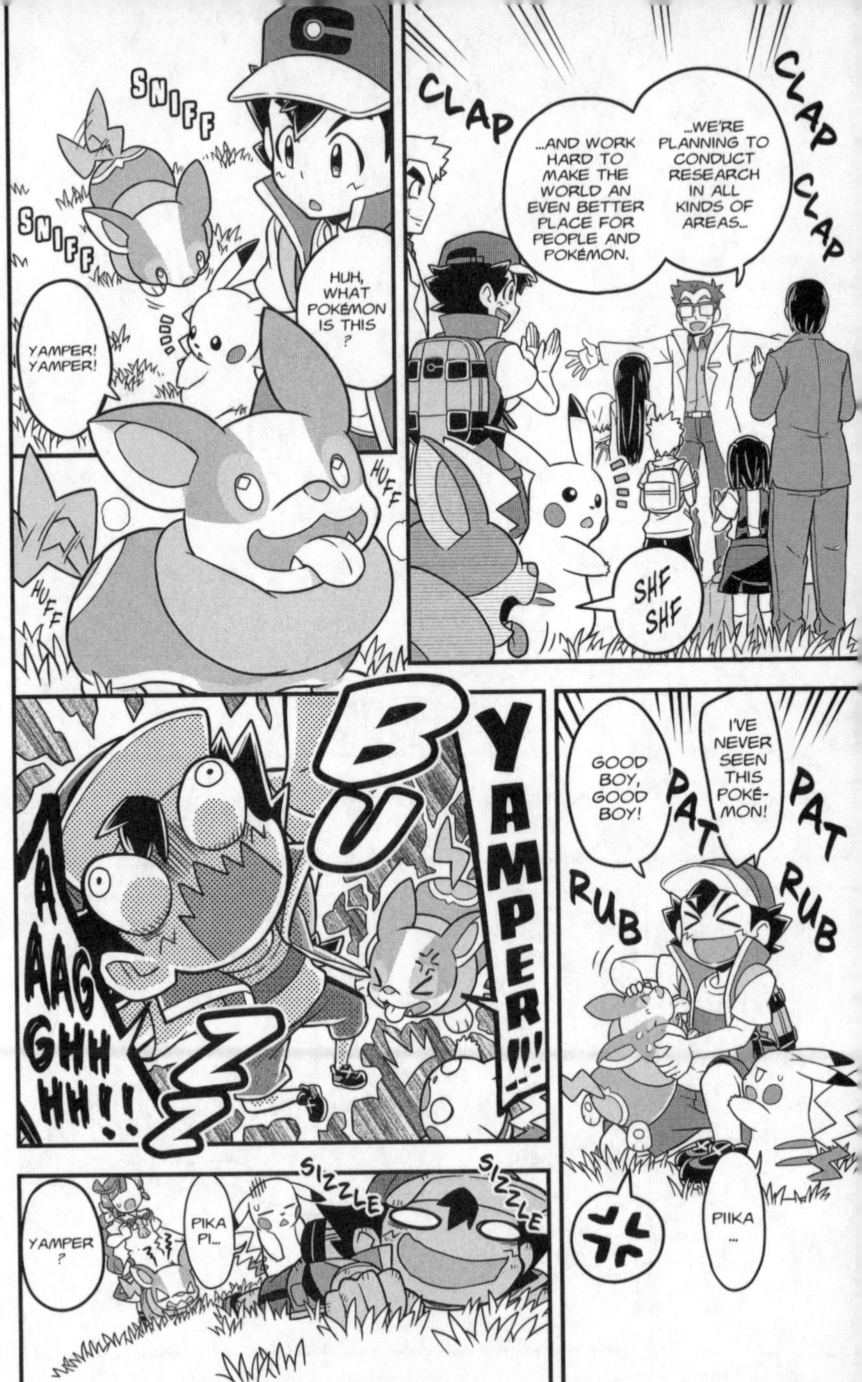
CLAP
CLAP
CLAP
...WE'RE PLANNING TO CONDUCT RESEARCH IN ALL KINDS OF AREAS...
...AND WORK HARD TO MAKE THE WORLD AN EVEN BETTER PLACE FOR PEOPLE AND POKÉMON.
CLAP
SHF SHF
SNIFF
SNIFF
HUH, WHAT POKÉMON IS THIS?
YAMPER! YAMPER!
HUFF
HUFF
I'VE NEVER SEEN THIS POKÉMON!
PAT
PAT
GOOD BOY, GOOD BOY!
PAT
RUB
RUB
PIIKA...
BZZ
YAMPER!!!
AAAGGHHHH!!
SIZZLE
SIZZLE
PIKA PI...
YAMPER?

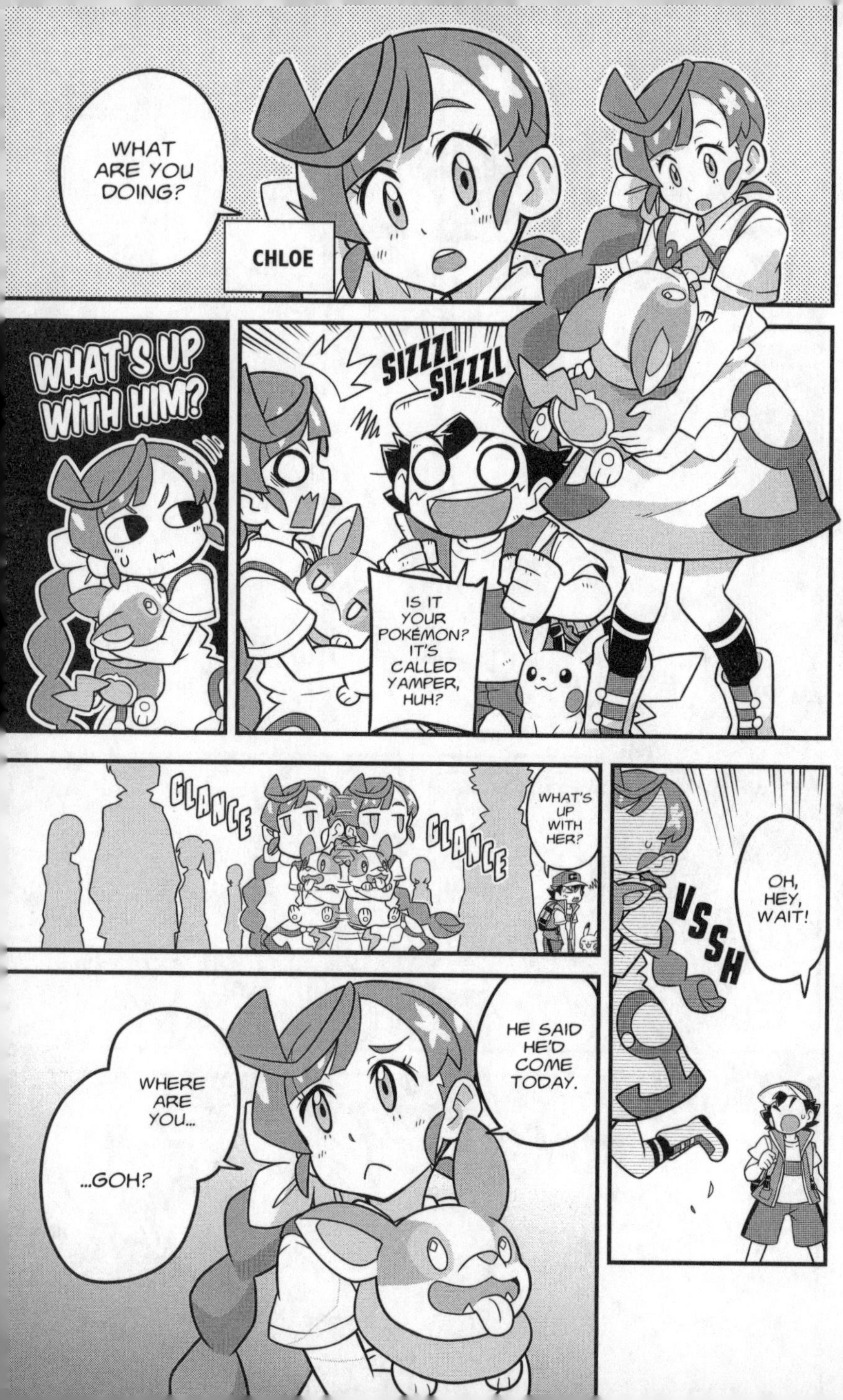
WHAT ARE YOU DOING?
CHLOE
SIZZZL SIZZZL
IS IT YOUR POKÉMON? IT'S CALLED YAMPER, HUH?
WHAT'S UP WITH HIM?
OH, HEY, WAIT!
VSSH
GLANCE
WHAT'S UP WITH HER?
GLANCE
HE SAID HE'D COME TODAY.
WHERE ARE YOU...
...GOH?

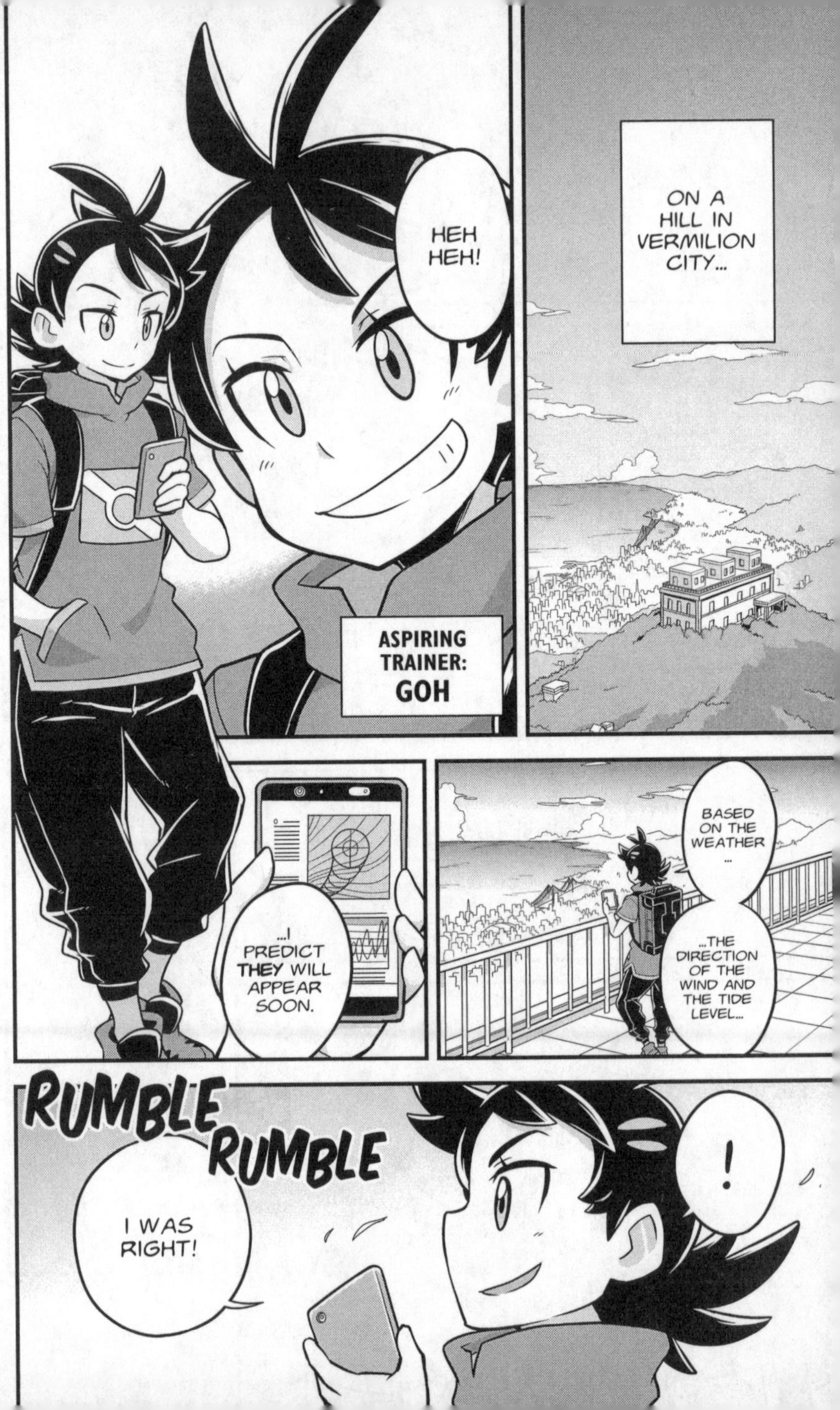
ON A HILL IN VERMILION CITY...
HEH HEH!
ASPIRING TRAINER: GOH
BASED ON THE WEATHER...
...THE DIRECTION OF THE WIND AND THE TIDE LEVEL...
...I PREDICT THEY WILL APPEAR SOON.
!
RUMBLE RUMBLE
I WAS RIGHT!

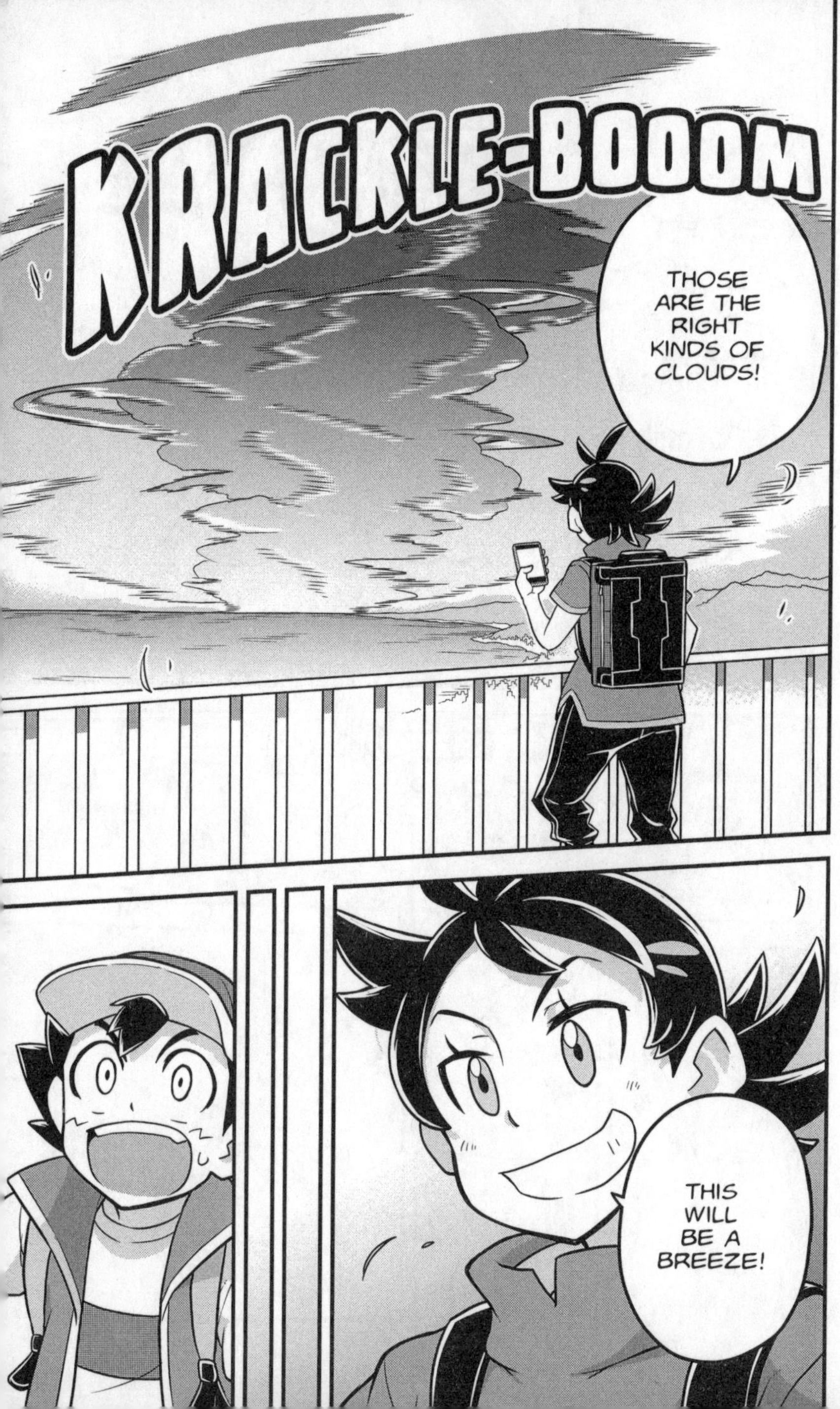
KRACKLE-BOOOM
THOSE ARE THE RIGHT KINDS OF CLOUDS!
THIS WILL BE A BREEZE!

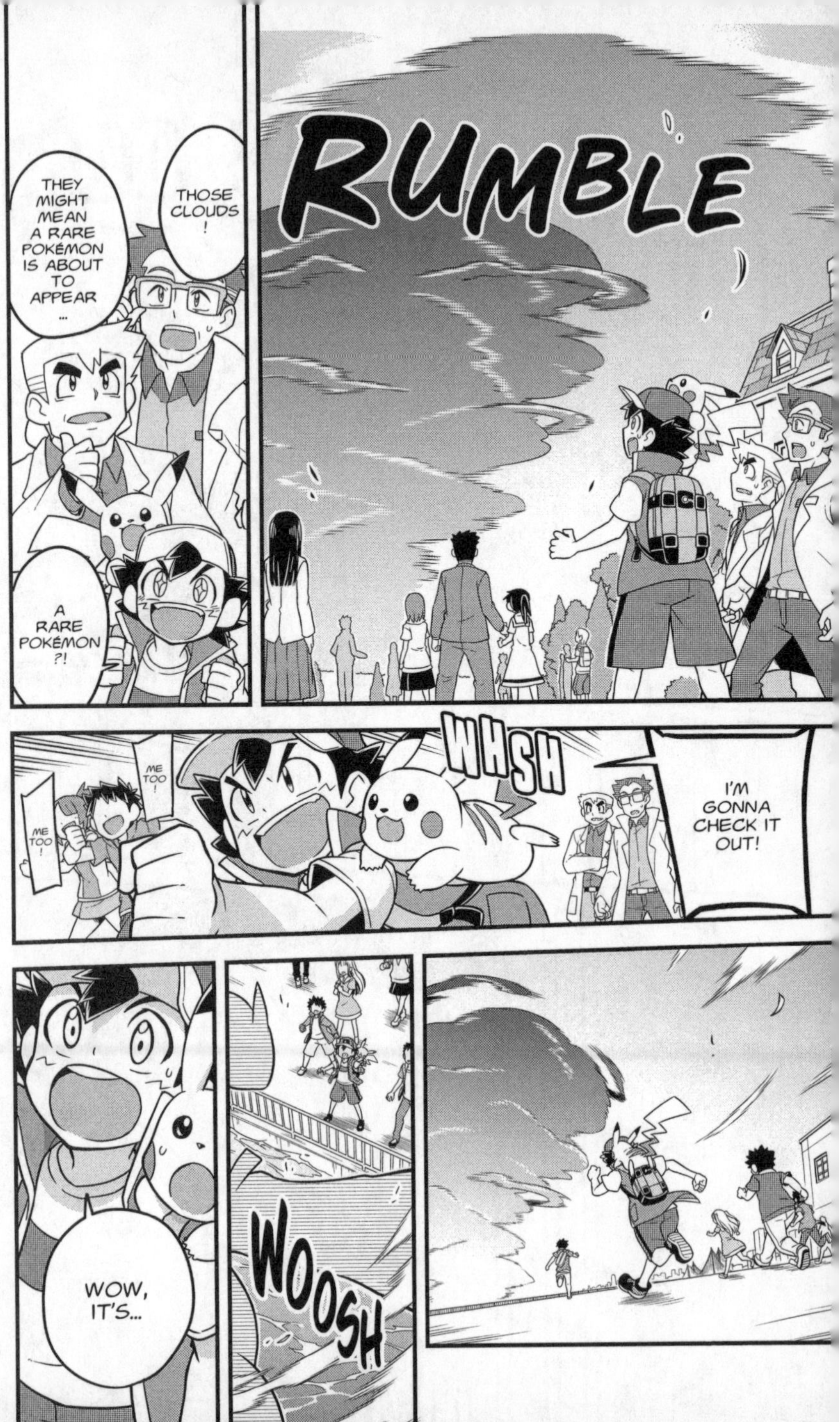
RUMBLE
THOSE CLOUDS!
THEY MIGHT MEAN A RARE POKÉMON IS ABOUT TO APPEAR...
A RARE POKÉMON?!
I'M GONNA CHECK IT OUT!
WHSH
ME TOO!
ME TOO!
WOOSH
WOW, IT'S...

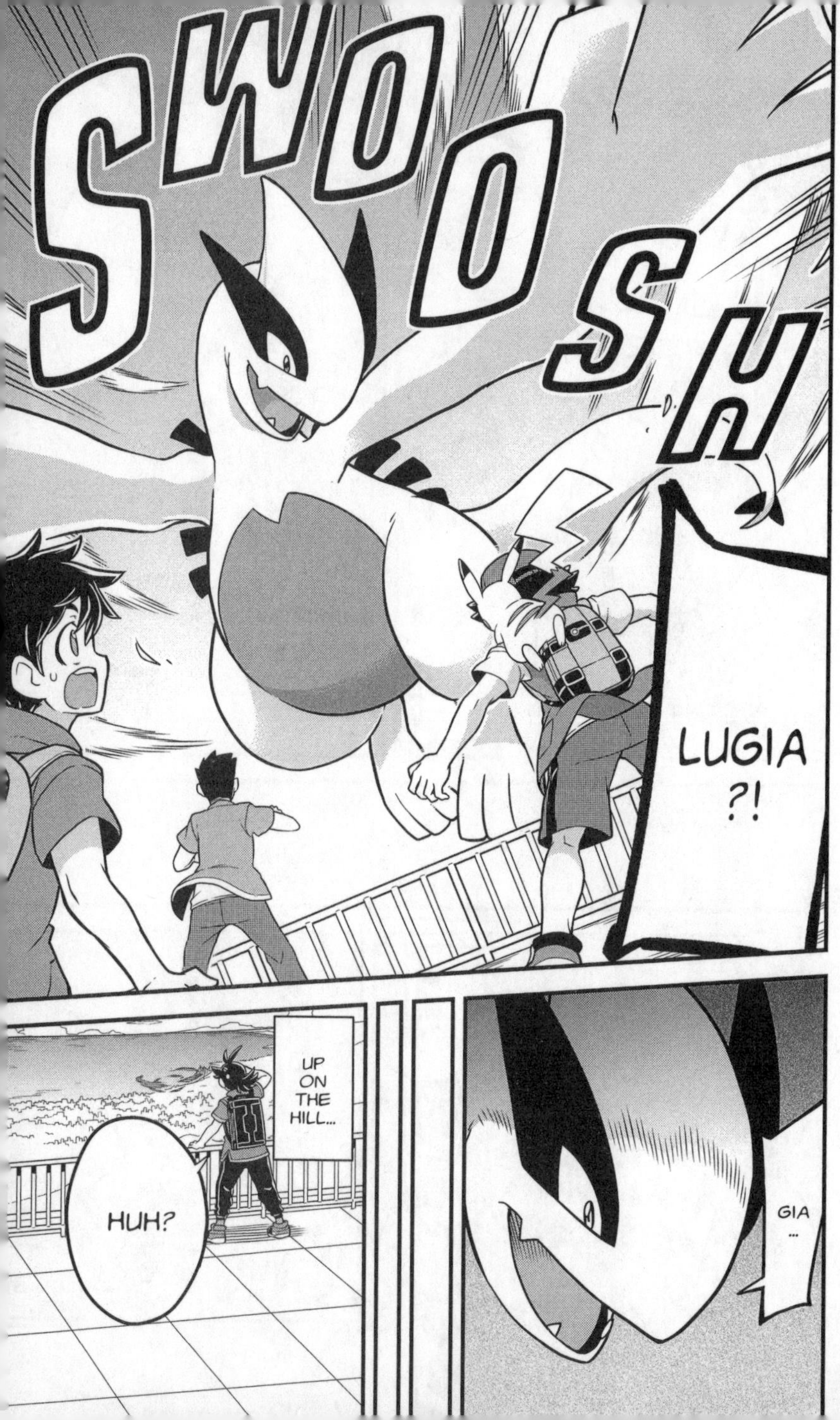
SWOOSH
LUGIA ?!
GIA ...
UP ON THE HILL...
HUH?

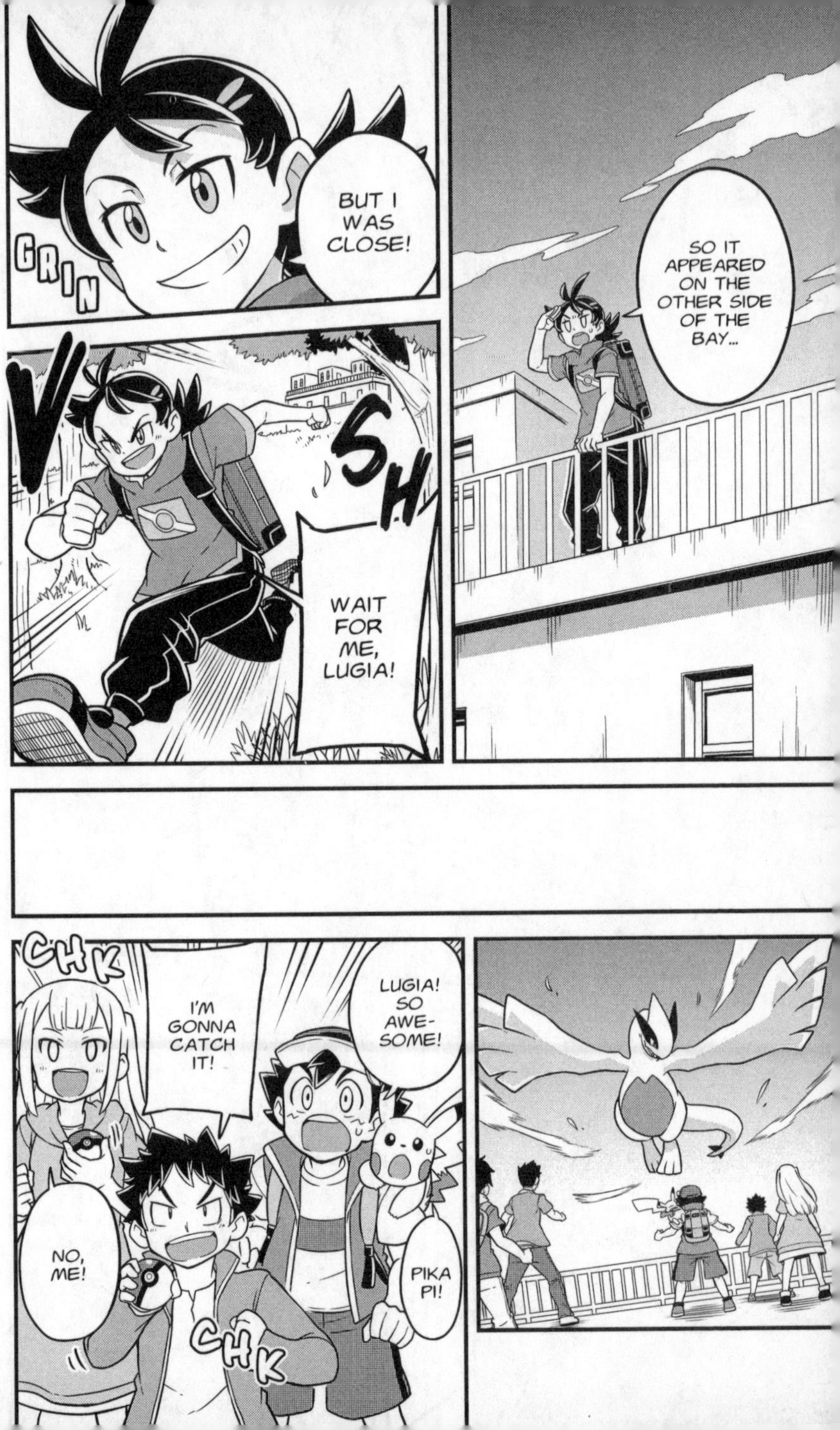
SO IT APPEARED ON THE OTHER SIDE OF THE BAY...
BUT I WAS CLOSE!
GRIN
SH
WAIT FOR ME, LUGIA!
V
LUGIA! SO AWE-SOME!
I'M GONNA CATCH IT!
CHK
PIKA PI!
NO, ME!
CHK

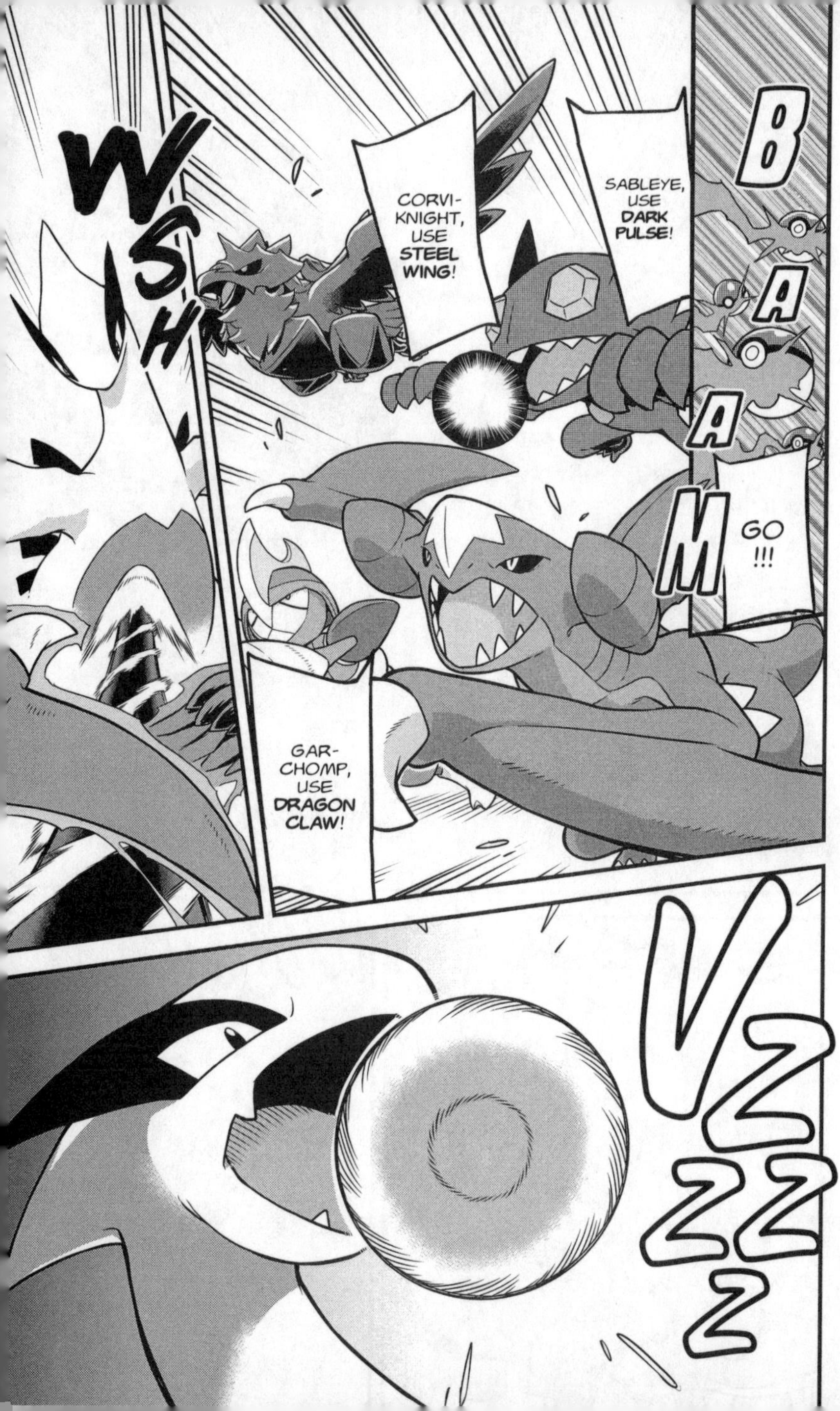
BAAMM
GO!!!
SABLEYE, USE DARK PULSE!
CORVI-KNIGHT, USE STEEL WING!
WSH
GAR-CHOMP, USE DRAGON CLAW!
VZZZZ

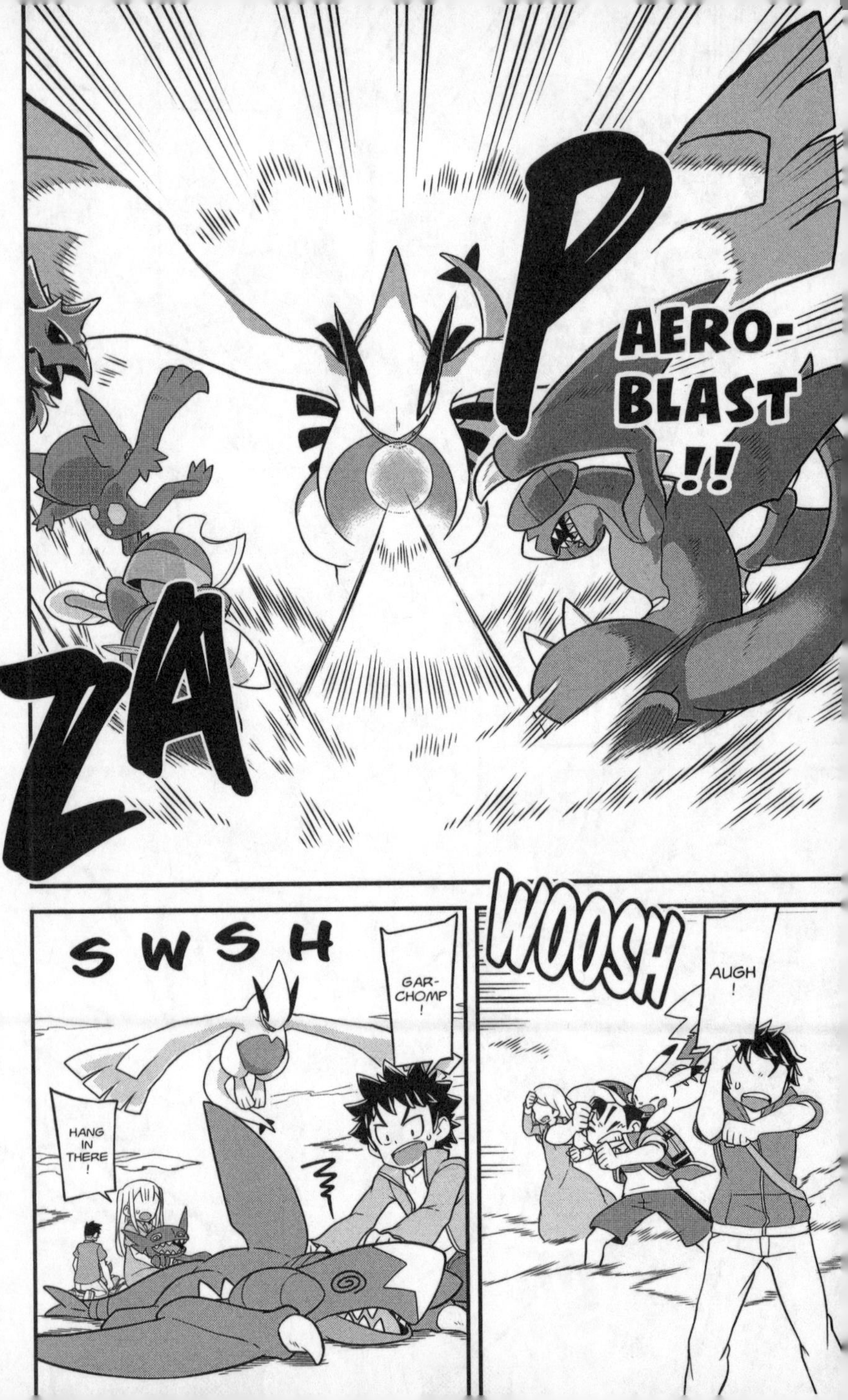
ZAP
AERO-BLAST!!
WOOSH
AUGH!
SWSH
GARCHOMP!
HANG IN THERE!

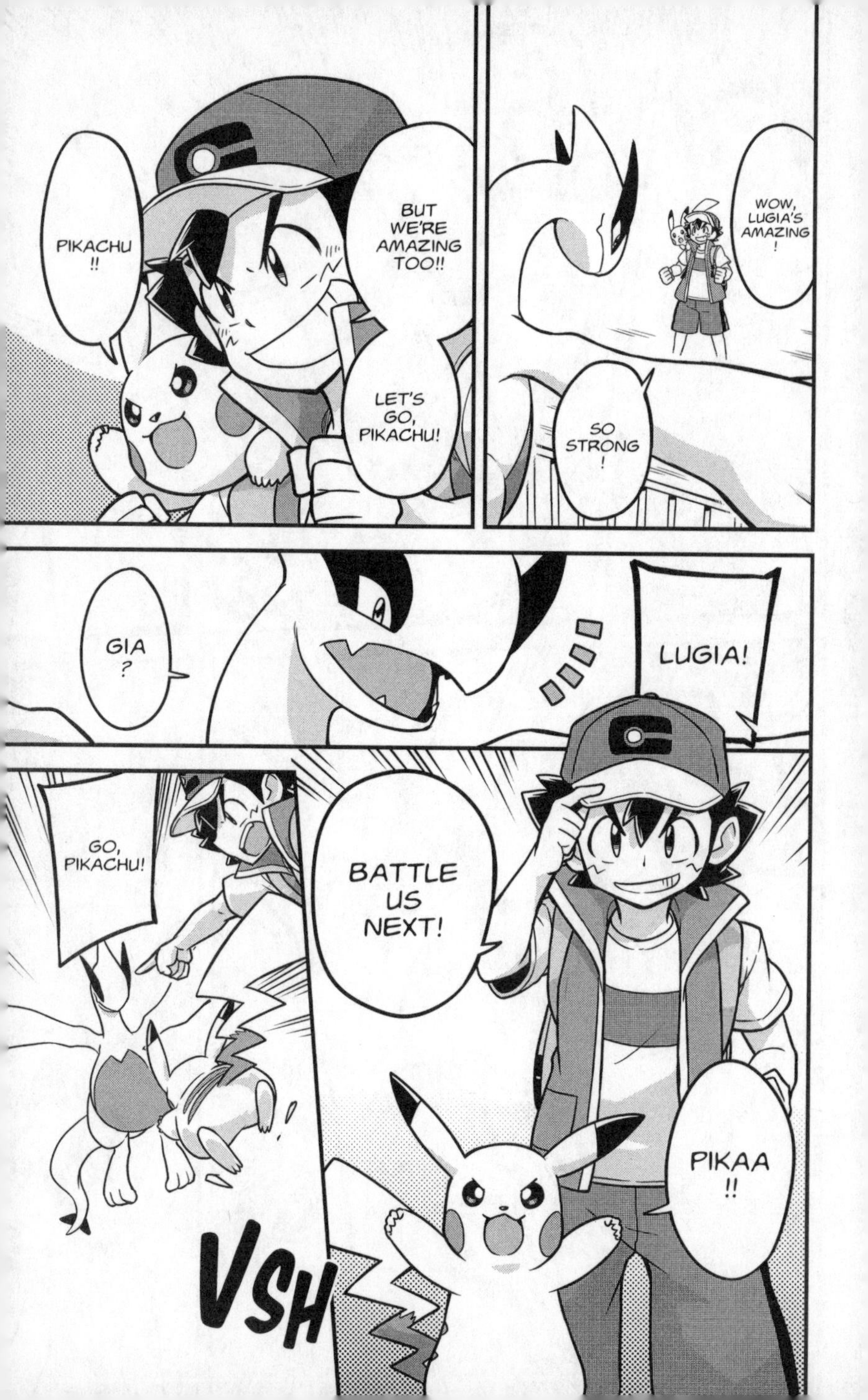
WOW, LUGIA'S AMAZING!
SO STRONG!
BUT WE'RE AMAZING TOO!!
LET'S GO, PIKACHU!
PIKACHU!!
LUGIA!
GIA?
BATTLE US NEXT!
PIKAA!!
GO, PIKACHU!
VSH

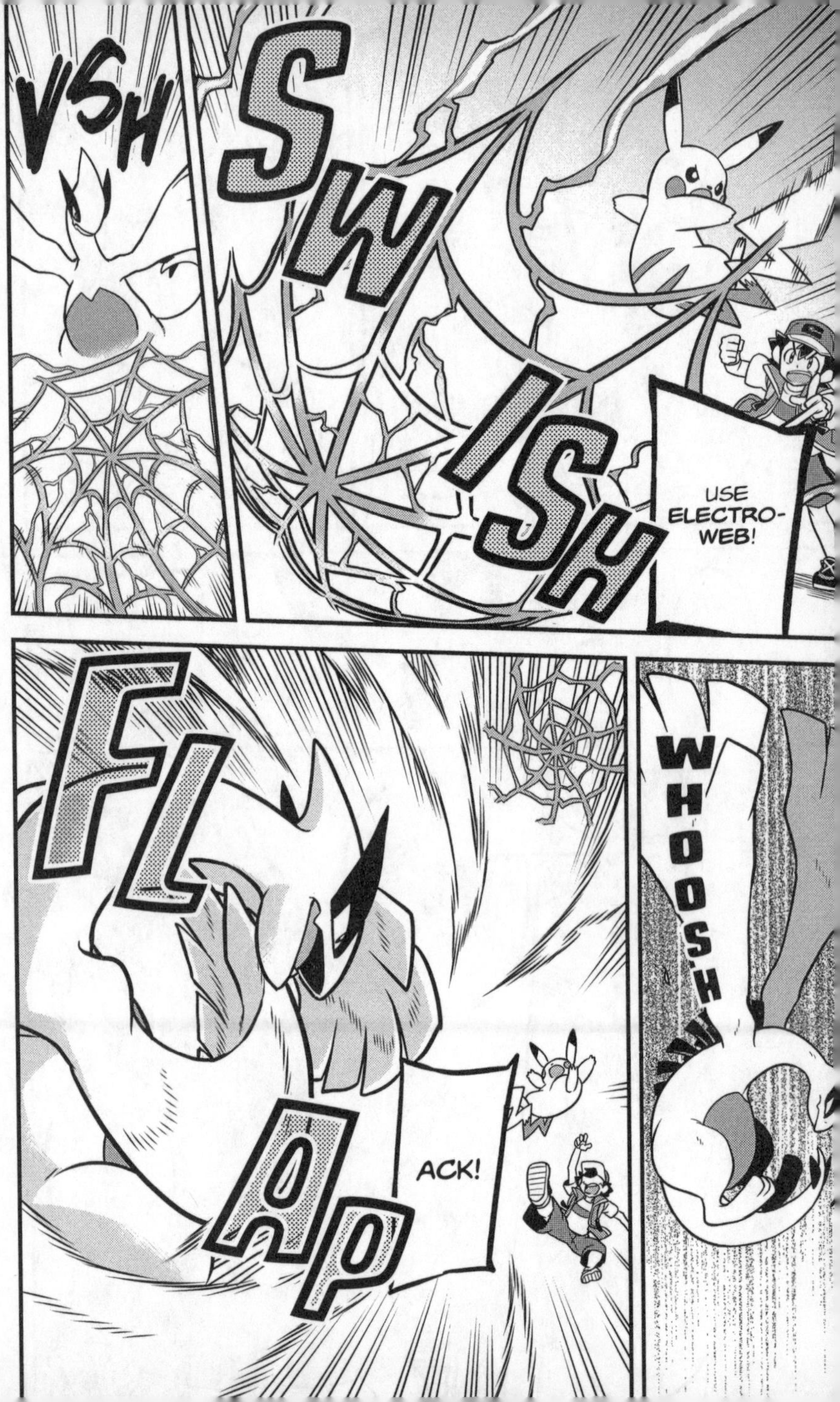
USE ELECTRO-WEB!
SWISH
VSH
WHOOOSH
FLAP
ACK!

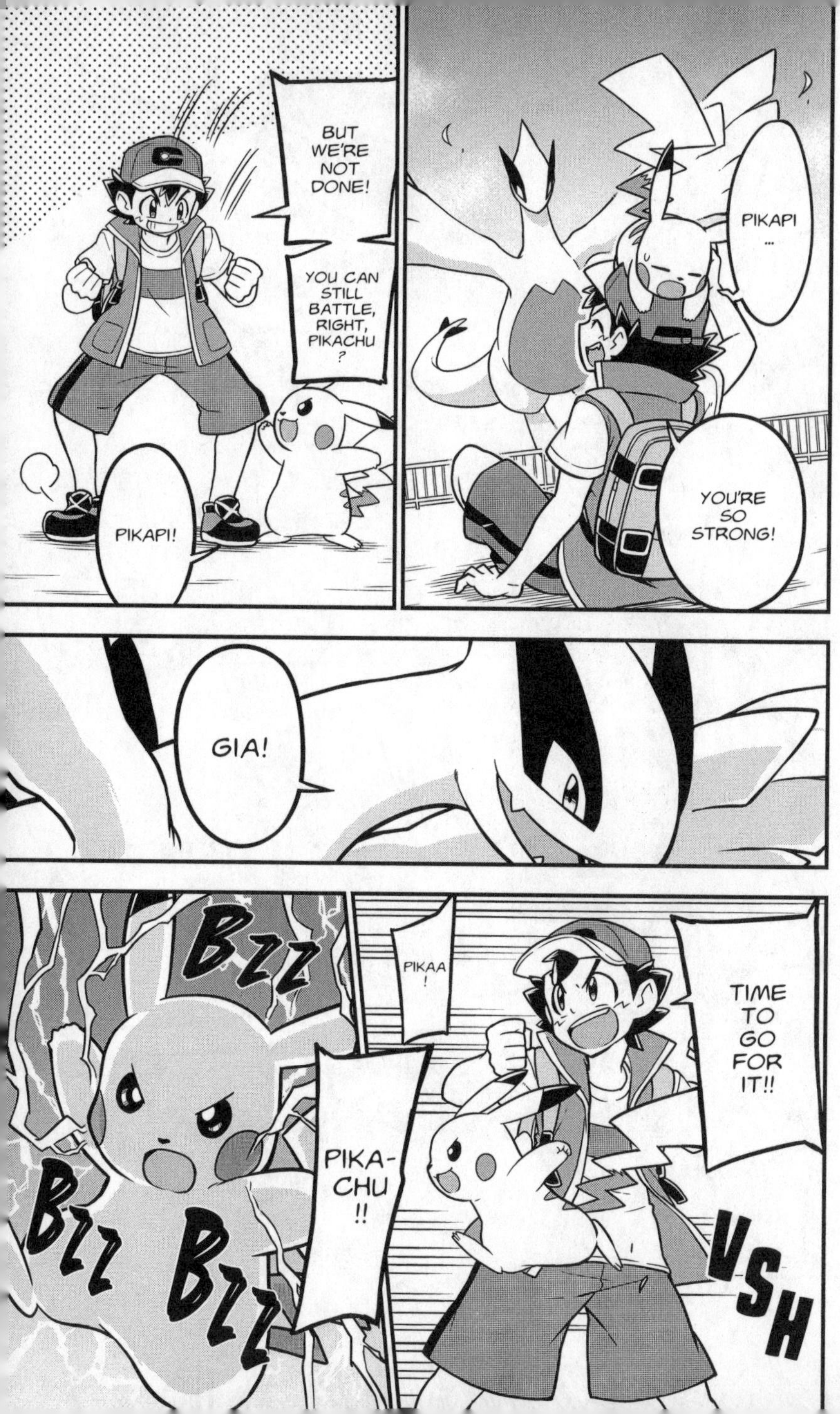
PIKAPI ...
YOU'RE SO STRONG!
BUT WE'RE NOT DONE!
YOU CAN STILL BATTLE, RIGHT, PIKACHU?
PIKAPI!
GIA!
TIME TO GO FOR IT!!
PIKAA!
VSH
BZZ
PIKA-CHU!!
BZZ
BZZ

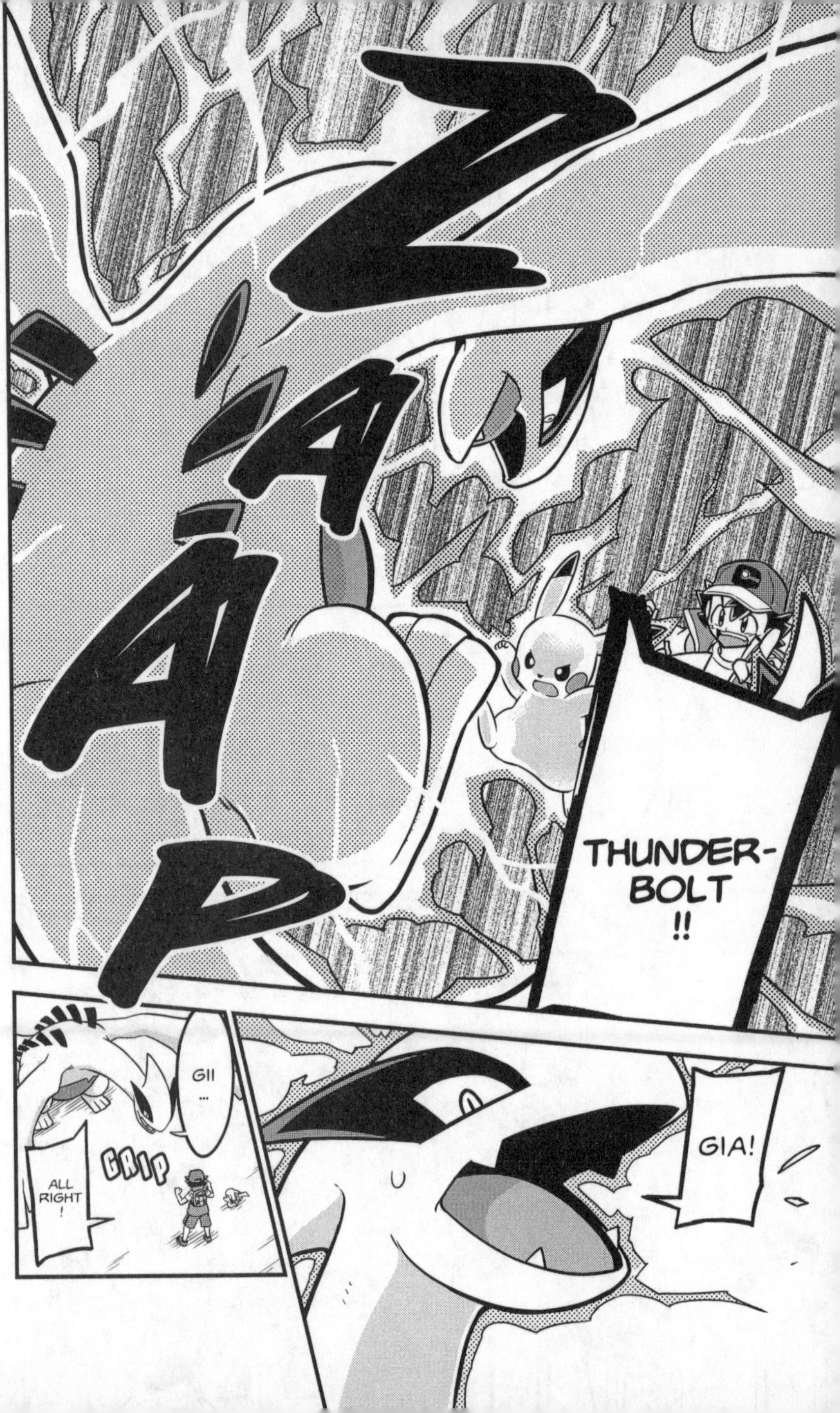
ZAAAP
THUNDER-BOLT !!
GIA!
GII ...
GRIP
ALL RIGHT !

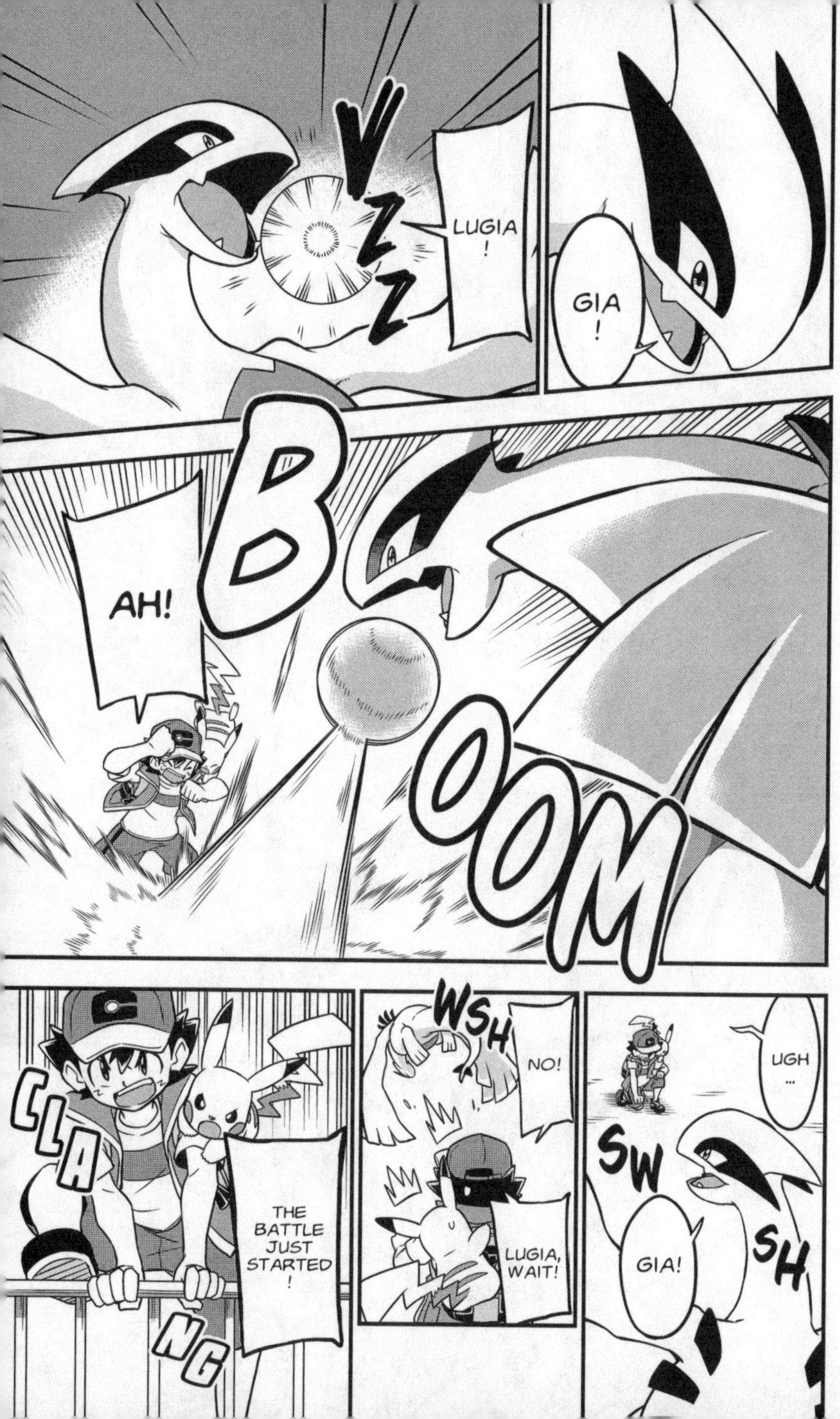
GIA!
VZZZ
LUGIA!
BOOOM
AH!
UGH...
SWSH
GIA!
WSH
NO!
LUGIA, WAIT!
CLANG
THE BATTLE JUST STARTED!

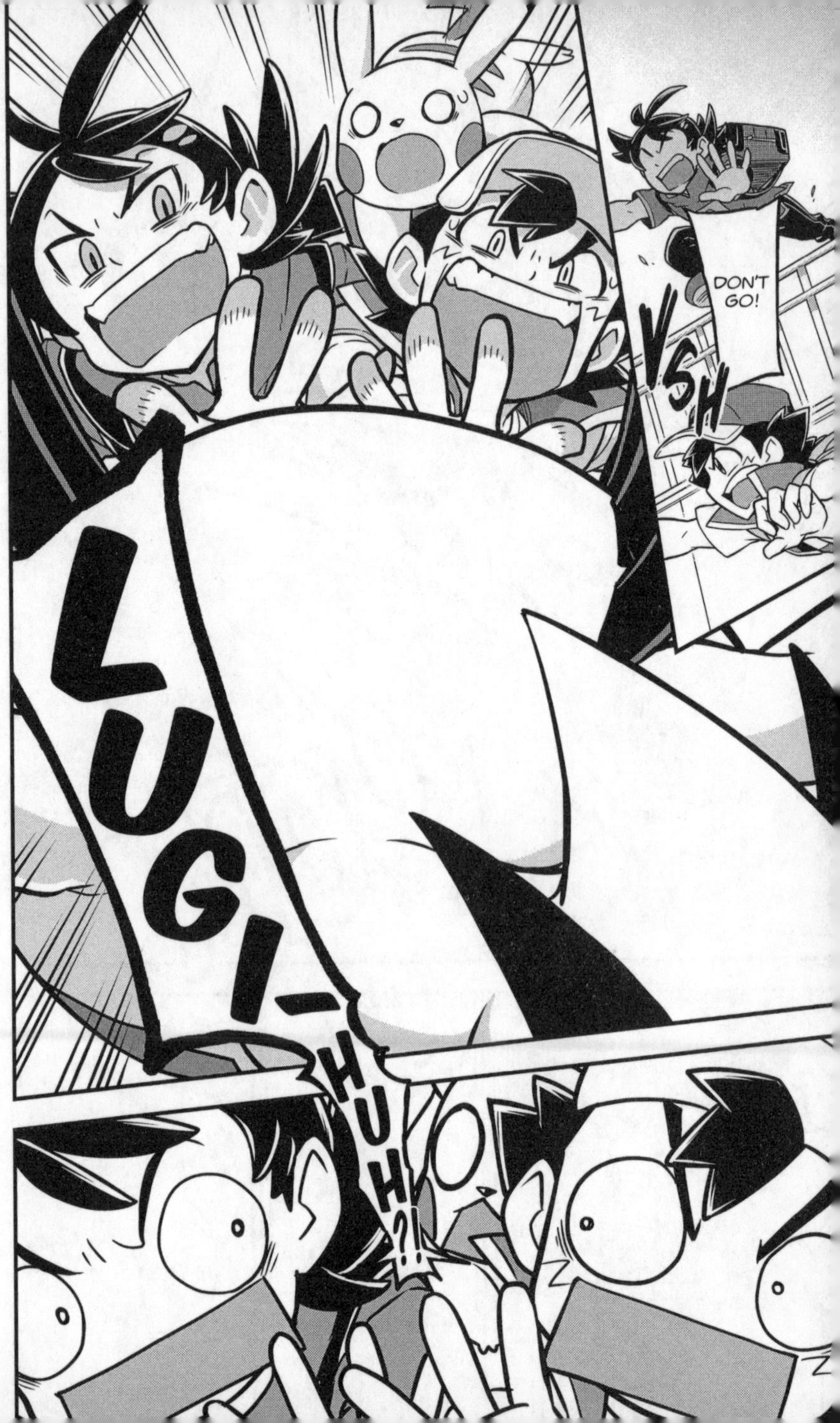
DON'T GO!
VSH
LUGI–
HUH?!

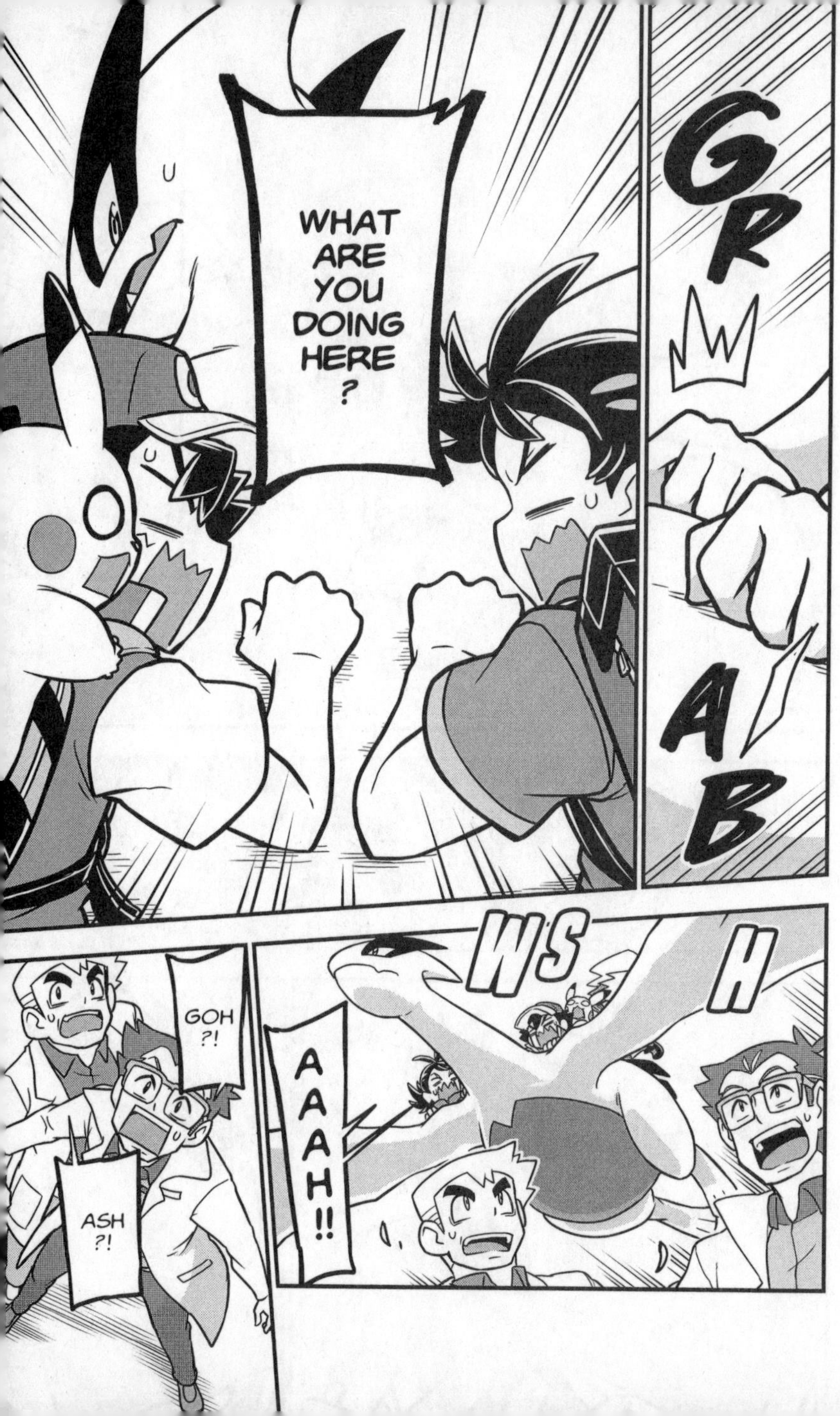
GRAB
WHAT ARE YOU DOING HERE?
WSH
AAAH!!
GOH?!
ASH?!

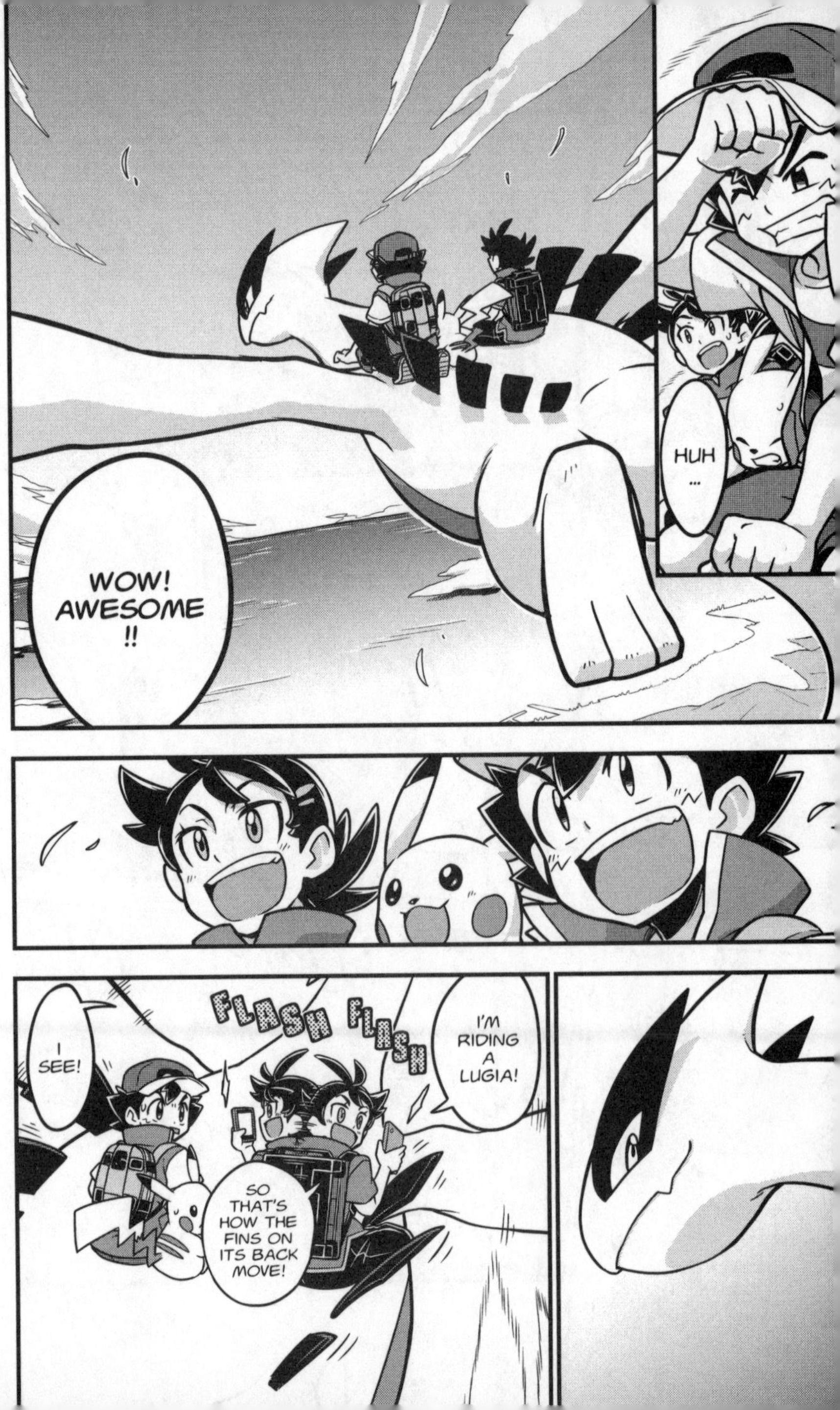
HUH...
WOW! AWESOME!!
I'M RIDING A LUGIA!
FLASH FLASH
I SEE!
SO THAT'S HOW THE FINS ON ITS BACK MOVE!

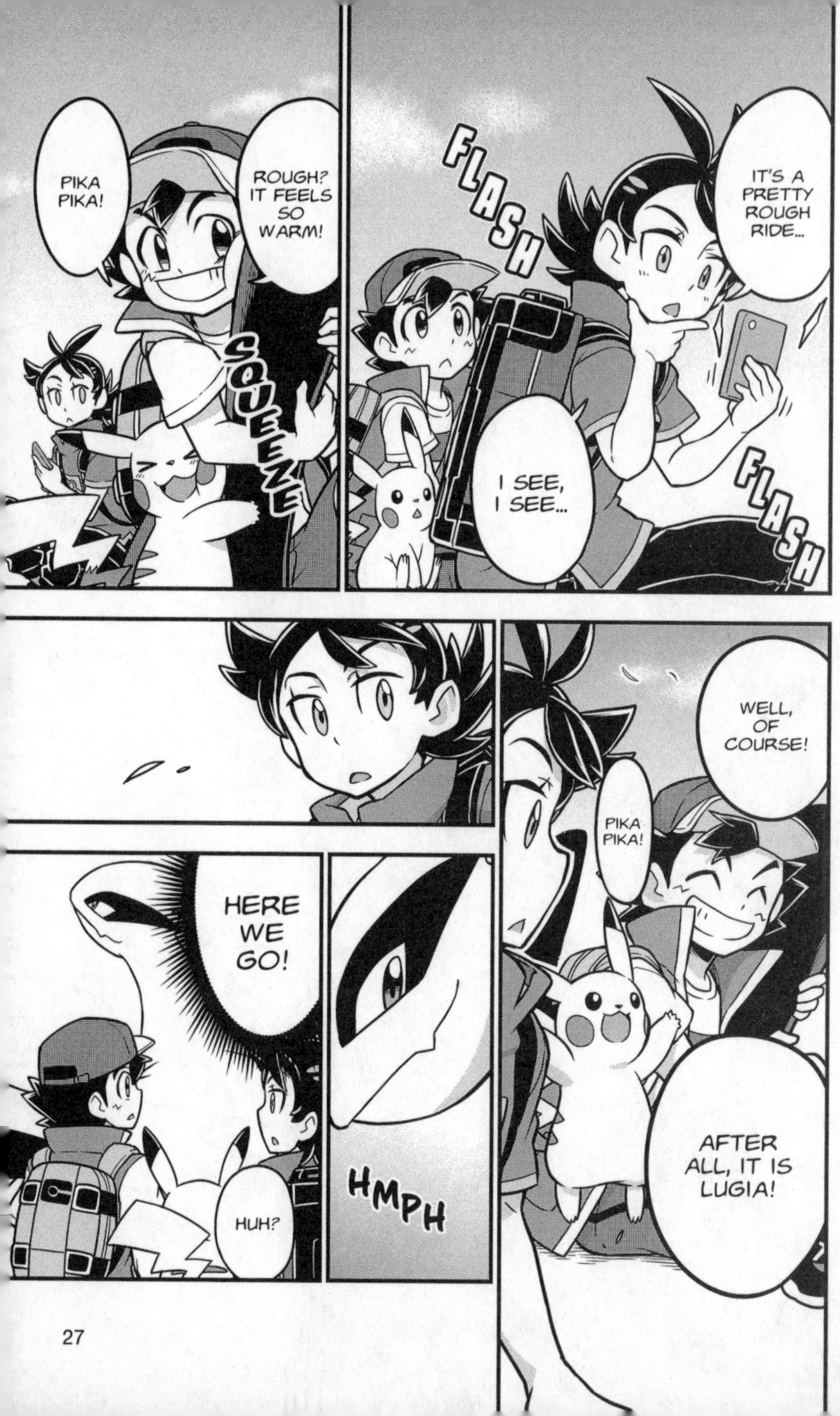
IT'S A PRETTY ROUGH RIDE...
FLASH
FLASH
I SEE, I SEE...
ROUGH? IT FEELS SO WARM!
PIKA PIKA!
SQUEEZE
WELL, OF COURSE!
PIKA PIKA!
AFTER ALL, IT IS LUGIA!
HMPH
HERE WE GO!
HUH?

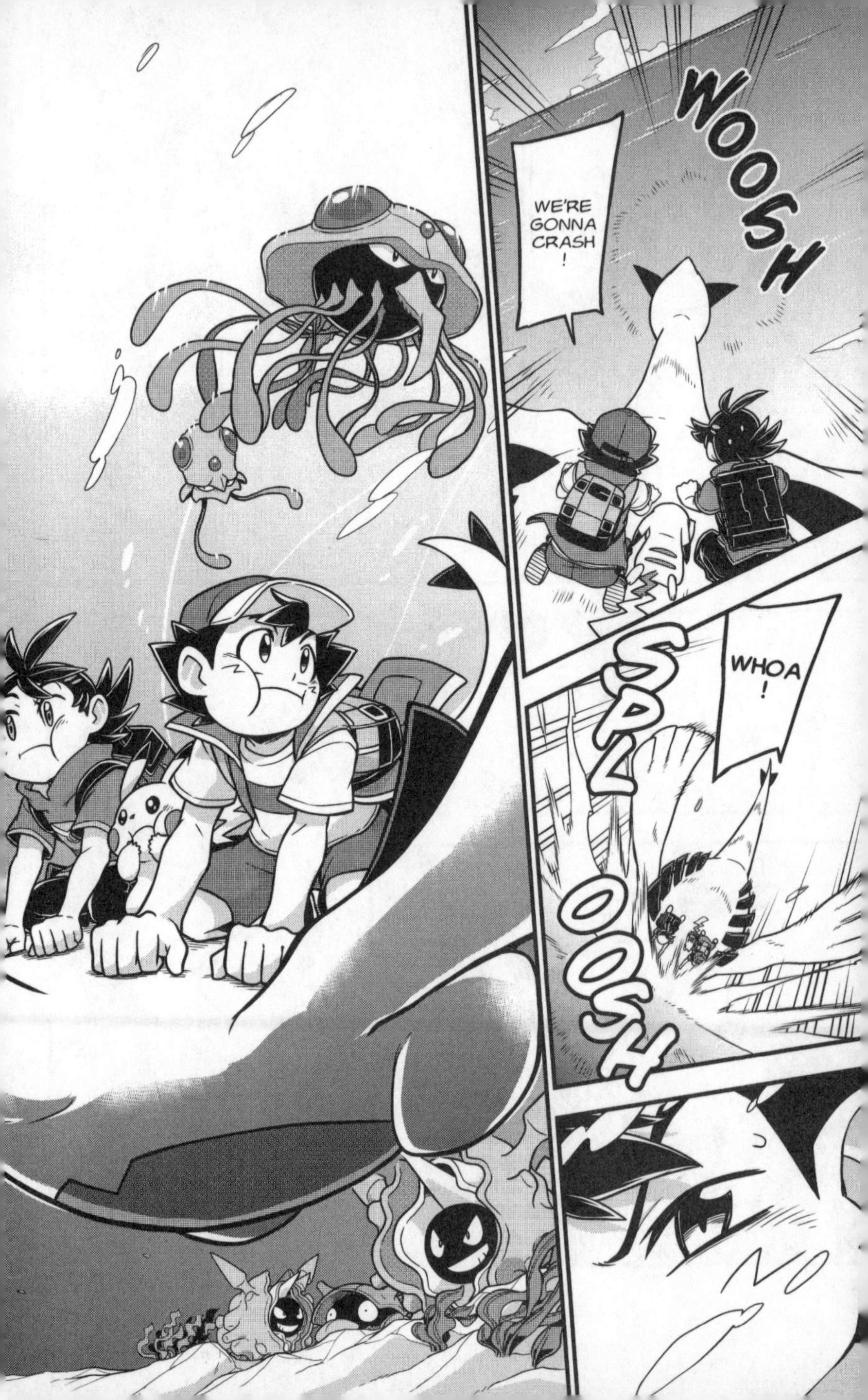
WOOSH
WE'RE GONNA CRASH!
SPLOOOSH
WHOA!

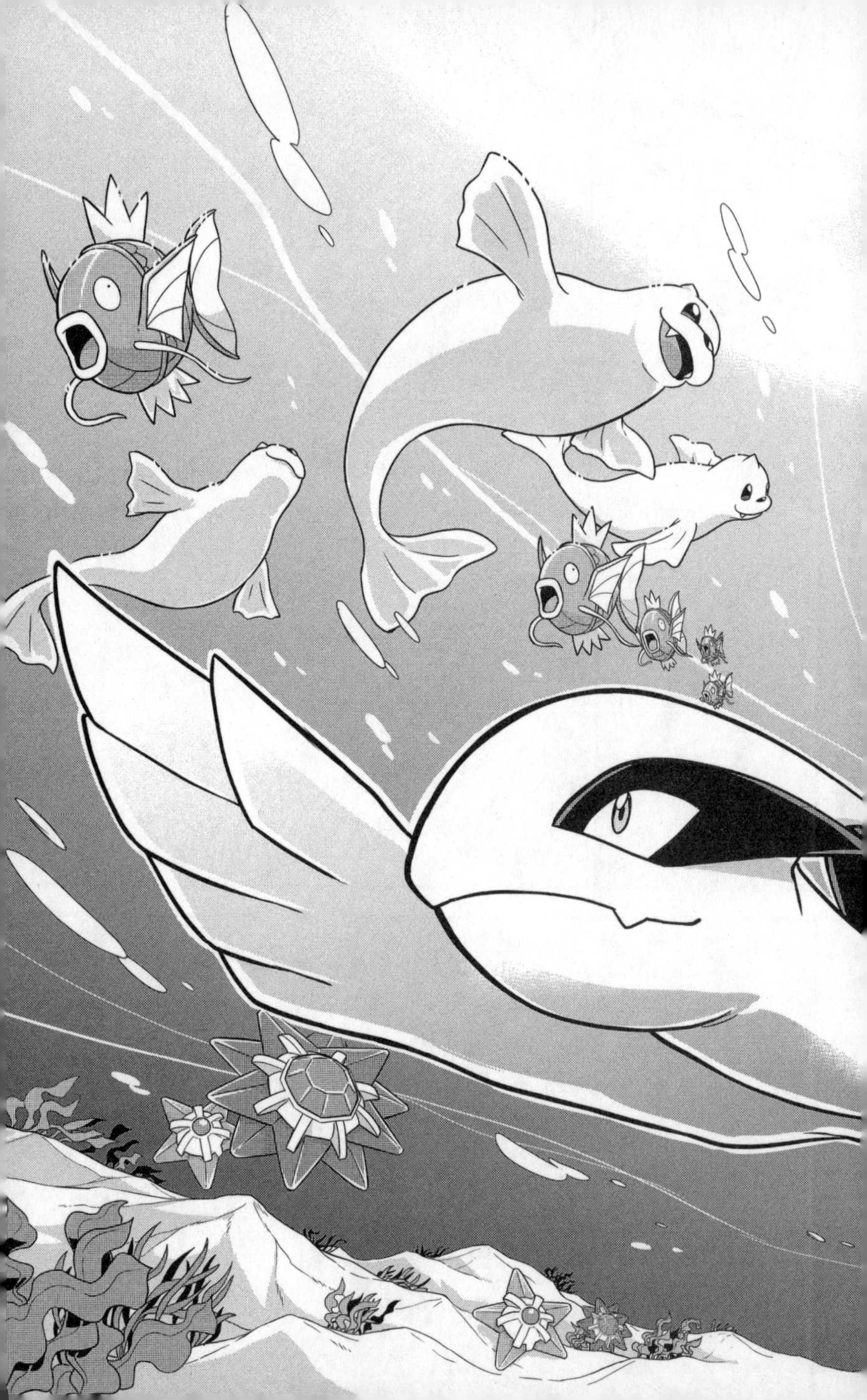

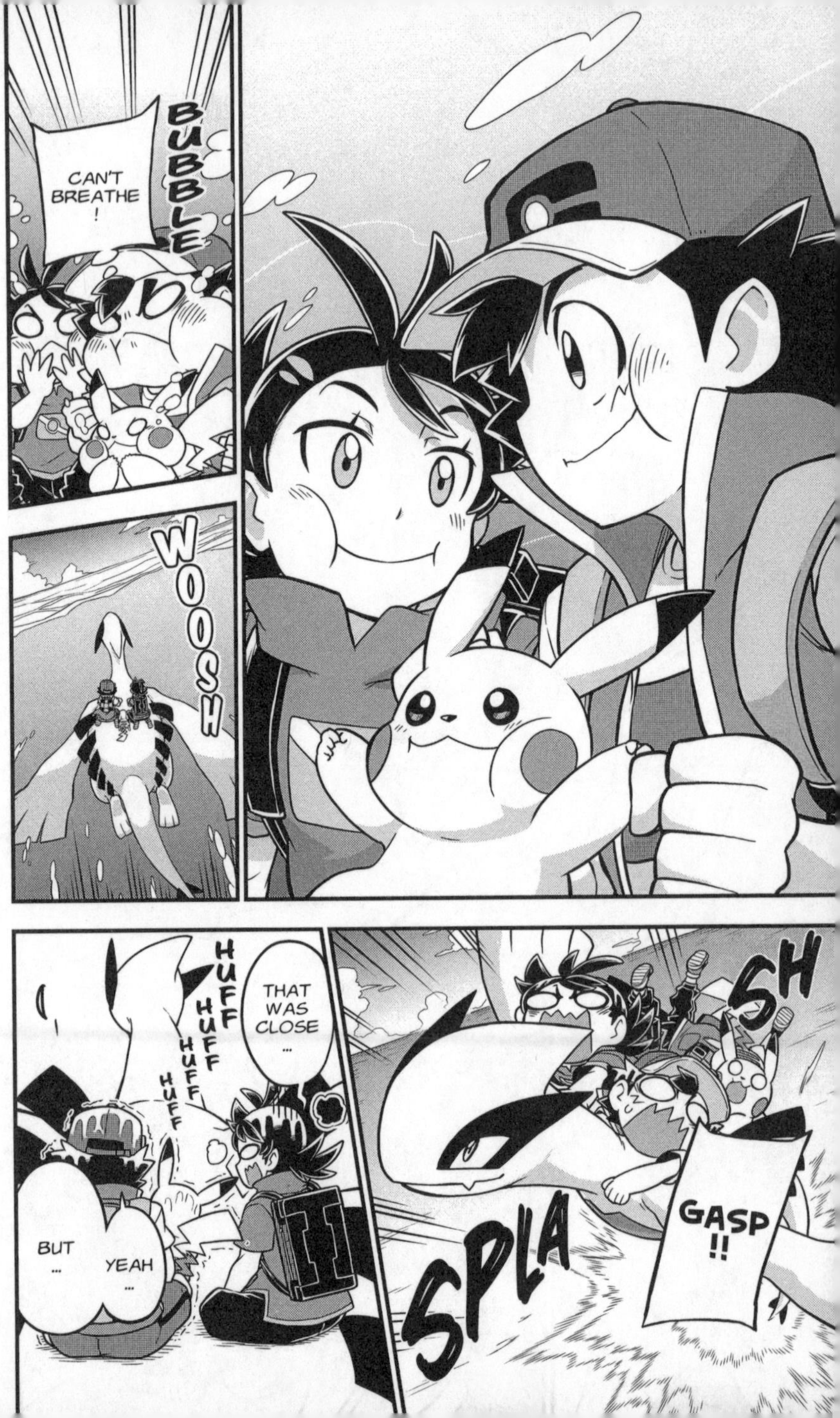
CAN'T BREATHE!
BUBBLE
WOOSH
SH
GASP!!
SPLA
THAT WAS CLOSE...
HUFF HUFF HUFF HUFF
YEAH... BUT...

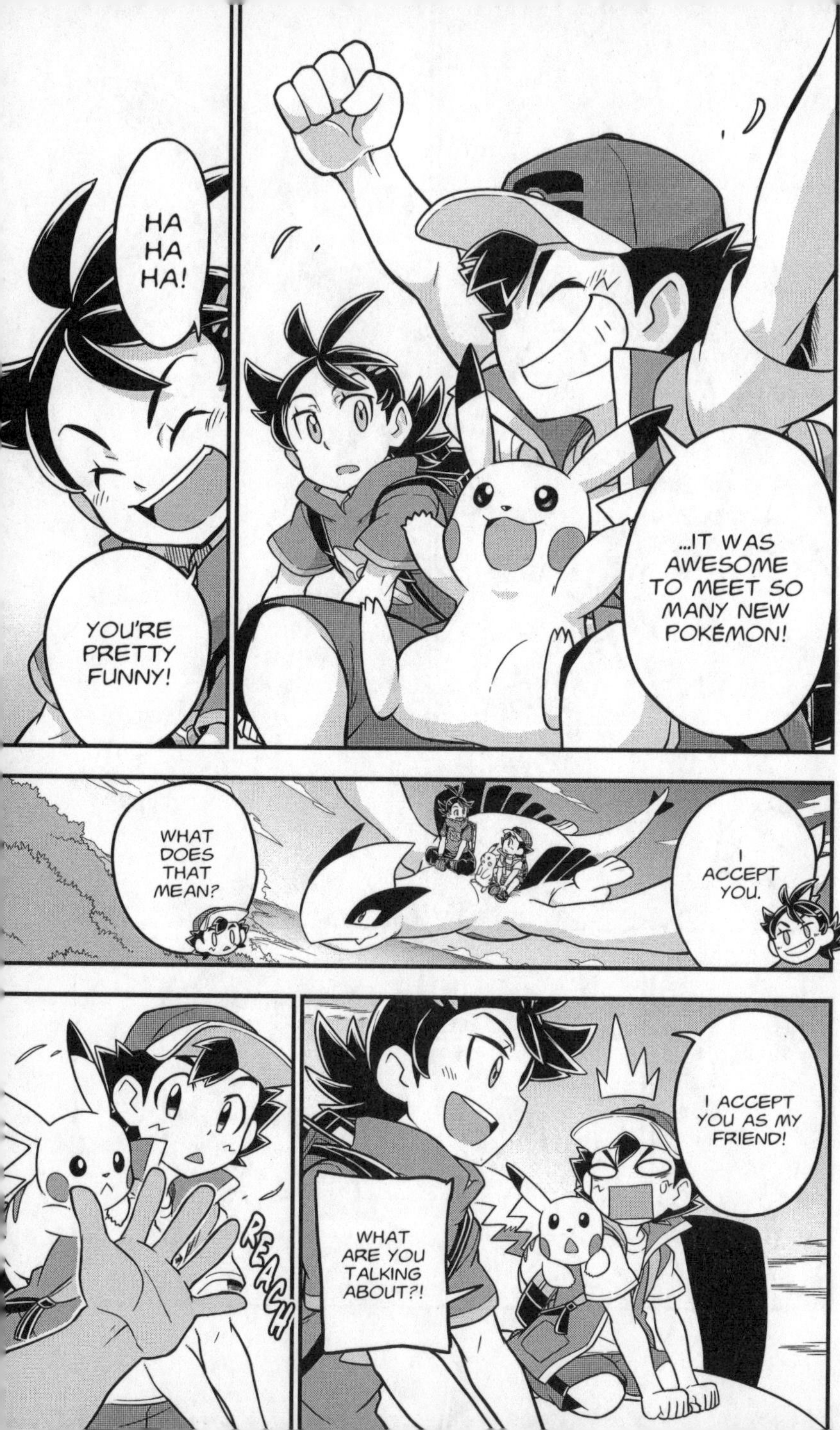
...IT WAS AWESOME TO MEET SO MANY NEW POKÉMON!
HA HA HA!
YOU'RE PRETTY FUNNY!
I ACCEPT YOU.
WHAT DOES THAT MEAN?
I ACCEPT YOU AS MY FRIEND!
WHAT ARE YOU TALKING ABOUT?!
REACH

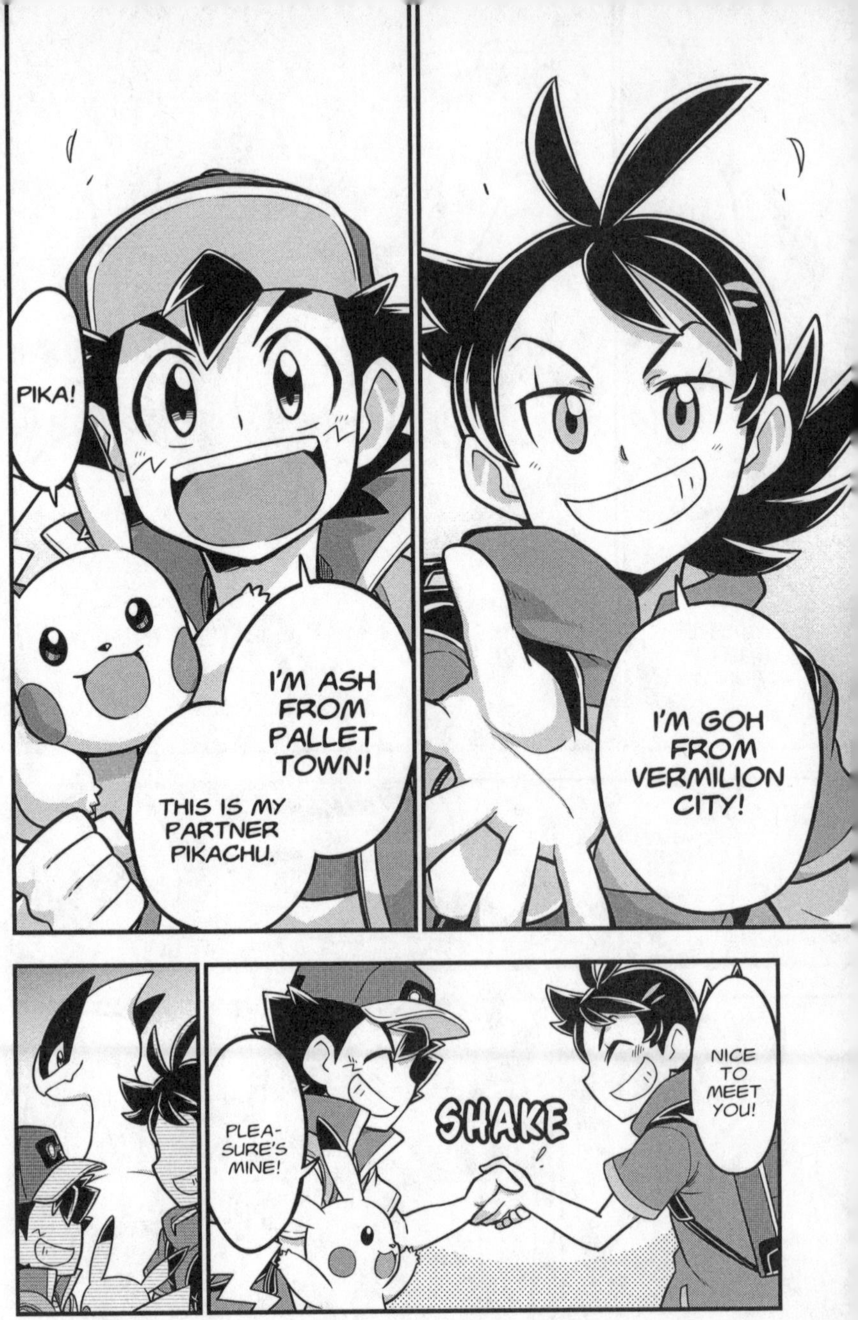
I'M GOH FROM VERMILION CITY!
I'M ASH FROM PALLET TOWN!
THIS IS MY PARTNER PIKACHU.
PIKA!
NICE TO MEET YOU!
SHAKE
PLEA-SURE'S MINE!

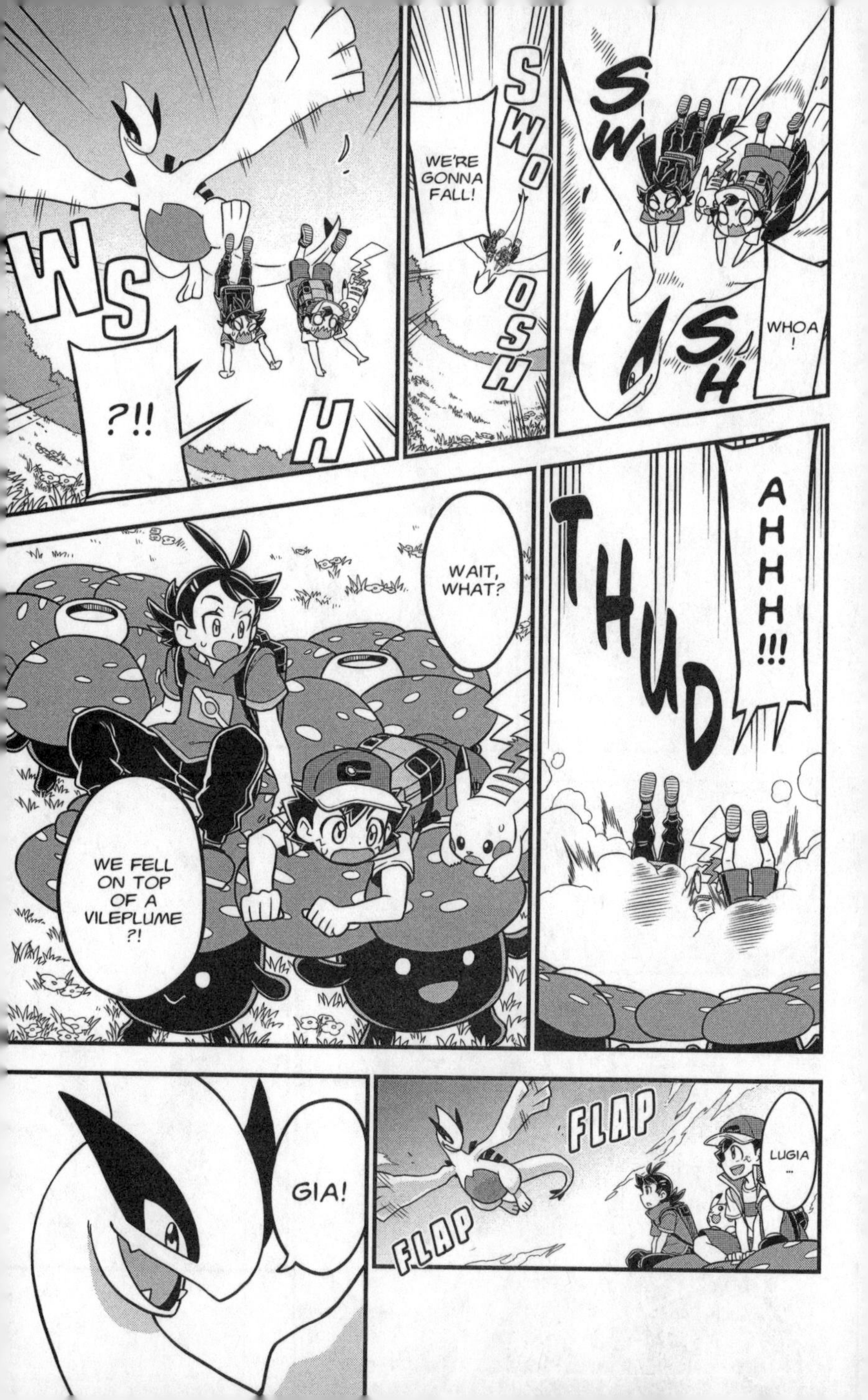
SWISH
WHOA!
SWOOSH
WE'RE GONNA FALL!
WS
H
?!!
AHHH!!!
THUD
WAIT, WHAT?
WE FELL ON TOP OF A VILEPLUME?!
LUGIA...
FLAP
FLAP
GIA!

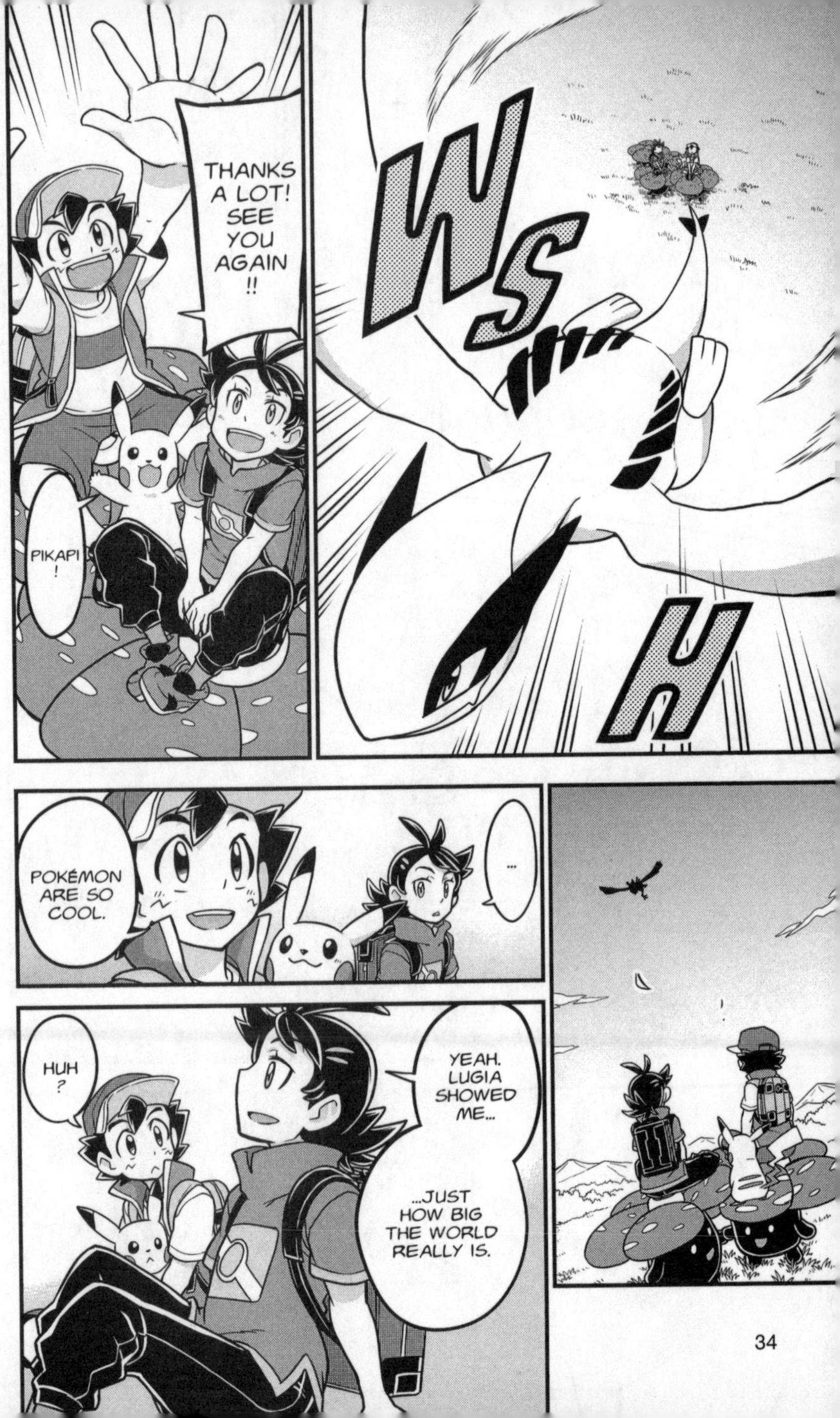
WSH
THANKS A LOT! SEE YOU AGAIN !!
PIKAPI !
...
POKÉMON ARE SO COOL.
YEAH. LUGIA SHOWED ME...
...JUST HOW BIG THE WORLD REALLY IS.
HUH ?

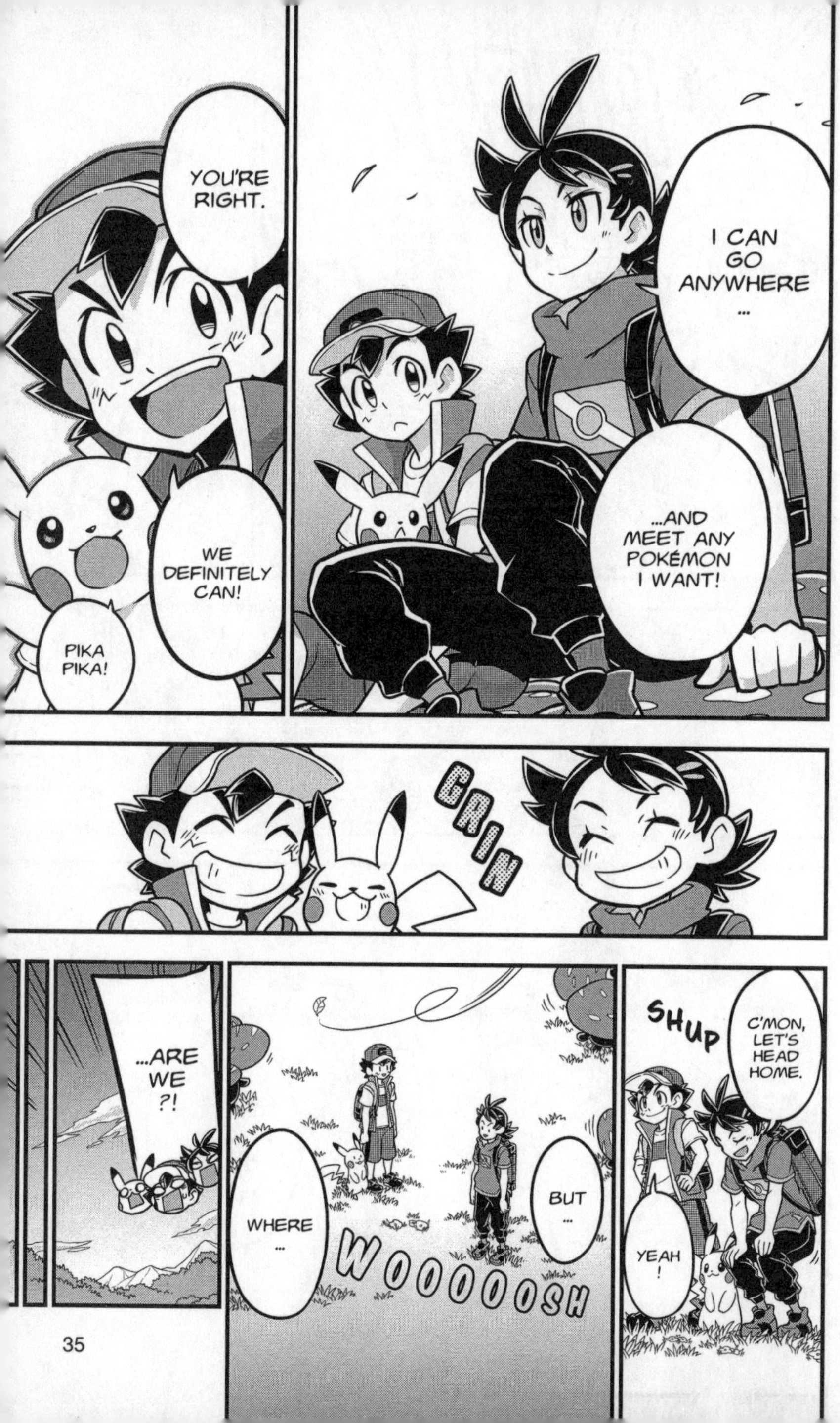
I CAN GO ANYWHERE ...
...AND MEET ANY POKÉMON I WANT!
YOU'RE RIGHT.
WE DEFINITELY CAN!
PIKA PIKA!
GRIN
SHUP
C'MON, LET'S HEAD HOME.
YEAH!
BUT ...
WOOOOOOSH
WHERE ...
...ARE WE ?!

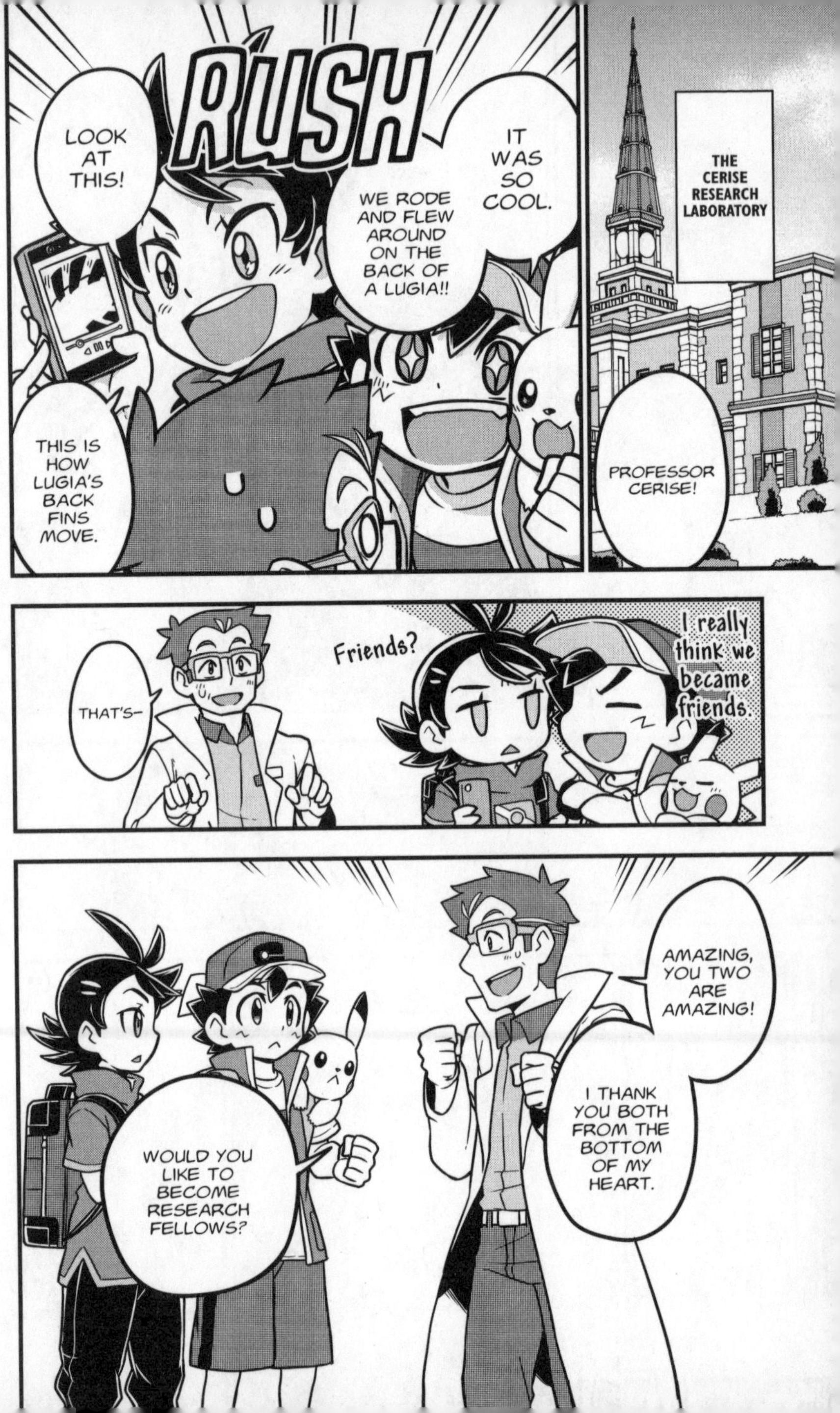
THE CERISE RESEARCH LABORATORY
PROFESSOR CERISE!
IT WAS SO COOL.
WE RODE AND FLEW AROUND ON THE BACK OF A LUGIA!!
RUSH
LOOK AT THIS!
THIS IS HOW LUGIA'S BACK FINS MOVE.
I really think we became friends.
Friends?
THAT'S—
AMAZING, YOU TWO ARE AMAZING!
I THANK YOU BOTH FROM THE BOTTOM OF MY HEART.
WOULD YOU LIKE TO BECOME RESEARCH FELLOWS?

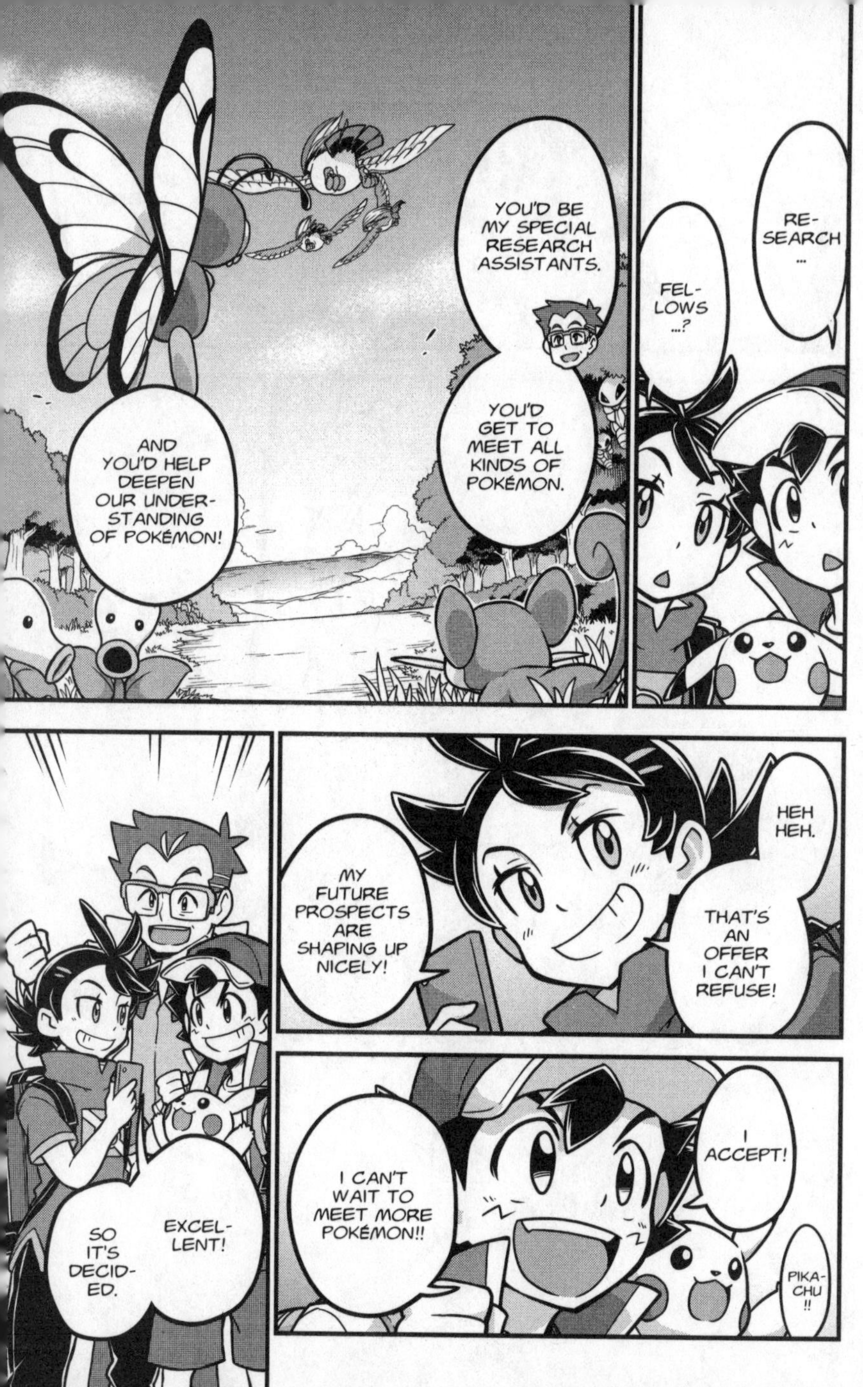
RE- SEARCH ...
FEL- LOWS ...?
YOU'D BE MY SPECIAL RESEARCH ASSISTANTS.
YOU'D GET TO MEET ALL KINDS OF POKÉMON.
AND YOU'D HELP DEEPEN OUR UNDER- STANDING OF POKÉMON!
HEH HEH.
THAT'S AN OFFER I CAN'T REFUSE!
MY FUTURE PROSPECTS ARE SHAPING UP NICELY!
I ACCEPT!
PIKA- CHU !!
I CAN'T WAIT TO MEET MORE POKÉMON!!
EXCEL- LENT!
SO IT'S DECID- ED.

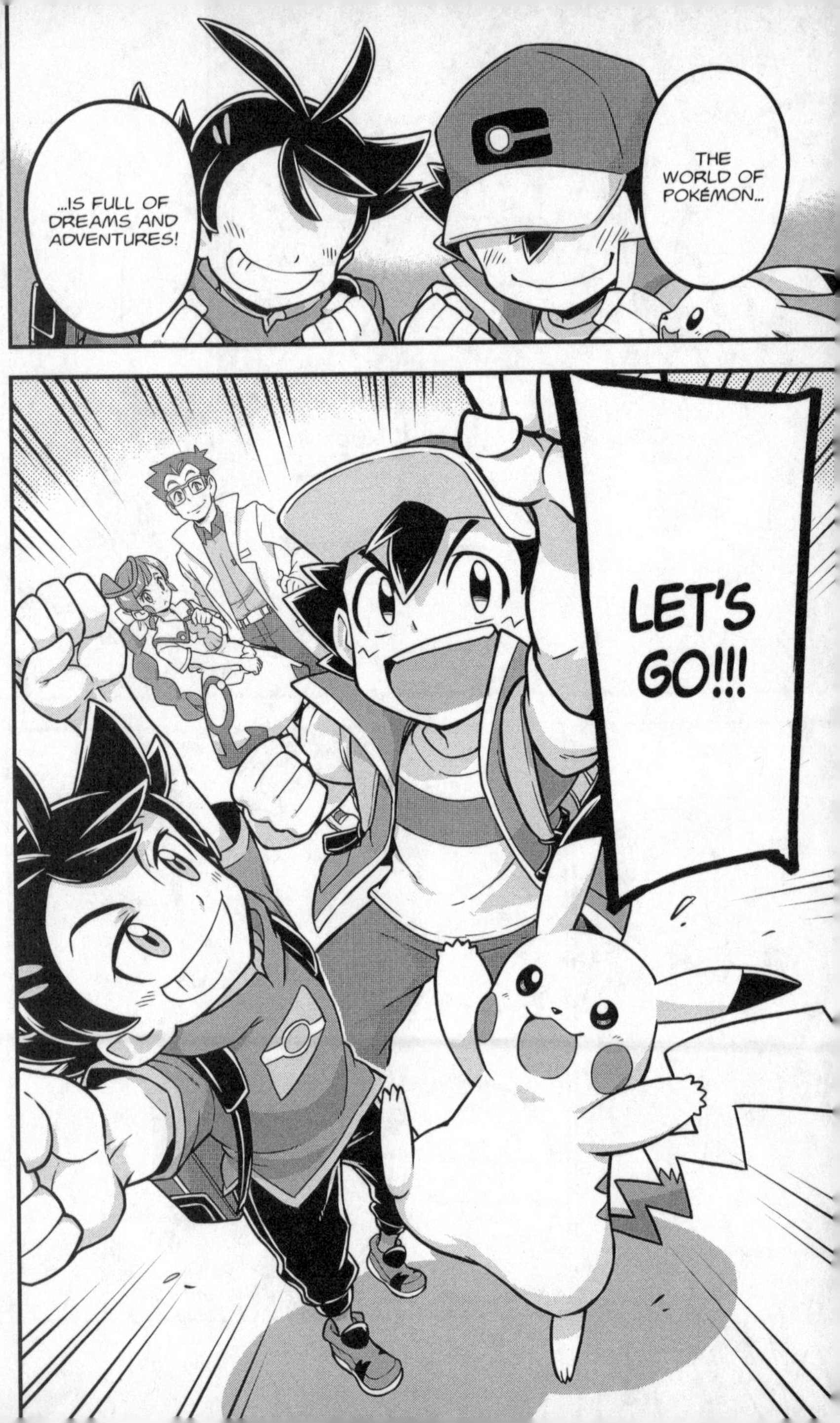
THE WORLD OF POKÉMON...
...IS FULL OF DREAMS AND ADVENTURES!
LET'S GO!!!

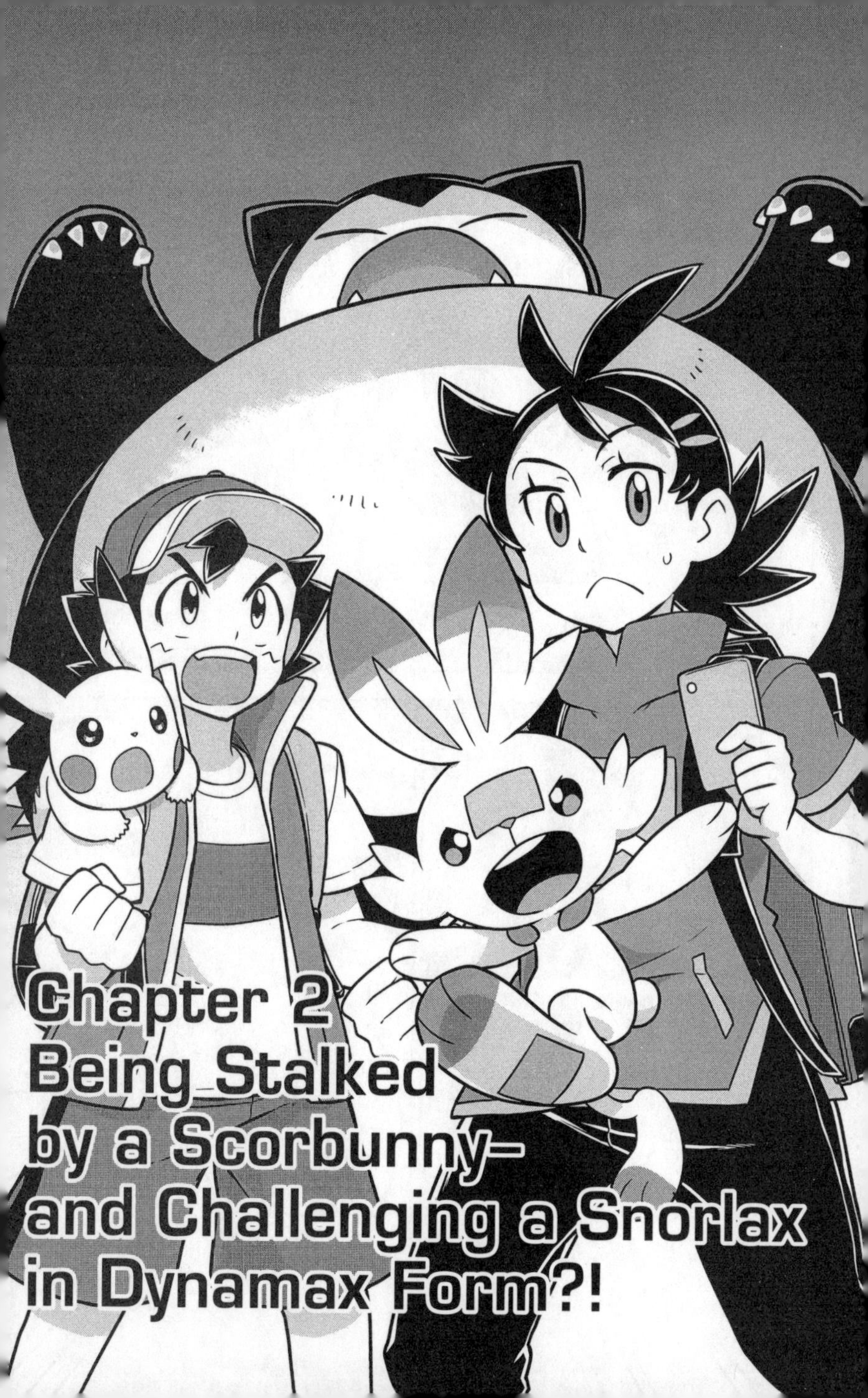

Chapter 2
Being Stalked by a Scorbunny—and Challenging a Snorlax in Dynamax Form?!

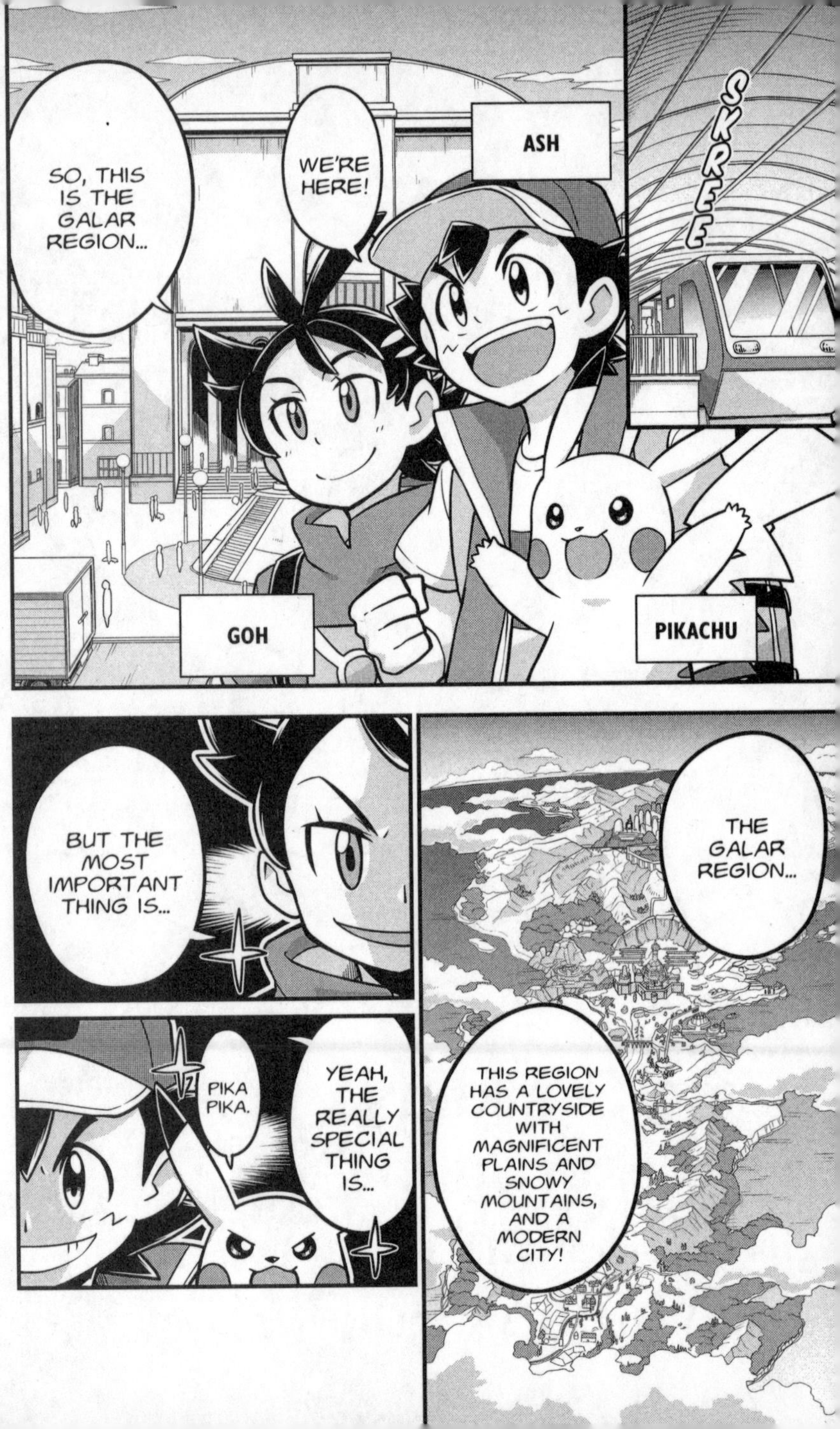
SKREE
ASH
WE'RE HERE!
SO, THIS IS THE GALAR REGION...
PIKACHU
GOH
THE GALAR REGION...
THIS REGION HAS A LOVELY COUNTRYSIDE WITH MAGNIFICENT PLAINS AND SNOWY MOUNTAINS, AND A MODERN CITY!
BUT THE MOST IMPORTANT THING IS...
YEAH, THE REALLY SPECIAL THING IS...
PIKA PIKA.

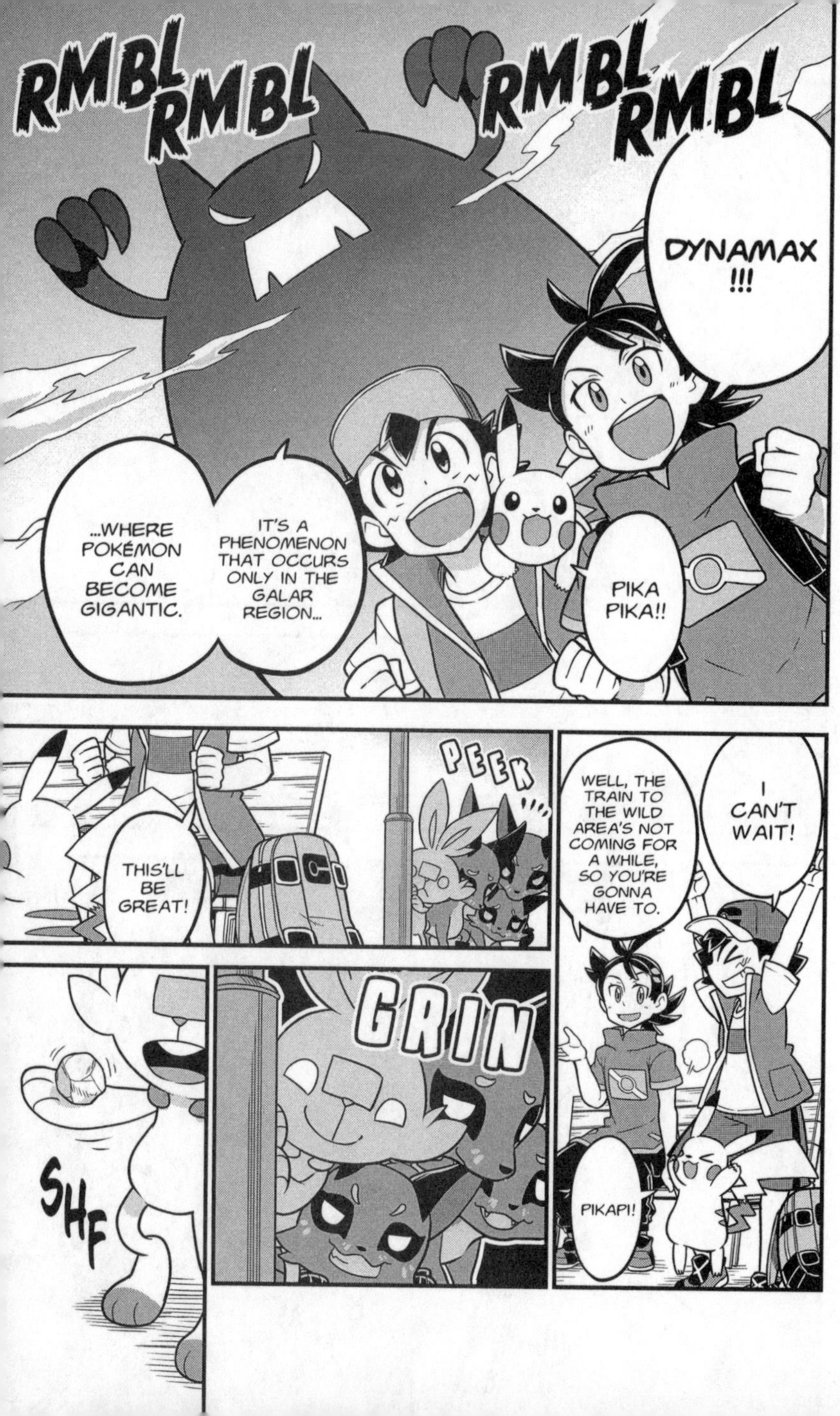
RMBL RMBL
RMBL RMBL
DYNAMAX!!!
PIKA PIKA!!
IT'S A PHENOMENON THAT OCCURS ONLY IN THE GALAR REGION...
...WHERE POKÉMON CAN BECOME GIGANTIC.
I CAN'T WAIT!
WELL, THE TRAIN TO THE WILD AREA'S NOT COMING FOR A WHILE, SO YOU'RE GONNA HAVE TO.
PIKAPI!
PEEK
THIS'LL BE GREAT!
GRIN
SHF

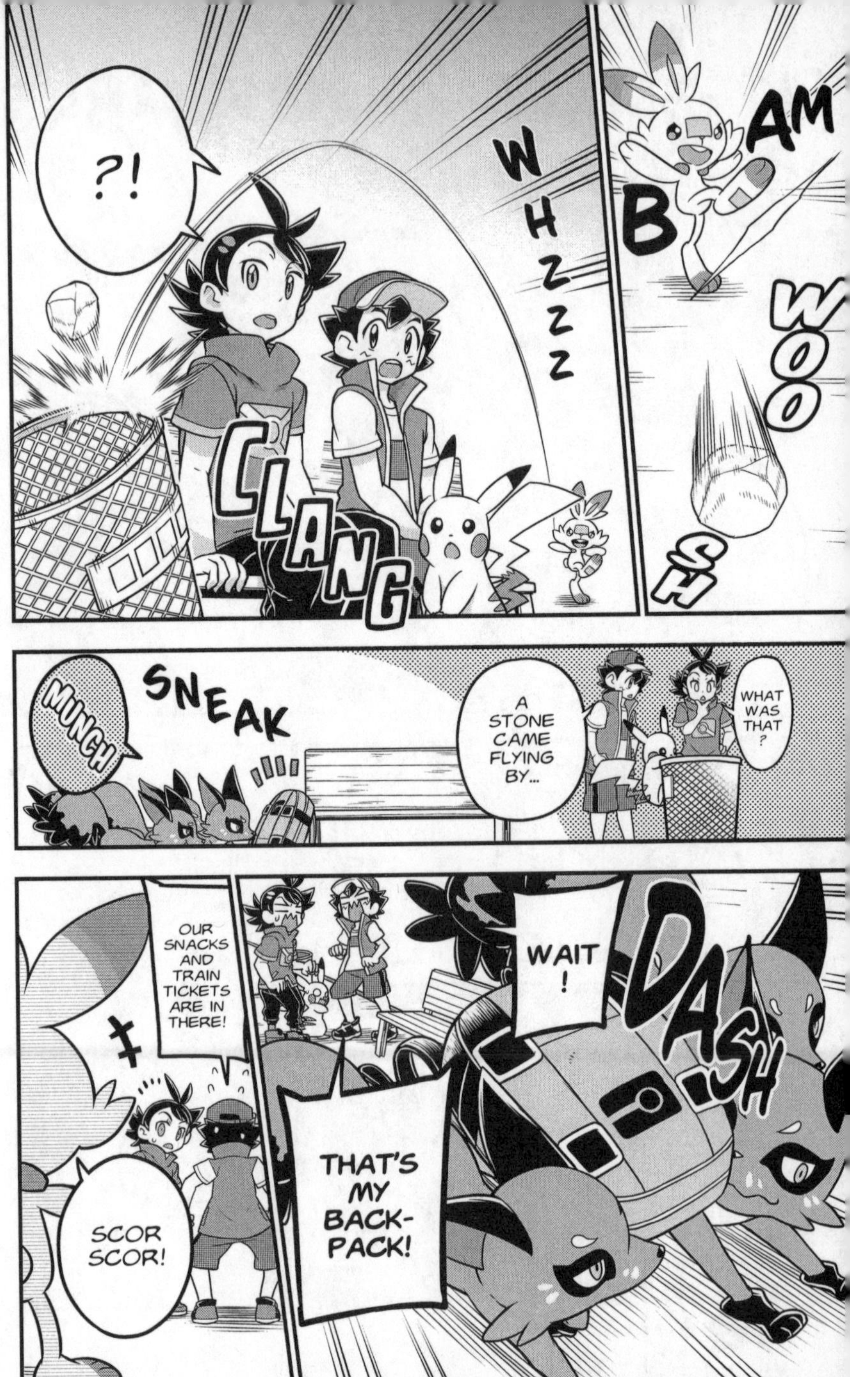
BAM
WOOSH
WHZZZ
?!
CLANG
WHAT WAS THAT?
A STONE CAME FLYING BY...
SNEAK
MUNCH
DASH
WAIT!
THAT'S MY BACK-PACK!
OUR SNACKS AND TRAIN TICKETS ARE IN THERE!
SCOR SCOR!

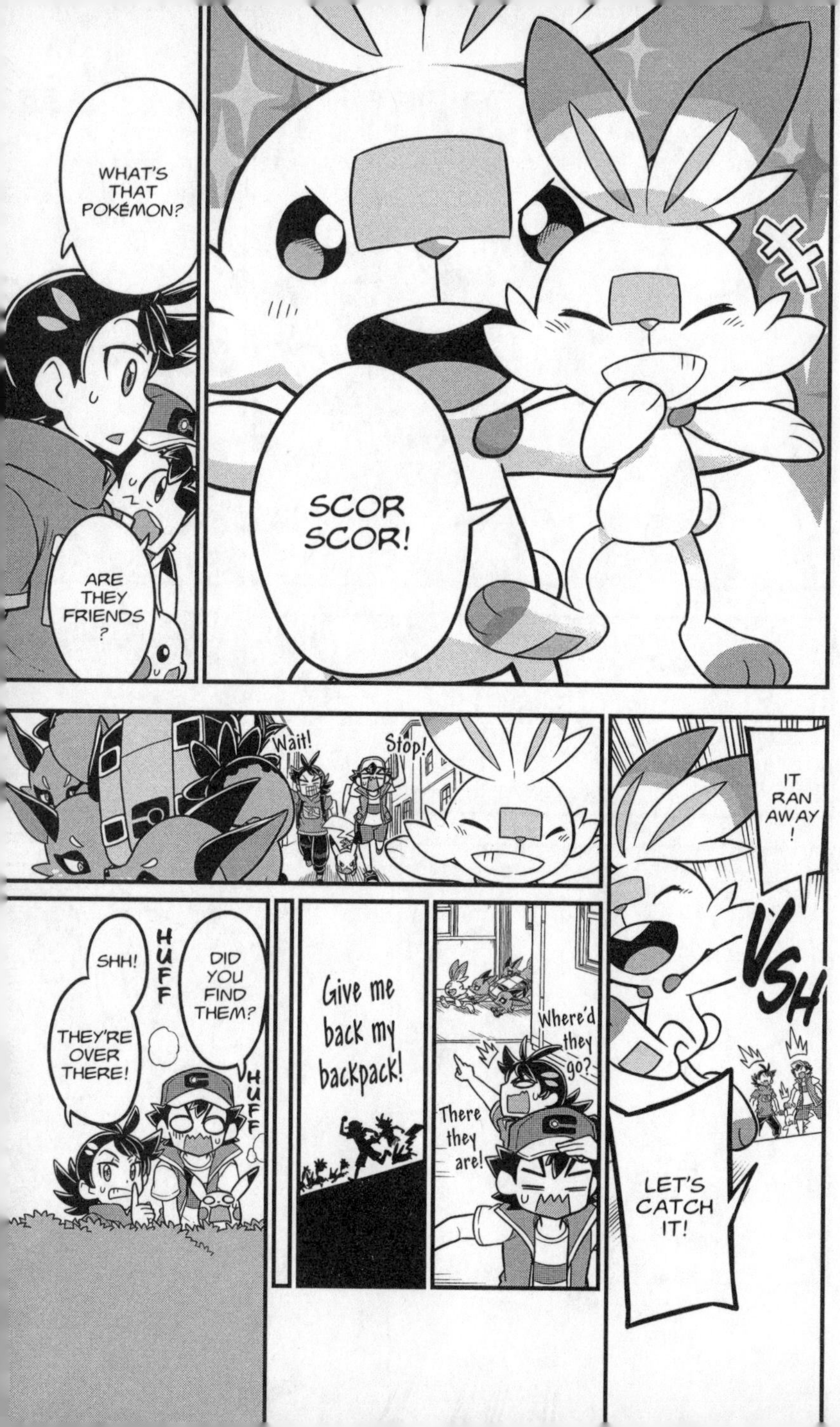

SCOR SCOR!
WHAT'S THAT POKÉMON?
ARE THEY FRIENDS?
IT RAN AWAY!
VSH
LET'S CATCH IT!
Stop!
Wait!
Where'd they go?
There they are!
Give me back my backpack!
DID YOU FIND THEM?
HUFF
HUFF
SHH!
THEY'RE OVER THERE!

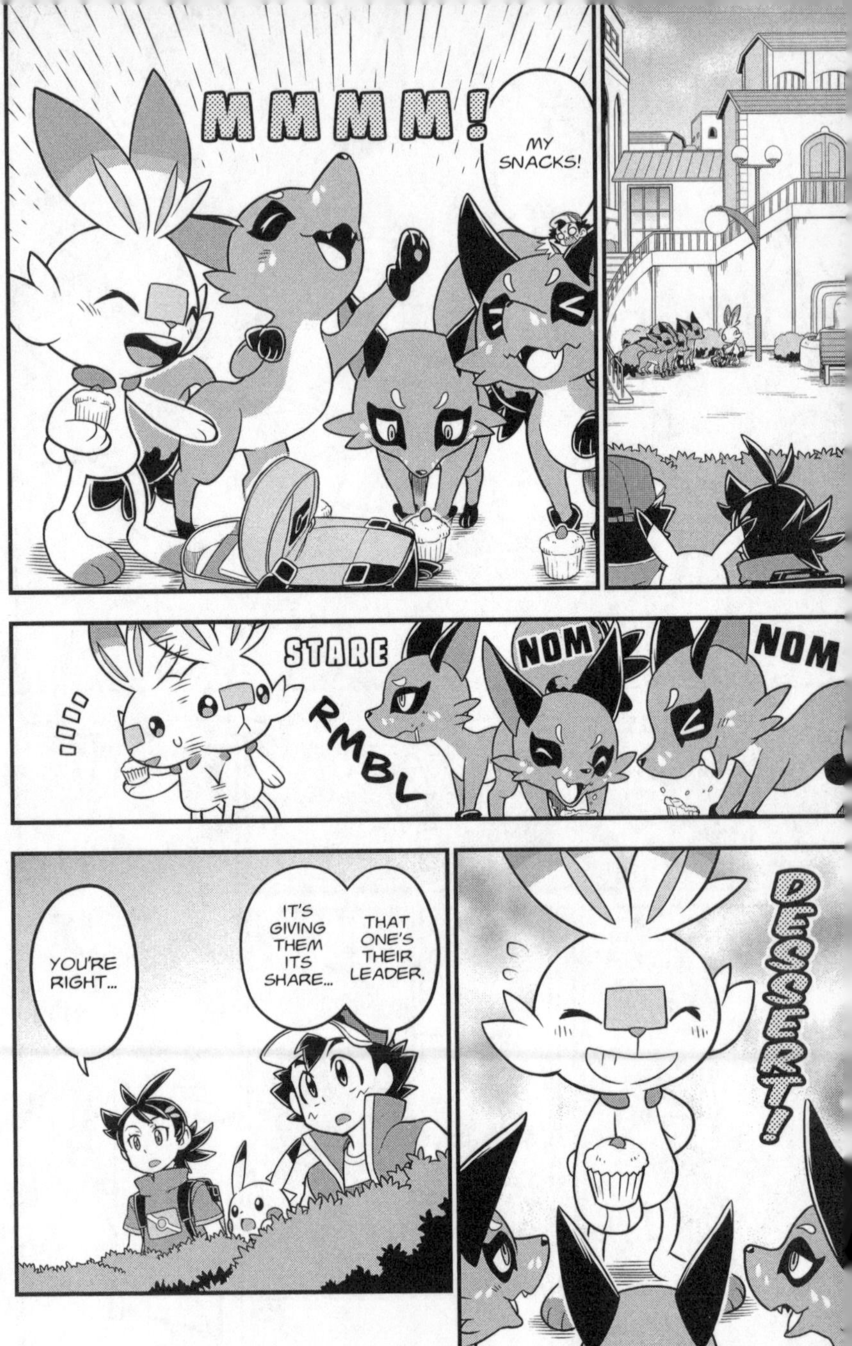
MY SNACKS!
MMMMM!
NOM
NOM
STARE
RMBL
DESSERT!
THAT ONE'S THEIR LEADER.
IT'S GIVING THEM ITS SHARE...
YOU'RE RIGHT...

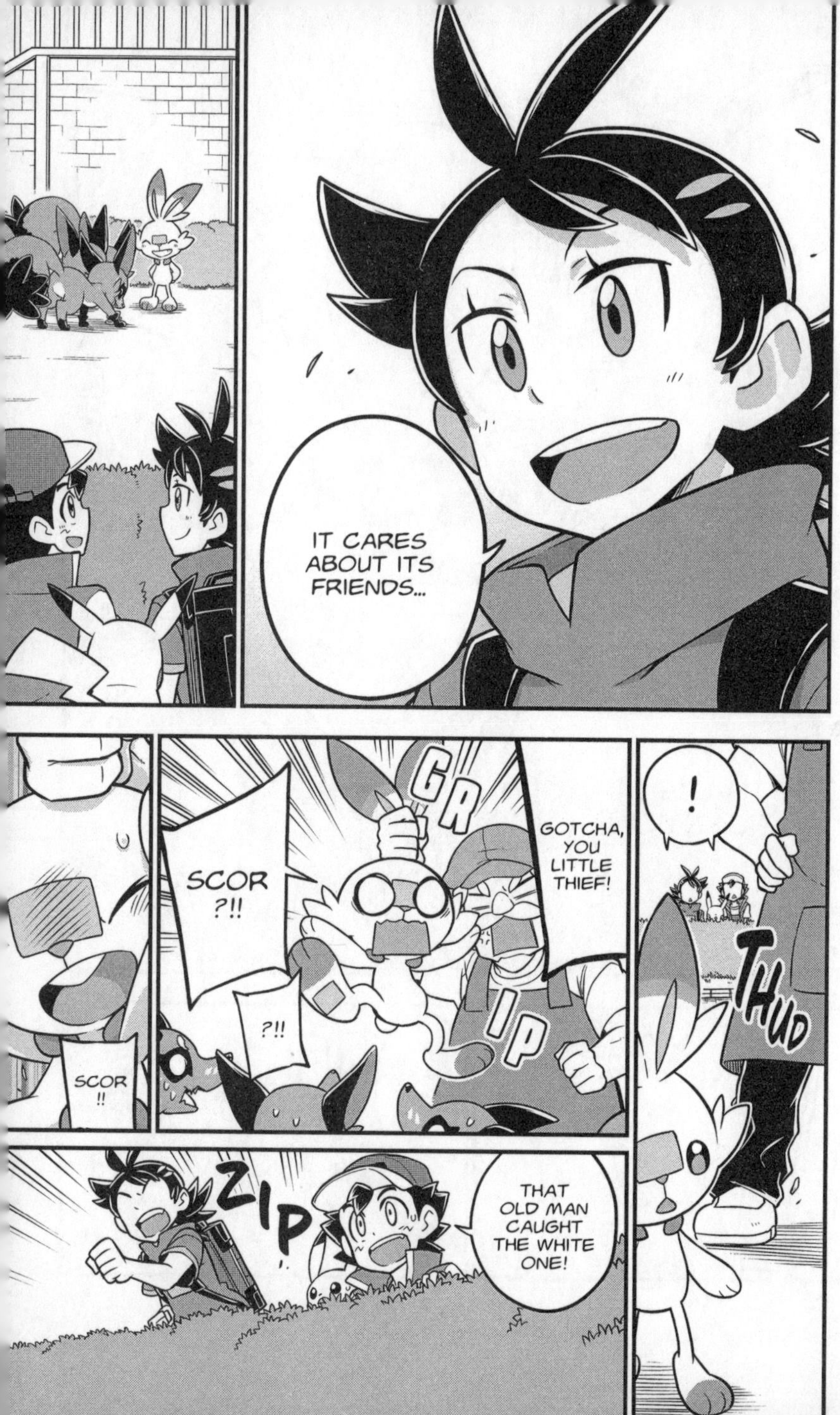
IT CARES ABOUT ITS FRIENDS...
!
THUD
GOTCHA, YOU LITTLE THIEF!
GRIP
SCOR ?!!
?!!
SCOR !!
THAT OLD MAN CAUGHT THE WHITE ONE!
ZIP

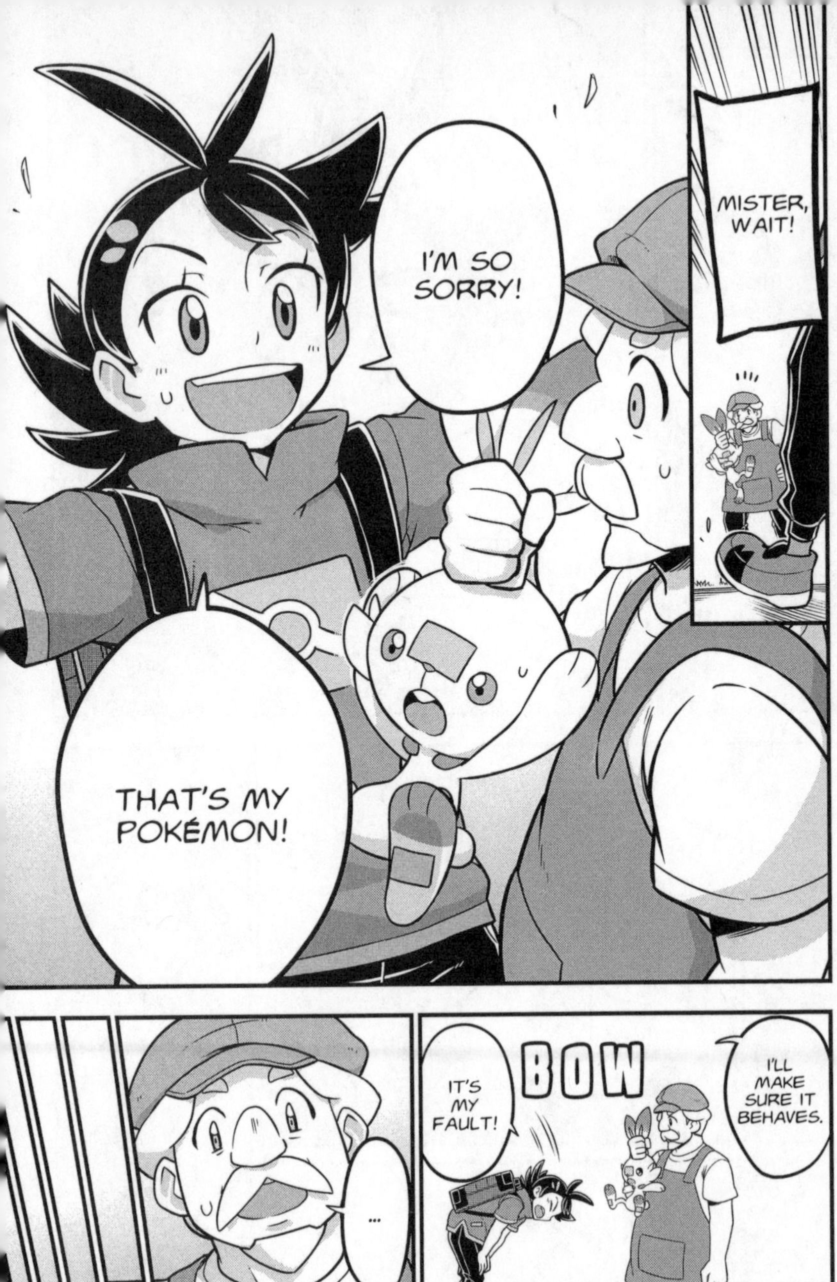
MISTER, WAIT!
I'M SO SORRY!
THAT'S MY POKÉMON!
I'LL MAKE SURE IT BEHAVES.
BOW
IT'S MY FAULT!
...

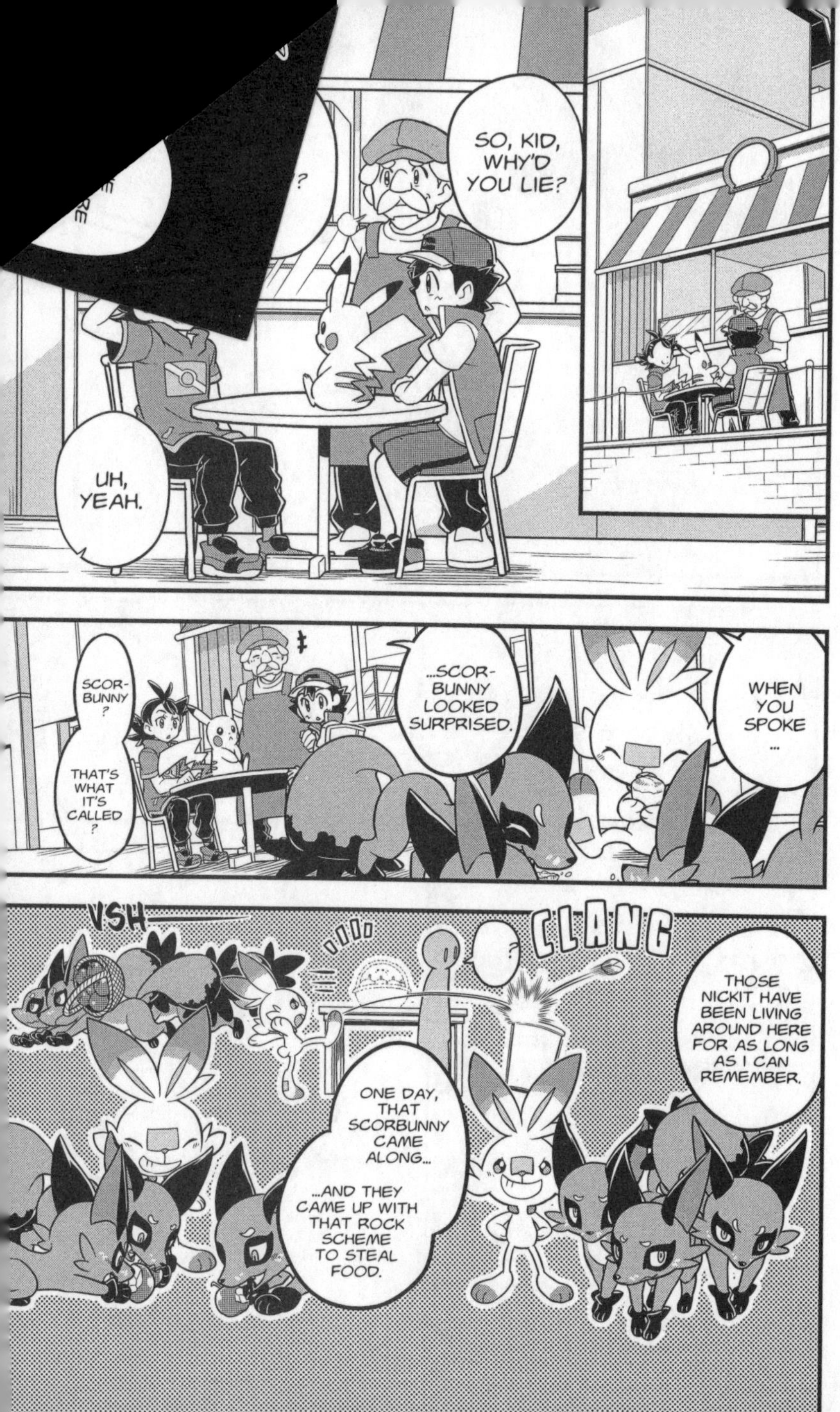
SO, KID, WHY'D YOU LIE?
UH, YEAH.
WHEN YOU SPOKE...
...SCORBUNNY LOOKED SURPRISED.
SCORBUNNY?
THAT'S WHAT IT'S CALLED?
CLANG
THOSE NICKIT HAVE BEEN LIVING AROUND HERE FOR AS LONG AS I CAN REMEMBER.
VSH
ONE DAY, THAT SCORBUNNY CAME ALONG...
...AND THEY CAME UP WITH THAT ROCK SCHEME TO STEAL FOOD.

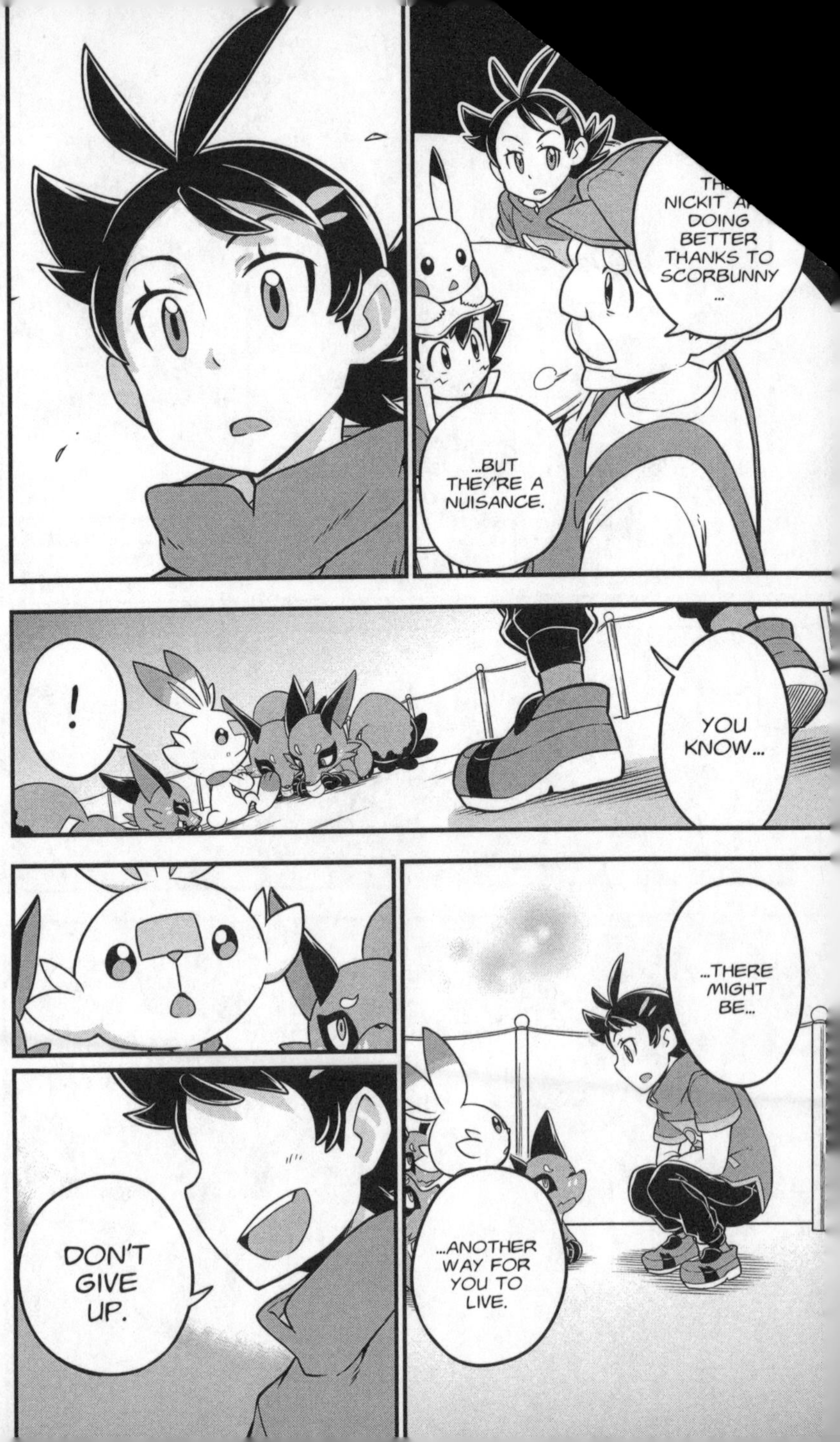
THE NICKIT A DOING BETTER THANKS TO SCORBUNNY ...
...BUT THEY'RE A NUISANCE.
YOU KNOW...
!
...THERE MIGHT BE...
...ANOTHER WAY FOR YOU TO LIVE.
DON'T GIVE UP.

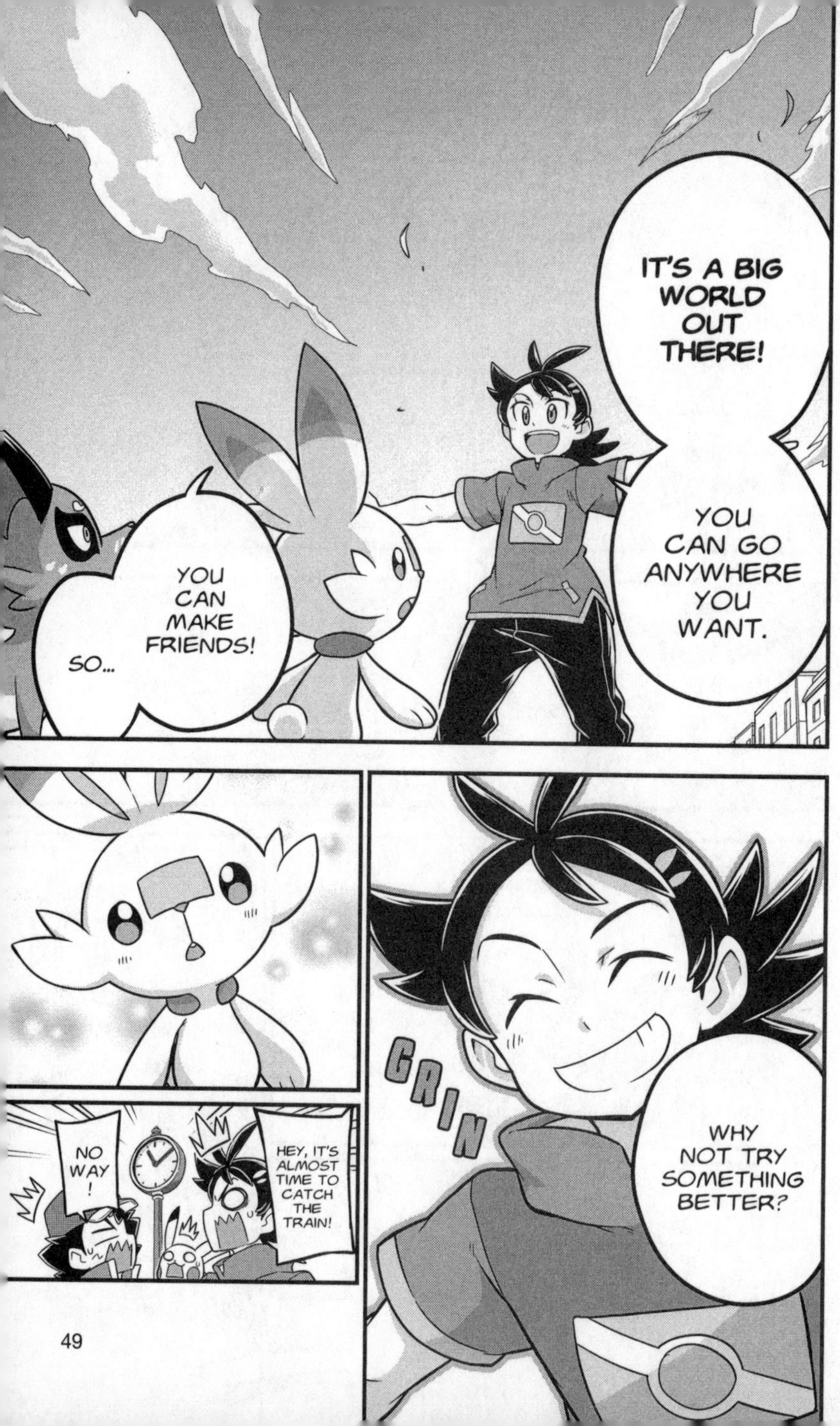

IT'S A BIG WORLD OUT THERE!
YOU CAN GO ANYWHERE YOU WANT.
YOU CAN MAKE FRIENDS!
SO...
GRIN
WHY NOT TRY SOMETHING BETTER?
HEY, IT'S ALMOST TIME TO CATCH THE TRAIN!
NO WAY!

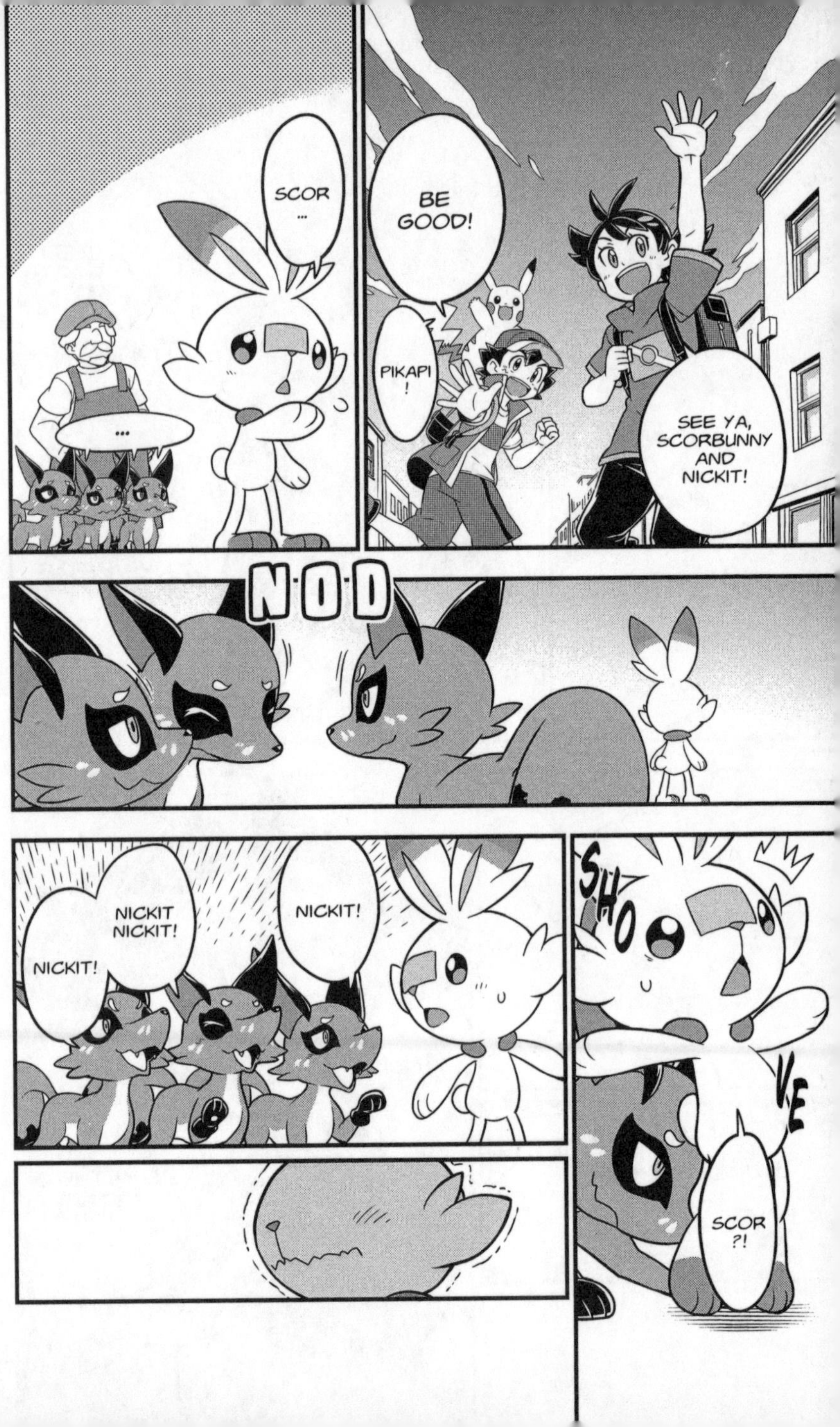
SEE YA, SCORBUNNY AND NICKIT!
BE GOOD!
PIKAPI!
SCOR...
...
NOD
SHOVE
SCOR?!
NICKIT!
NICKIT NICKIT!
NICKIT!

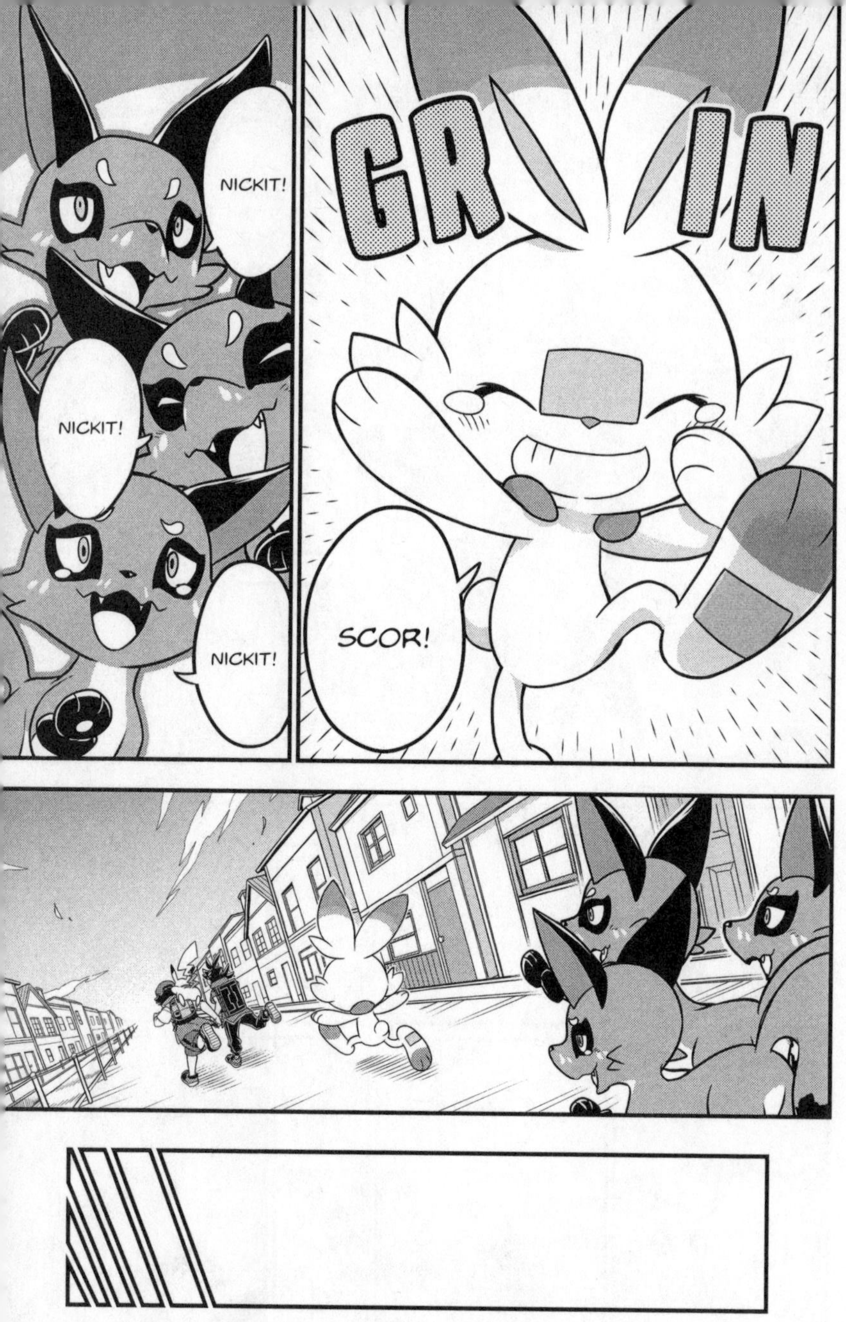
GR IN
SCOR!
NICKIT!
NICKIT!
NICKIT!

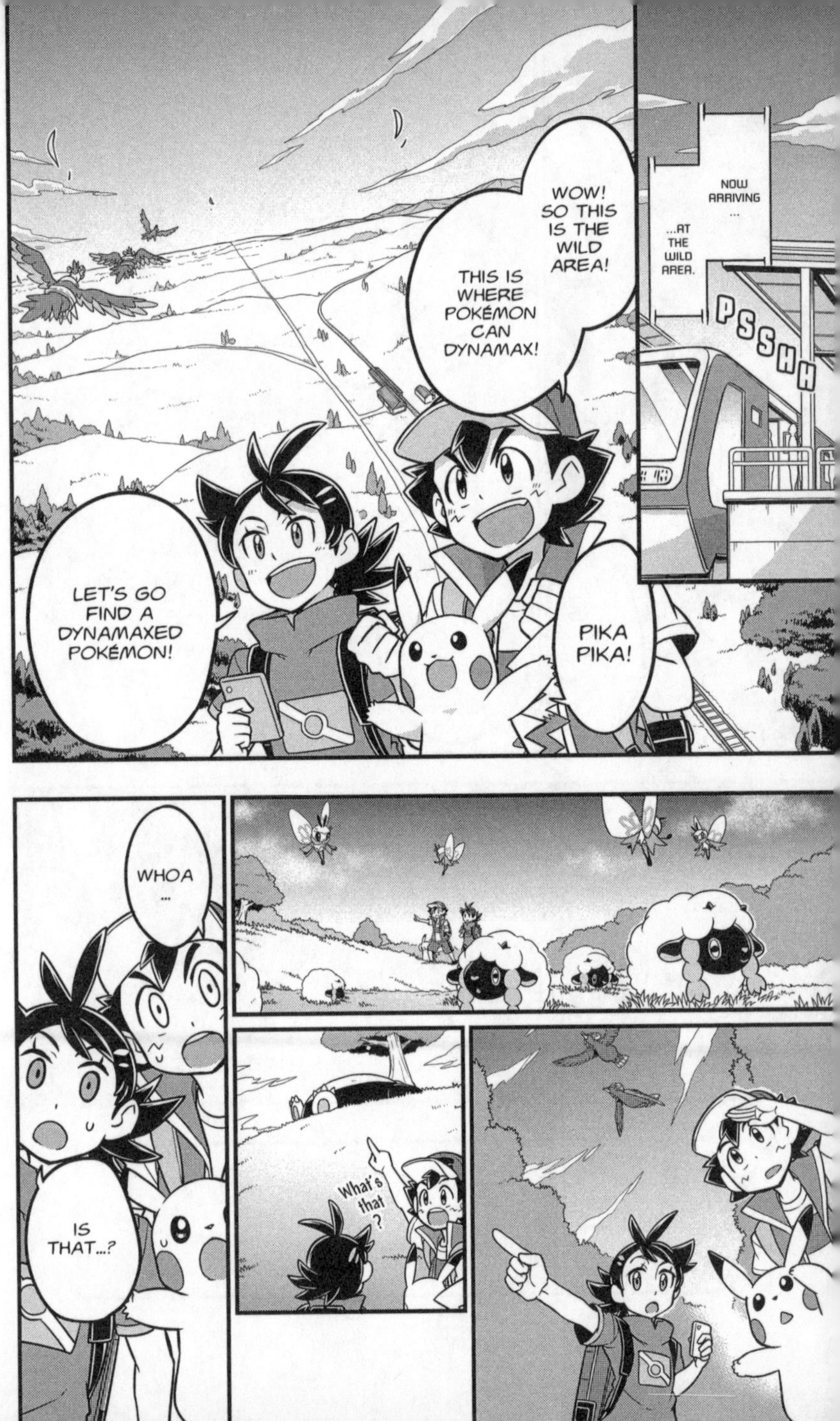
NOW ARRIVING ...
...AT THE WILD AREA.
PSSHH
WOW! SO THIS IS THE WILD AREA!
THIS IS WHERE POKÉMON CAN DYNAMAX!
PIKA PIKA!
LET'S GO FIND A DYNAMAXED POKÉMON!
What's that?
WHOA ...
IS THAT...?

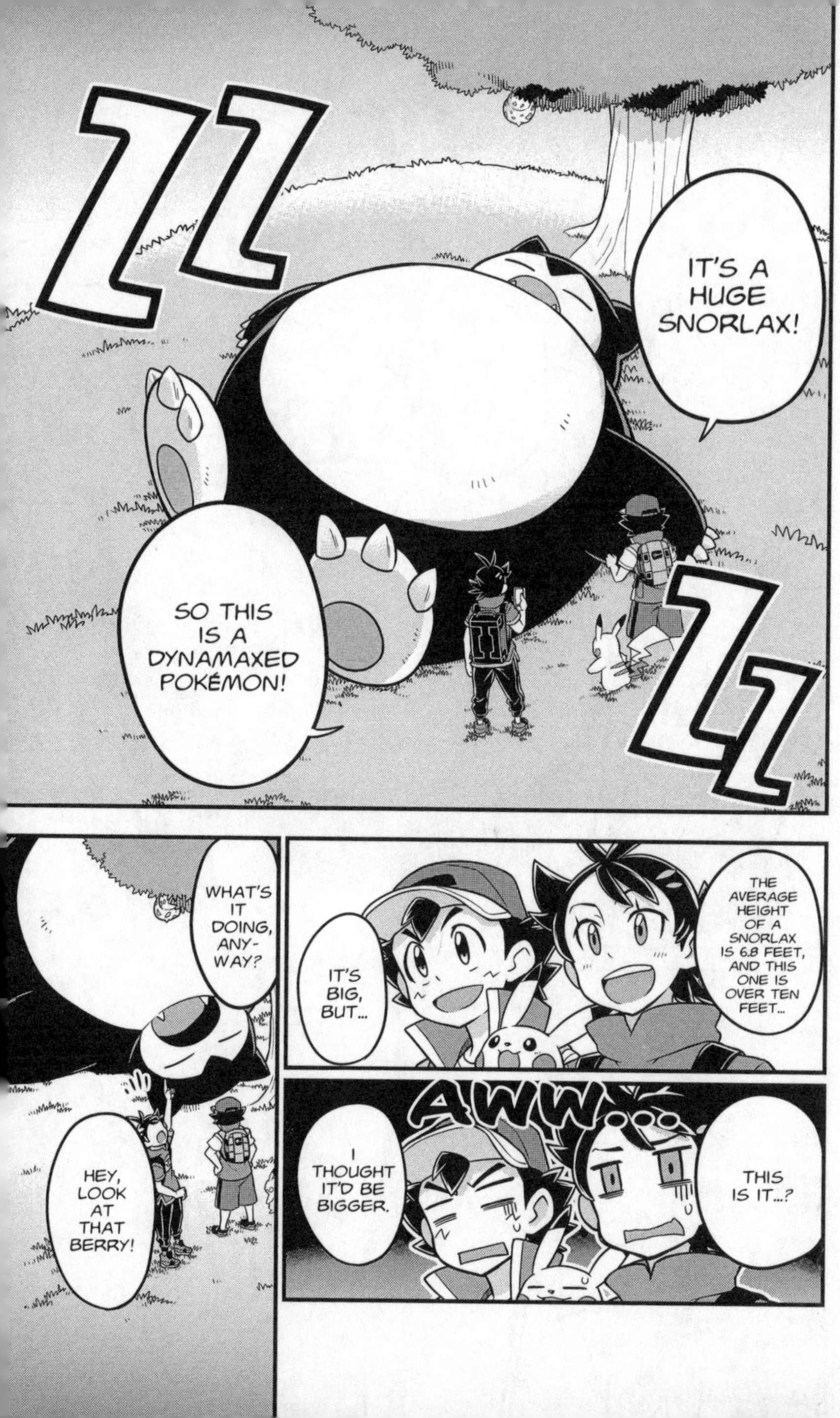
ZZ
IT'S A HUGE SNORLAX!
SO THIS IS A DYNAMAXED POKÉMON!
ZZ
THE AVERAGE HEIGHT OF A SNORLAX IS 6.8 FEET, AND THIS ONE IS OVER TEN FEET...
IT'S BIG, BUT...
AWW...
THIS IS IT...?
I THOUGHT IT'D BE BIGGER.
WHAT'S IT DOING, ANY-WAY?
HEY, LOOK AT THAT BERRY!

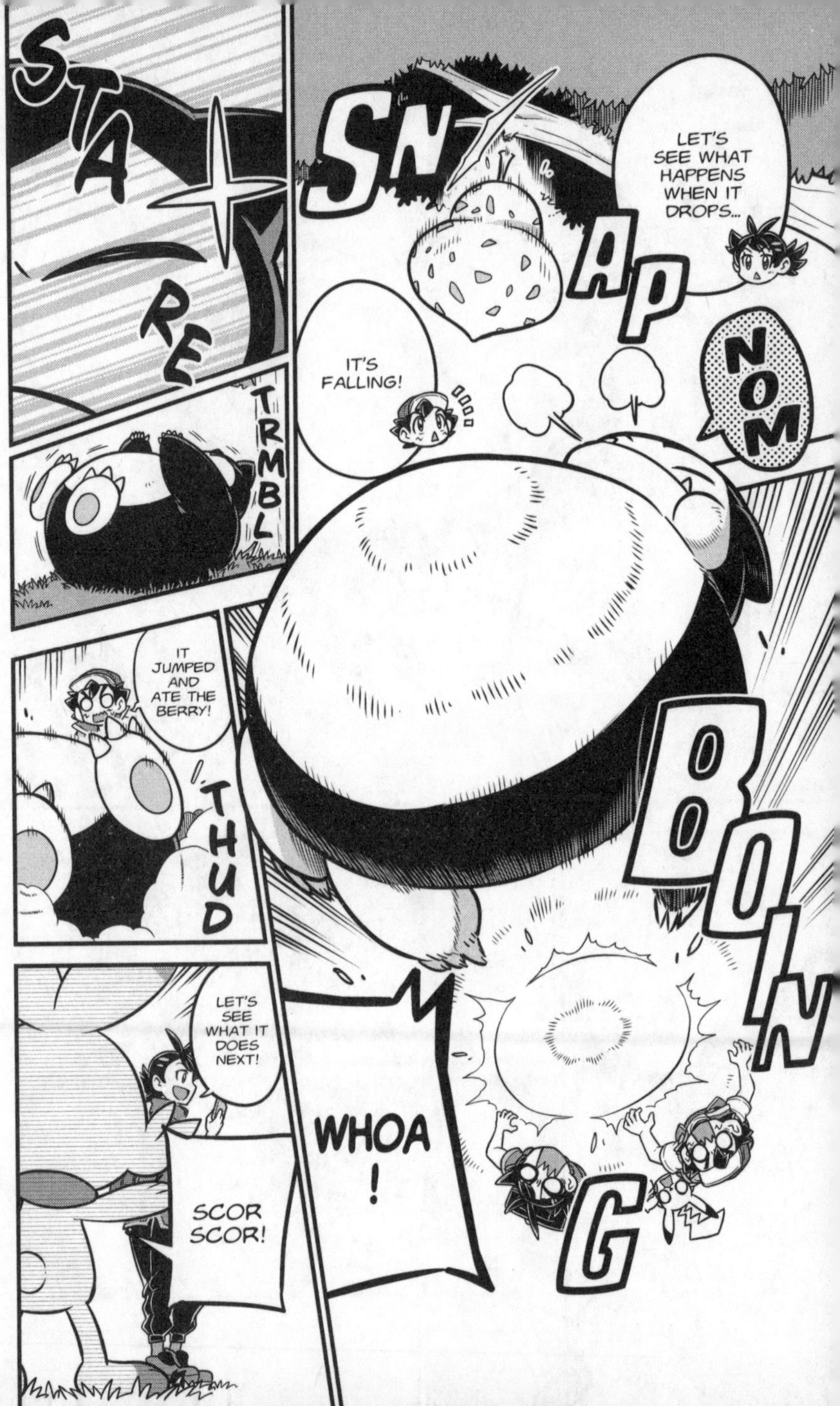
SNAP
LET'S SEE WHAT HAPPENS WHEN IT DROPS...
IT'S FALLING!
NOM
BOOOING
WHOA!
STARE
TRMBL
IT JUMPED AND ATE THE BERRY!
THUD
LET'S SEE WHAT IT DOES NEXT!
SCOR SCOR!

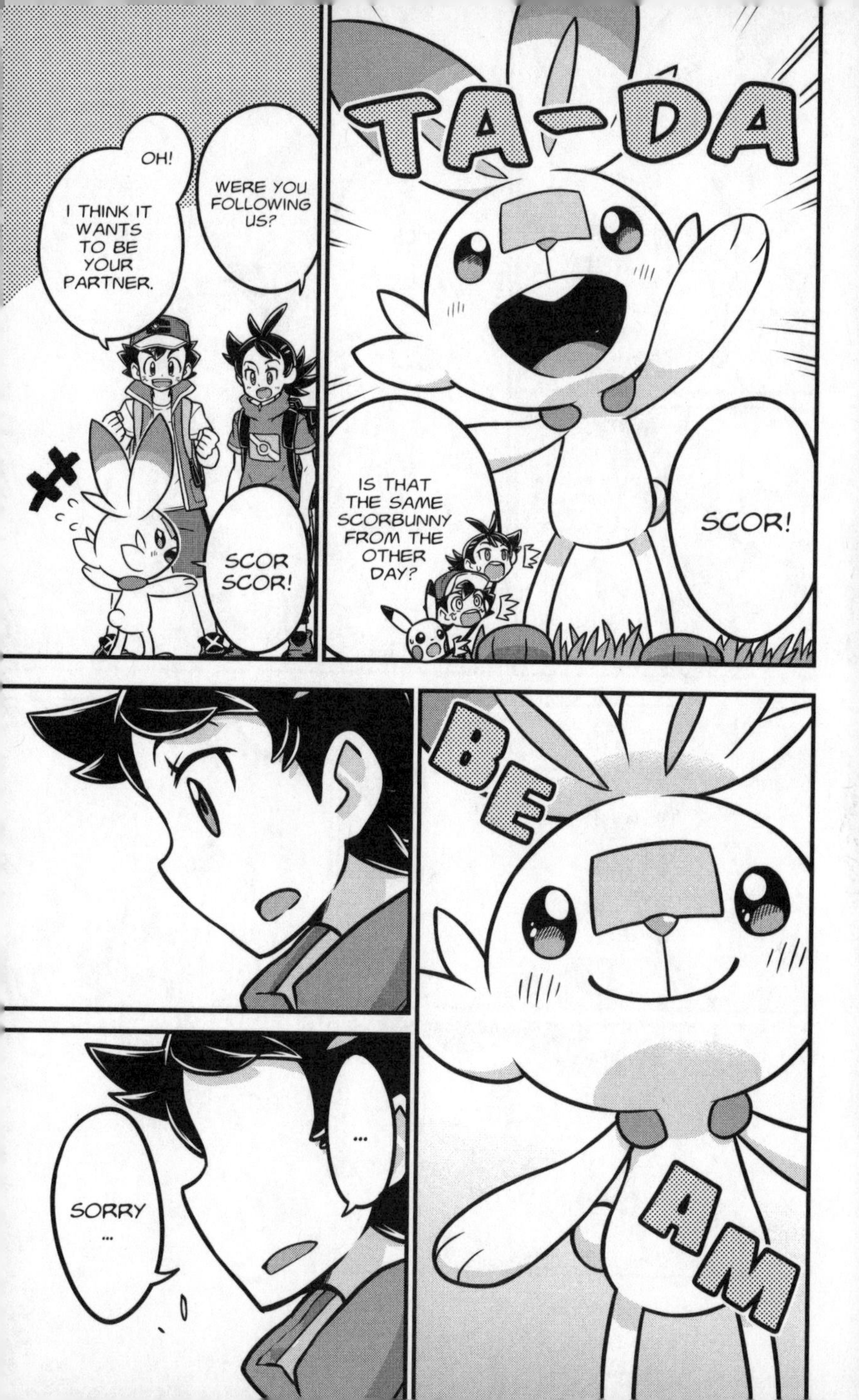
TA-DA
SCOR!
IS THAT THE SAME SCORBUNNY FROM THE OTHER DAY?
WERE YOU FOLLOWING US?
OH!
I THINK IT WANTS TO BE YOUR PARTNER.
SCOR SCOR!
BEAM
...
SORRY ...

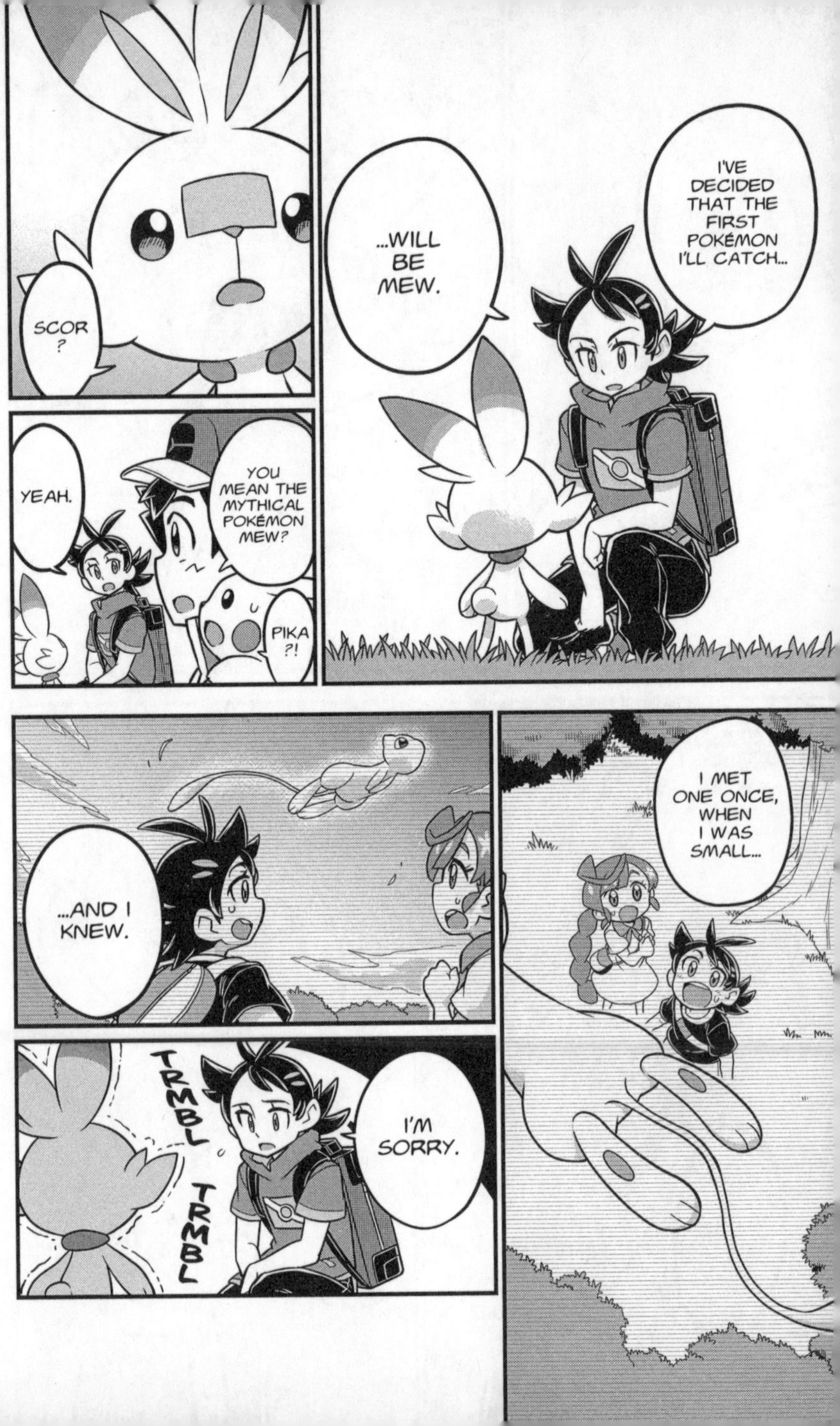

I'VE DECIDED THAT THE FIRST POKÉMON I'LL CATCH...
...WILL BE MEW.
SCOR ?
YOU MEAN THE MYTHICAL POKÉMON MEW?
PIKA ?!
YEAH.
I MET ONE ONCE, WHEN I WAS SMALL...
...AND I KNEW.
I'M SORRY.
TRMBL TRMBL

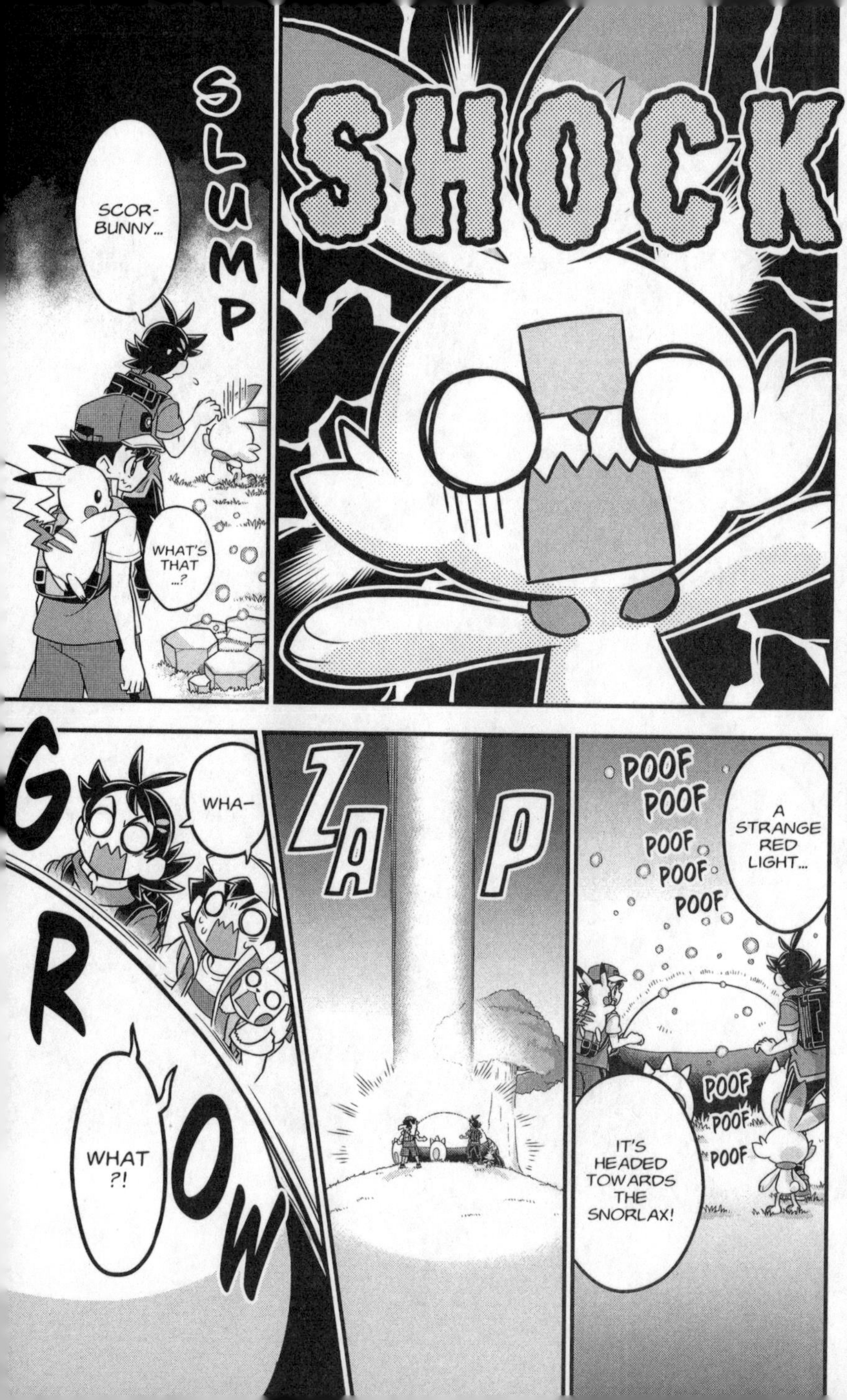
SHOCK
SLUMP
SCOR-BUNNY...
WHAT'S THAT ...?
A STRANGE RED LIGHT...
POOF POOF POOF POOF POOF
IT'S HEADED TOWARDS THE SNORLAX!
POOF POOF POOF
ZAP
GROW
WHA-
WHAT?!

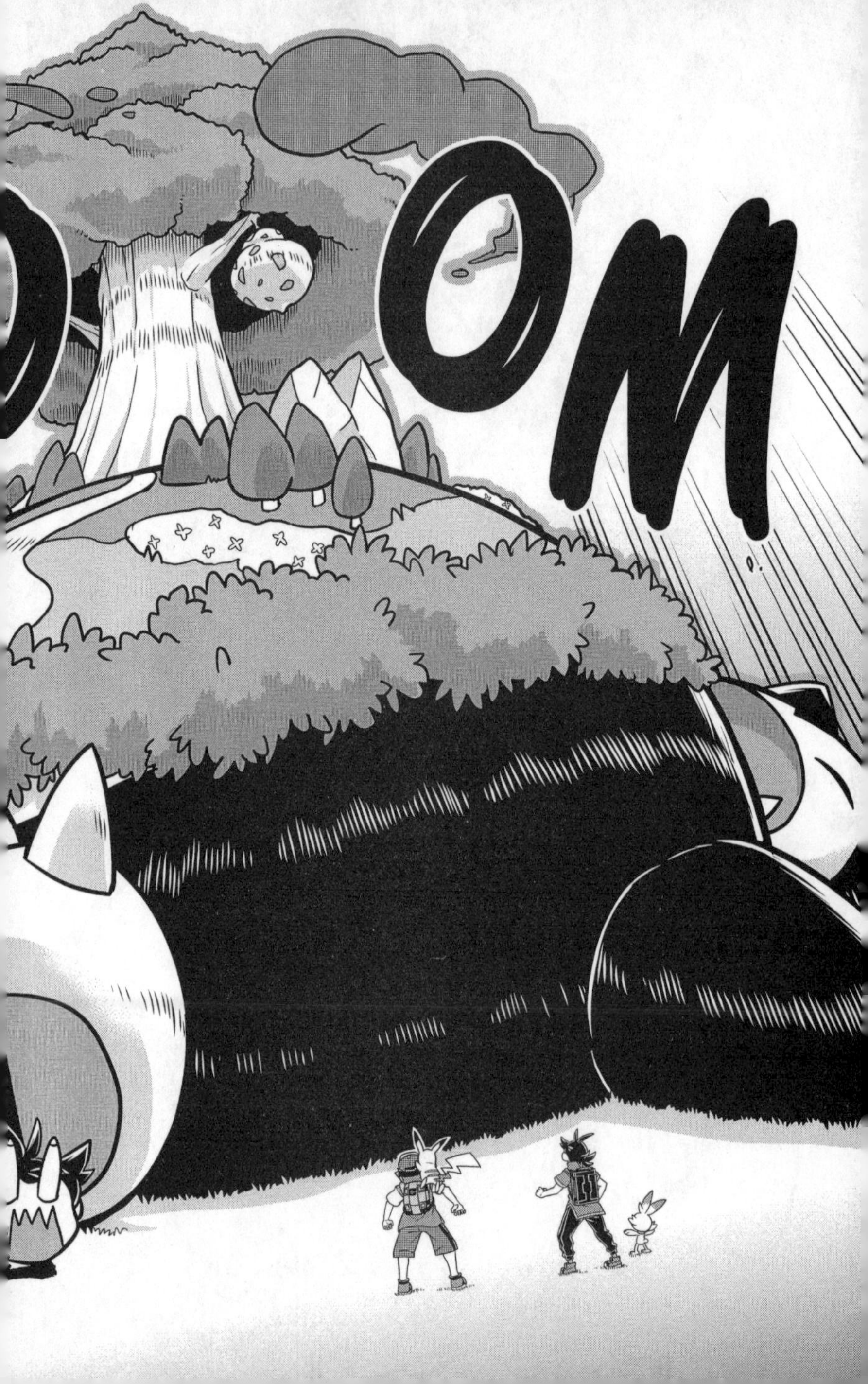
OOM

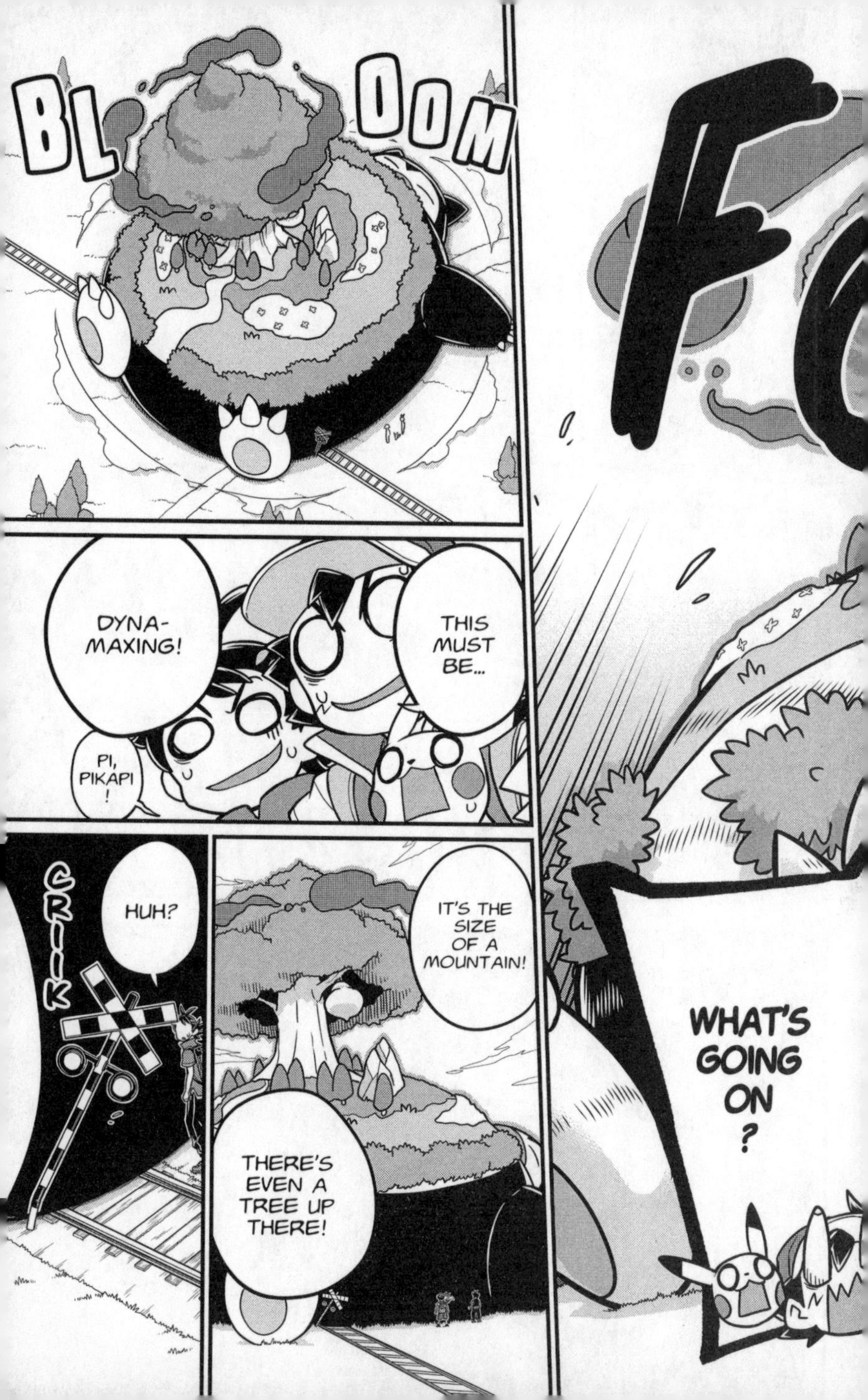
FO
WHAT'S GOING ON?
BLOOM
THIS MUST BE...
DYNA-MAXING!
PI, PIKAPI!
IT'S THE SIZE OF A MOUNTAIN!
THERE'S EVEN A TREE UP THERE!
HUH?
CR—K

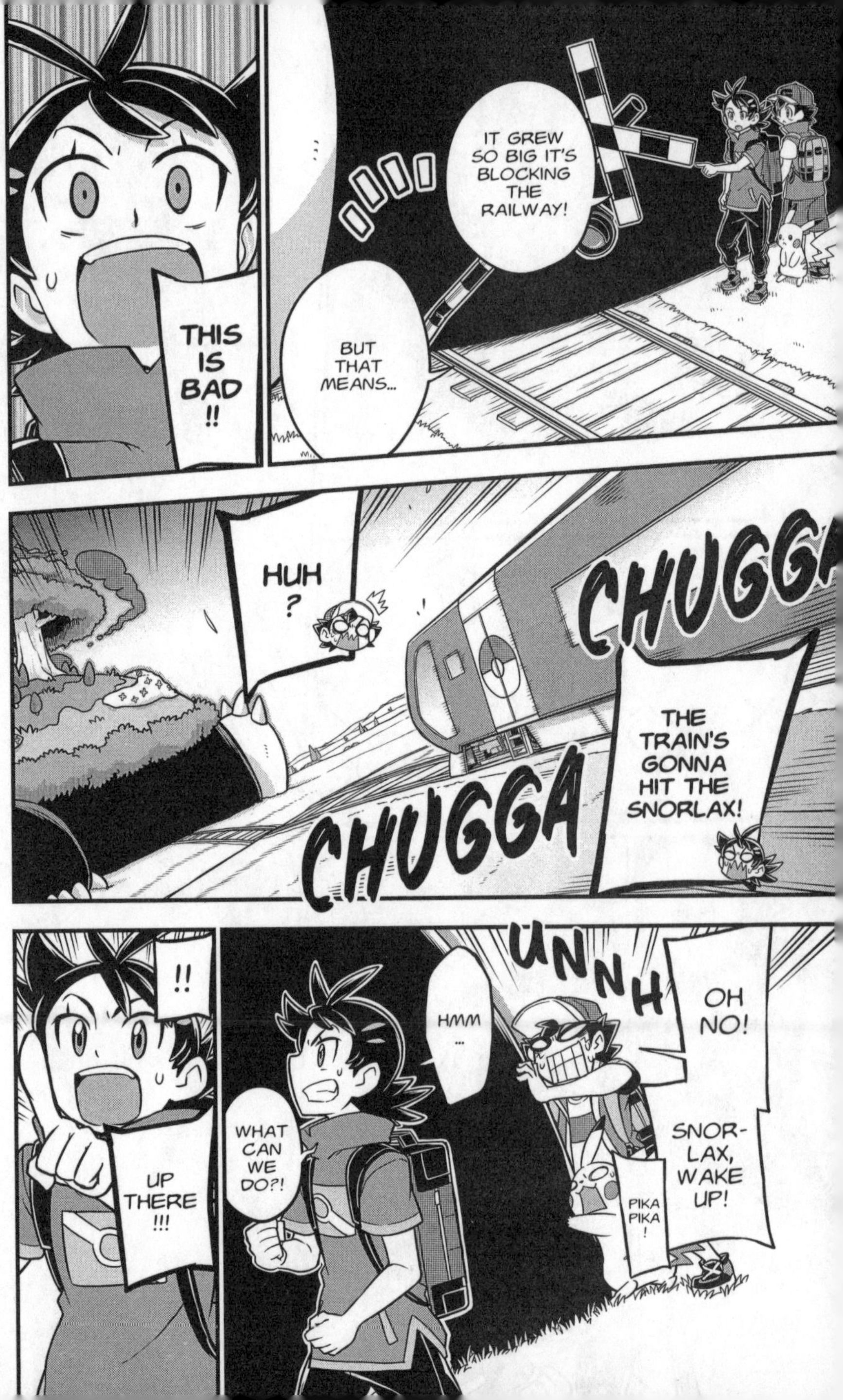
IT GREW SO BIG IT'S BLOCKING THE RAILWAY!
BUT THAT MEANS...
THIS IS BAD !!
CHUGGA
THE TRAIN'S GONNA HIT THE SNORLAX!
HUH ?
CHUGGA
OH NO!
UNNH
HMM ...
SNOR-LAX, WAKE UP!
PIKA PIKA !
WHAT CAN WE DO?!
!!
UP THERE !!!

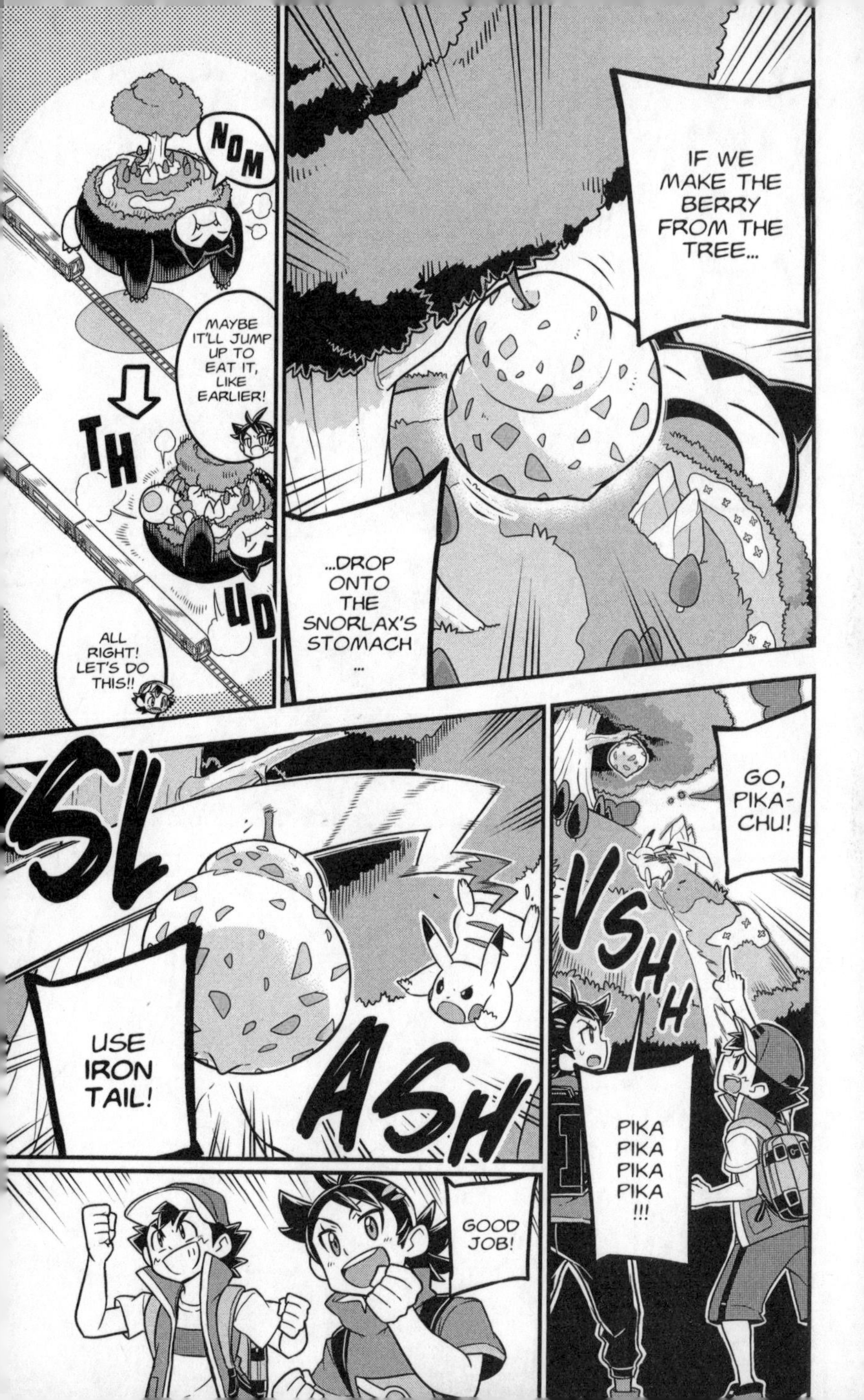
IF WE MAKE THE BERRY FROM THE TREE...
...DROP ONTO THE SNORLAX'S STOMACH...
NOM
MAYBE IT'LL JUMP UP TO EAT IT, LIKE EARLIER!
THUD
ALL RIGHT! LET'S DO THIS!!
GO, PIKA-CHU!
VSHH
PIKA PIKA PIKA PIKA!!!
SLASH
USE IRON TAIL!
GOOD JOB!

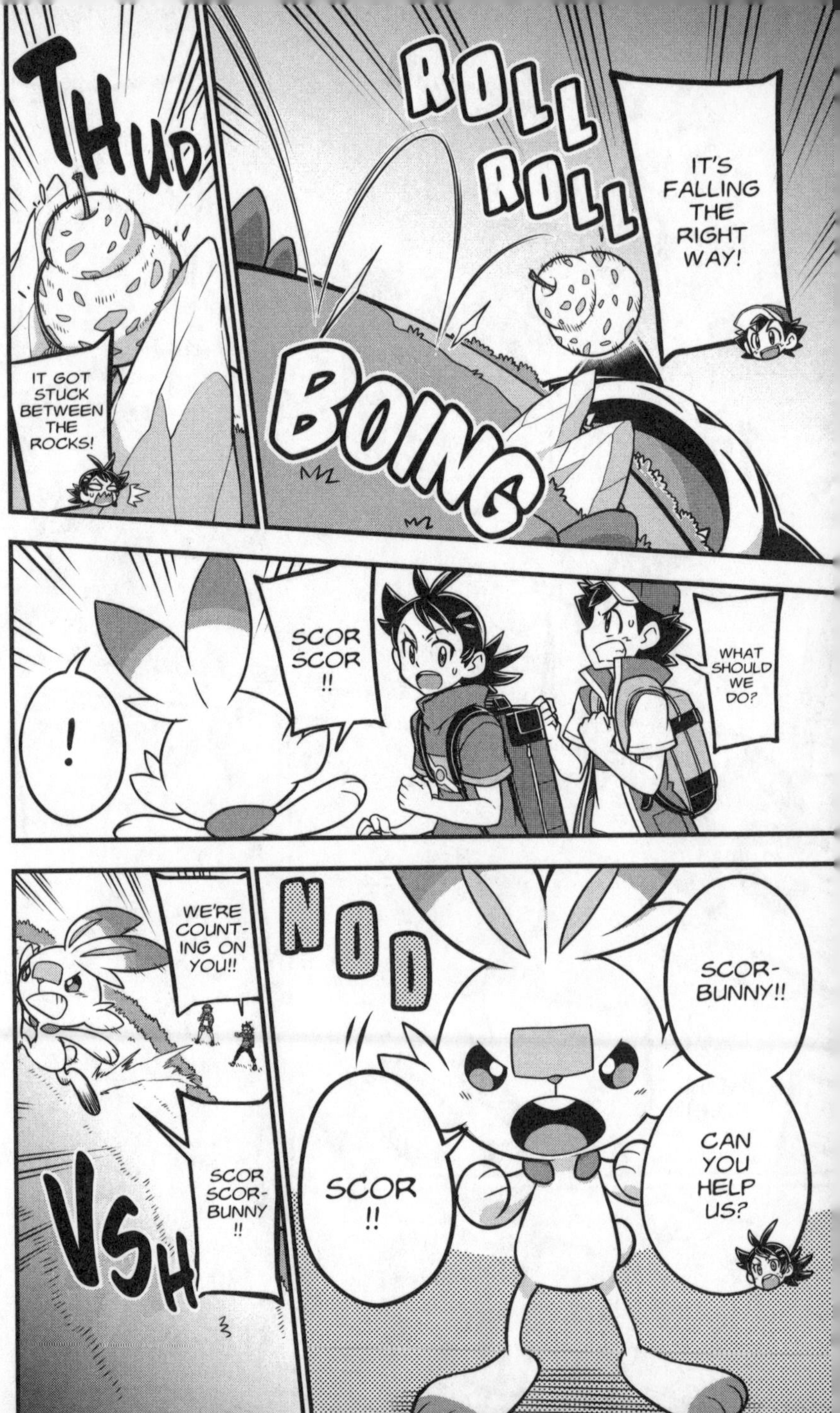

ROLL ROLL
IT'S FALLING THE RIGHT WAY!
BOING
THUD
IT GOT STUCK BETWEEN THE ROCKS!
WHAT SHOULD WE DO?
SCOR SCOR !!
!
SCOR-BUNNY!!
NOD
CAN YOU HELP US?
SCOR !!
WE'RE COUNTING ON YOU!!
SCOR SCOR-BUNNY !!
VSH

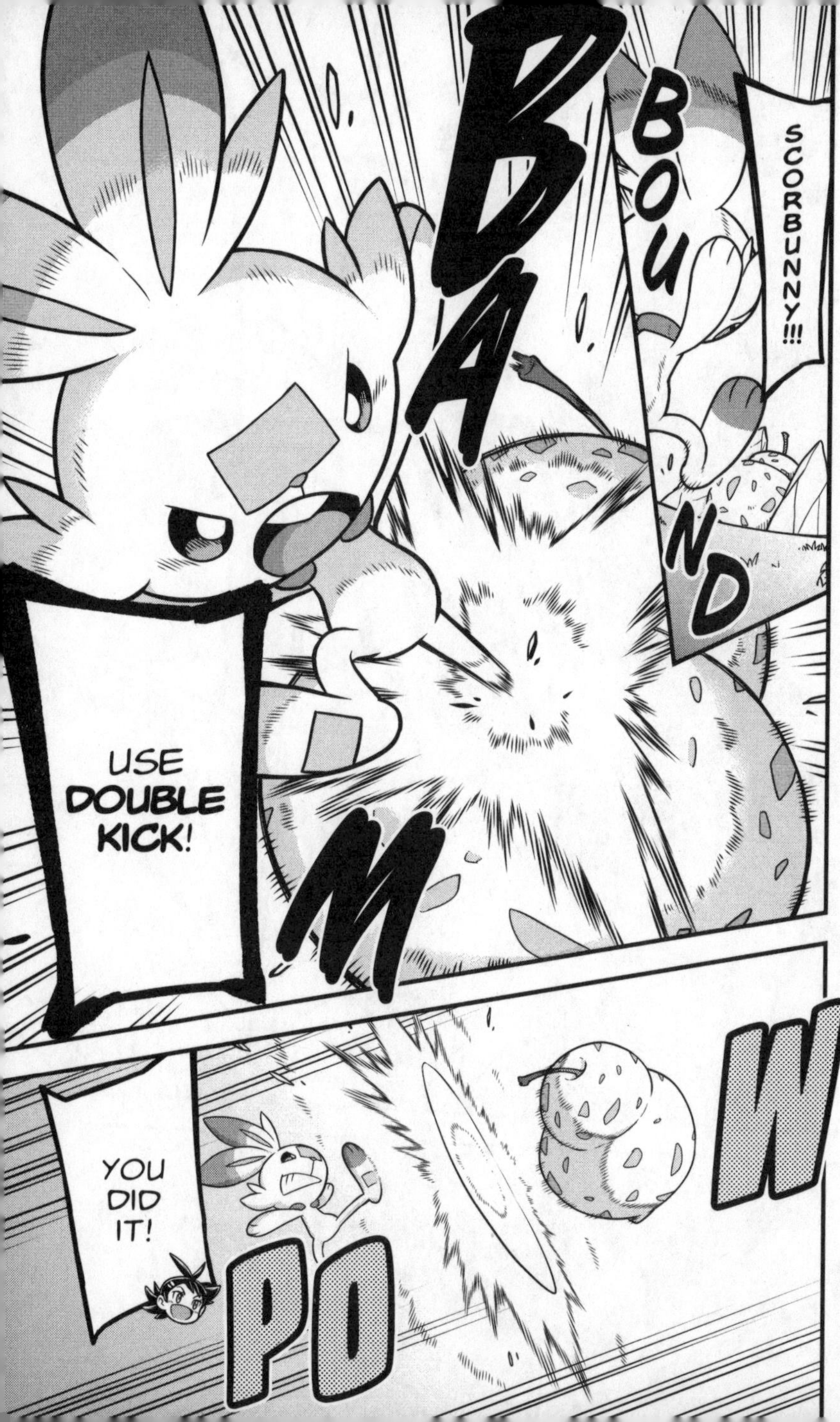
SCORBUNNY!!!
BOUND
BAAM
USE **DOUBLE KICK!**
POW
YOU DID IT!

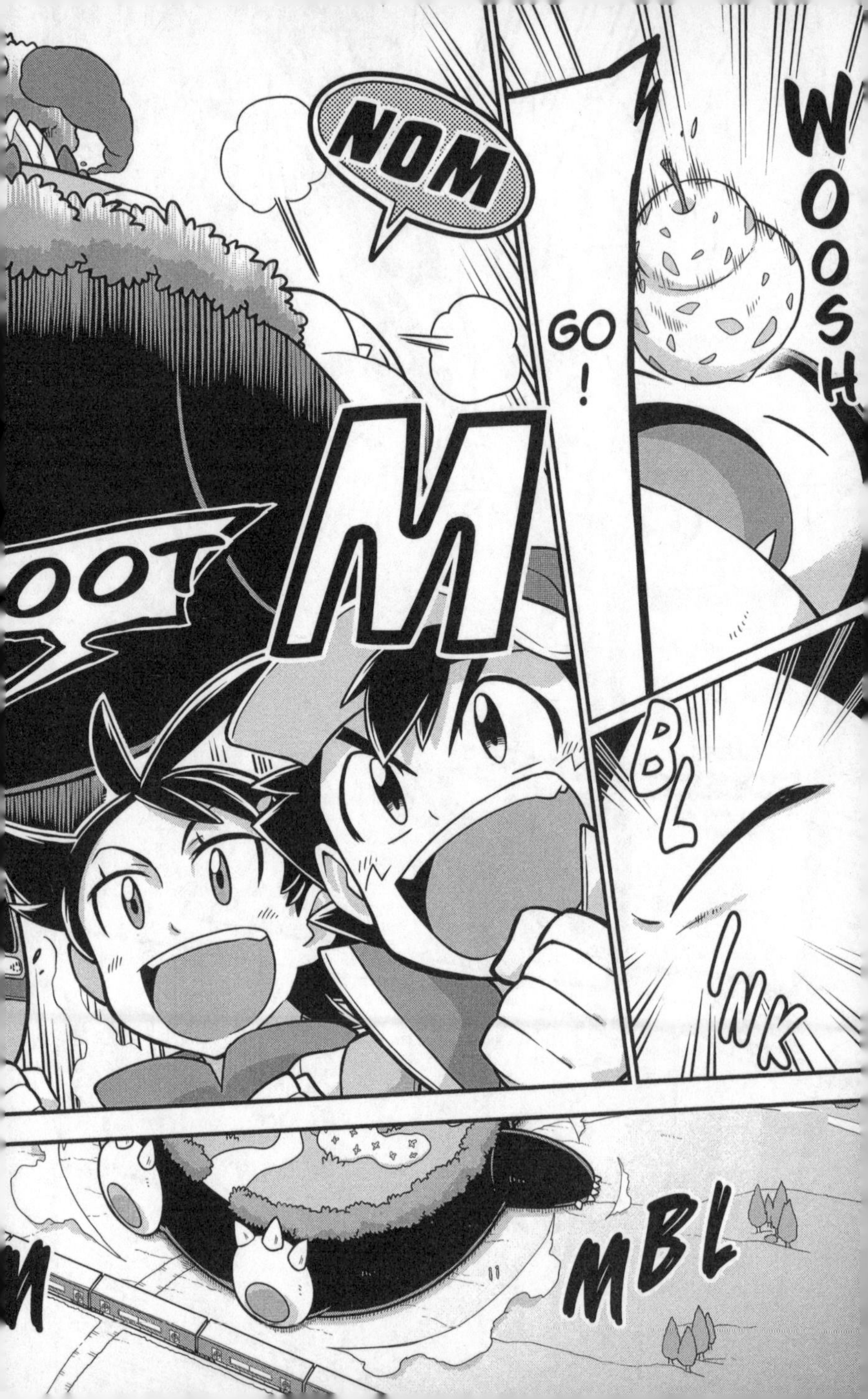
WOOSH
GO!
BLINK
NOM
M
OOT
MBL
N

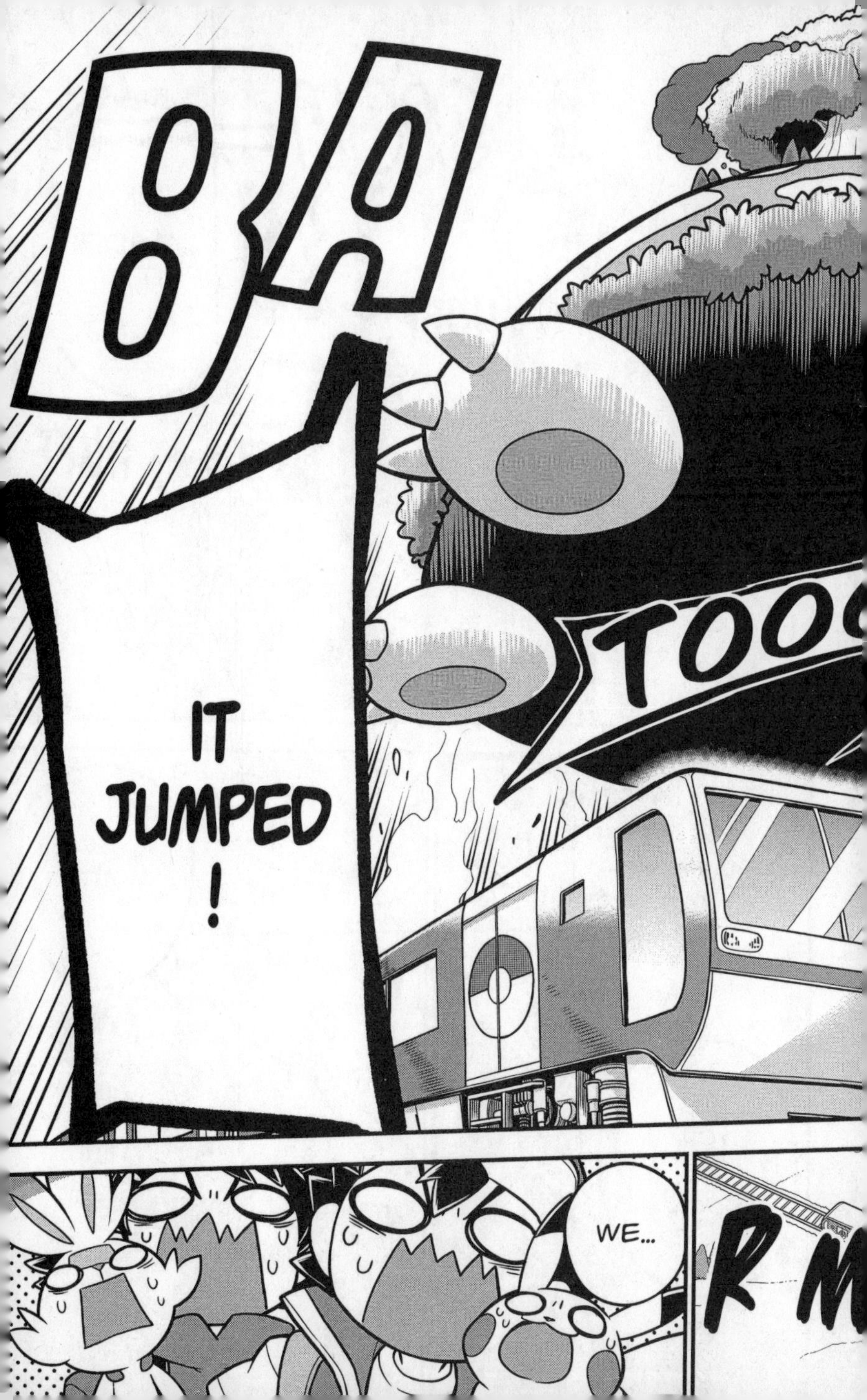
IT JUMPED!
WE...

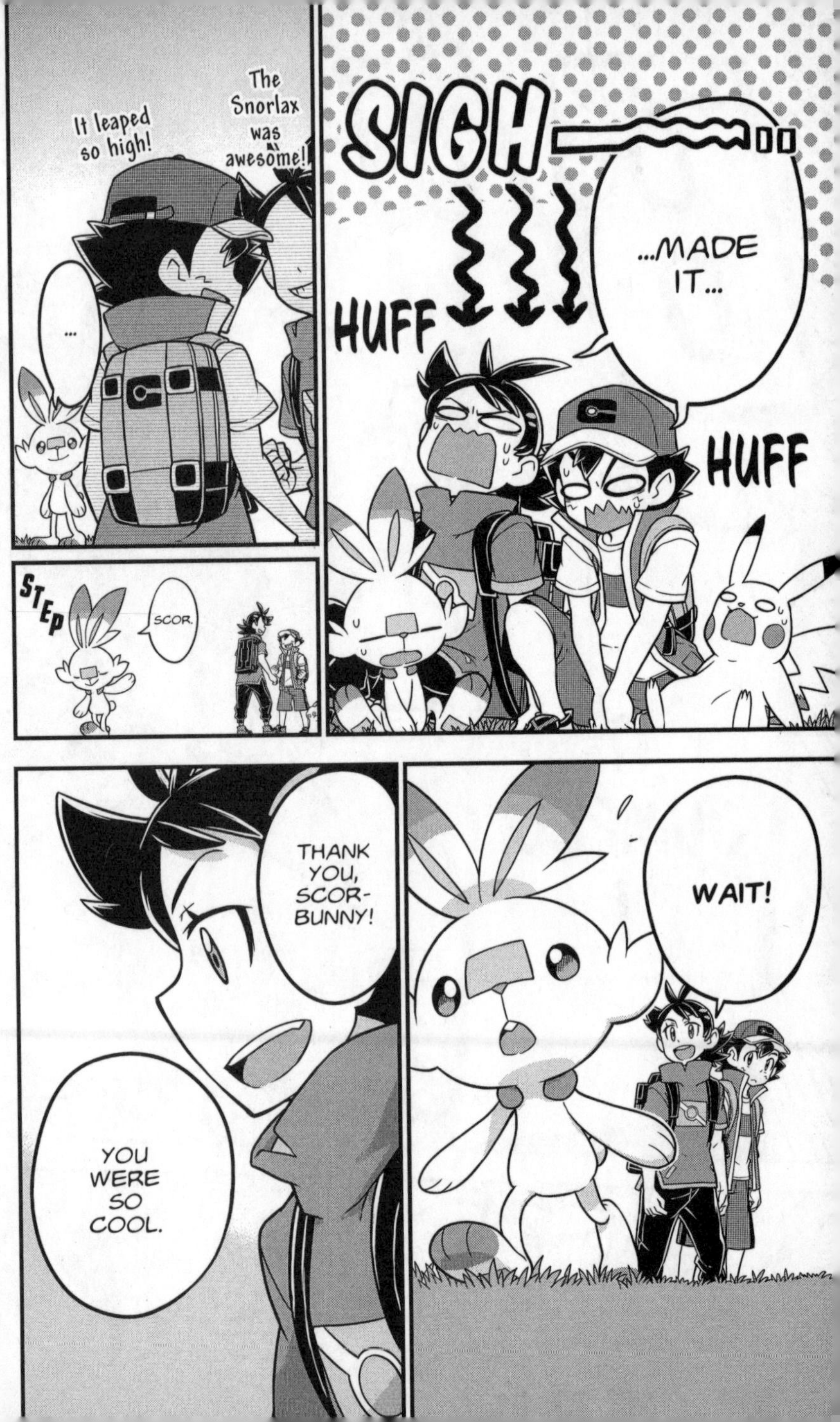
SIGH—
...MADE IT...
HUFF
HUFF
The Snorlax was awesome!
It leaped so high!
...
STEP
SCOR.
WAIT!
THANK YOU, SCORBUNNY!
YOU WERE SO COOL.

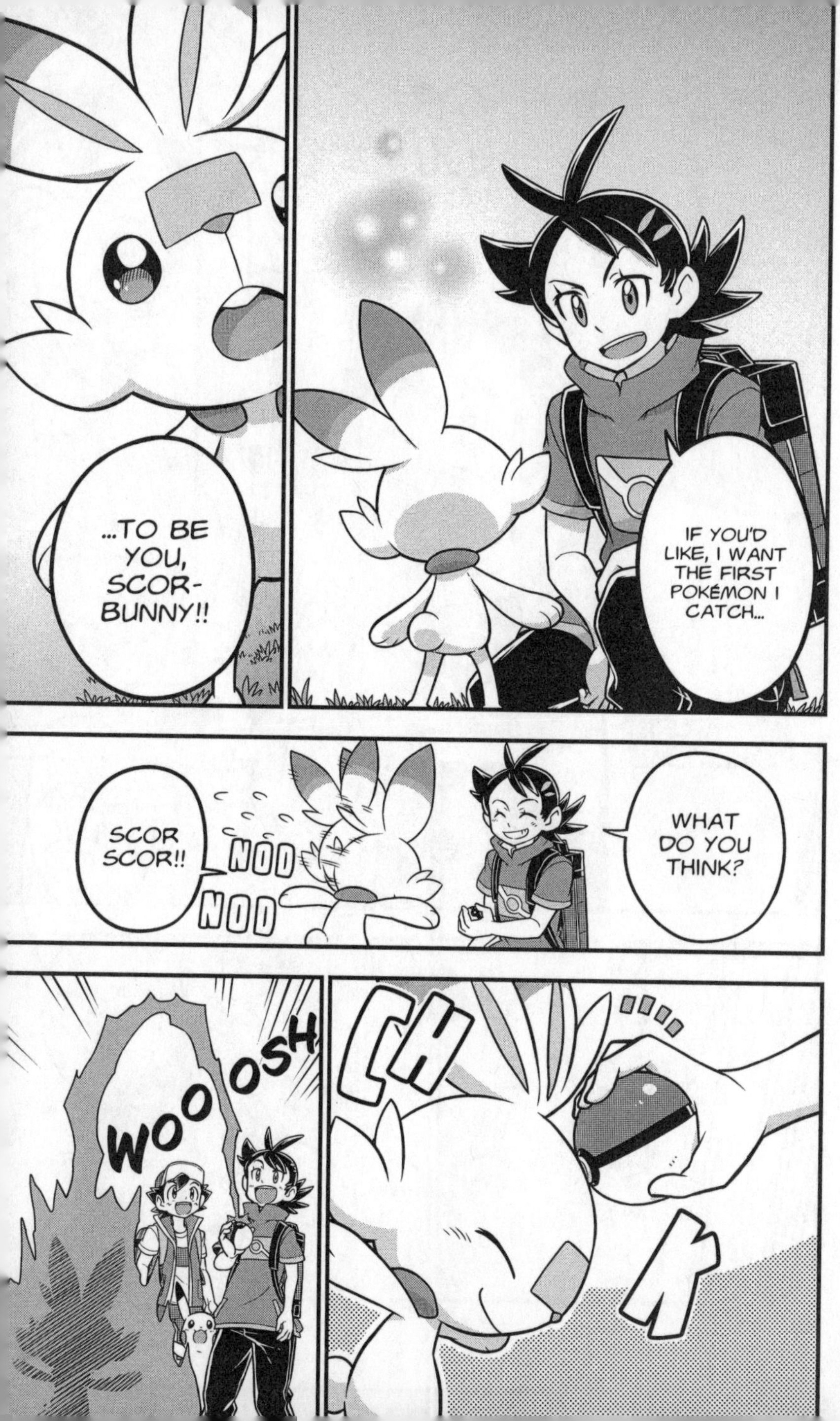
IF YOU'D LIKE, I WANT THE FIRST POKÉMON I CATCH...
...TO BE YOU, SCOR-BUNNY!!
WHAT DO YOU THINK?
NOD NOD
SCOR SCOR!!
....
CH
K
WOOOSH

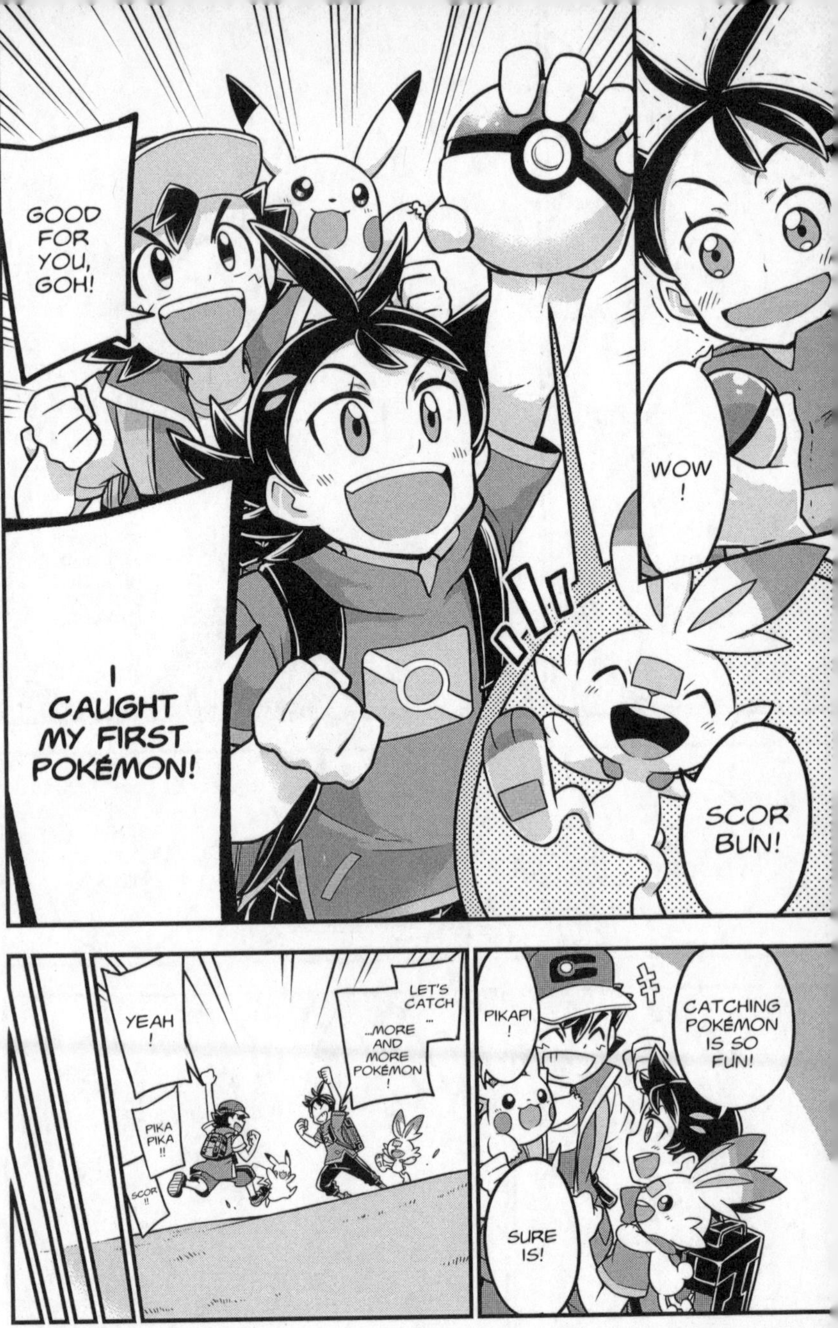
WOW!
I CAUGHT MY FIRST POKéMON!
SCOR BUN!
GOOD FOR YOU, GOH!
CATCHING POKéMON IS SO FUN!
PIKAPI!
SURE IS!
LET'S CATCH... ...MORE AND MORE POKéMON!
YEAH!
PIKA PIKA!!
SCOR!!

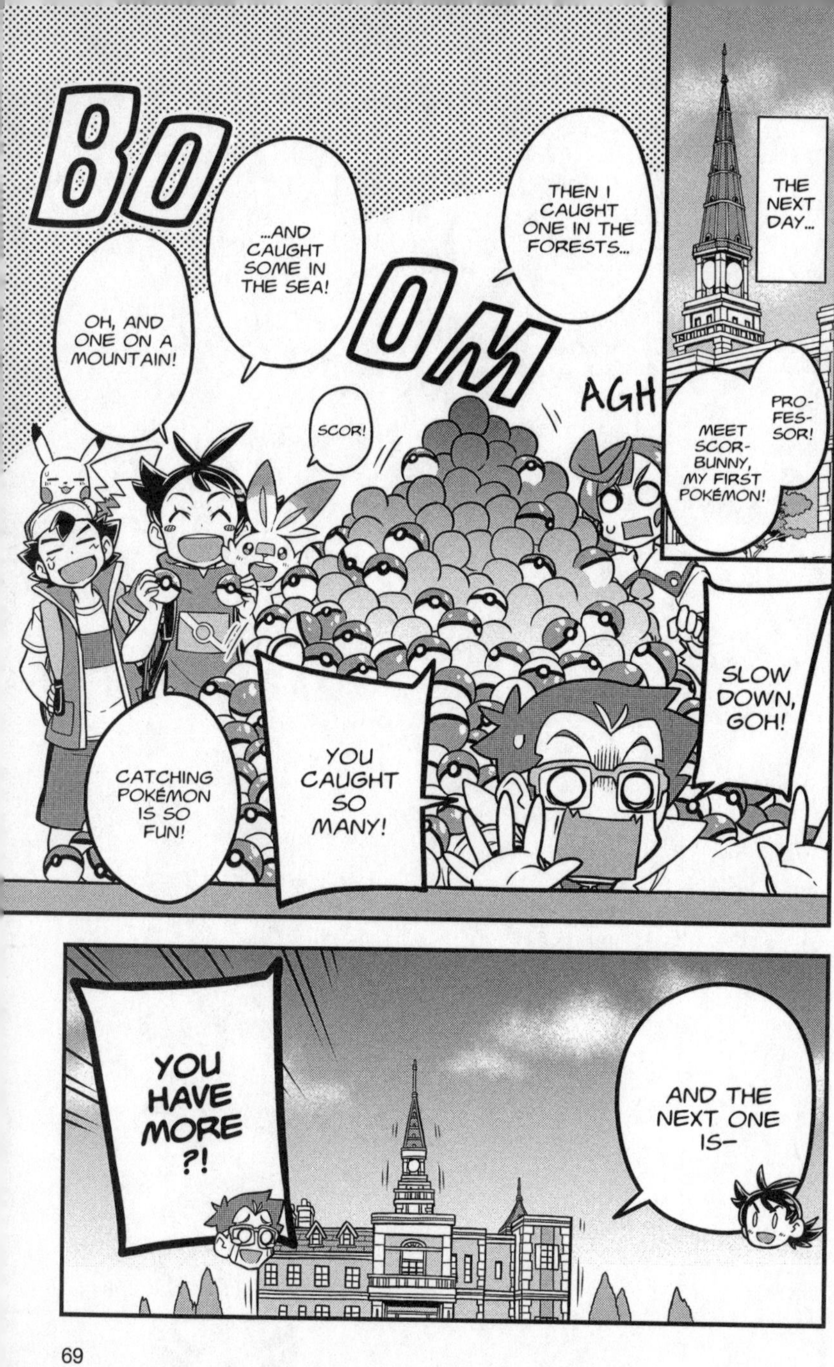
THE NEXT DAY...
PRO-FES-SOR! MEET SCOR-BUNNY, MY FIRST POKÉMON!
AGH
BOOM
THEN I CAUGHT ONE IN THE FORESTS...
...AND CAUGHT SOME IN THE SEA!
OH, AND ONE ON A MOUNTAIN!
SCOR!
SLOW DOWN, GOH!
YOU CAUGHT SO MANY!
CATCHING POKÉMON IS SO FUN!
AND THE NEXT ONE IS—
YOU HAVE MORE?!

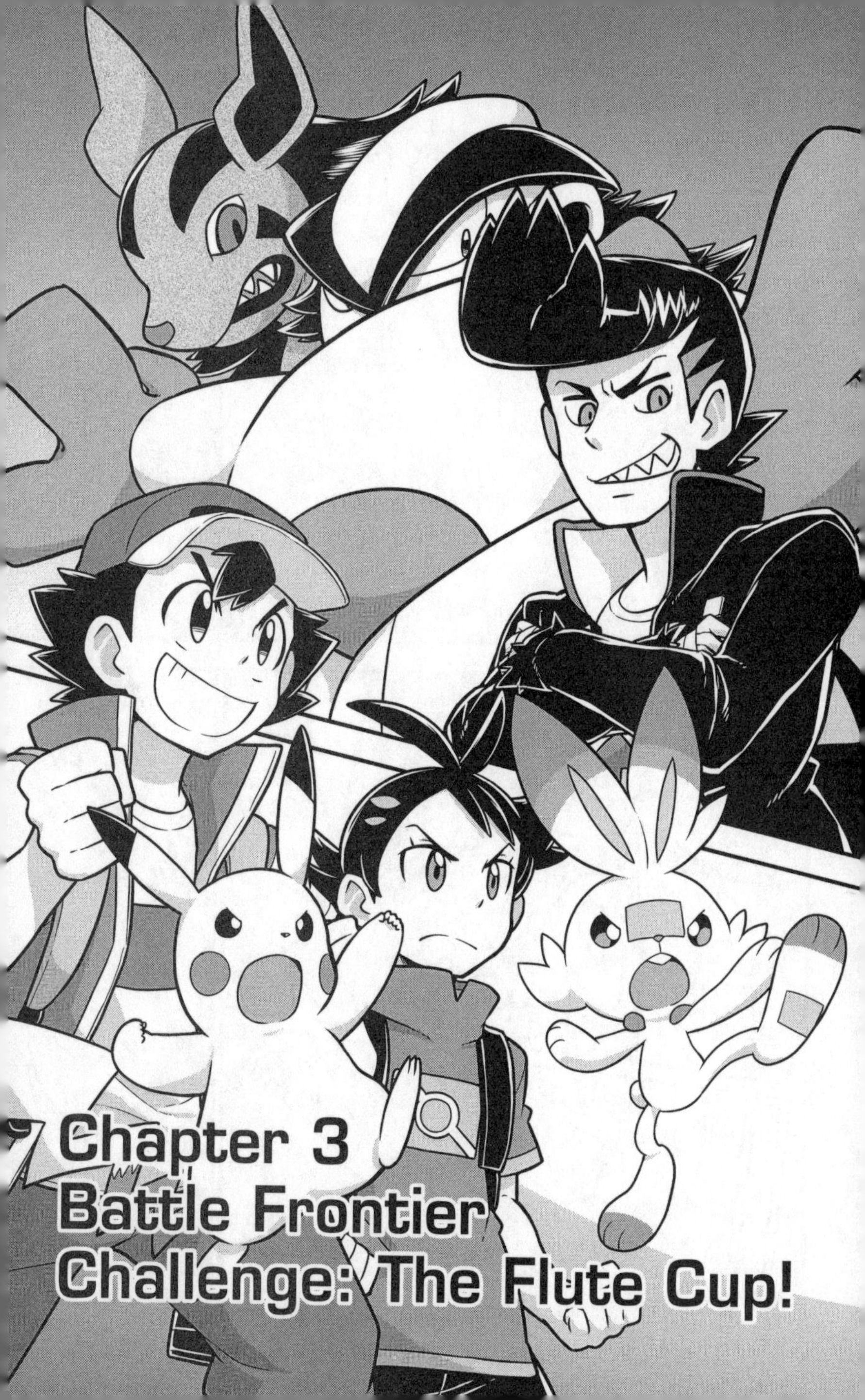
Chapter 3
Battle Frontier
Challenge: The Flute Cup!

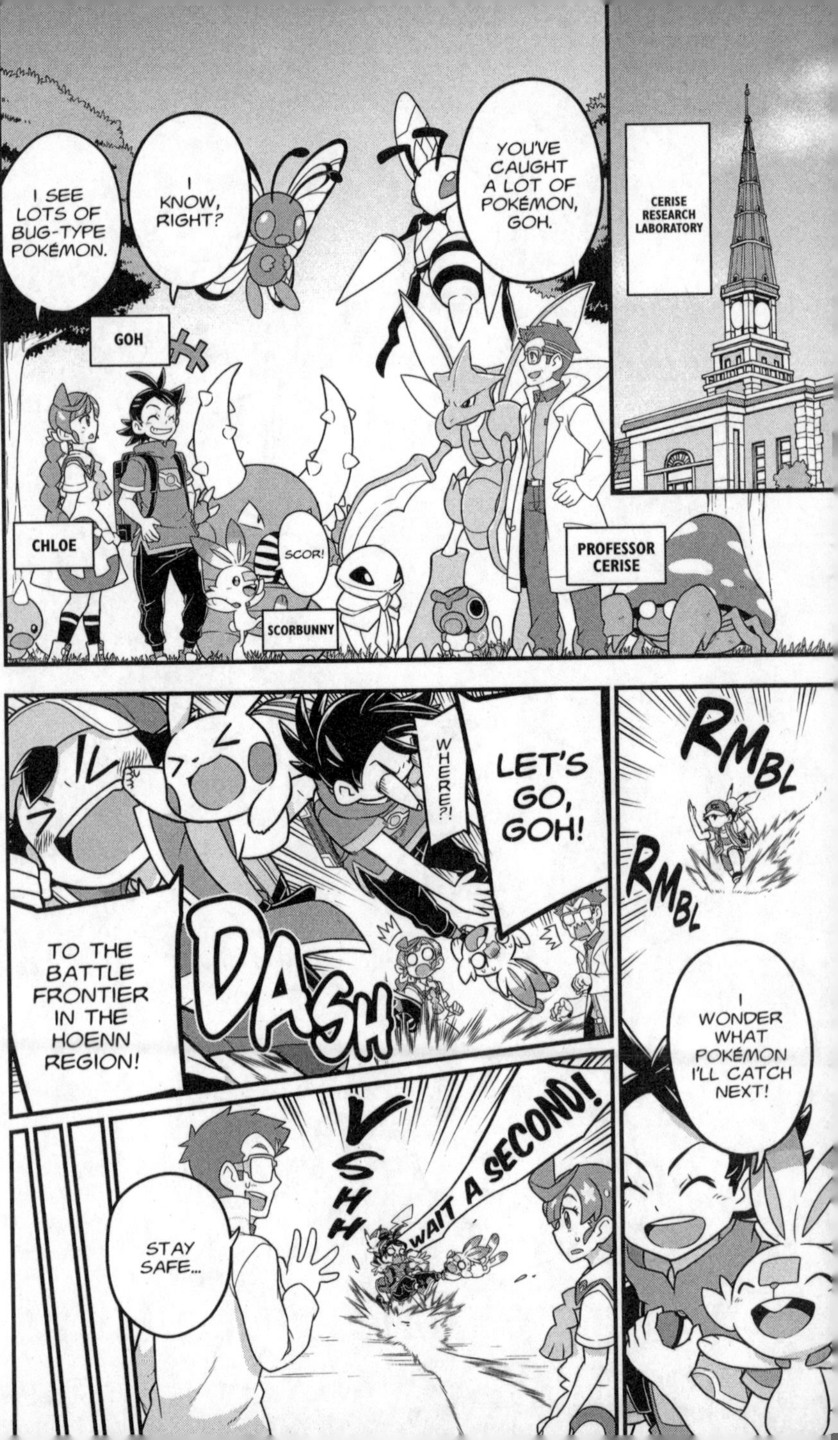
CERISE RESEARCH LABORATORY
YOU'VE CAUGHT A LOT OF POKÉMON, GOH.
I KNOW, RIGHT?
I SEE LOTS OF BUG-TYPE POKÉMON.
GOH
PROFESSOR CERISE
SCOR!
SCORBUNNY
CHLOE
RMBL
RMBL
LET'S GO, GOH!
WHERE?!
TO THE BATTLE FRONTIER IN THE HOENN REGION!
DASH
I WONDER WHAT POKÉMON I'LL CATCH NEXT!
WAIT A SECOND!
SHHH
STAY SAFE...

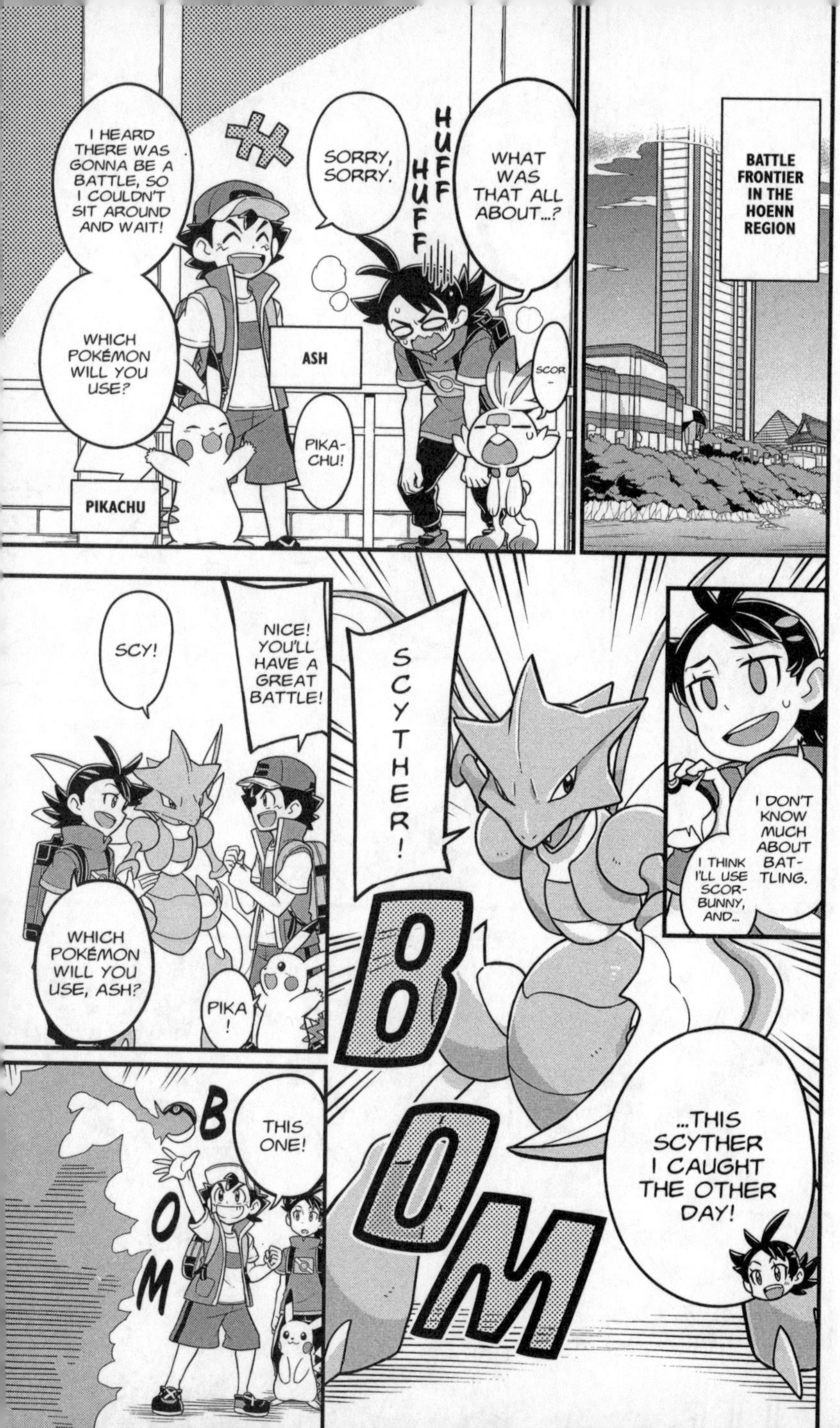
BATTLE FRONTIER IN THE HOENN REGION
WHAT WAS THAT ALL ABOUT...?
HUFF HUFF
SORRY, SORRY.
I HEARD THERE WAS GONNA BE A BATTLE, SO I COULDN'T SIT AROUND AND WAIT!
SCOR-
ASH
WHICH POKÉMON WILL YOU USE?
PIKA-CHU!
PIKACHU
I DON'T KNOW MUCH ABOUT BAT-TLING.
I THINK I'LL USE SCOR-BUNNY, AND...
...THIS SCYTHER I CAUGHT THE OTHER DAY!
SCYTHER!
BOOM
NICE! YOU'LL HAVE A GREAT BATTLE!
SCY!
WHICH POKÉMON WILL YOU USE, ASH?
PIKA!
THIS ONE!
BOOM

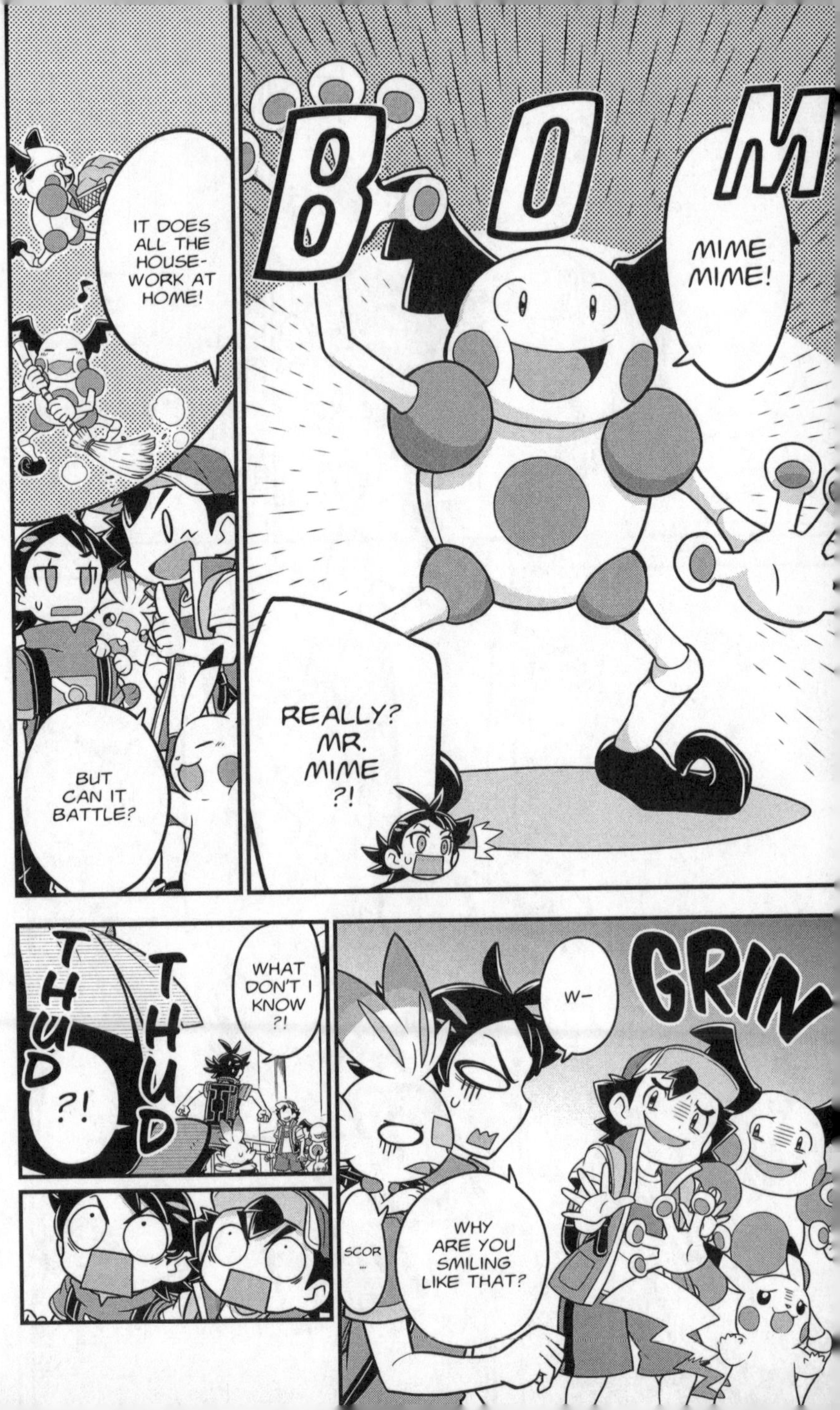
BOM
MIME MIME!
REALLY? MR. MIME ?!
IT DOES ALL THE HOUSE-WORK AT HOME!
BUT CAN IT BATTLE?
GRIN
W–
WHY ARE YOU SMILING LIKE THAT?
SCOR...
WHAT DON'T I KNOW ?!
THUD
THUD
?!

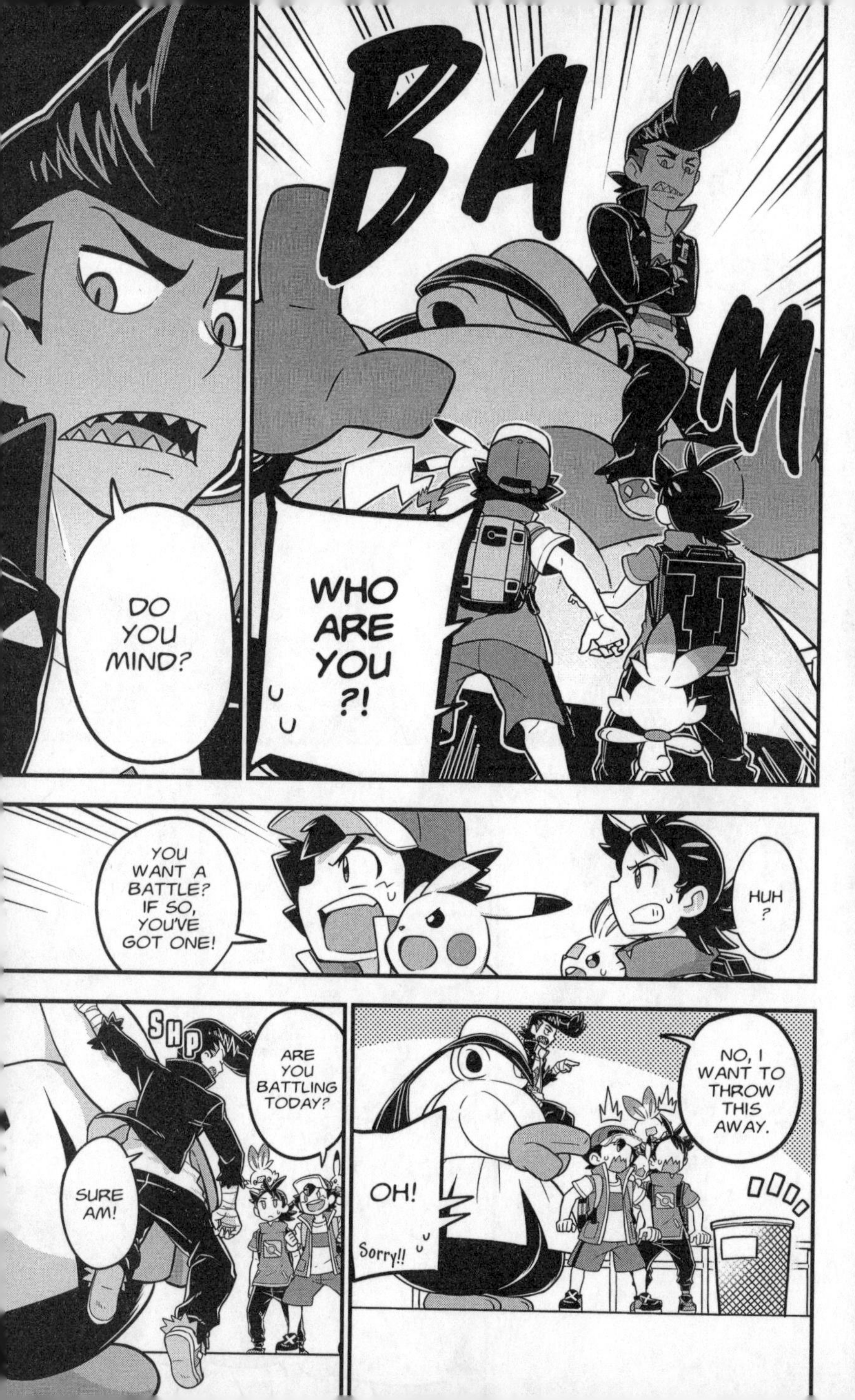
BAM
WHO ARE YOU ?!
DO YOU MIND?
HUH ?
YOU WANT A BATTLE? IF SO, YOU'VE GOT ONE!
NO, I WANT TO THROW THIS AWAY.
OH!
Sorry!!
SHP
ARE YOU BATTLING TODAY?
SURE AM!

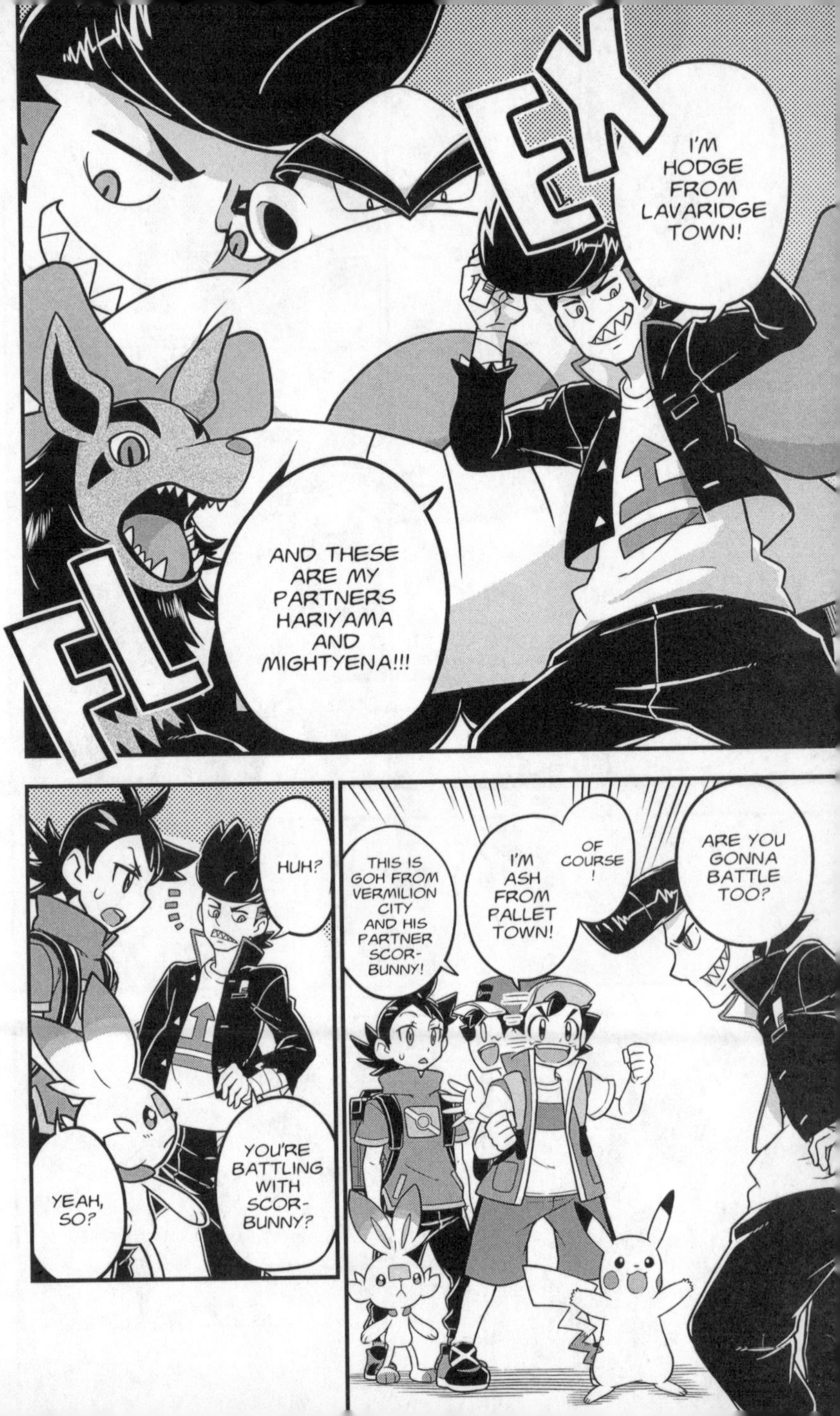
EX
I'M HODGE FROM LAVARIDGE TOWN!
AND THESE ARE MY PARTNERS HARIYAMA AND MIGHTYENA!!!
FL
ARE YOU GONNA BATTLE TOO?
OF COURSE!
I'M ASH FROM PALLET TOWN!
THIS IS GOH FROM VERMILION CITY AND HIS PARTNER SCOR-BUNNY!
HUH?
YOU'RE BATTLING WITH SCOR-BUNNY?
YEAH, SO?

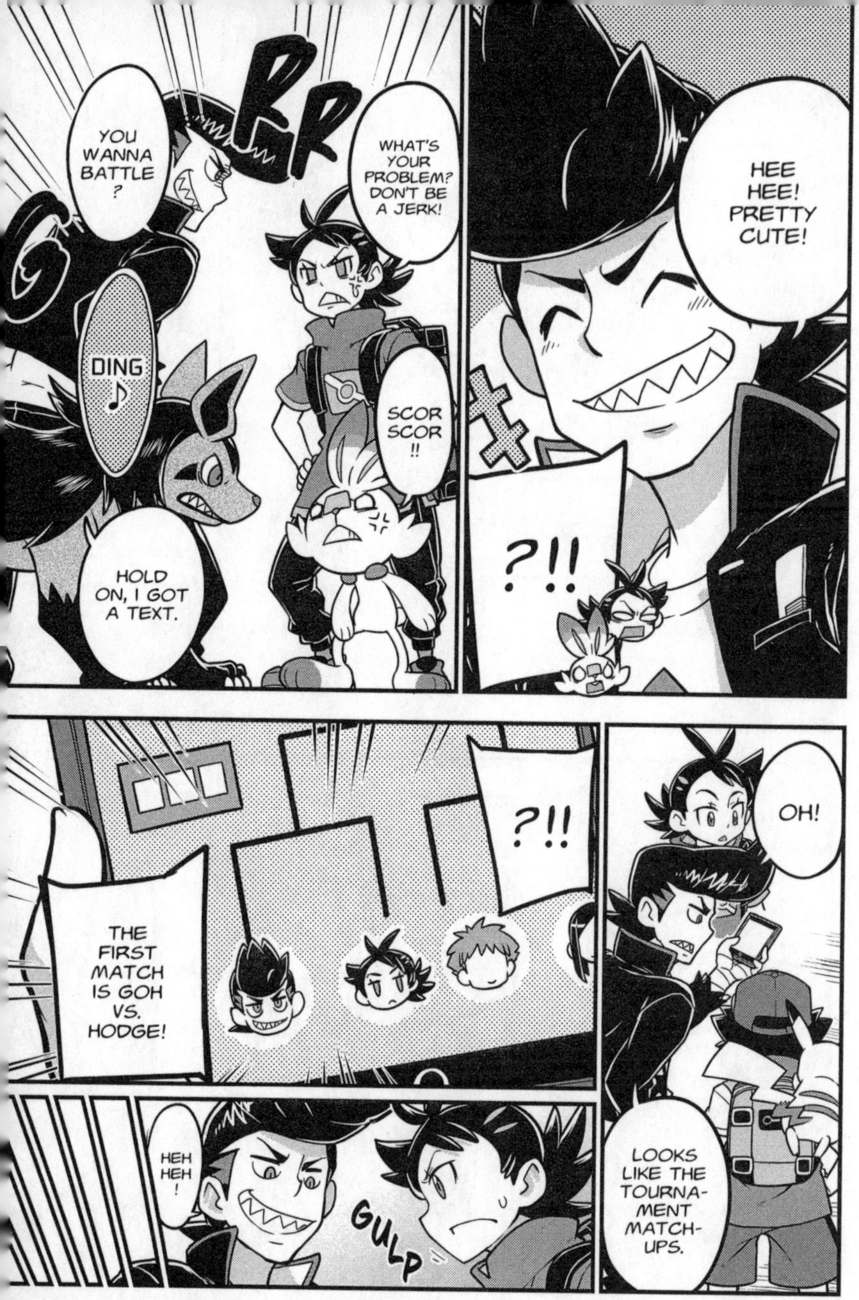
HEE HEE! PRETTY CUTE!
?!!
WHAT'S YOUR PROBLEM? DON'T BE A JERK!
RR
YOU WANNA BATTLE?
SCOR SCOR!!
DING ♪
HOLD ON, I GOT A TEXT.
OH!
LOOKS LIKE THE TOURNAMENT MATCH-UPS.
?!!
THE FIRST MATCH IS GOH VS. HODGE!
HEH HEH!
GULP

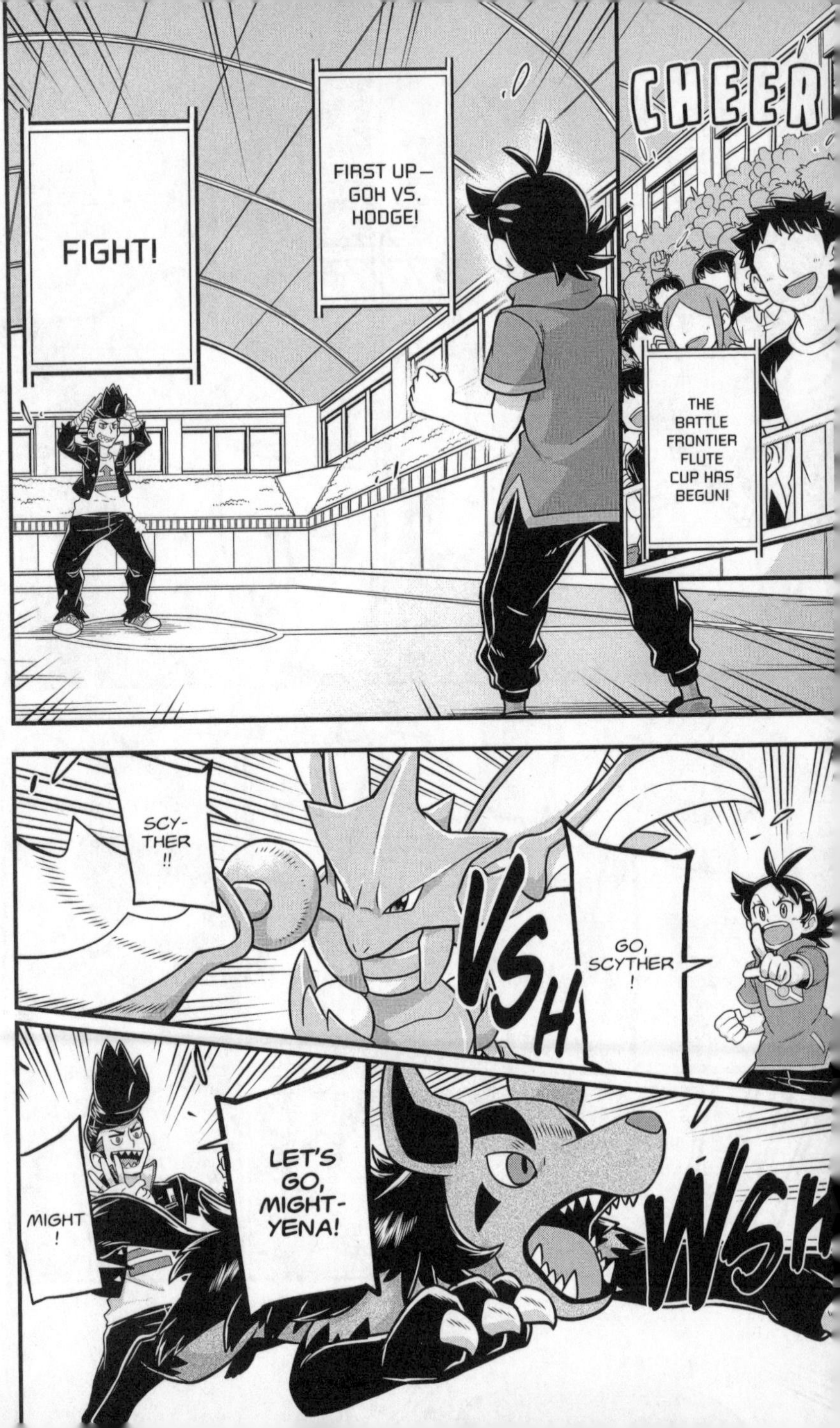
CHEER
THE BATTLE FRONTIER FLUTE CUP HAS BEGUN!
FIRST UP—GOH VS. HODGE!
FIGHT!
GO, SCYTHER!
VSH
SCY-THER!!
WSH
LET'S GO, MIGHT-YENA!
MIGHT!

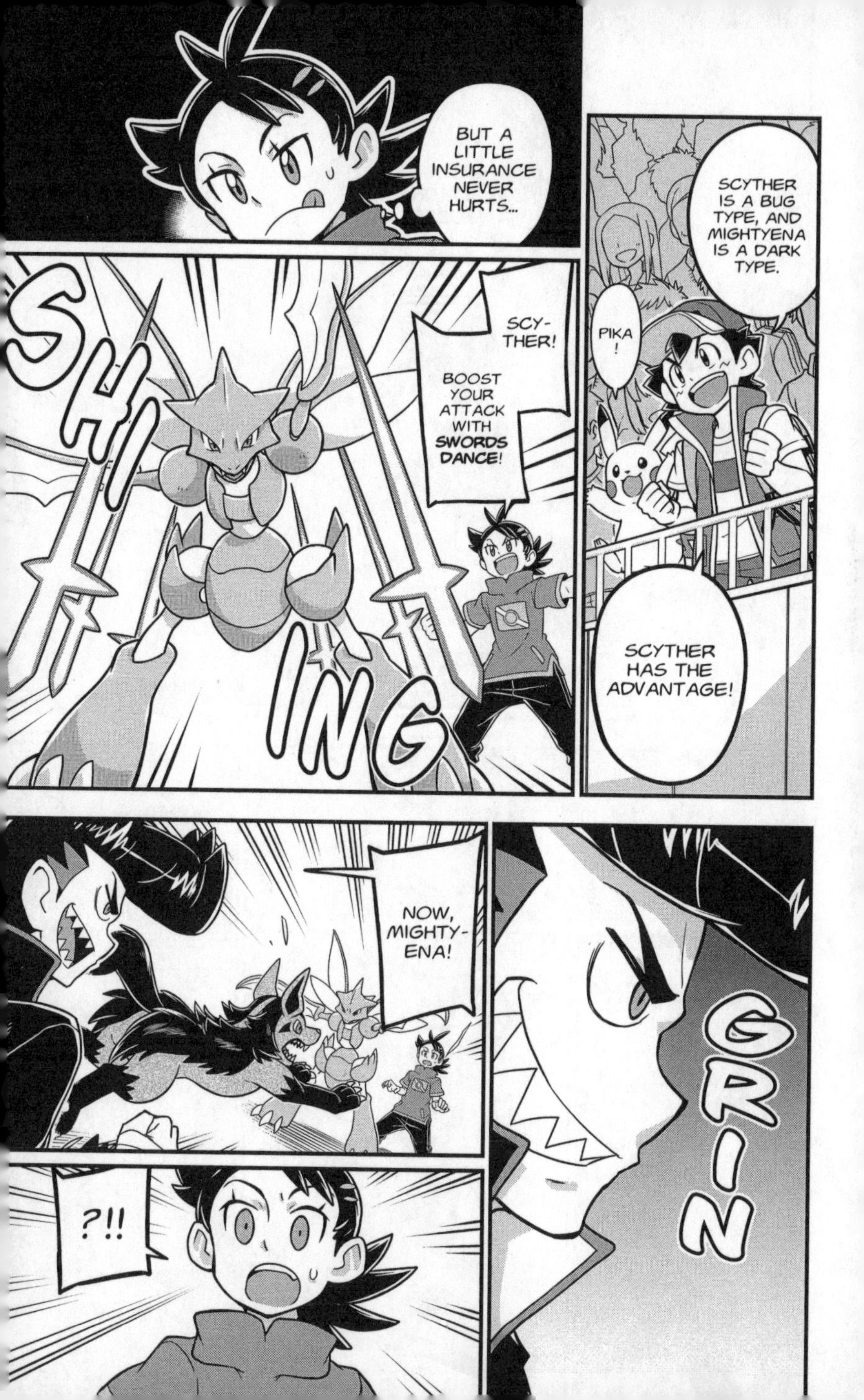
BUT A LITTLE INSURANCE NEVER HURTS...
SCYTHER IS A BUG TYPE, AND MIGHTYENA IS A DARK TYPE.
PIKA!
SCYTHER HAS THE ADVANTAGE!
SCY-THER!
BOOST YOUR ATTACK WITH **SWORDS DANCE**!
SHIING
GRIN
NOW, MIGHTY-ENA!
?!!

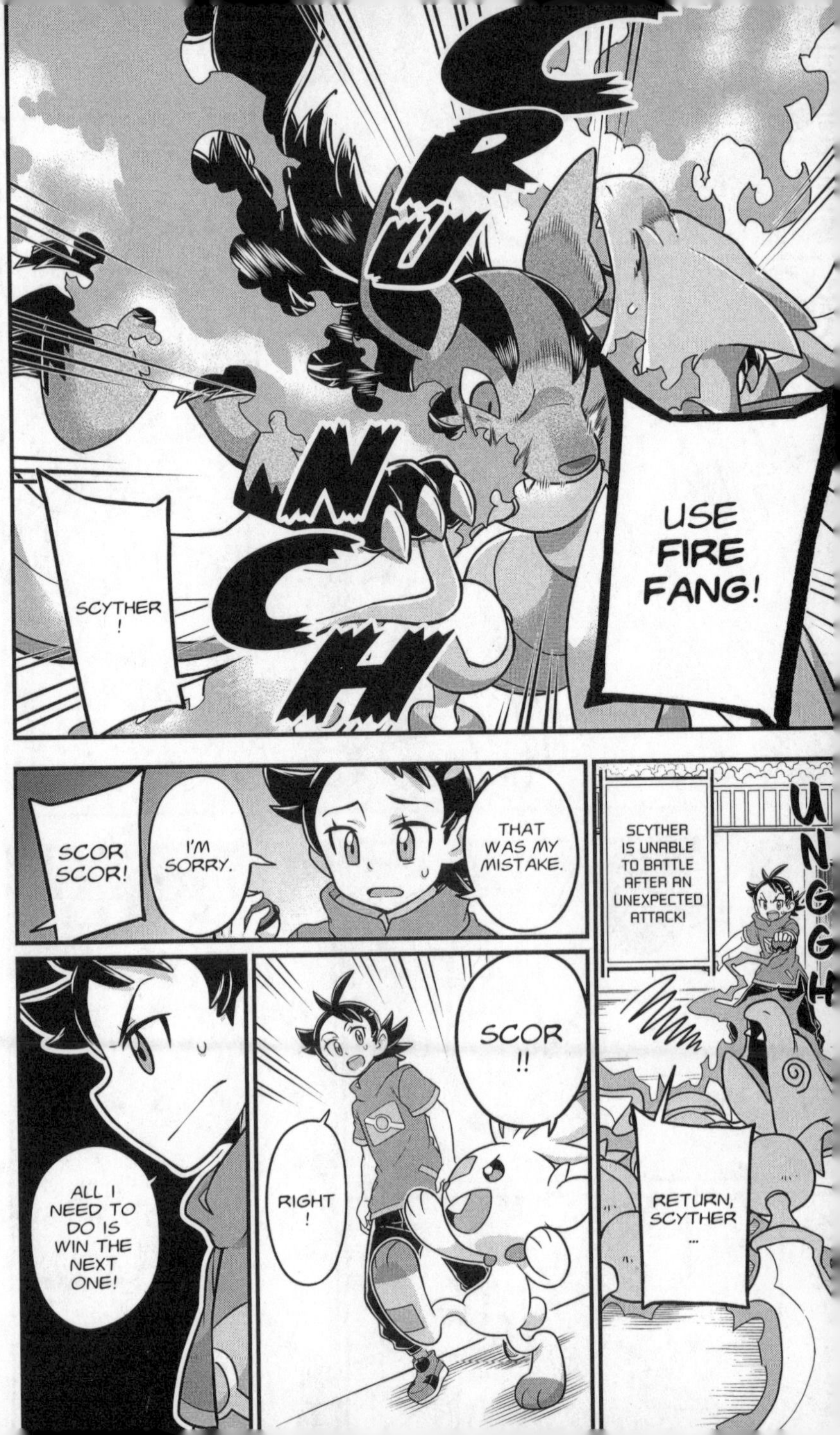
USE FIRE FANG!
CRUNCH
SCYTHER!
SCYTHER IS UNABLE TO BATTLE AFTER AN UNEXPECTED ATTACK!
UNGGH
RETURN, SCYTHER...
THAT WAS MY MISTAKE.
I'M SORRY.
SCOR SCOR!
SCOR!!
RIGHT!
ALL I NEED TO DO IS WIN THE NEXT ONE!

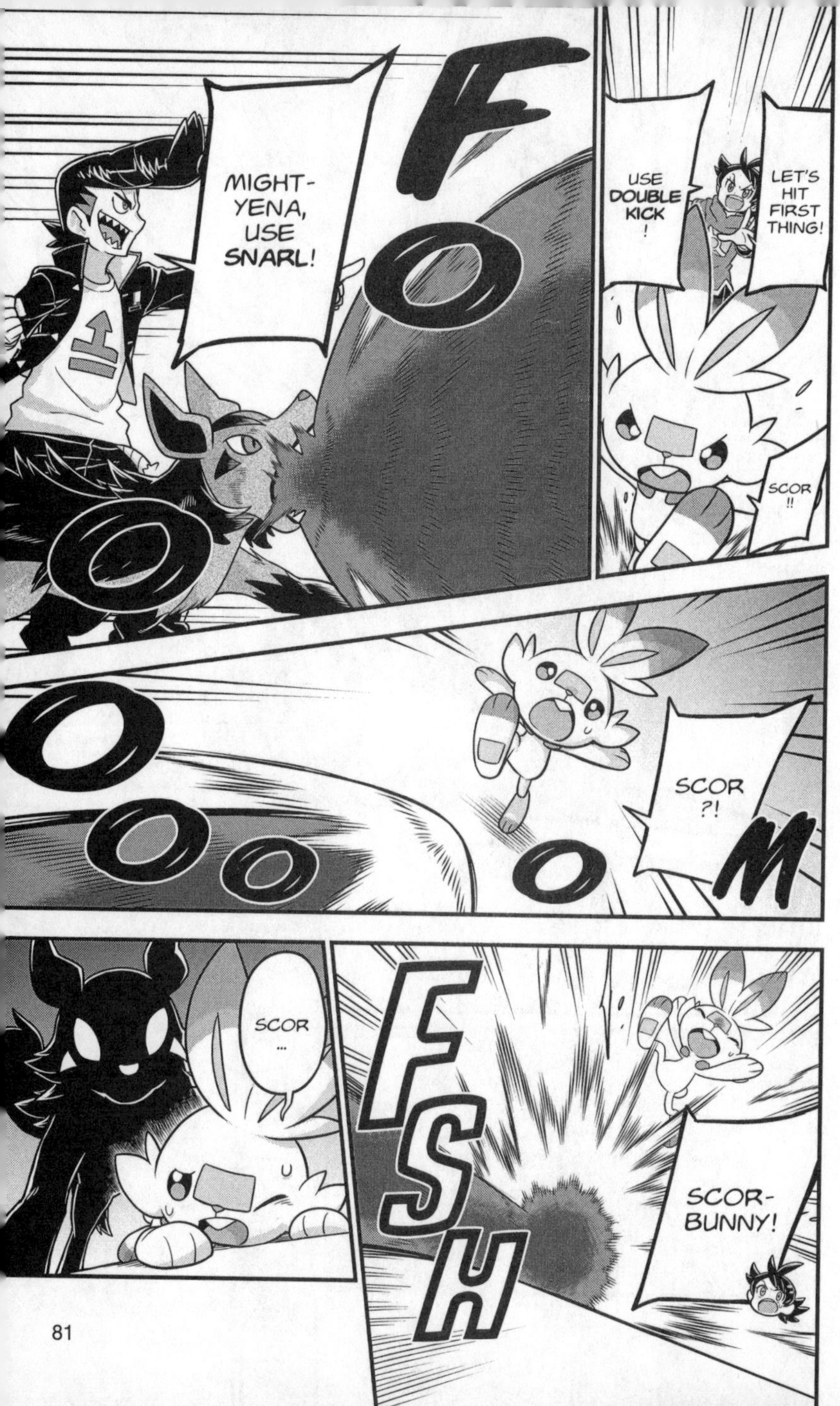
LET'S HIT FIRST THING!
USE DOUBLE KICK!
SCOR!!
MIGHTY-YENA, USE SNARL!
FOOOOOOM
SCOR?!
SCOR-BUNNY!
FSH
SCOR...

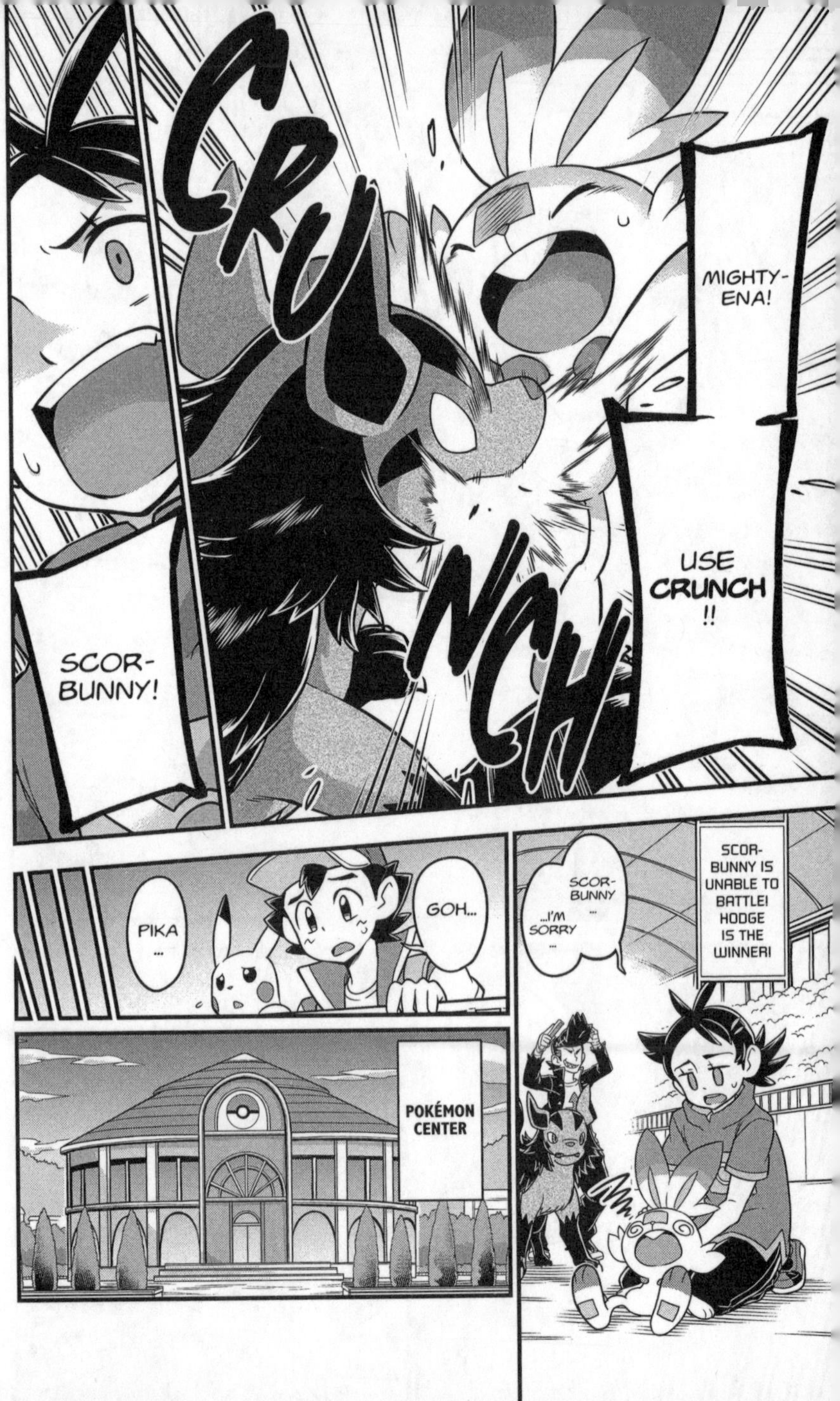
MIGHTY-ENA!
USE CRUNCH!!
CRUNCH
SCOR-BUNNY!
SCOR-BUNNY IS UNABLE TO BATTLE! HODGE IS THE WINNER!
SCOR-BUNNY... ...I'M SORRY...
GOH...
PIKA...
POKÉMON CENTER

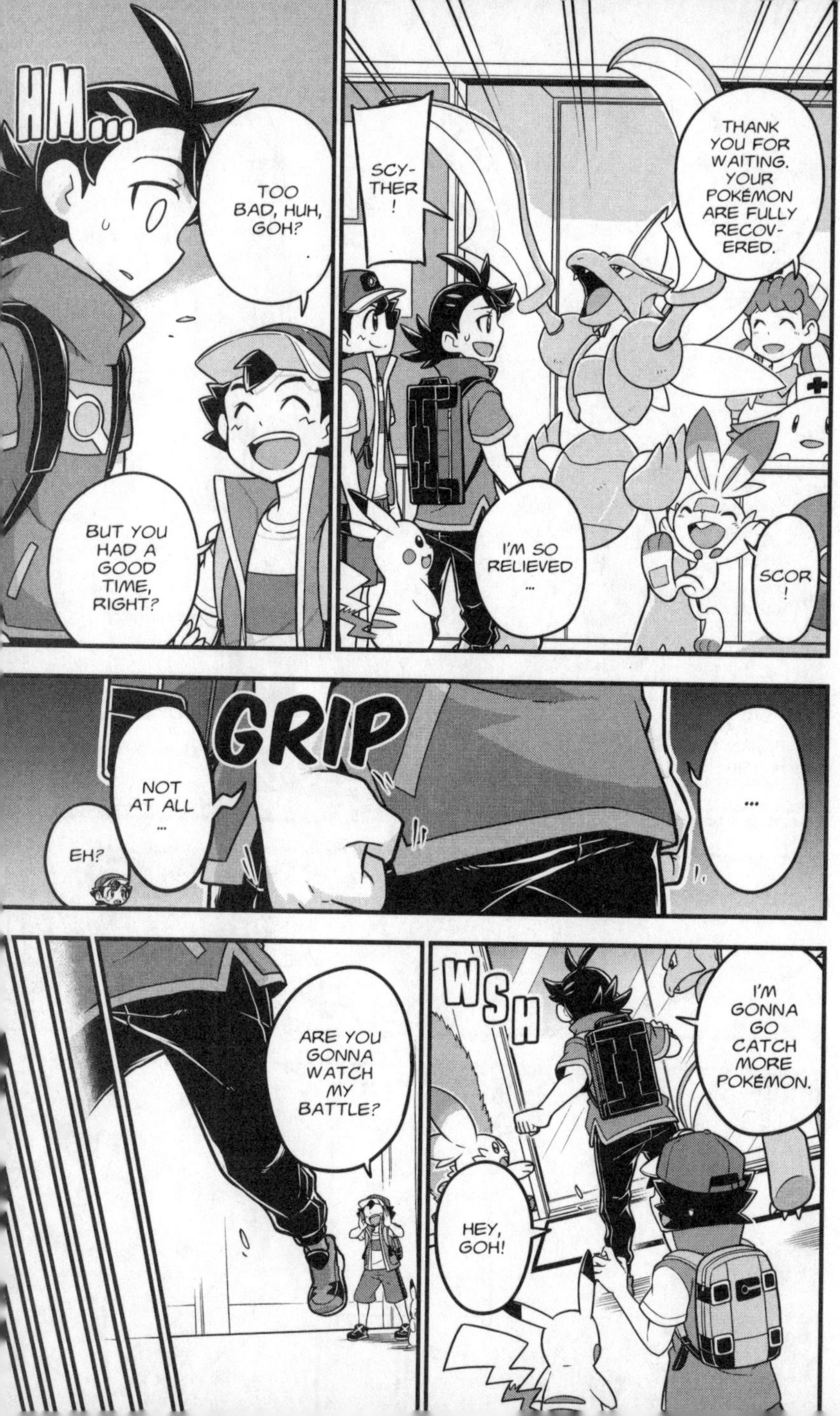
THANK YOU FOR WAITING. YOUR POKÉMON ARE FULLY RECOVERED.
SCYTHER!
SCOR!
I'M SO RELIEVED...
HM...
TOO BAD, HUH, GOH?
BUT YOU HAD A GOOD TIME, RIGHT?
...
GRIP
NOT AT ALL...
EH?
I'M GONNA GO CATCH MORE POKÉMON.
WSH
HEY, GOH!
ARE YOU GONNA WATCH MY BATTLE?

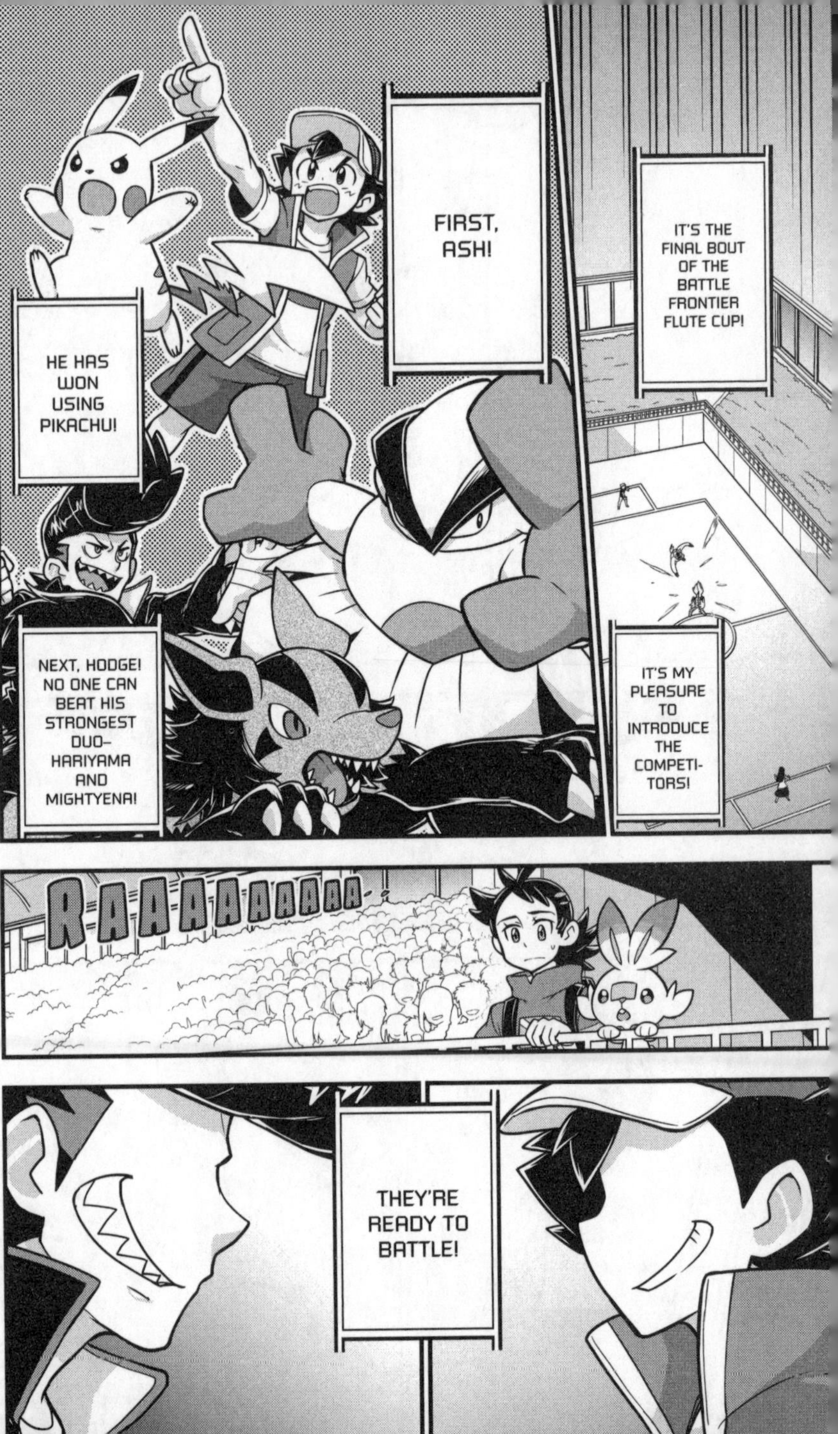
IT'S THE FINAL BOUT OF THE BATTLE FRONTIER FLUTE CUP!
IT'S MY PLEASURE TO INTRODUCE THE COMPETI-TORS!
FIRST, ASH!
HE HAS WON USING PIKACHU!
NEXT, HODGE! NO ONE CAN BEAT HIS STRONGEST DUO–HARIYAMA AND MIGHTYENA!
RAAAAAAAAA
THEY'RE READY TO BATTLE!

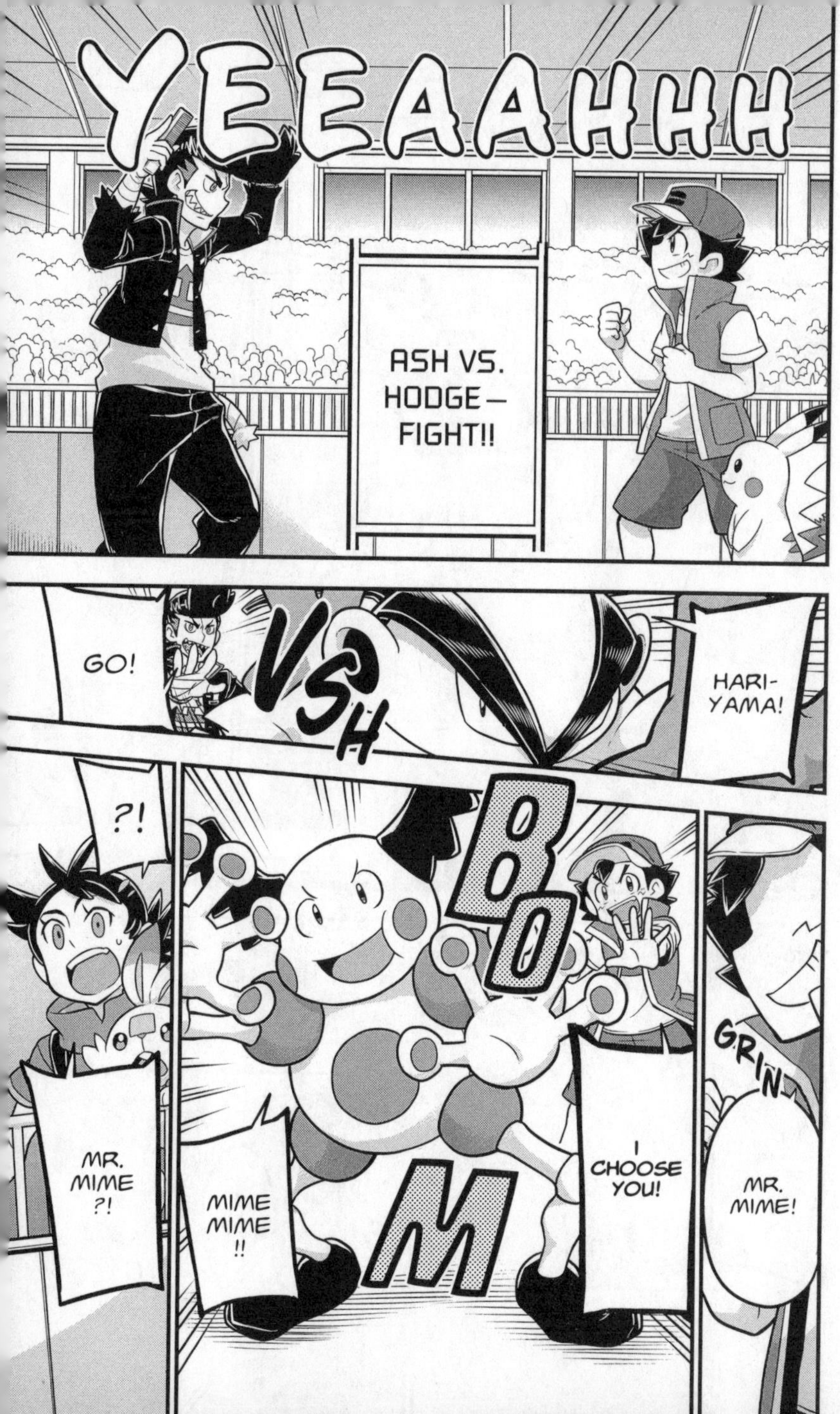
YEEAAHHH
ASH VS. HODGE—FIGHT!!
HARI-YAMA!
VSH
GO!
GRIN
MR. MIME!
BOOM
I CHOOSE YOU!
MIME MIME !!
?!
MR. MIME ?!

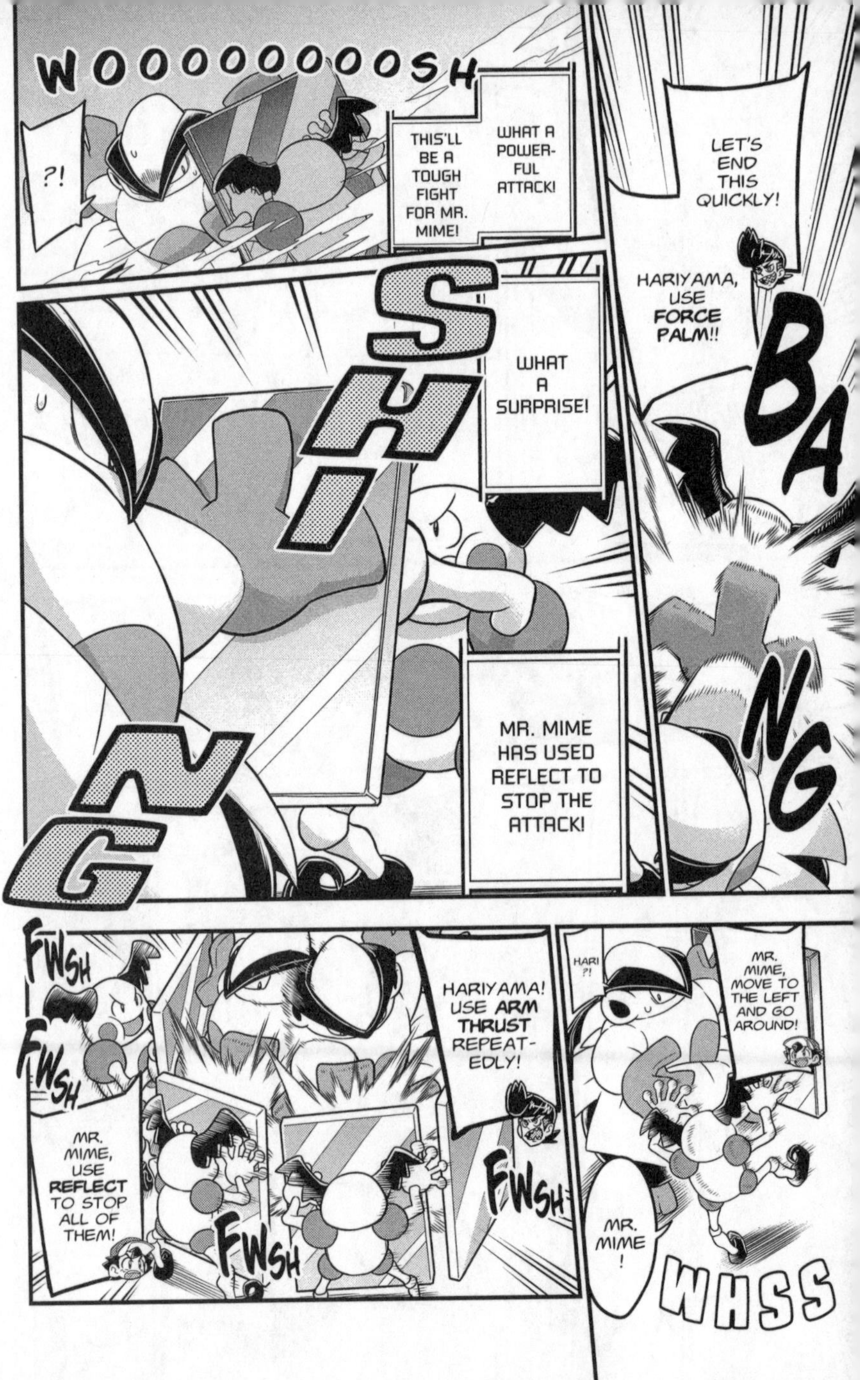

LET'S END THIS QUICKLY!
HARIYAMA, USE FORCE PALM!!
BANG
WOOOOOOOOSH
?!
WHAT A POWERFUL ATTACK!
THIS'LL BE A TOUGH FIGHT FOR MR. MIME!
SHING
WHAT A SURPRISE!
MR. MIME HAS USED REFLECT TO STOP THE ATTACK!
MR. MIME, MOVE TO THE LEFT AND GO AROUND!
HARI ?!
MR. MIME!
WHSS
HARIYAMA! USE ARM THRUST REPEATEDLY!
FWSH
FWSH
FWSH
FWSH
MR. MIME, USE REFLECT TO STOP ALL OF THEM!

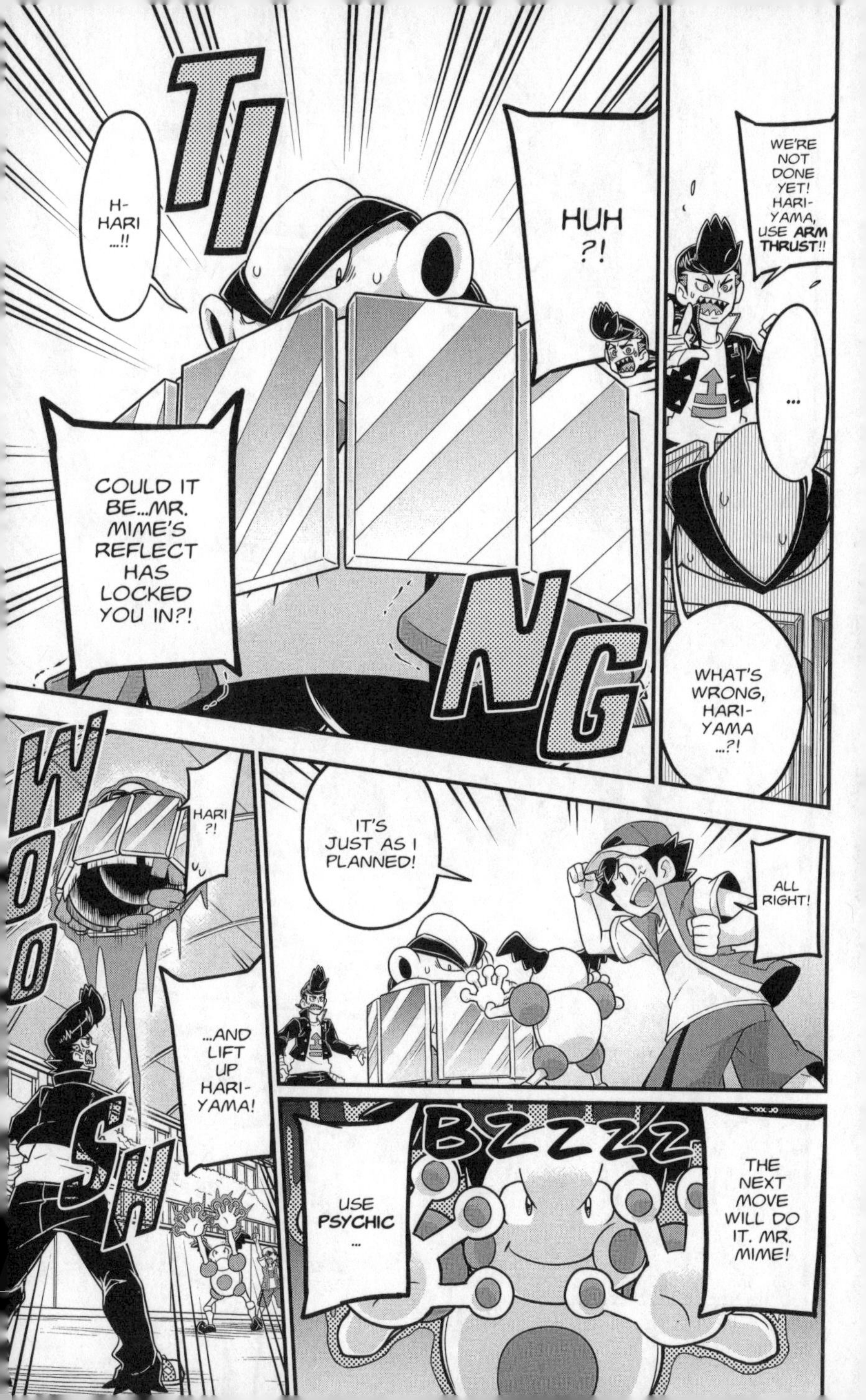
WE'RE NOT DONE YET! HARI-YAMA, USE **ARM THRUST**!!
...
WHAT'S WRONG, HARI-YAMA ...?!
HUH ?!
TI
H-HARI ...!!
COULD IT BE...MR. MIME'S REFLECT HAS LOCKED YOU IN?!
NG
ALL RIGHT!
IT'S JUST AS I PLANNED!
THE NEXT MOVE WILL DO IT. MR. MIME!
BZZZZ
USE **PSYCHIC** ...
WOOOSH
HARI ?!
...AND LIFT UP HARI-YAMA!

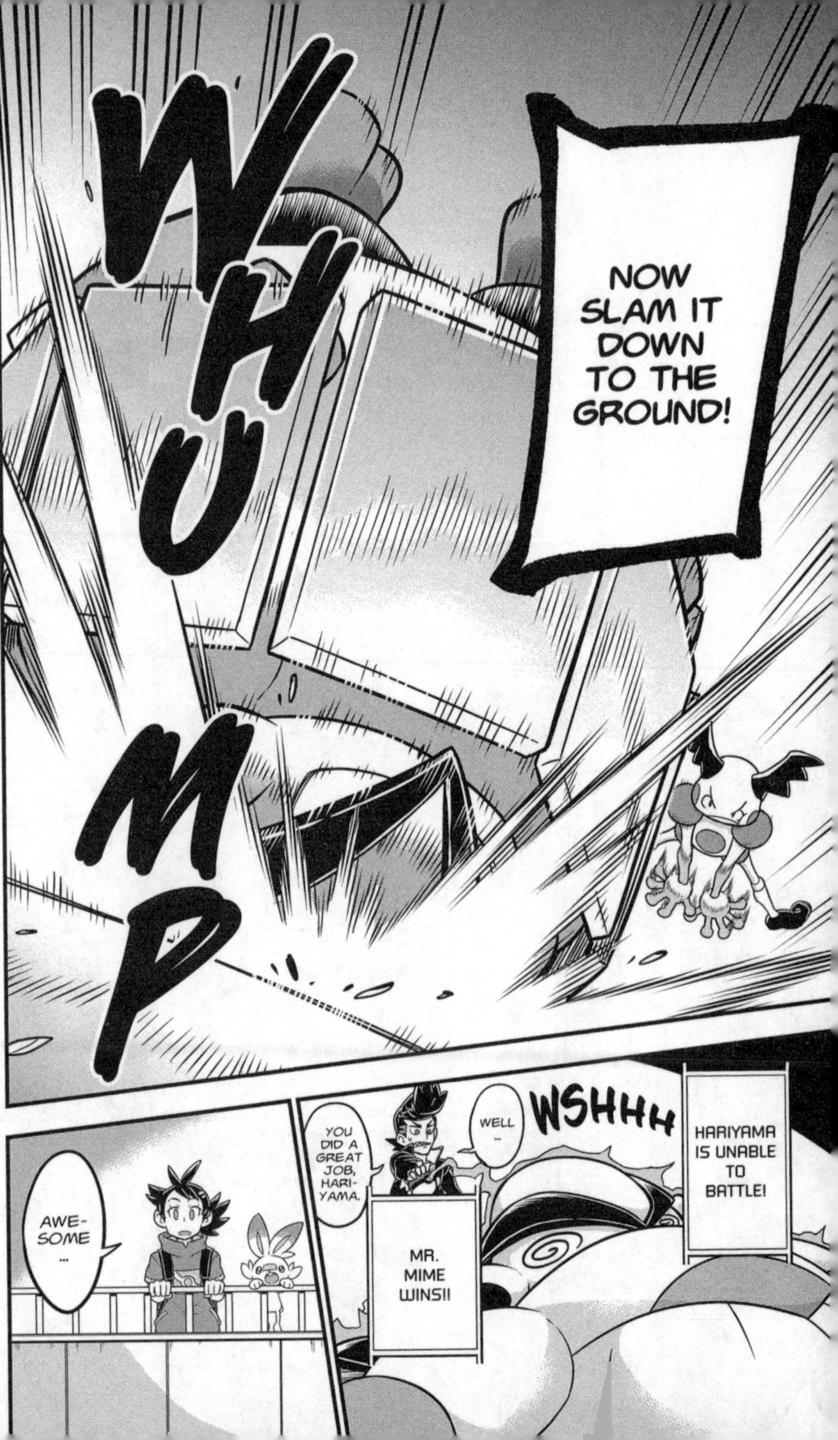
NOW SLAM IT DOWN TO THE GROUND!
WHUMP
HARIYAMA IS UNABLE TO BATTLE!
WSHHH
WELL...
YOU DID A GREAT JOB, HARIYAMA.
MR. MIME WINS!!
AWESOME...

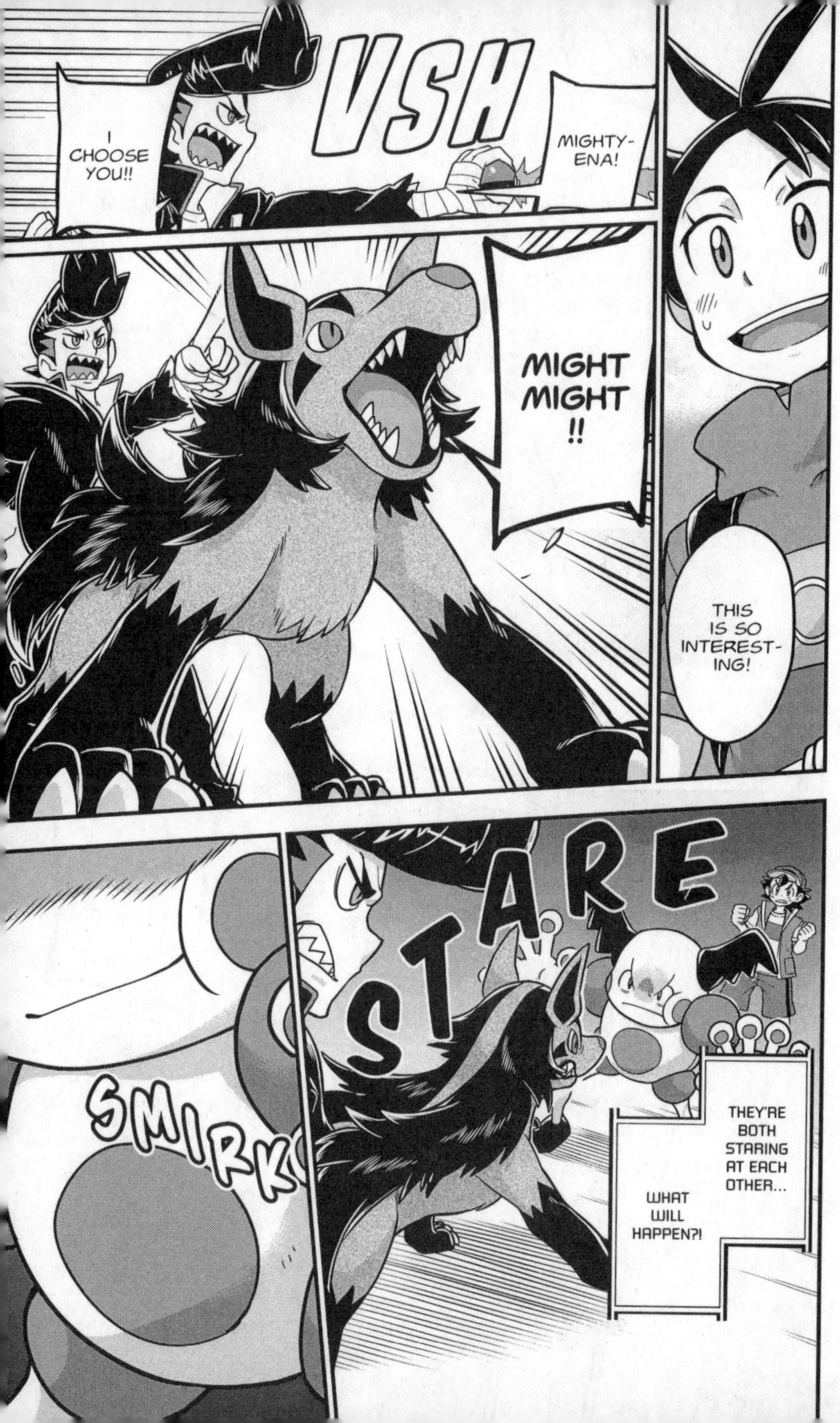
THIS IS SO INTERESTING!
VSH
MIGHTY-ENA!
I CHOOSE YOU!!
MIGHT MIGHT !!
STARE
THEY'RE BOTH STARING AT EACH OTHER...
WHAT WILL HAPPEN?!
SMIRK

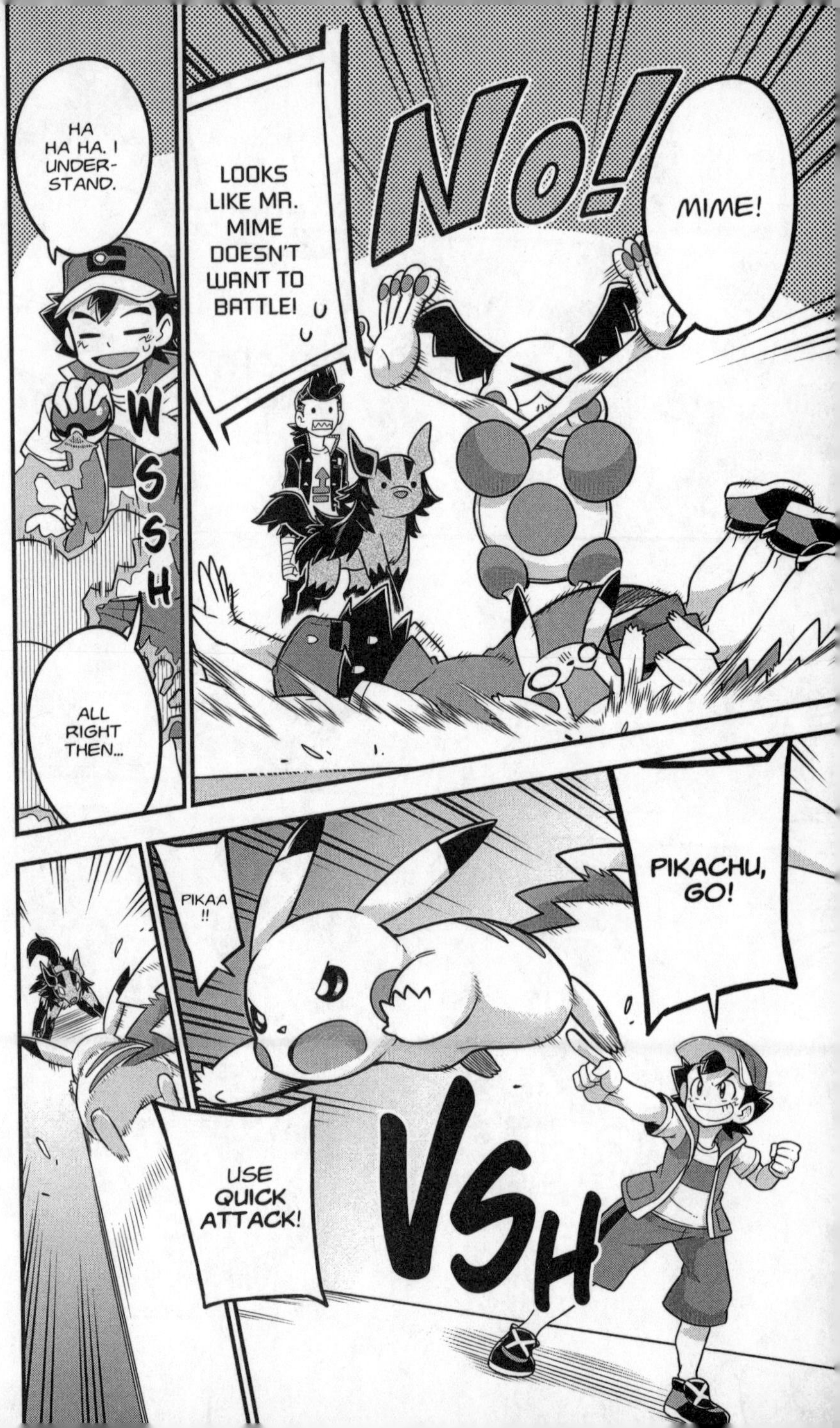
MIME!
NO!
LOOKS LIKE MR. MIME DOESN'T WANT TO BATTLE!
HA HA HA. I UNDER-STAND.
WSSH
ALL RIGHT THEN...
PIKACHU, GO!
PIKAA!!
USE QUICK ATTACK!
VSH

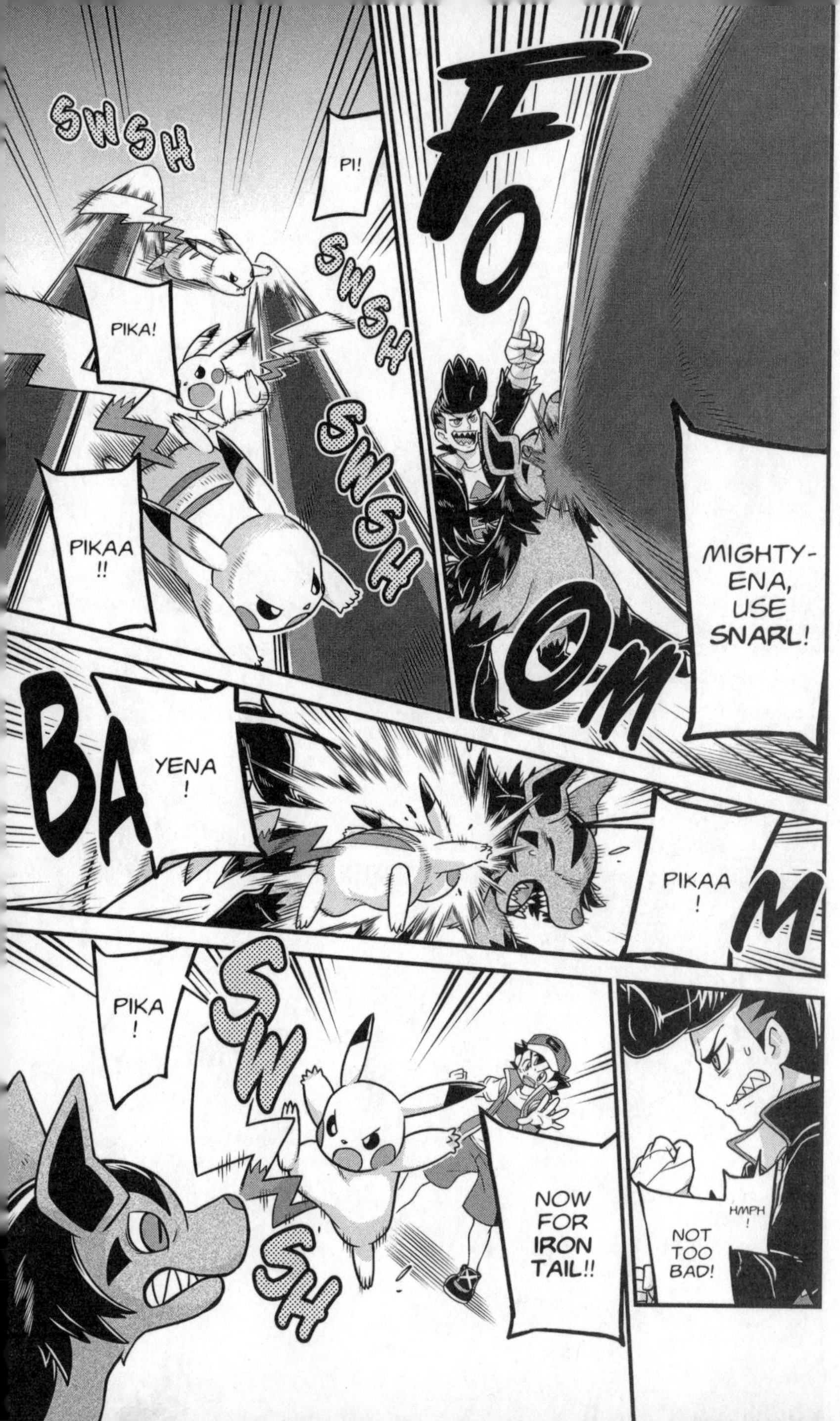
MIGHTY-ENA, USE SNARL!
FOOM
PI!
SWSH
SWSH
SWSH
PIKA!
SWSH
PIKAA!!
PIKAA!
BAM
YENA!
HMPH!
NOT TOO BAD!
NOW FOR IRON TAIL!!
PIKA!
SWSH

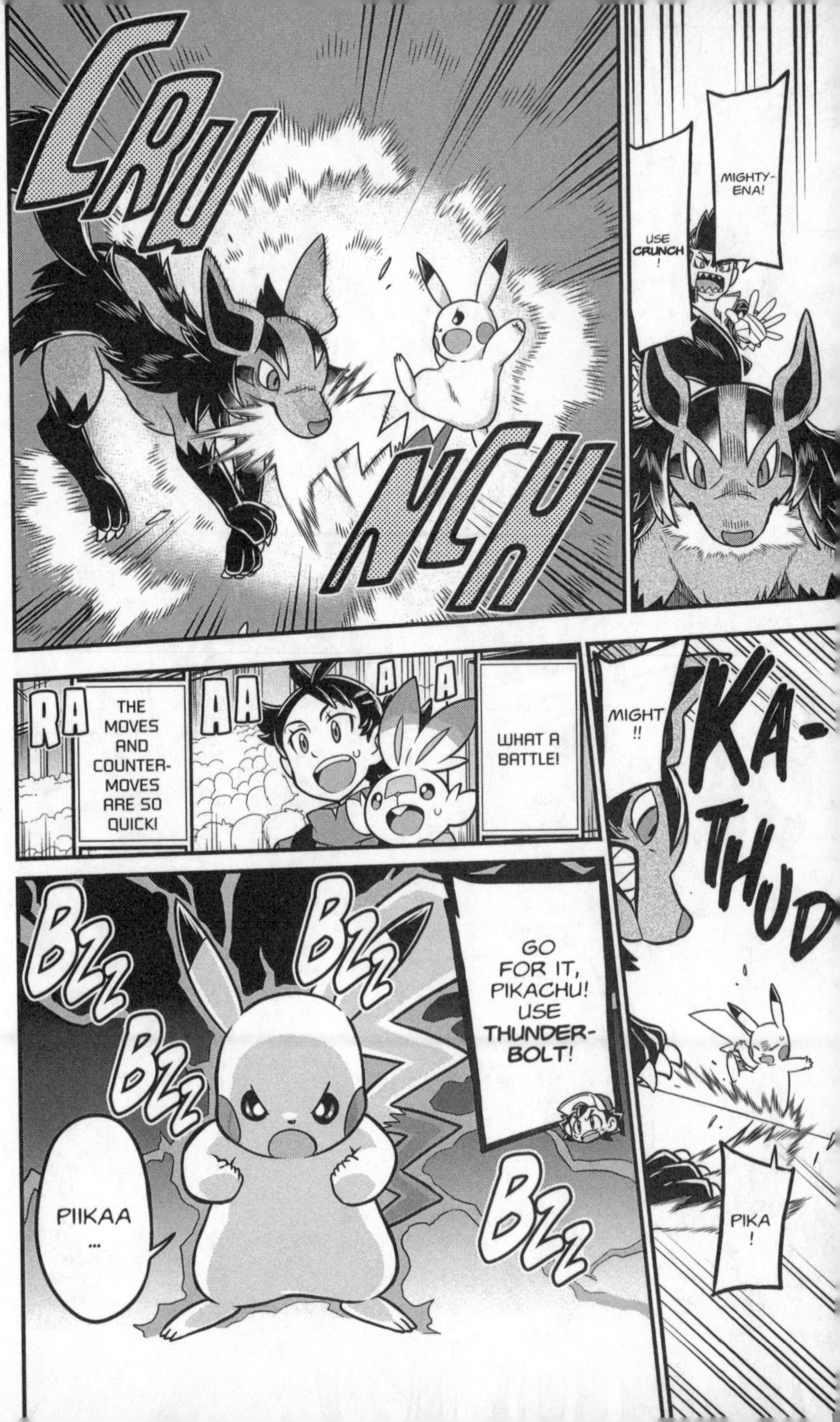
MIGHTY-ENA!
USE CRUNCH!
CRU
NCH
MIGHT!!
KA-THUD
PIKA!
WHAT A BATTLE!
A
A
AA
THE MOVES AND COUNTER-MOVES ARE SO QUICK!
RA
GO FOR IT, PIKACHU! USE THUNDER-BOLT!
BZZ
BZZ
BZZ
BZZ
PIIKAA ...

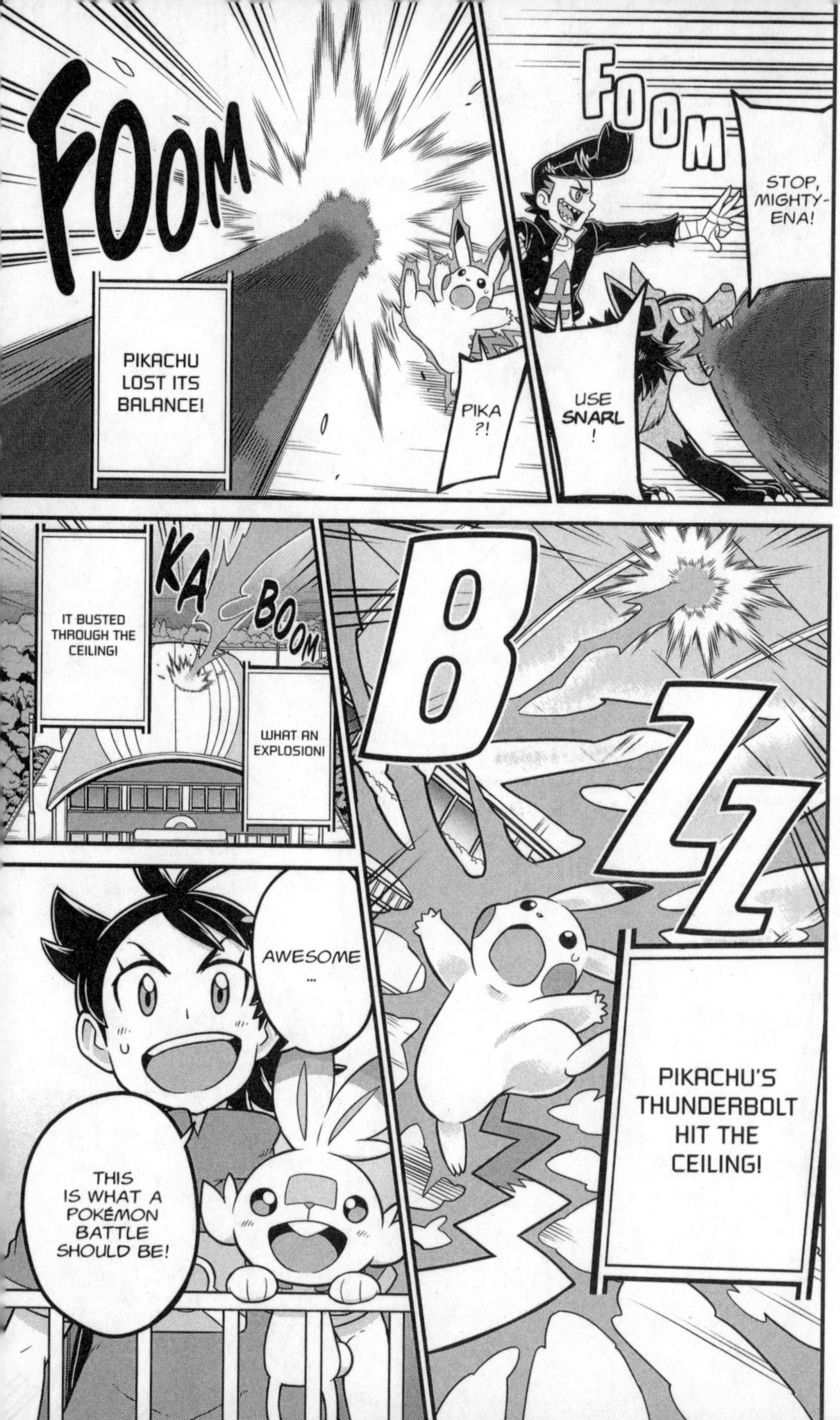
FOOM
STOP, MIGHTY-ENA!
USE SNARL!
PIKA ?!
FOOM
PIKACHU LOST ITS BALANCE!
BZZ
PIKACHU'S THUNDERBOLT HIT THE CEILING!
KA-BOOM
WHAT AN EXPLOSION!
IT BUSTED THROUGH THE CEILING!
AWESOME...
THIS IS WHAT A POKÉMON BATTLE SHOULD BE!

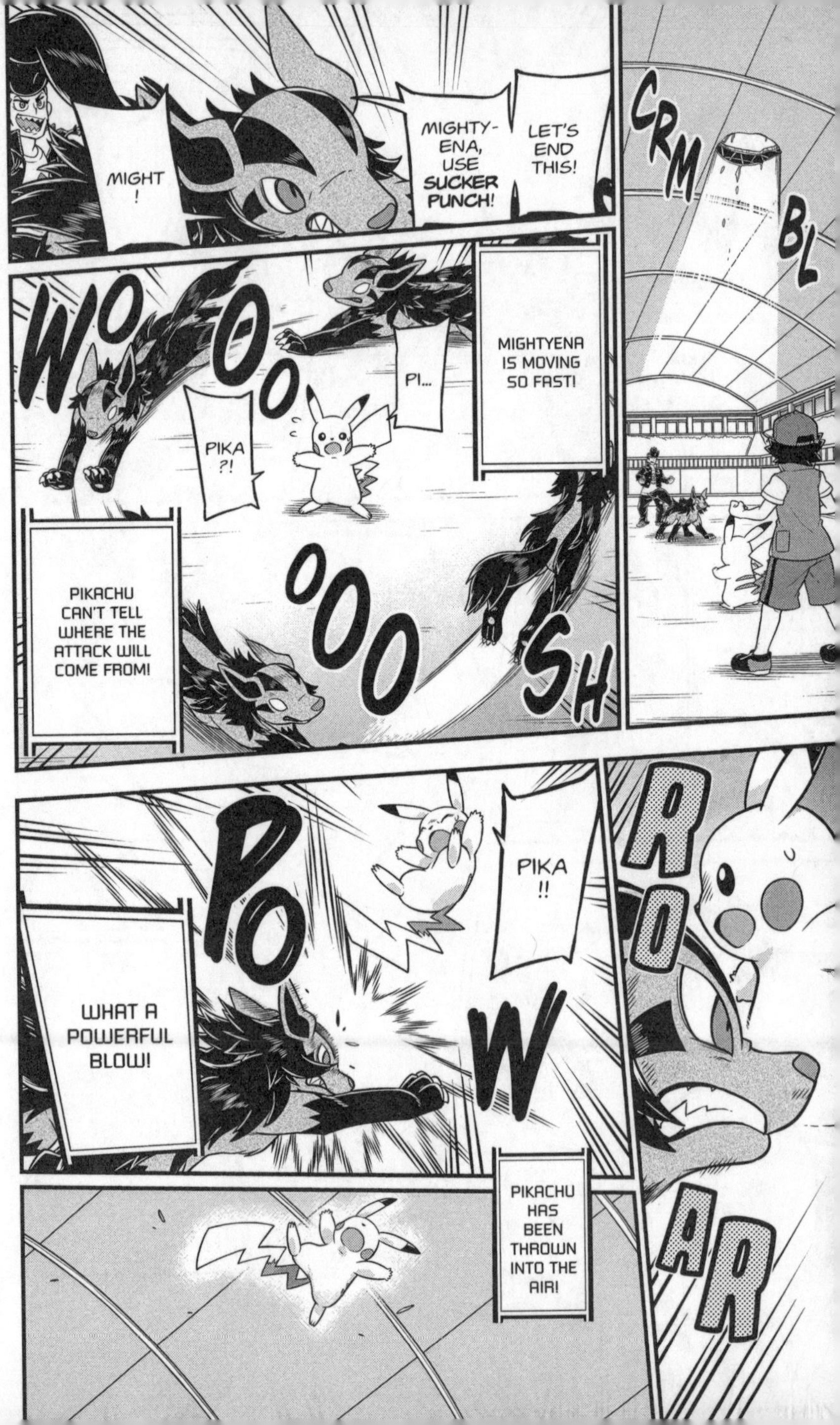
CRMBL
LET'S END THIS!
MIGHTY-ENA, USE SUCKER PUNCH!
MIGHT!
MIGHTYENA IS MOVING SO FAST!
PI...
PIKA?!
WOOOOOOOSH
PIKACHU CAN'T TELL WHERE THE ATTACK WILL COME FROM!
ROOAR
PIKA!!
POW
WHAT A POWERFUL BLOW!
PIKACHU HAS BEEN THROWN INTO THE AIR!

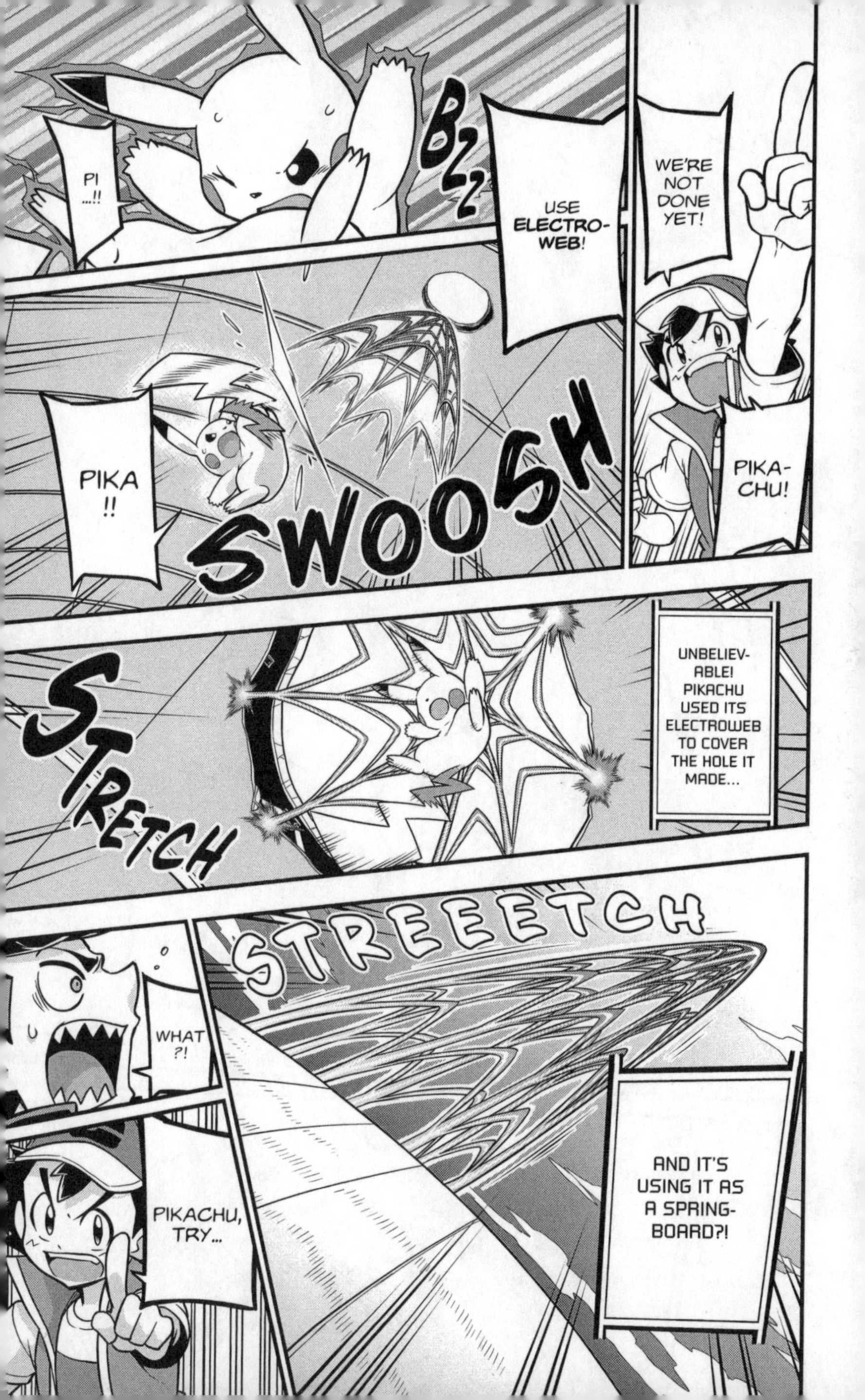
WE'RE NOT DONE YET!
USE ELECTRO-WEB!
PIKA-CHU!
BZZ
PI ...!!
SWOOSH
PIKA !!
UNBELIEVABLE! PIKACHU USED ITS ELECTROWEB TO COVER THE HOLE IT MADE...
STRETCH
STREEETCH
AND IT'S USING IT AS A SPRING-BOARD?!
WHAT ?!
PIKACHU, TRY...

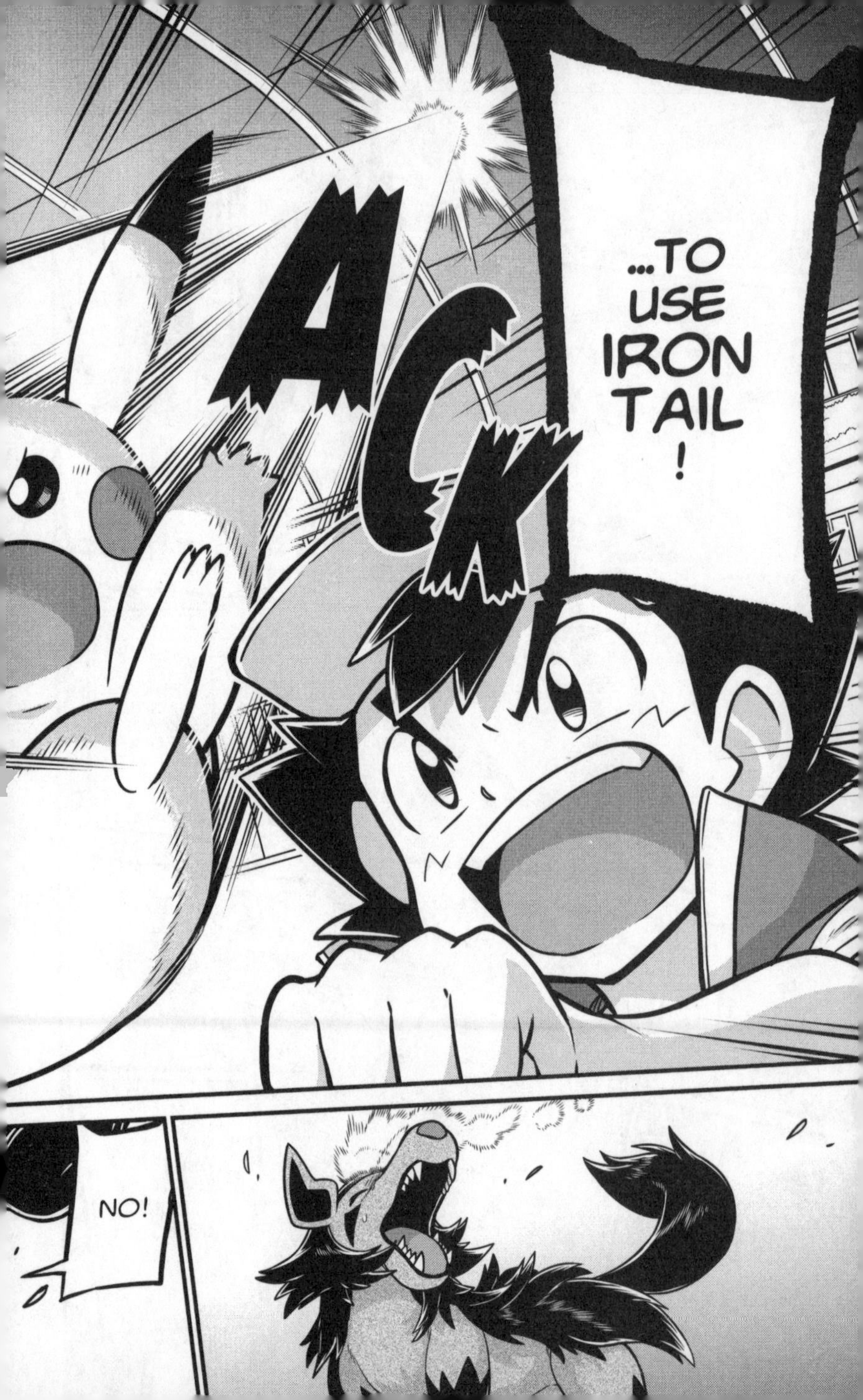
...TO USE IRON TAIL!
ACK
NO!

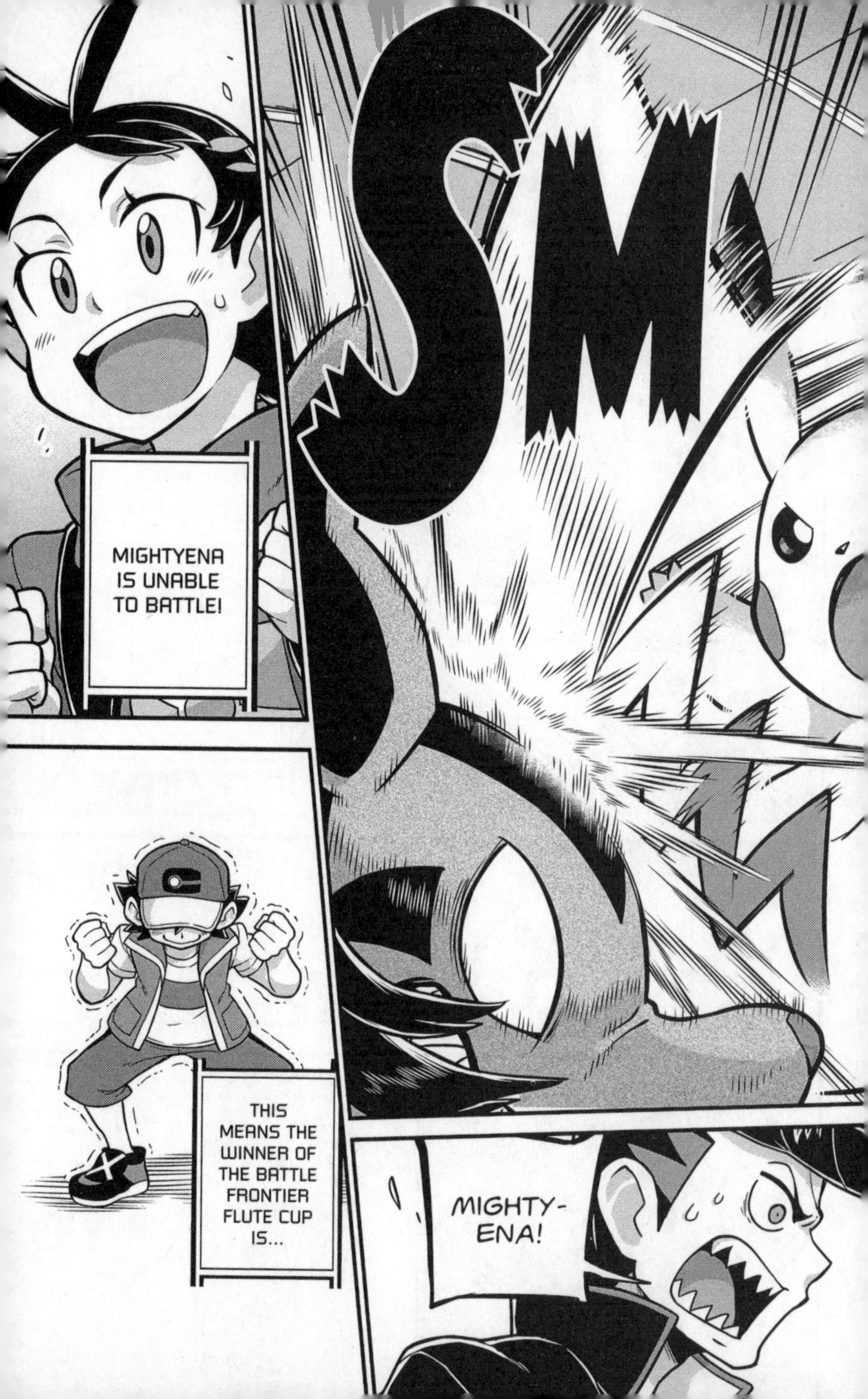
SM
MIGHTYENA IS UNABLE TO BATTLE!
MIGHTY-ENA!
THIS MEANS THE WINNER OF THE BATTLE FRONTIER FLUTE CUP IS...

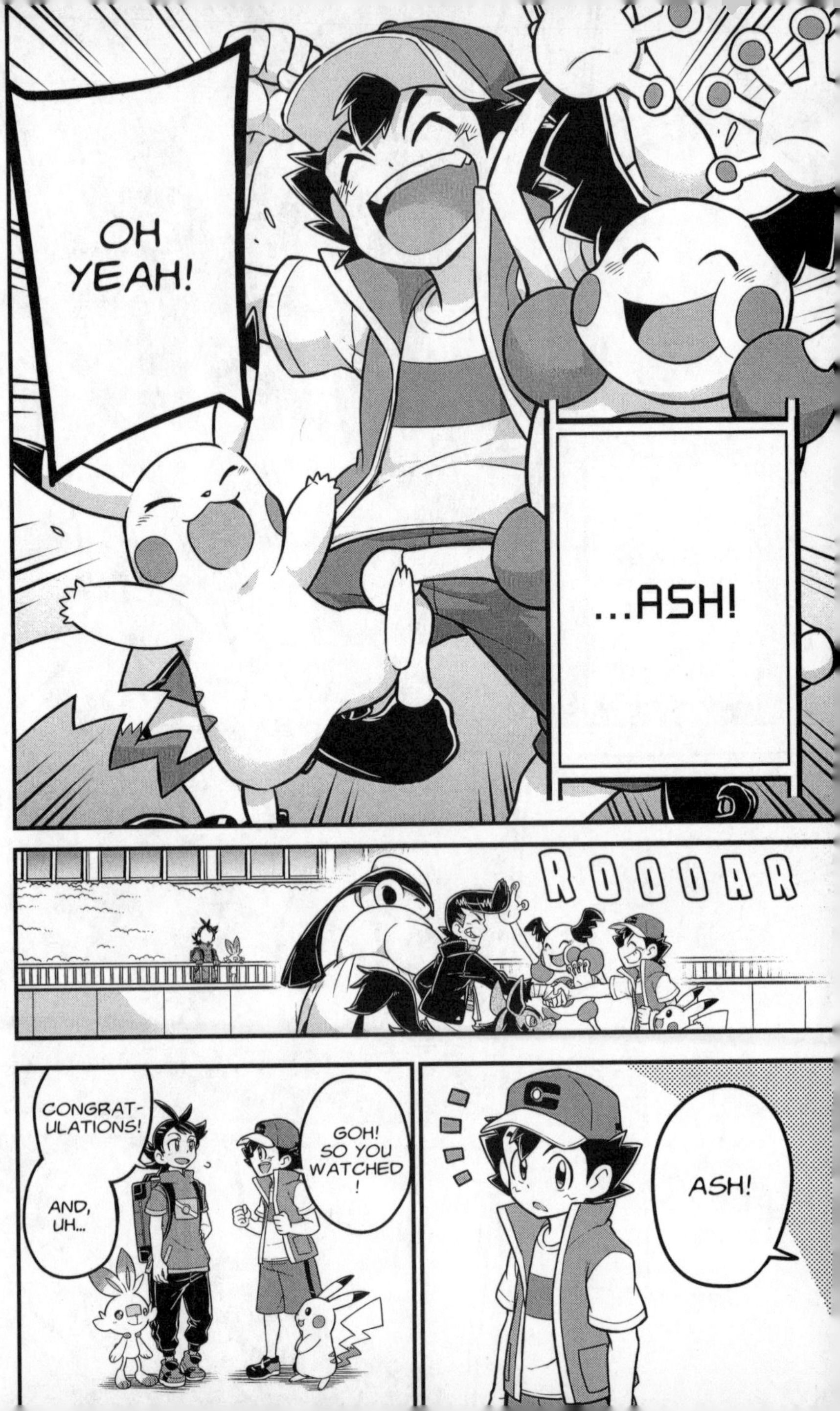
...ASH!
OH YEAH!
ROOOAR
ASH!
GOH! SO YOU WATCHED!
CONGRATULATIONS!
AND, UH...

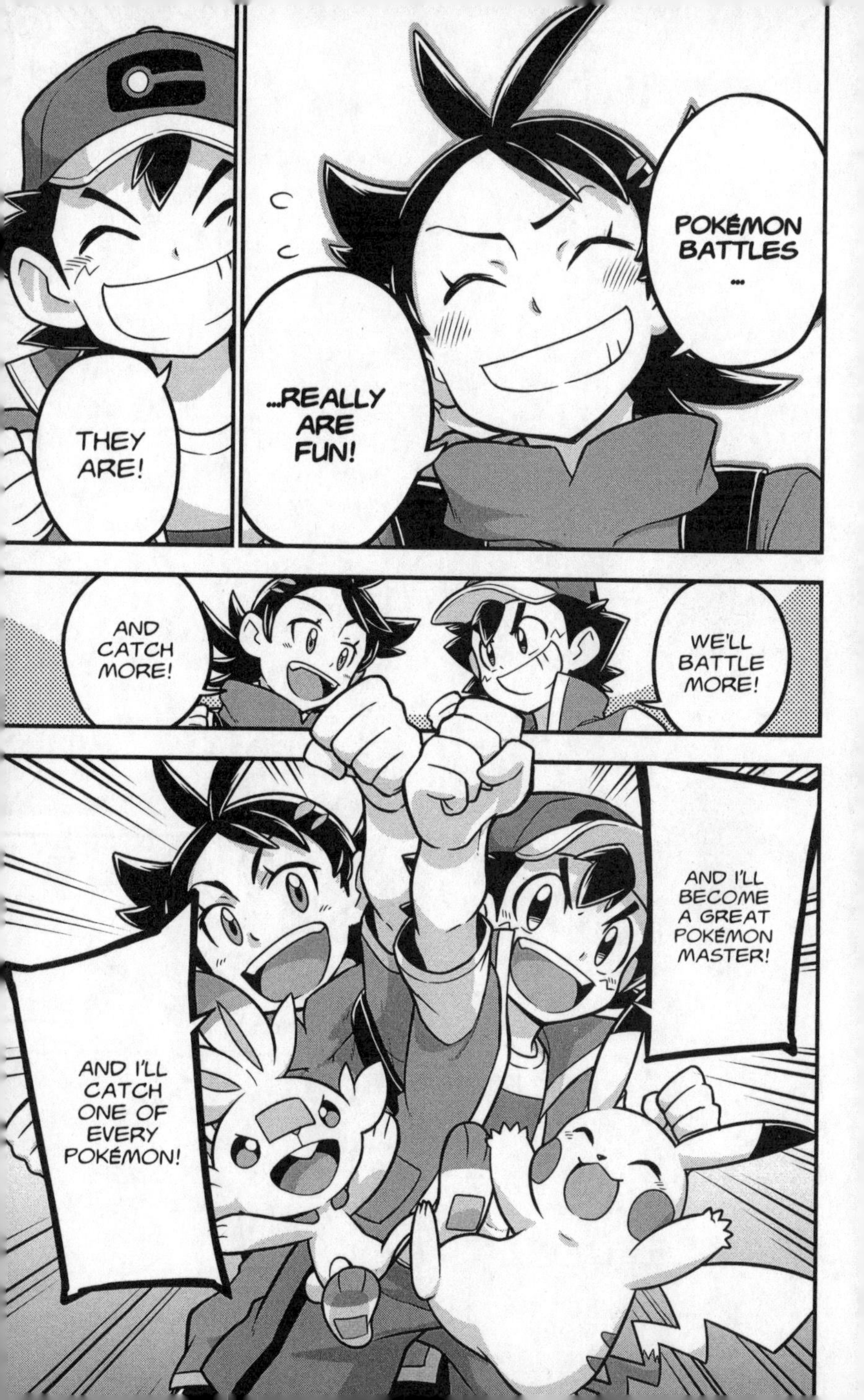
POKÉMON BATTLES ...
...REALLY ARE FUN!
THEY ARE!
WE'LL BATTLE MORE!
AND CATCH MORE!
AND I'LL BECOME A GREAT POKÉMON MASTER!
AND I'LL CATCH ONE OF EVERY POKÉMON!

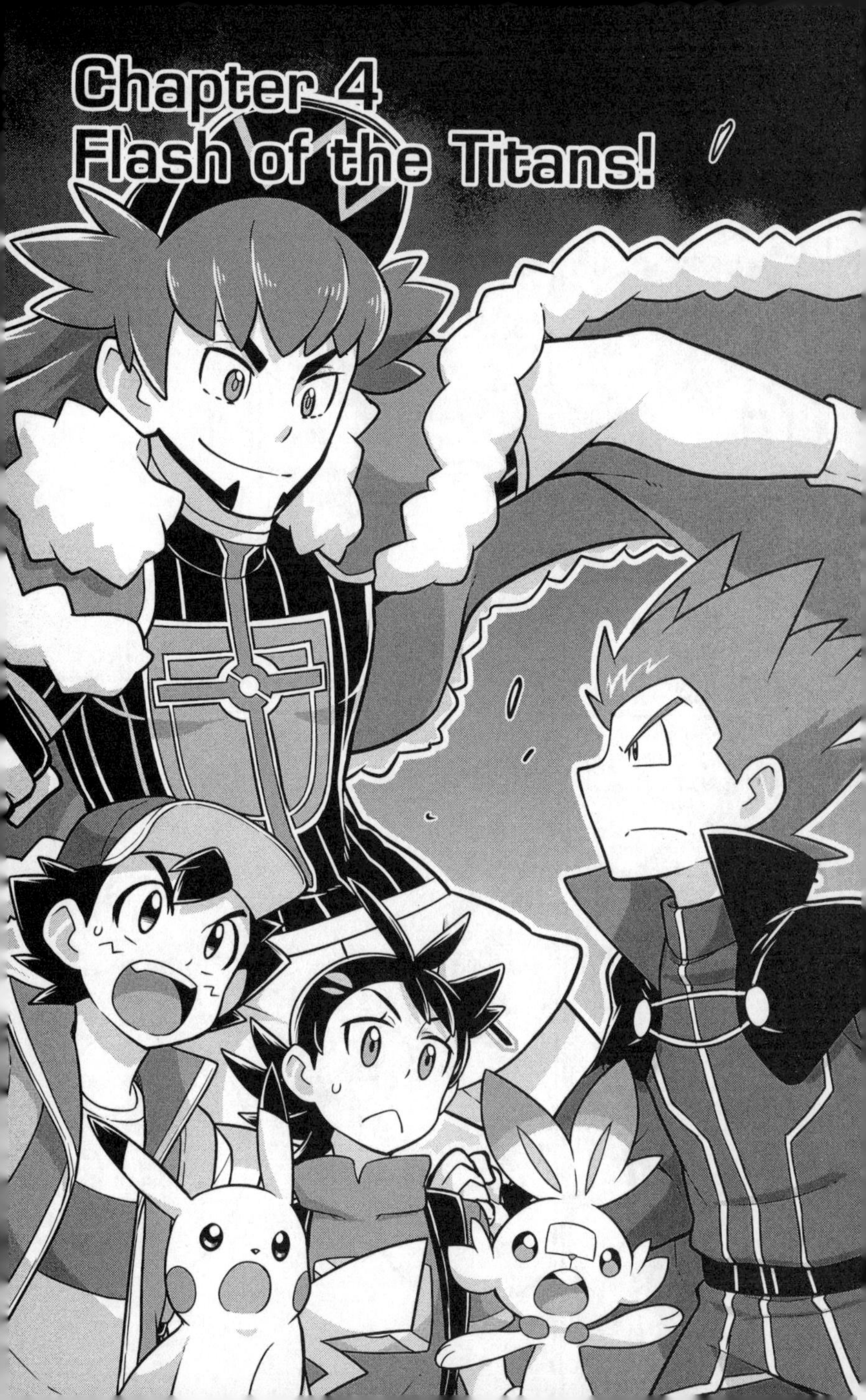
Chapter 4
Flash of the Titans!

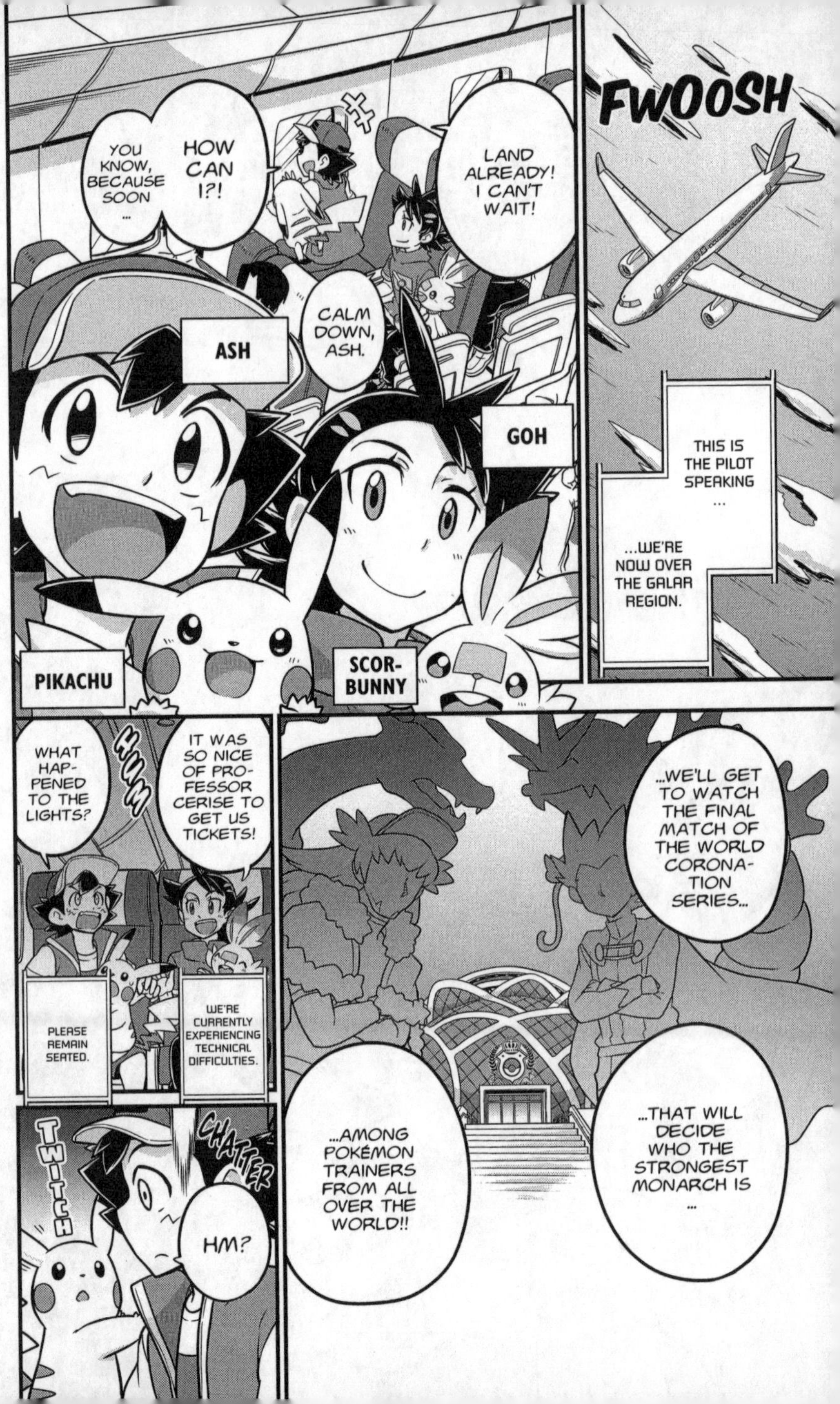
FWOOSH
THIS IS THE PILOT SPEAKING ...
...WE'RE NOW OVER THE GALAR REGION.
LAND ALREADY! I CAN'T WAIT!
HOW CAN I?!
YOU KNOW, BECAUSE SOON ...
CALM DOWN, ASH.
ASH
GOH
SCOR-BUNNY
PIKACHU
...WE'LL GET TO WATCH THE FINAL MATCH OF THE WORLD CORONA-TION SERIES...
...THAT WILL DECIDE WHO THE STRONGEST MONARCH IS ...
...AMONG POKÉMON TRAINERS FROM ALL OVER THE WORLD!!
IT WAS SO NICE OF PRO-FESSOR CERISE TO GET US TICKETS!
HUM
WHAT HAP-PENED TO THE LIGHTS?
WE'RE CURRENTLY EXPERIENCING TECHNICAL DIFFICULTIES.
PLEASE REMAIN SEATED.
CHATTER
HM?
TWITCH

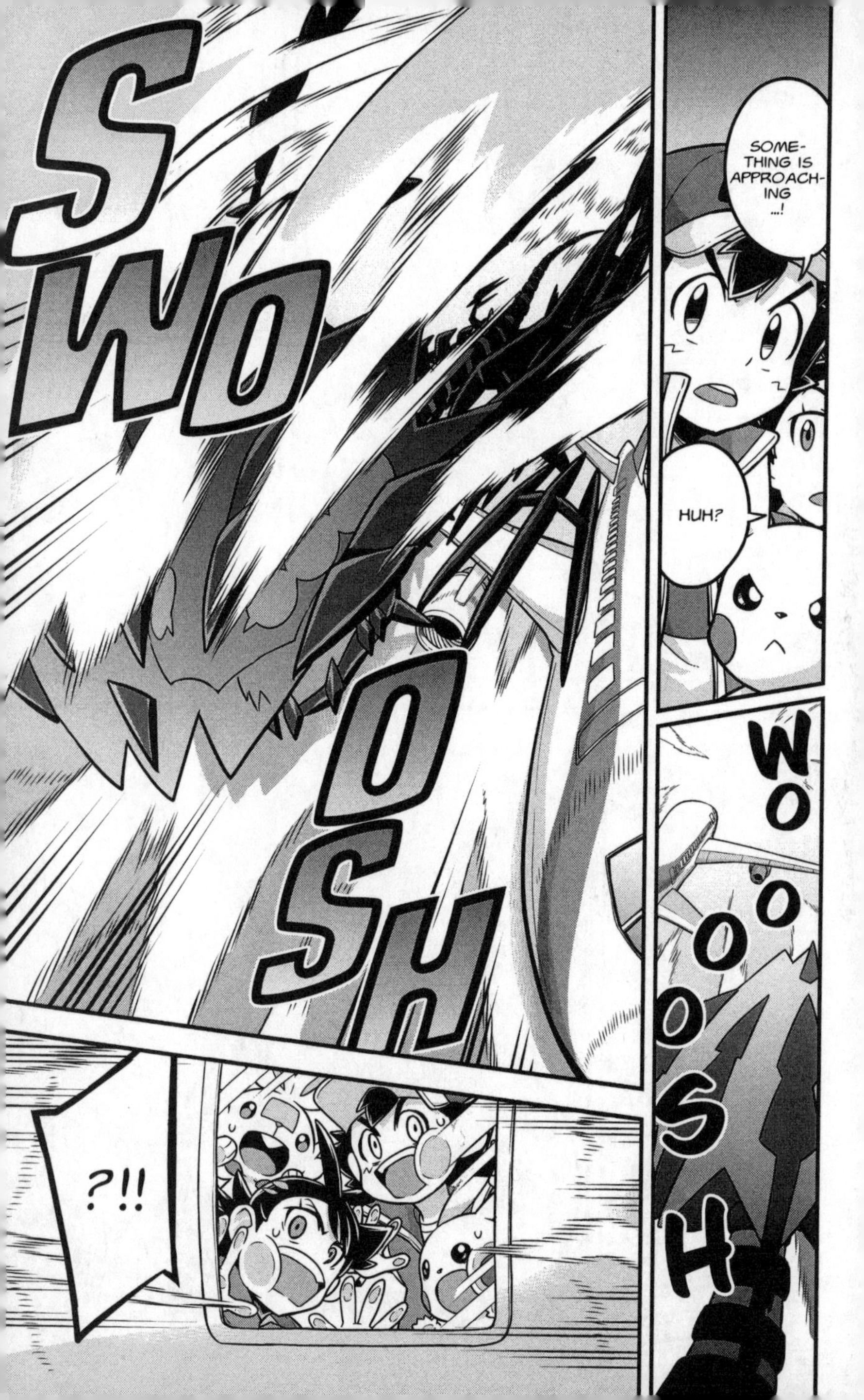

SOME-THING IS APPROACH-ING ...!
HUH?
SWOOSH
WOOOOOSH
?!!

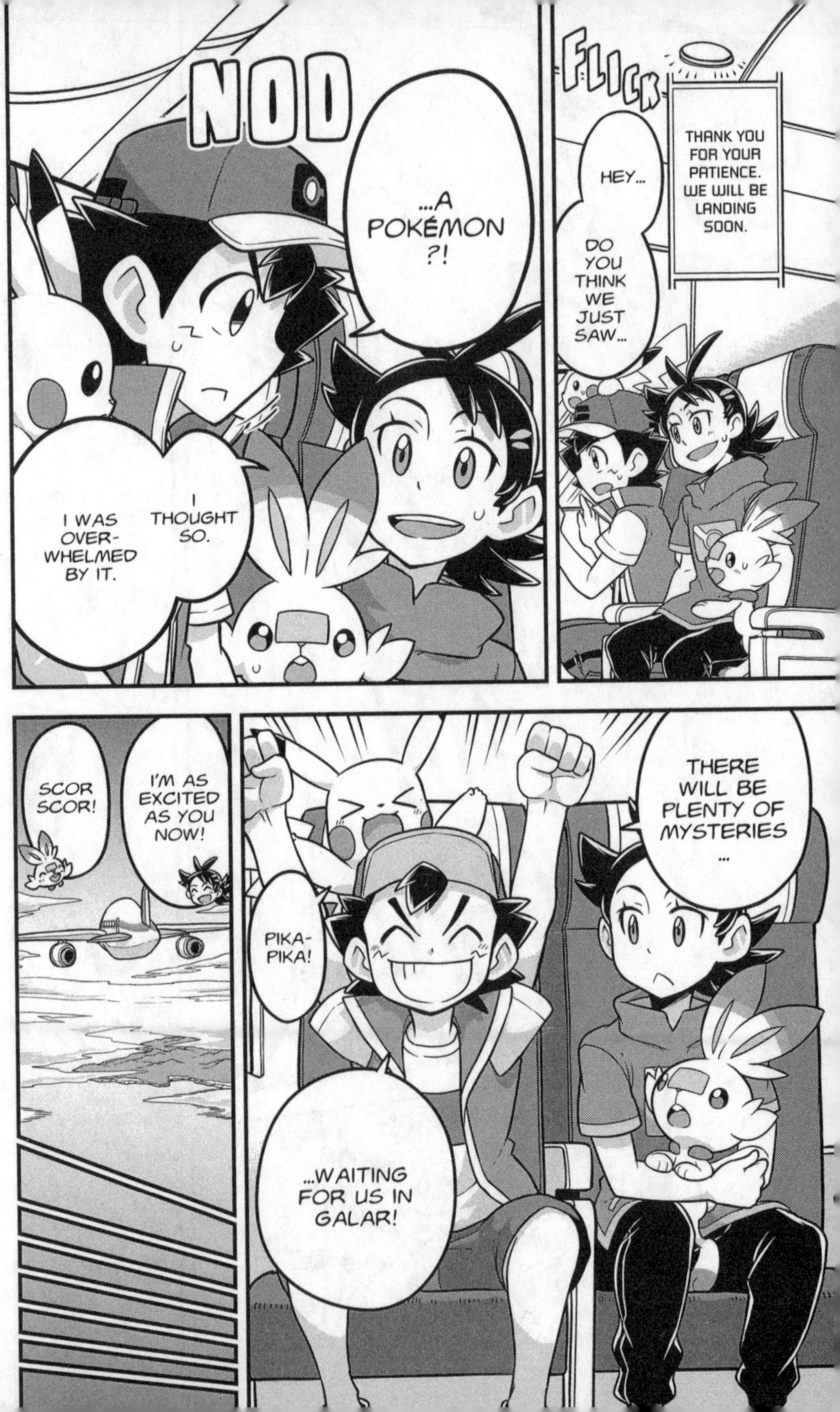
FLICK
THANK YOU FOR YOUR PATIENCE. WE WILL BE LANDING SOON.
HEY...
DO YOU THINK WE JUST SAW...
NOD
...A POKÉMON ?!
I THOUGHT SO.
I WAS OVER-WHELMED BY IT.
THERE WILL BE PLENTY OF MYSTERIES ...
PIKA-PIKA!
...WAITING FOR US IN GALAR!
I'M AS EXCITED AS YOU NOW!
SCOR SCOR!

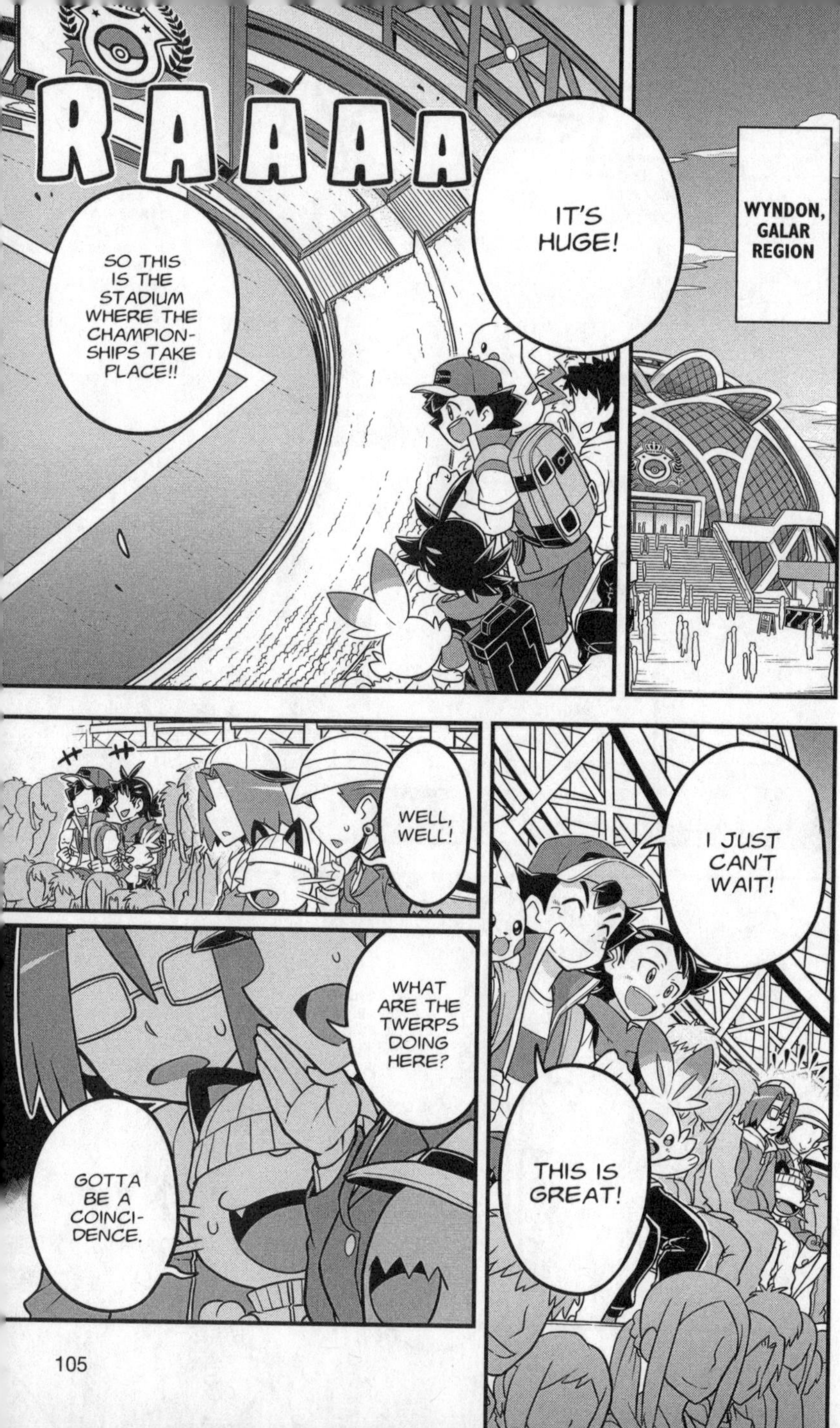
WYNDON, GALAR REGION
RAAAAA
SO THIS IS THE STADIUM WHERE THE CHAMPIONSHIPS TAKE PLACE!!
IT'S HUGE!
I JUST CAN'T WAIT!
THIS IS GREAT!
WELL, WELL!
WHAT ARE THE TWERPS DOING HERE?
GOTTA BE A COINCIDENCE.

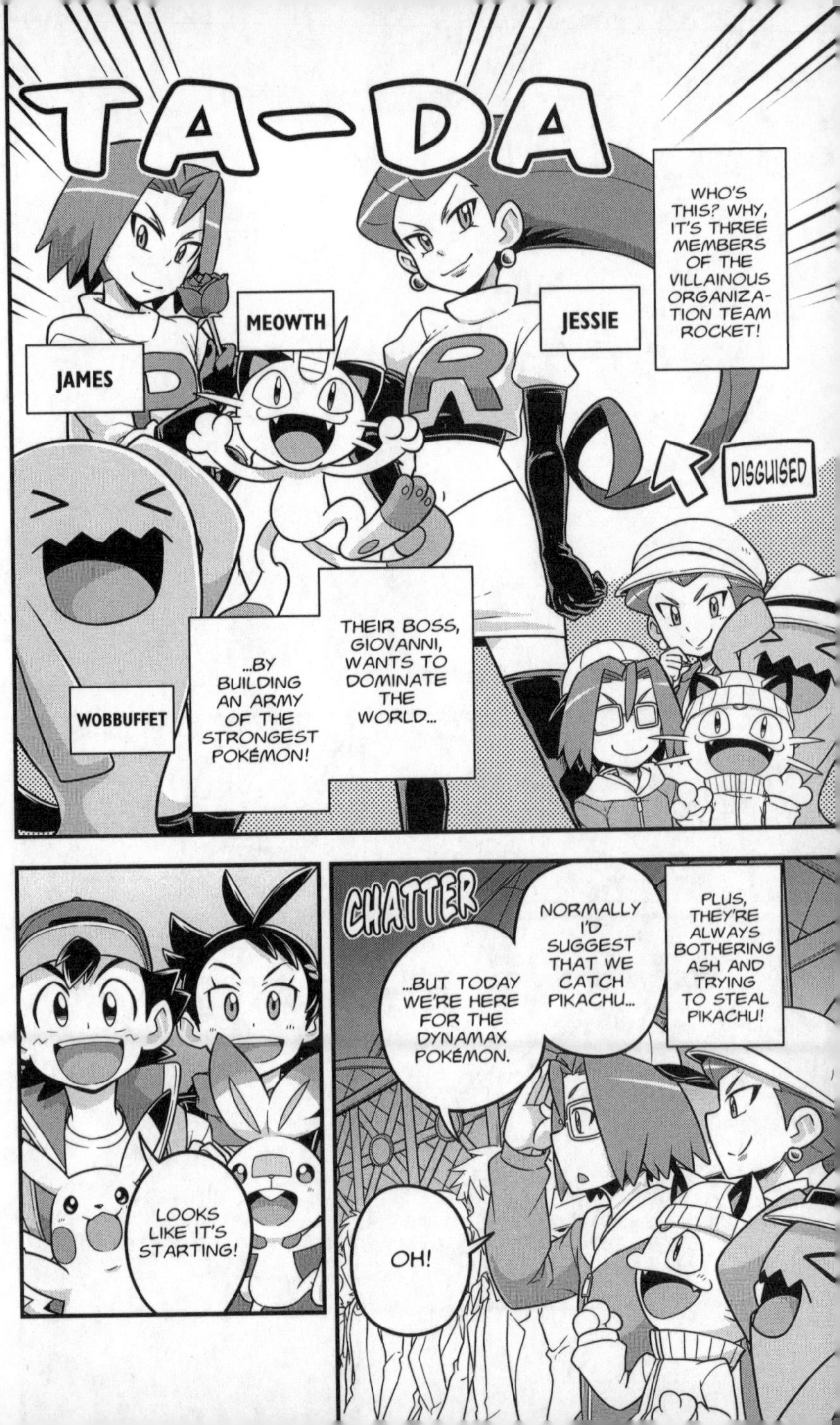
TA-DA
WHO'S THIS? WHY, IT'S THREE MEMBERS OF THE VILLAINOUS ORGANIZATION TEAM ROCKET!
JESSIE
MEOWTH
JAMES
DISGUISED
THEIR BOSS, GIOVANNI, WANTS TO DOMINATE THE WORLD...
...BY BUILDING AN ARMY OF THE STRONGEST POKÉMON!
WOBBUFFET
CHATTER
PLUS, THEY'RE ALWAYS BOTHERING ASH AND TRYING TO STEAL PIKACHU!
NORMALLY I'D SUGGEST THAT WE CATCH PIKACHU...
...BUT TODAY WE'RE HERE FOR THE DYNAMAX POKÉMON.
OH!
LOOKS LIKE IT'S STARTING!

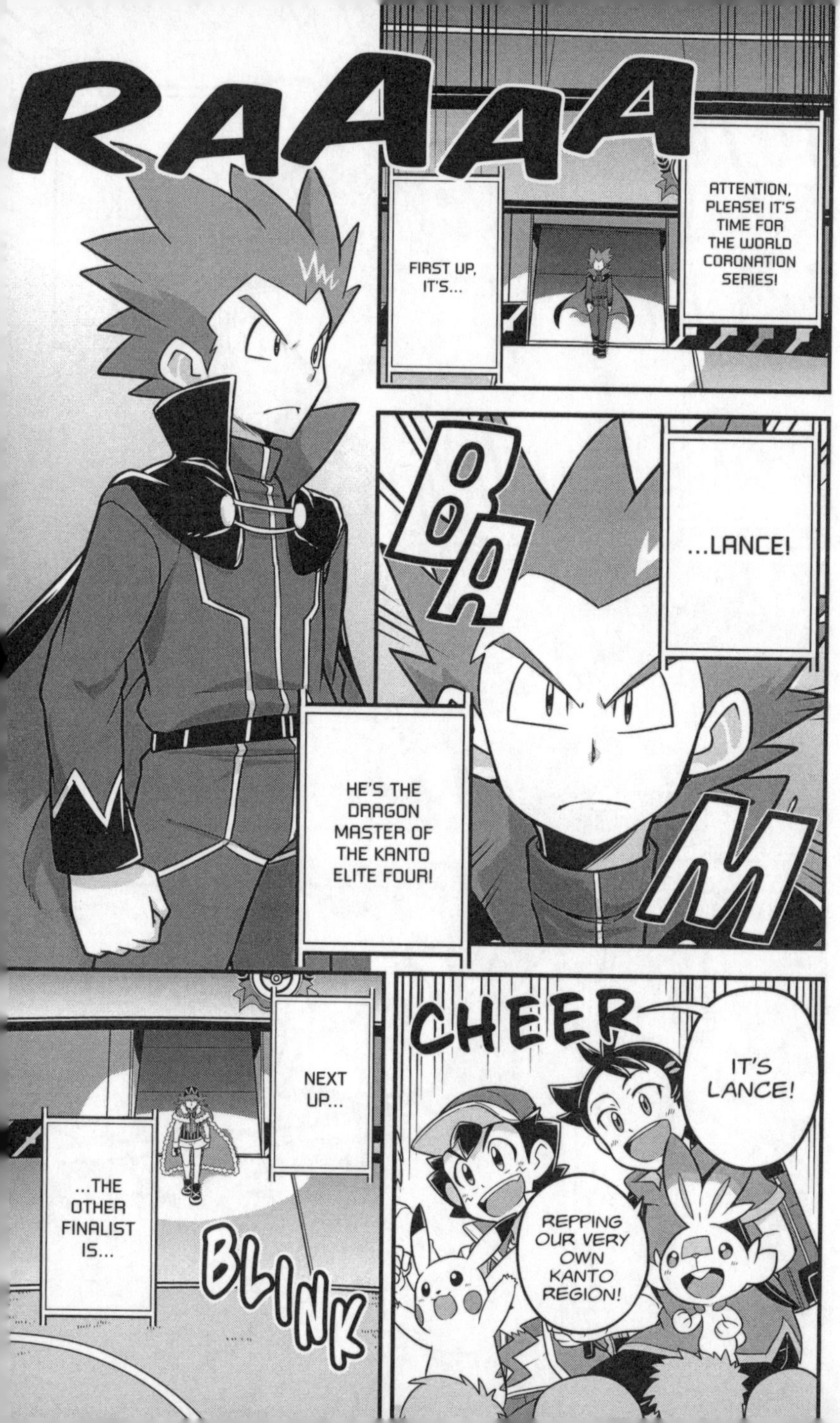
ATTENTION, PLEASE! IT'S TIME FOR THE WORLD CORONATION SERIES!
FIRST UP, IT'S...
...LANCE!
BOOM
RAAAA
HE'S THE DRAGON MASTER OF THE KANTO ELITE FOUR!
CHEER
IT'S LANCE!
REPPING OUR VERY OWN KANTO REGION!
NEXT UP...
...THE OTHER FINALIST IS...
BLINK

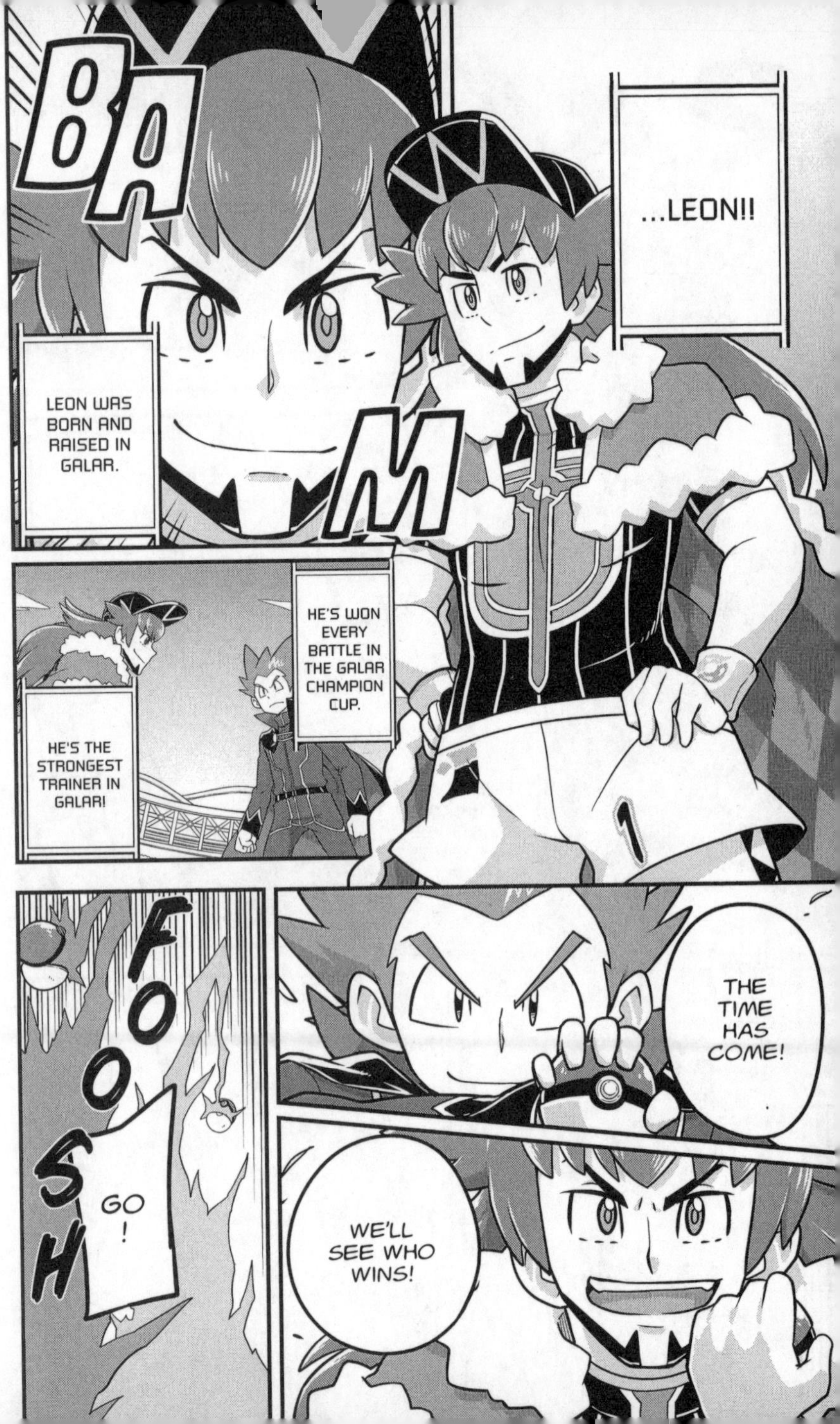
...LEON!!
BAM
LEON WAS BORN AND RAISED IN GALAR.
HE'S WON EVERY BATTLE IN THE GALAR CHAMPION CUP.
HE'S THE STRONGEST TRAINER IN GALAR!
THE TIME HAS COME!
WE'LL SEE WHO WINS!
FOOSH
GO!

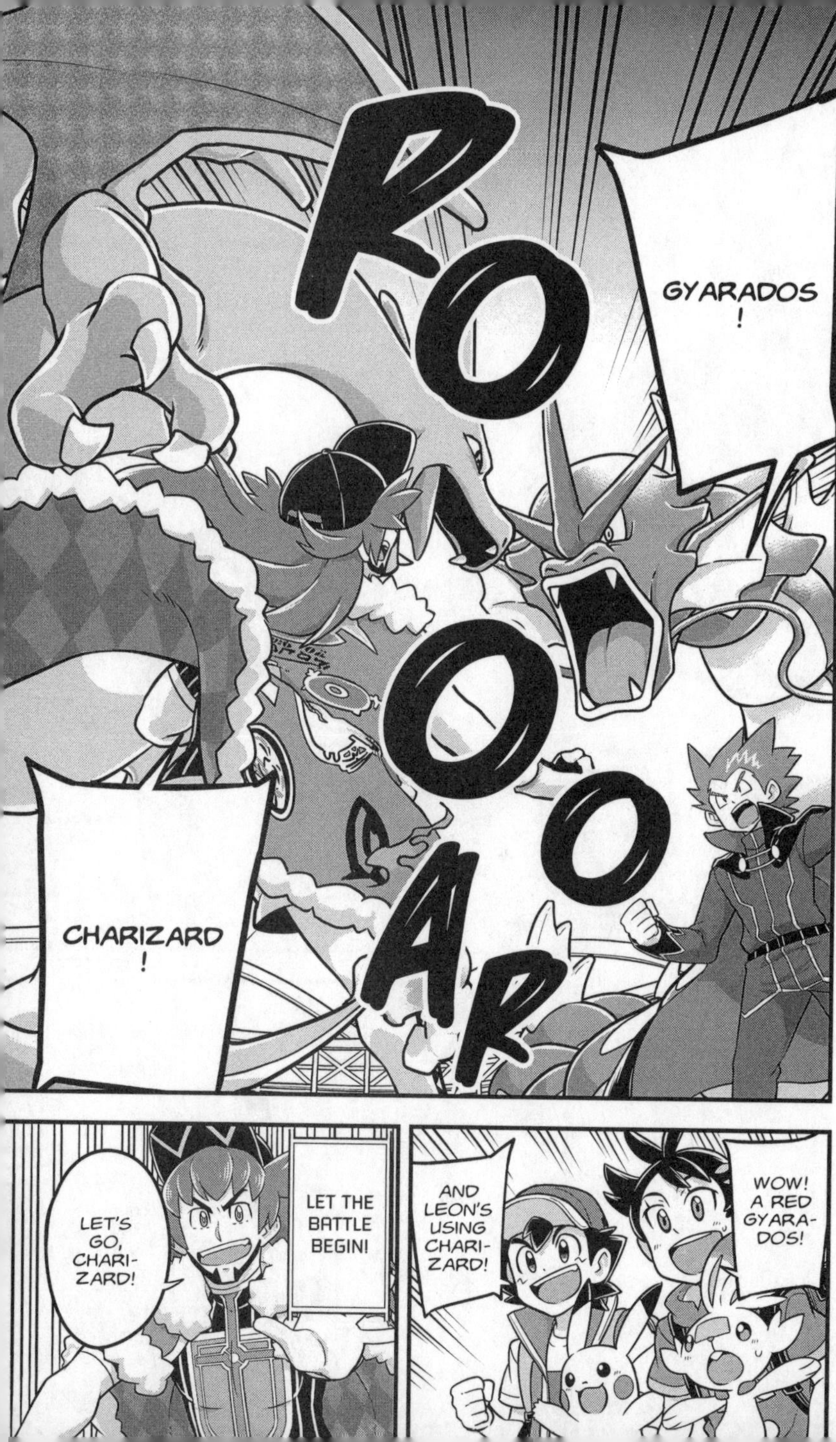
GYARADOS!
ROOOOAR
CHARIZARD!
WOW! A RED GYARADOS!
AND LEON'S USING CHARIZARD!
LET THE BATTLE BEGIN!
LET'S GO, CHARIZARD!

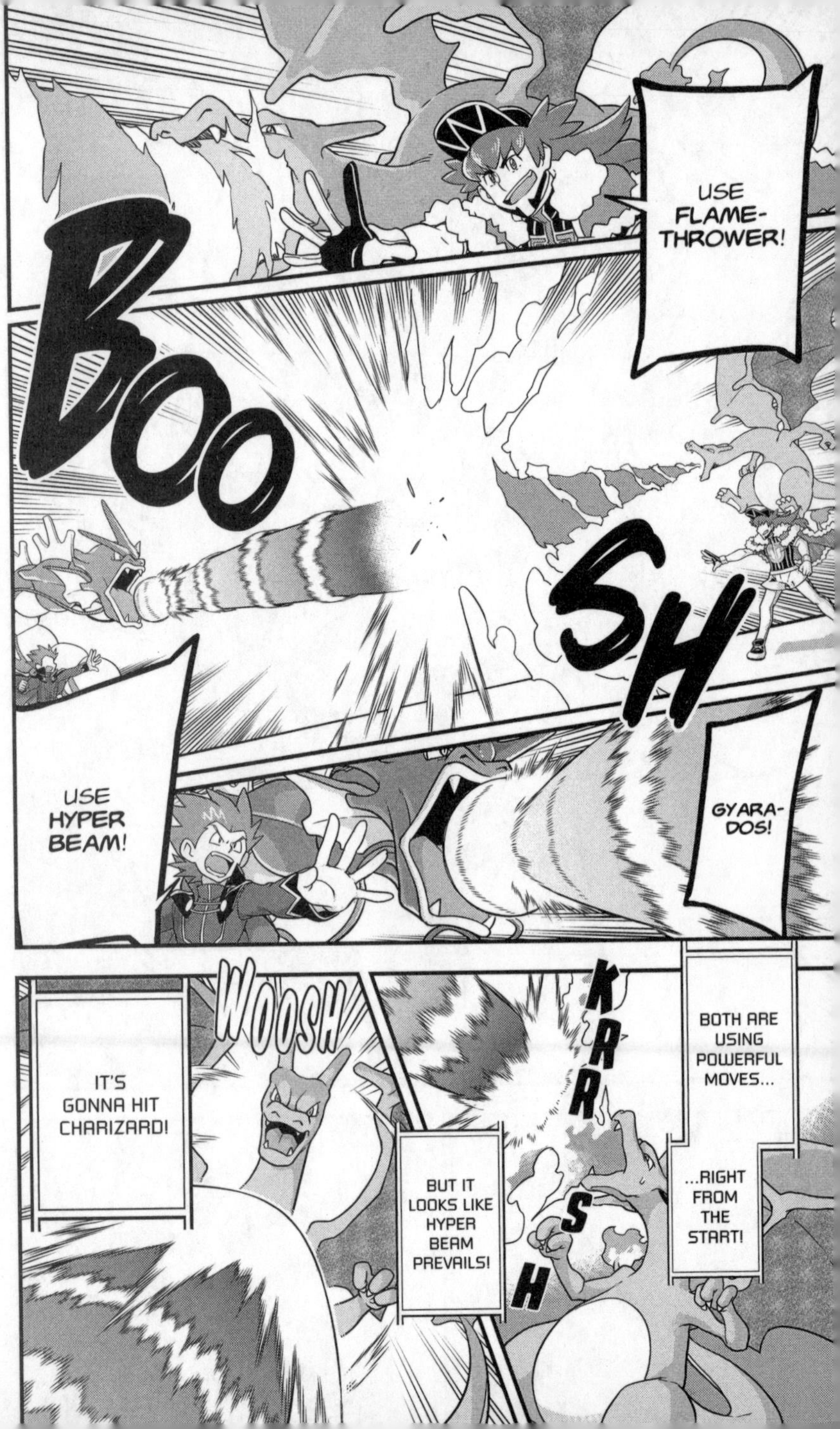
USE FLAME-THROWER!
BOOSH
GYARA-DOS!
USE HYPER BEAM!
BOTH ARE USING POWERFUL MOVES...
...RIGHT FROM THE START!
KRRSSH
BUT IT LOOKS LIKE HYPER BEAM PREVAILS!
WOOSH
IT'S GONNA HIT CHARIZARD!

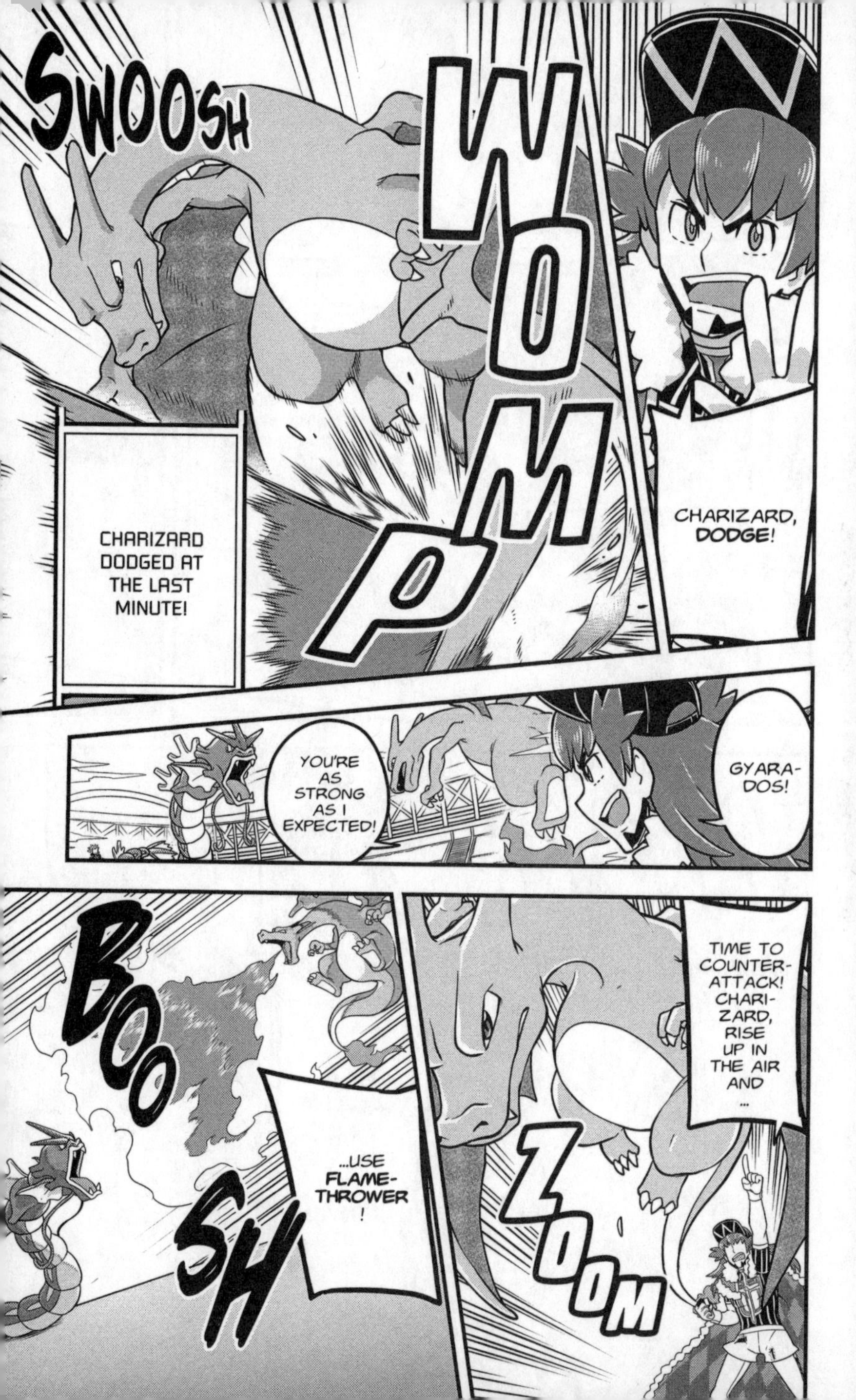
CHARIZARD, DODGE!
WOMP
SWOOSH
CHARIZARD DODGED AT THE LAST MINUTE!
GYARA-DOS!
YOU'RE AS STRONG AS I EXPECTED!
TIME TO COUNTER-ATTACK! CHARI-ZARD, RISE UP IN THE AIR AND ...
ZOOM
...USE FLAME-THROWER!
BOOSH

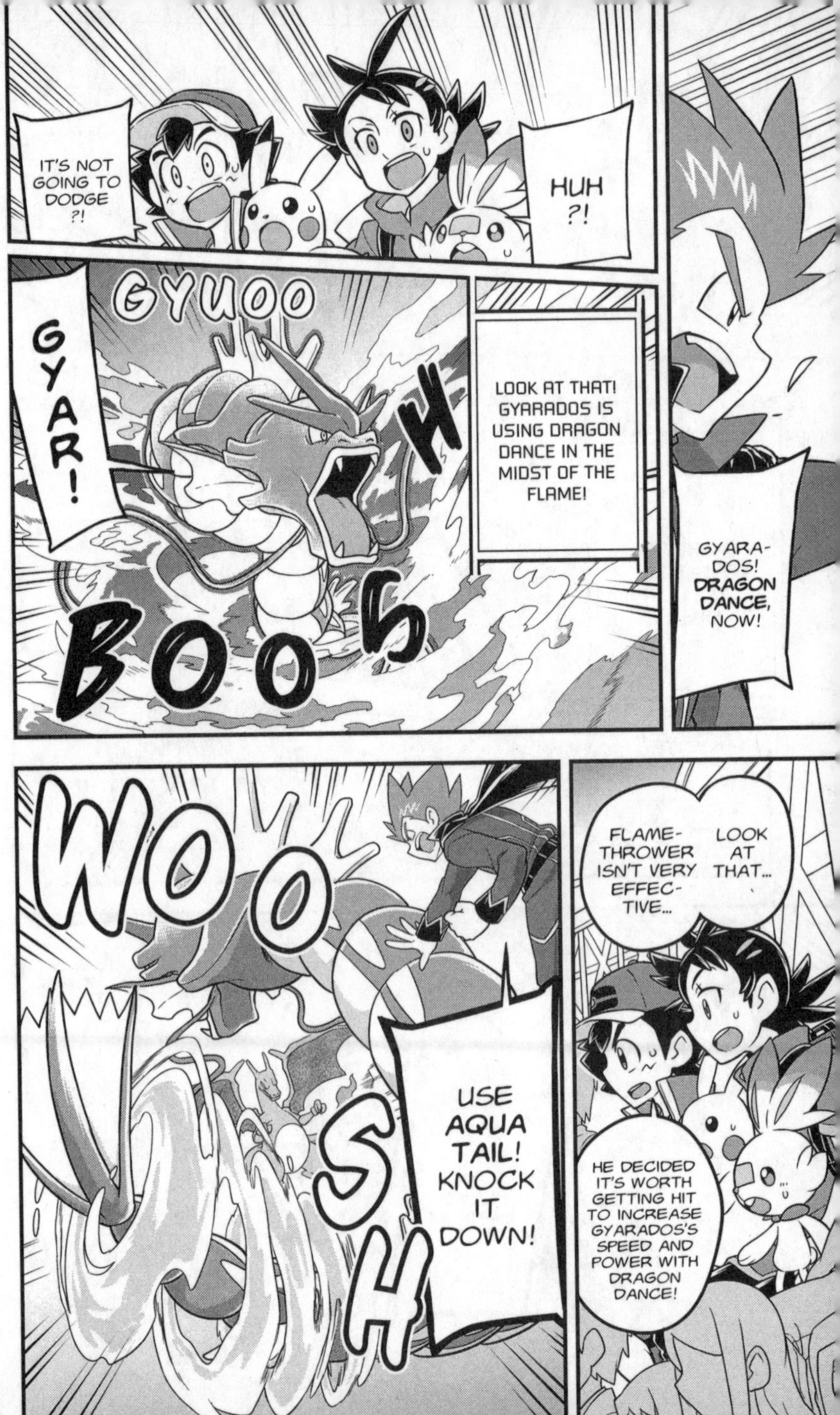
GYARADOS! DRAGON DANCE, NOW!
HUH?!
IT'S NOT GOING TO DODGE?!
LOOK AT THAT! GYARADOS IS USING DRAGON DANCE IN THE MIDST OF THE FLAME!
GYUOO
GYAR!
BOOHH
LOOK AT THAT...
FLAMETHROWER ISN'T VERY EFFECTIVE...
HE DECIDED IT'S WORTH GETTING HIT TO INCREASE GYARADOS'S SPEED AND POWER WITH DRAGON DANCE!
USE AQUA TAIL! KNOCK IT DOWN!
WOOSH

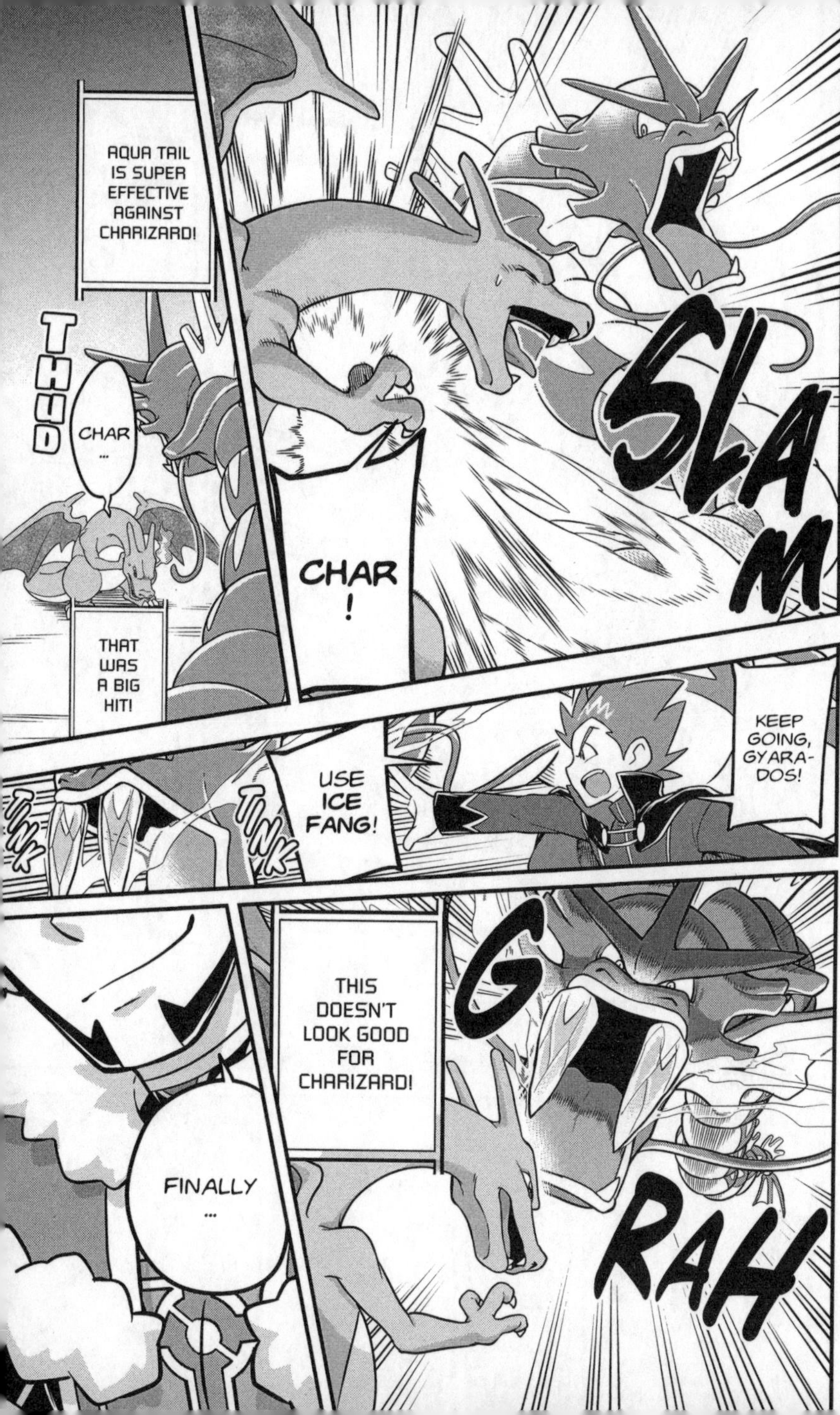
SLAM
CHAR!
AQUA TAIL IS SUPER EFFECTIVE AGAINST CHARIZARD!
THUD
CHAR ...
THAT WAS A BIG HIT!
KEEP GOING, GYARADOS!
USE ICE FANG!
TINK
TINK
THIS DOESN'T LOOK GOOD FOR CHARIZARD!
G
RAH
FINALLY ...

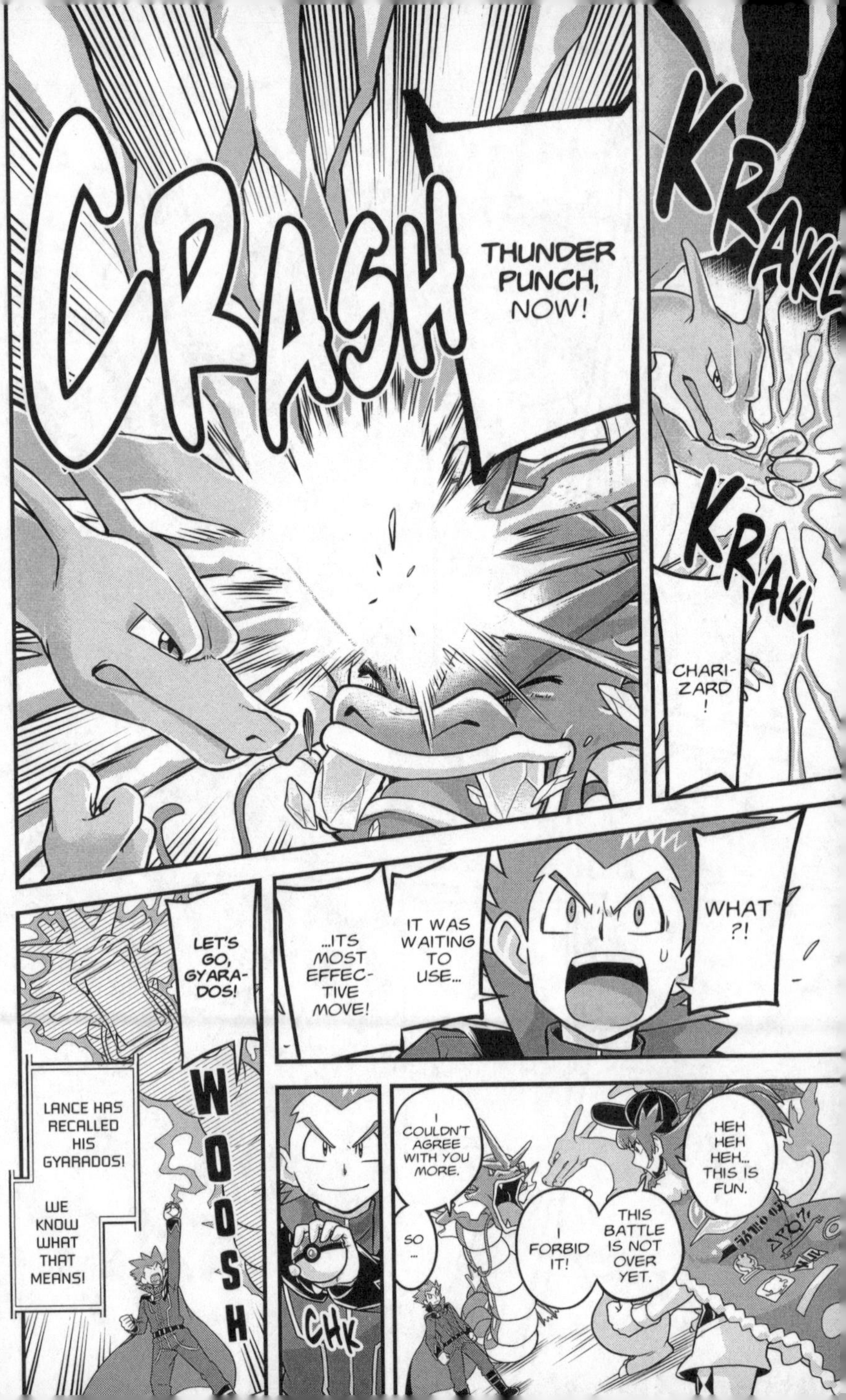
KRAKL
KRAKL
KRAKL
CHARIZARD!
CRASH
THUNDER PUNCH, NOW!
WHAT?!
IT WAS WAITING TO USE...
...ITS MOST EFFECTIVE MOVE!
HEH HEH HEH... THIS IS FUN.
THIS BATTLE IS NOT OVER YET.
I FORBID IT!
I COULDN'T AGREE WITH YOU MORE.
SO...
CHK
LET'S GO, GYARADOS!
WOOSH
LANCE HAS RECALLED HIS GYARADOS!
WE KNOW WHAT THAT MEANS!

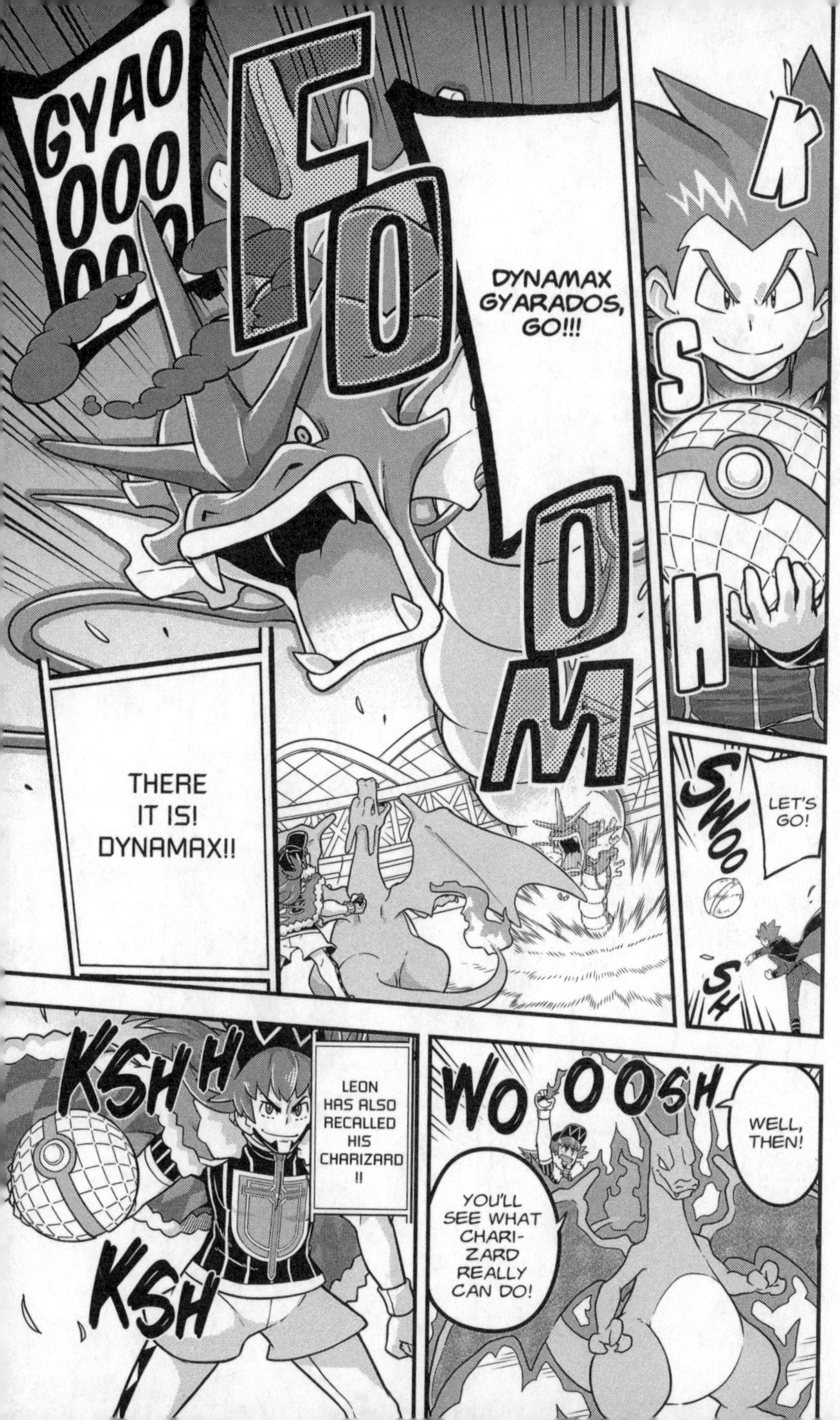
KSH
SWOO
LET'S GO!
SH
DYNAMAX GYARADOS, GO!!!
FOOM
GYAOOOOO
THERE IT IS! DYNAMAX!!
WOOOSH
WELL, THEN!
YOU'LL SEE WHAT CHARIZARD REALLY CAN DO!
KSHH
LEON HAS ALSO RECALLED HIS CHARIZARD!!
KSH

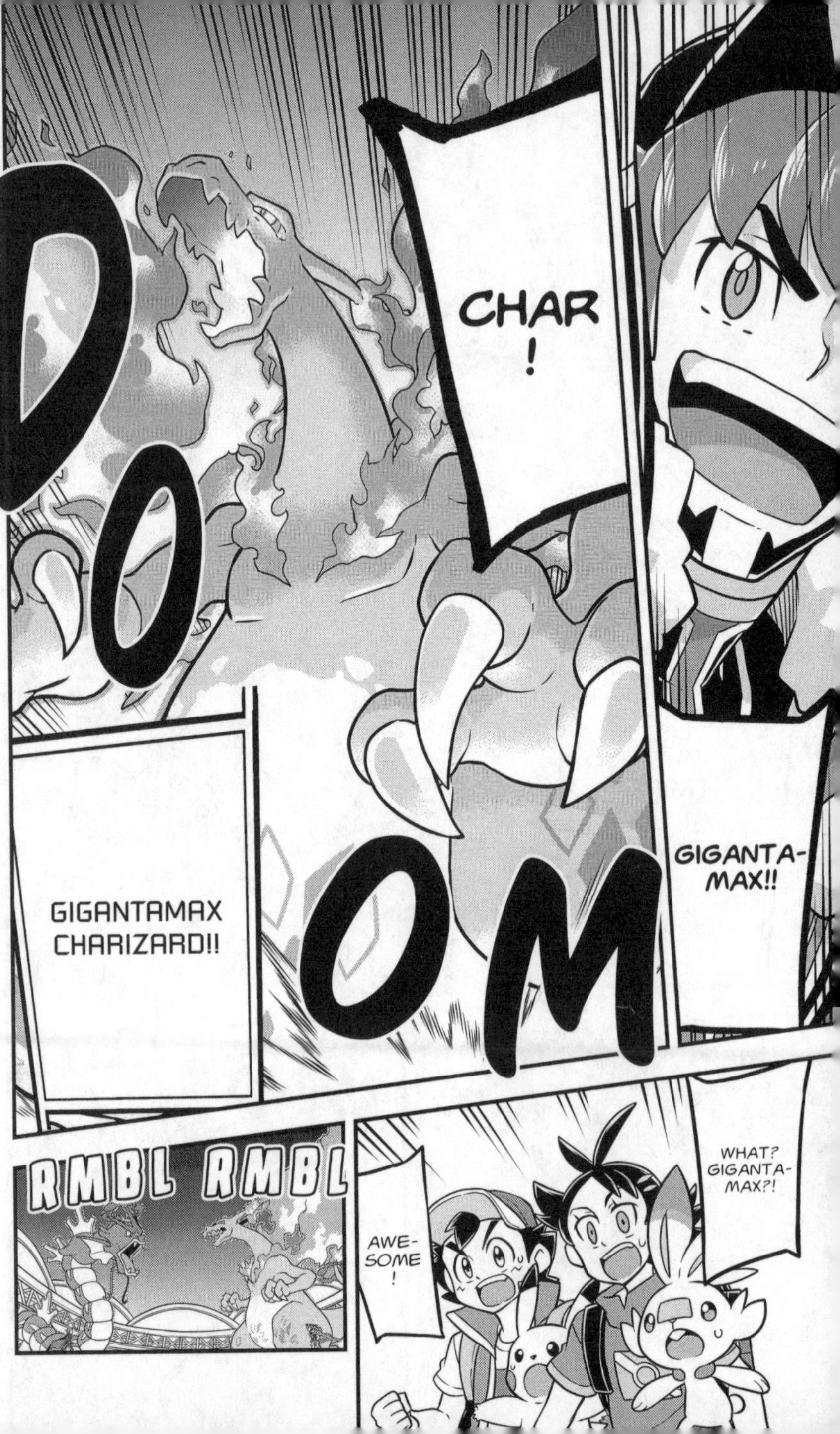
GIGANTA-MAX!!
CHAR!
DOOOM
GIGANTAMAX CHARIZARD!!
WHAT? GIGANTA-MAX?!
AWE-SOME!
RMBL RMBL

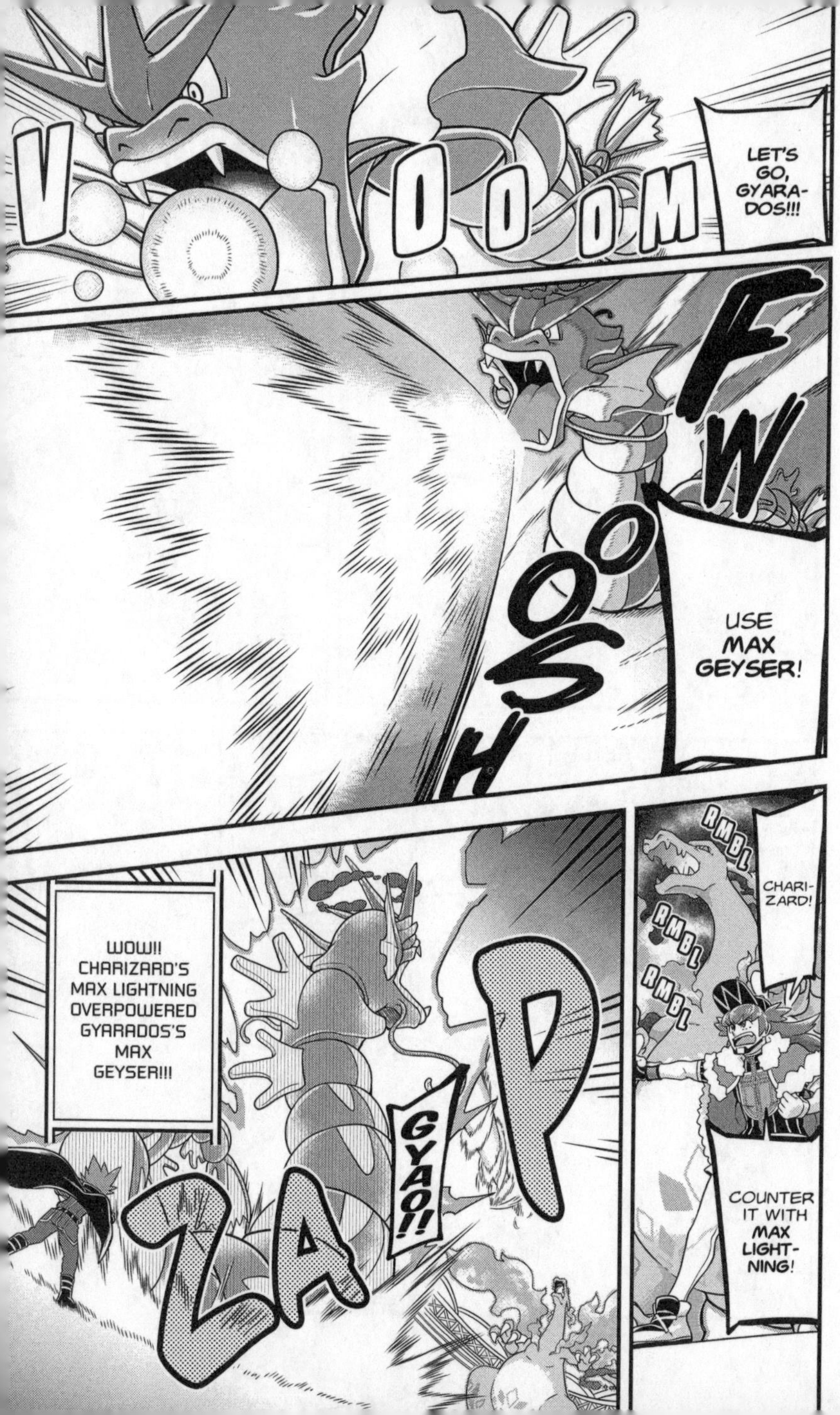
LET'S GO, GYARADOS!!!
VOOOM
FWOOSH
USE MAX GEYSER!
RMBL
CHARIZARD!
RMBL
RMBL
COUNTER IT WITH MAX LIGHTNING!
ZAP
GYAO!!
WOW!! CHARIZARD'S MAX LIGHTNING OVERPOWERED GYARADOS'S MAX GEYSER!!!

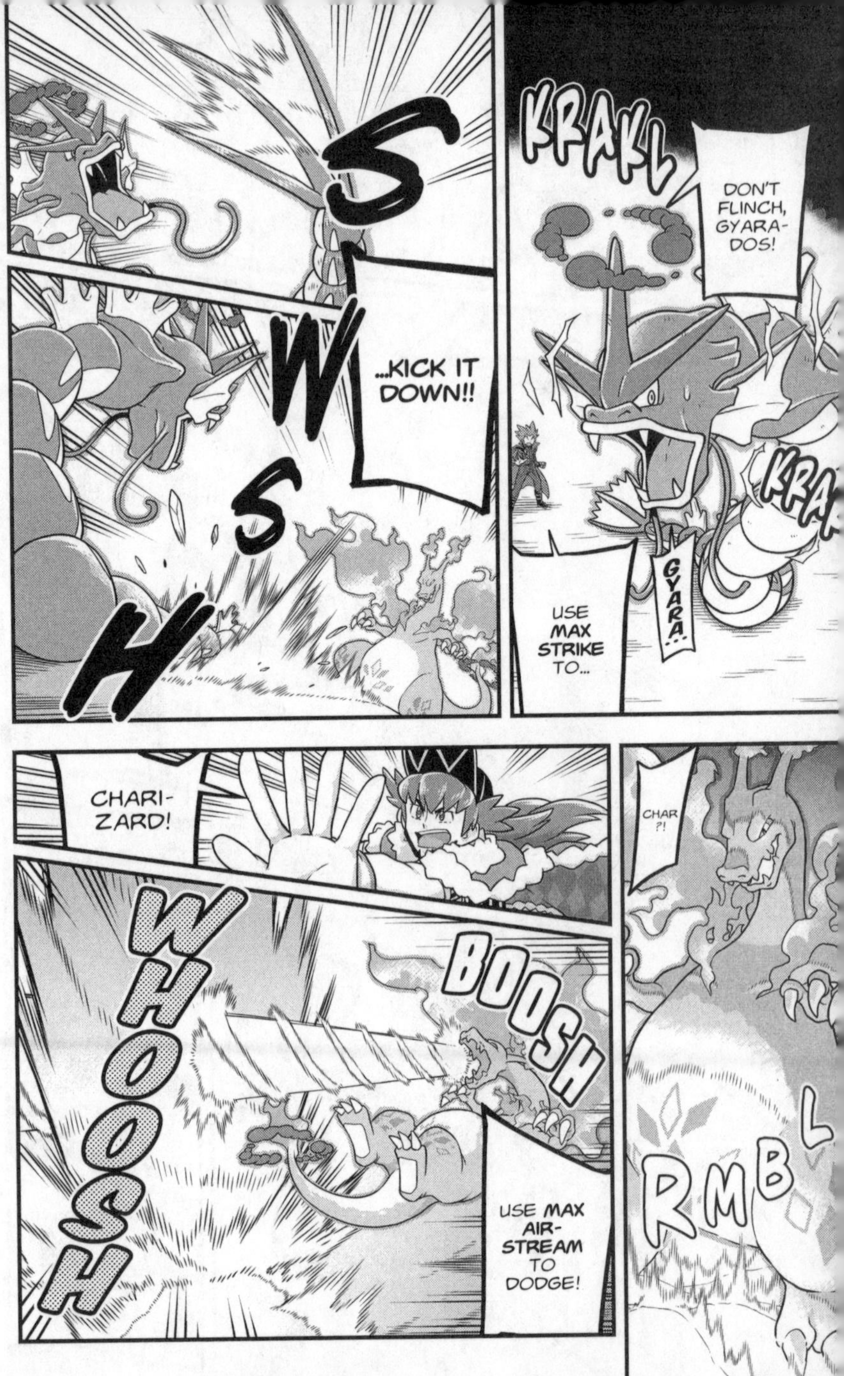
KRAKL
DON'T FLINCH, GYARADOS!
KRA
GYARA...
USE MAX STRIKE TO...
...KICK IT DOWN!!
SWSH
CHAR?!
RMBL
CHARIZARD!
BOOSH
WHOOSH
USE MAX AIR-STREAM TO DODGE!

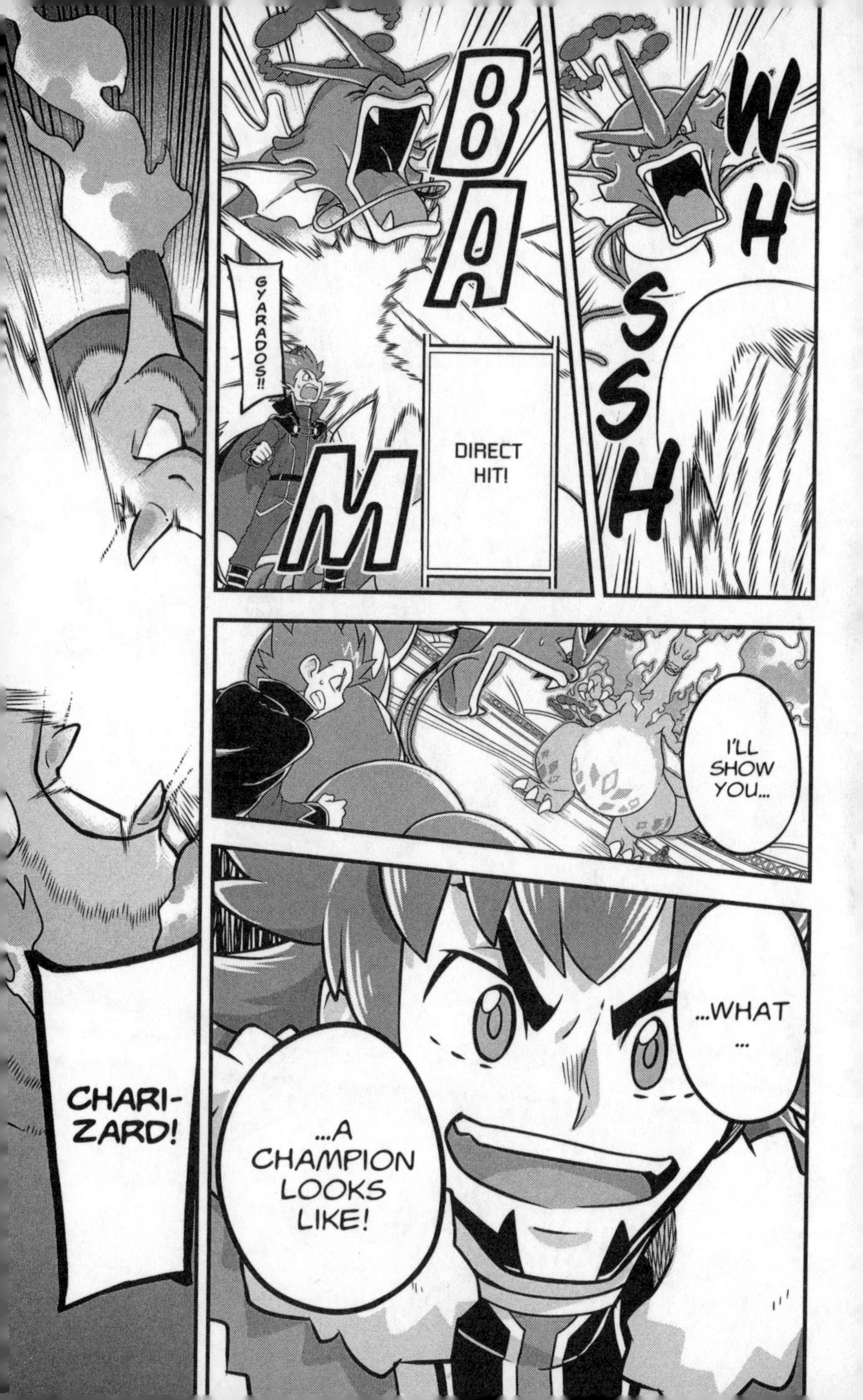
WHSSH
BAAM
GYARADOS!!
DIRECT HIT!
I'LL SHOW YOU...
...WHAT ...
...A CHAMPION LOOKS LIKE!
CHARI-ZARD!

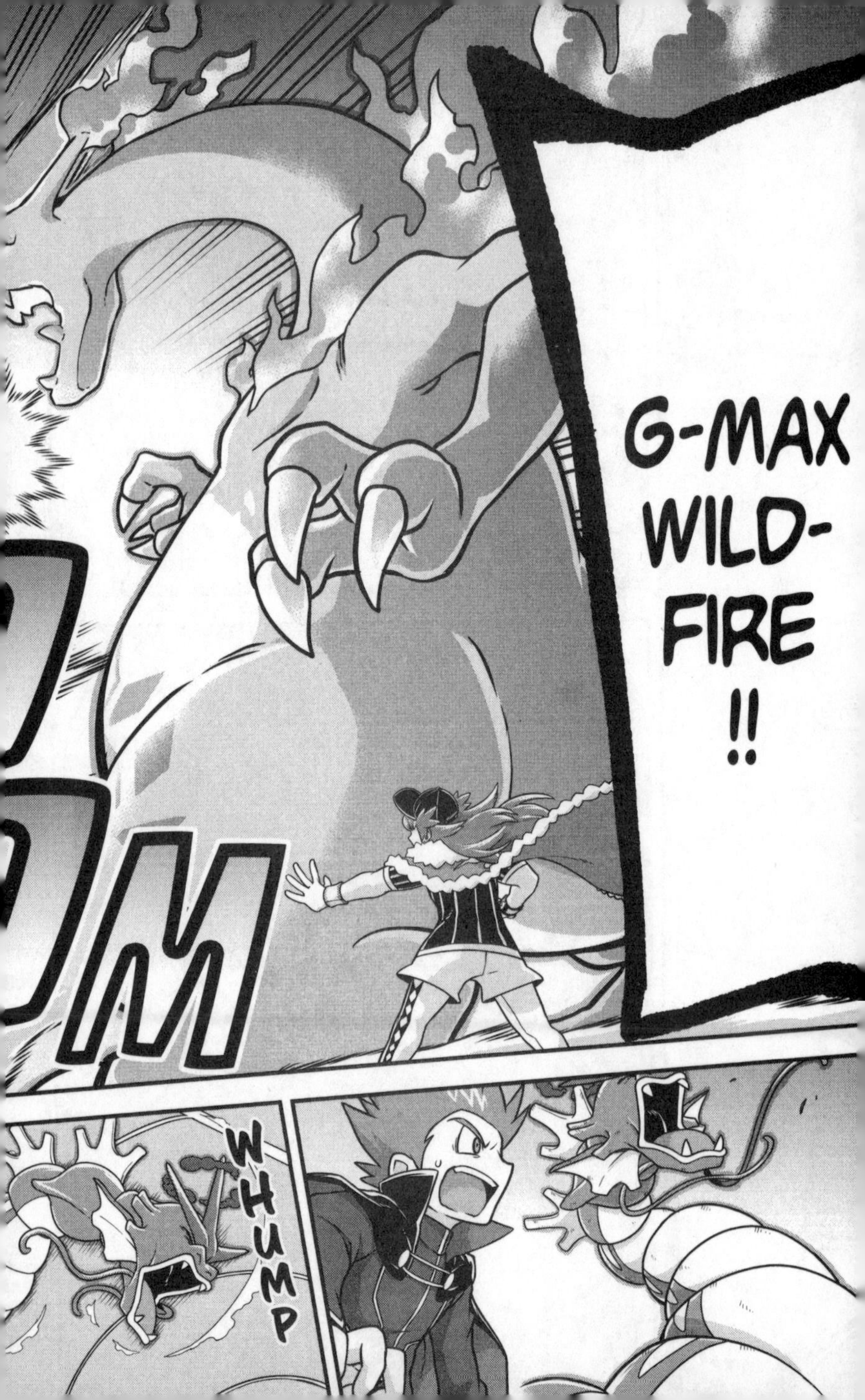
G-MAX WILD-FIRE !!
WHUMP

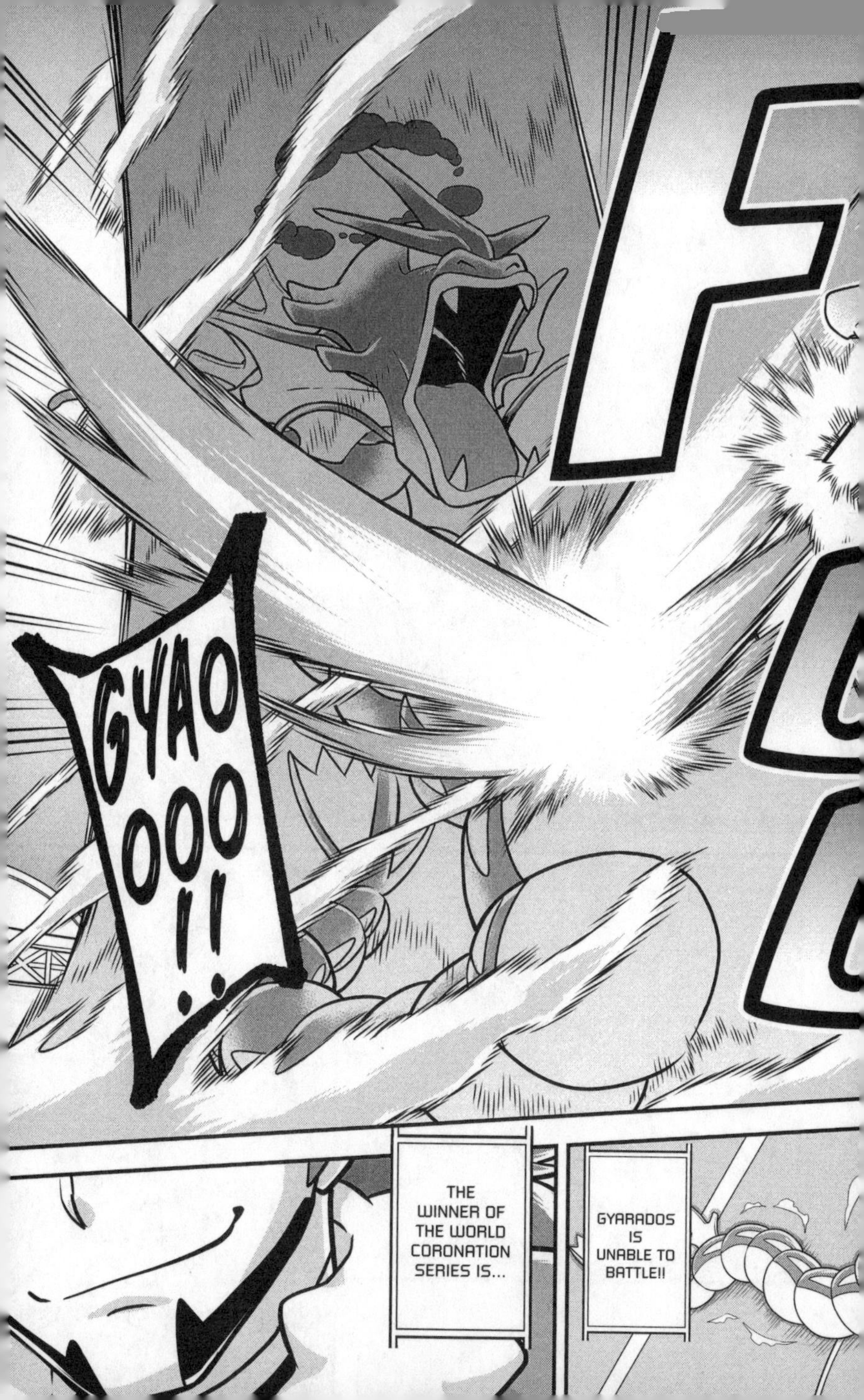
GYAOOOO!!
GYARADOS IS UNABLE TO BATTLE!!
THE WINNER OF THE WORLD CORONATION SERIES IS...

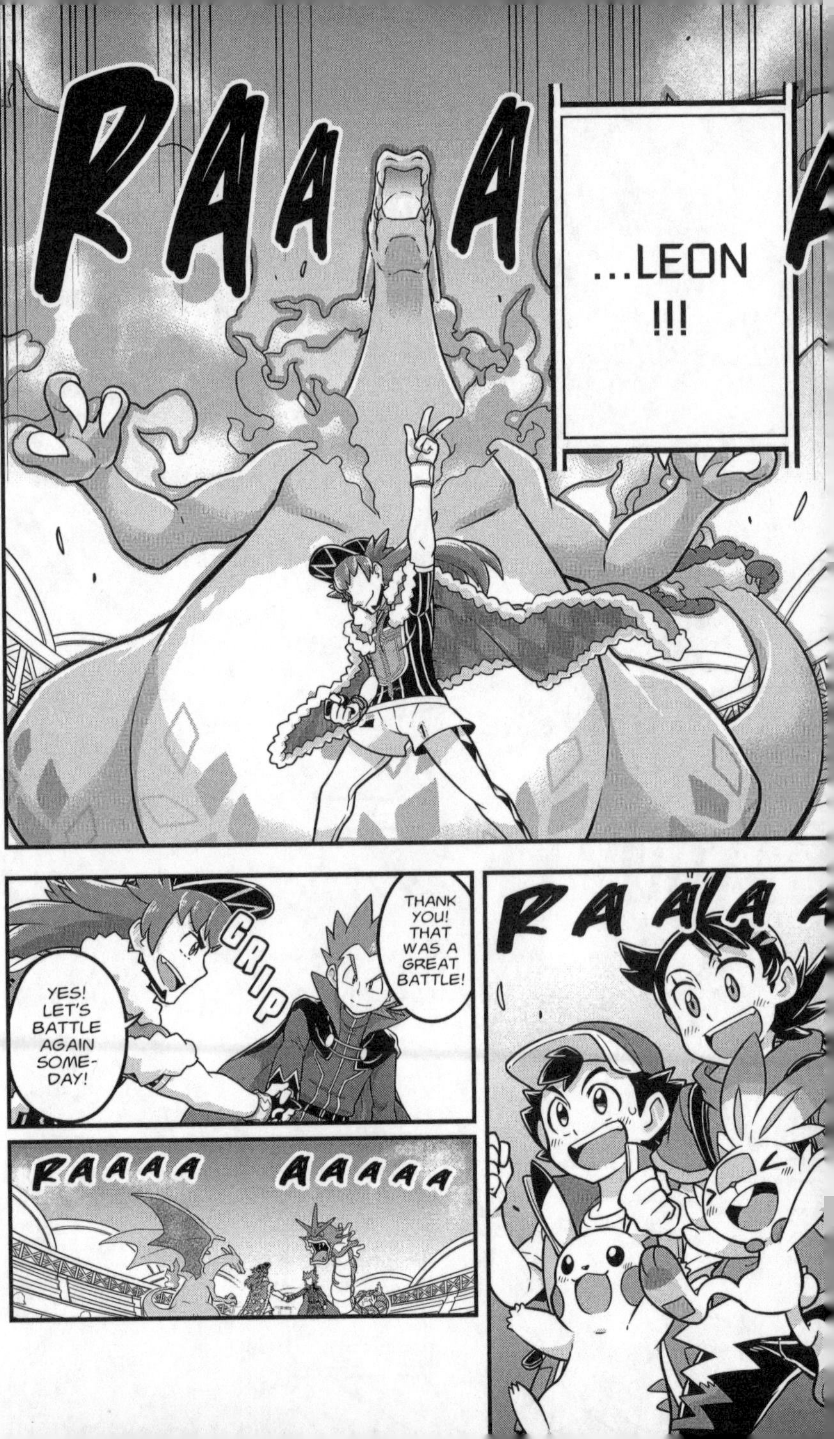
...LEON !!!
RAAAA
RAAAA
THANK YOU! THAT WAS A GREAT BATTLE!
GRIP
YES! LET'S BATTLE AGAIN SOME-DAY!
RAAAA AAAAA

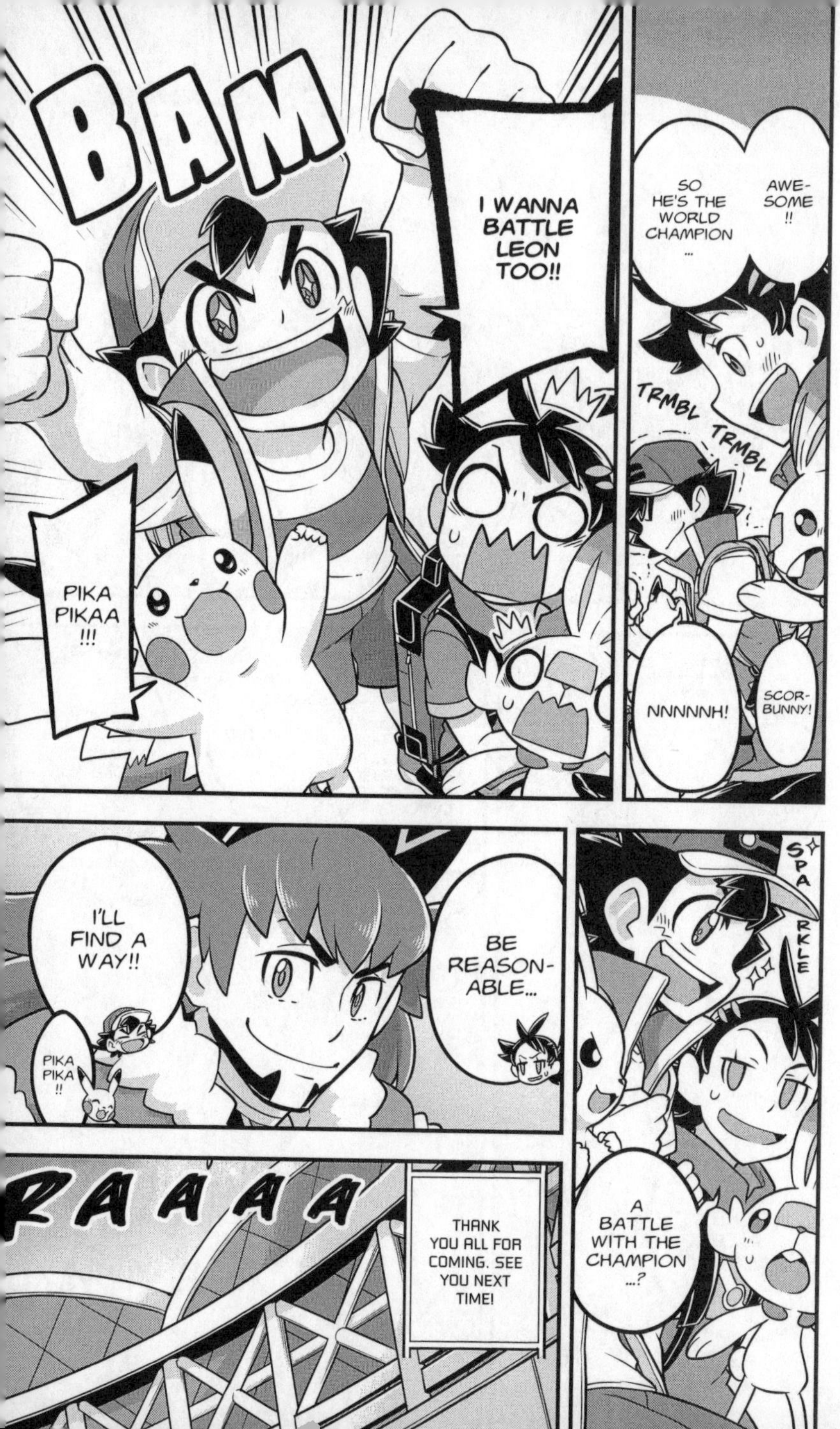
AWE-SOME!!
SO HE'S THE WORLD CHAMPION...
TRMBL TRMBL
SCOR-BUNNY!
NNNNNH!
I WANNA BATTLE LEON TOO!!
BAM
PIKA PIKAA!!!
SPARKLE
A BATTLE WITH THE CHAMPION...?
BE REASON-ABLE...
I'LL FIND A WAY!!
PIKA PIKA!!
THANK YOU ALL FOR COMING. SEE YOU NEXT TIME!
RAAAA

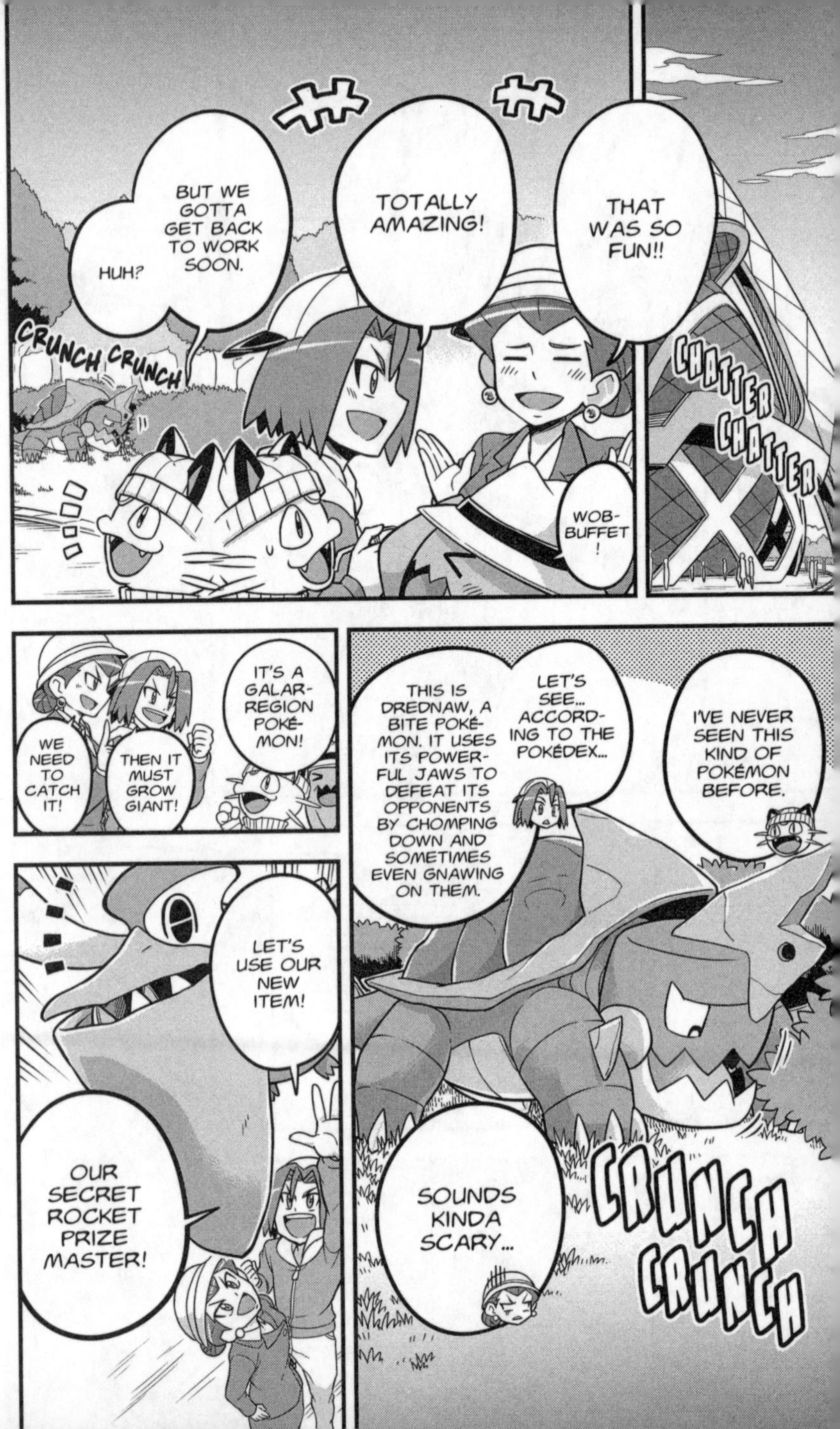
CHATTER CHATTER
THAT WAS SO FUN!!
TOTALLY AMAZING!
WOB-BUFFET!
BUT WE GOTTA GET BACK TO WORK SOON.
HUH?
CRUNCH CRUNCH
I'VE NEVER SEEN THIS KIND OF POKÉMON BEFORE.
LET'S SEE... ACCORDING TO THE POKÉDEX...
THIS IS DREDNAW, A BITE POKÉMON. IT USES ITS POWERFUL JAWS TO DEFEAT ITS OPPONENTS BY CHOMPING DOWN AND SOMETIMES EVEN GNAWING ON THEM.
SOUNDS KINDA SCARY...
CRUNCH CRUNCH
IT'S A GALAR-REGION POKÉMON!
THEN IT MUST GROW GIANT!
WE NEED TO CATCH IT!
LET'S USE OUR NEW ITEM!
OUR SECRET ROCKET PRIZE MASTER!

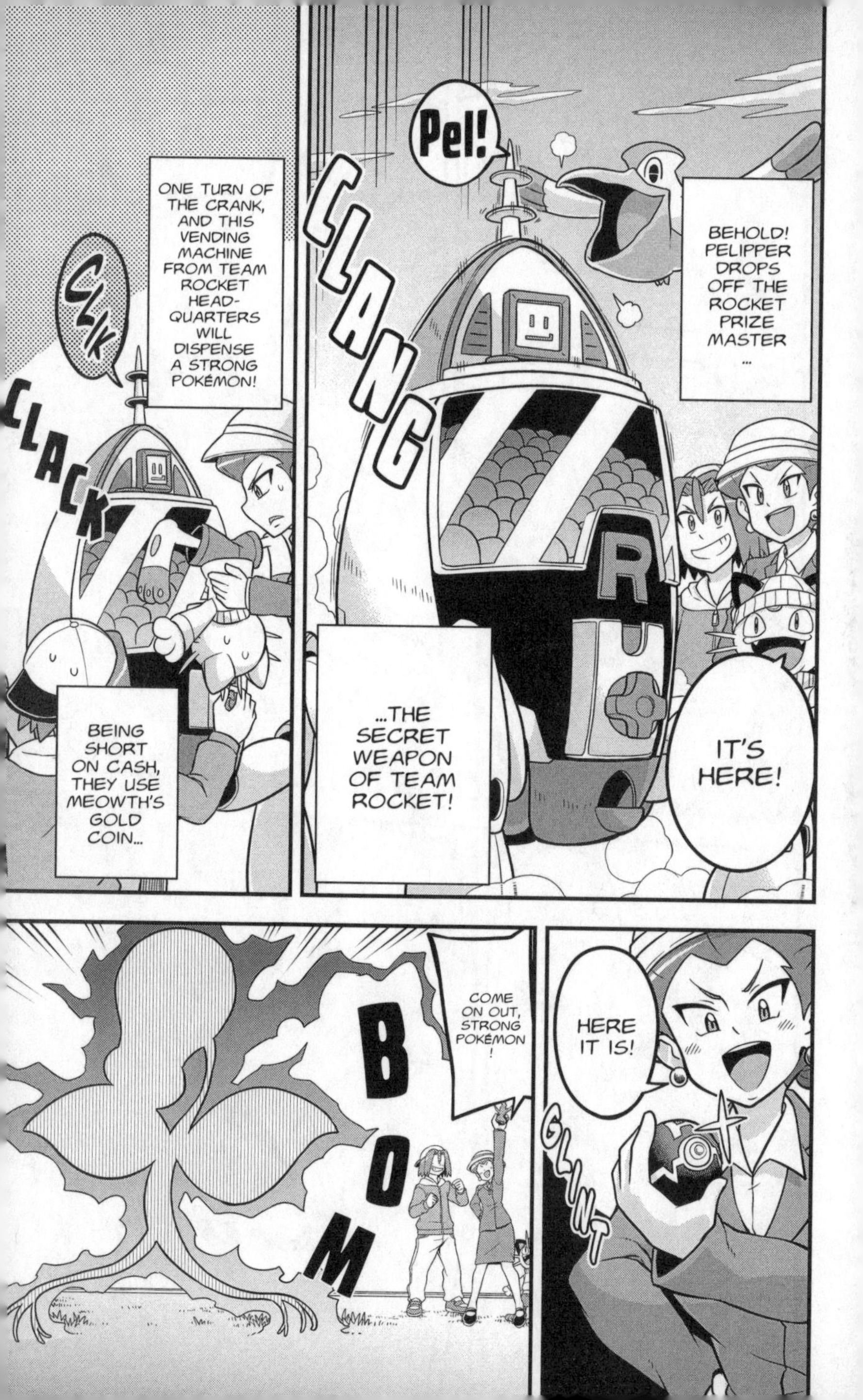
Pel!
BEHOLD! PELIPPER DROPS OFF THE ROCKET PRIZE MASTER ...
CLANG
...THE SECRET WEAPON OF TEAM ROCKET!
IT'S HERE!
ONE TURN OF THE CRANK, AND THIS VENDING MACHINE FROM TEAM ROCKET HEAD-QUARTERS WILL DISPENSE A STRONG POKÉMON!
CLIK
CLACK
BEING SHORT ON CASH, THEY USE MEOWTH'S GOLD COIN...
HERE IT IS!
GLINT
COME ON OUT, STRONG POKÉMON!
BOOM

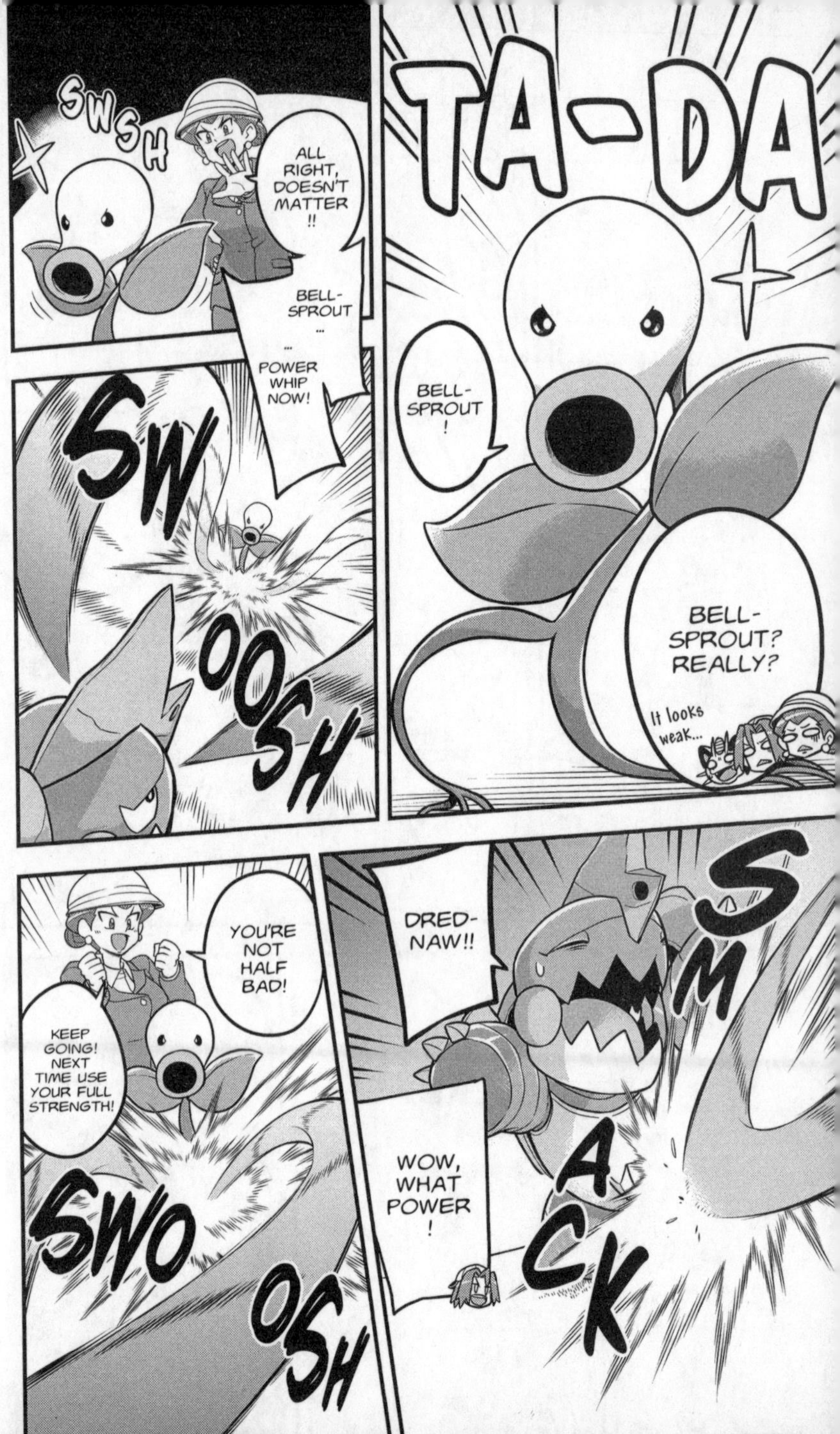
TA-DA
BELL-SPROUT!
BELL-SPROUT? REALLY?
It looks weak...
SWSH
ALL RIGHT, DOESN'T MATTER!!
BELL-SPROUT... ...POWER WHIP NOW!
SWOOSH
DRED-NAW!!
SMACK
WOW, WHAT POWER!
YOU'RE NOT HALF BAD!
KEEP GOING! NEXT TIME USE YOUR FULL STRENGTH!
SWOOOSH

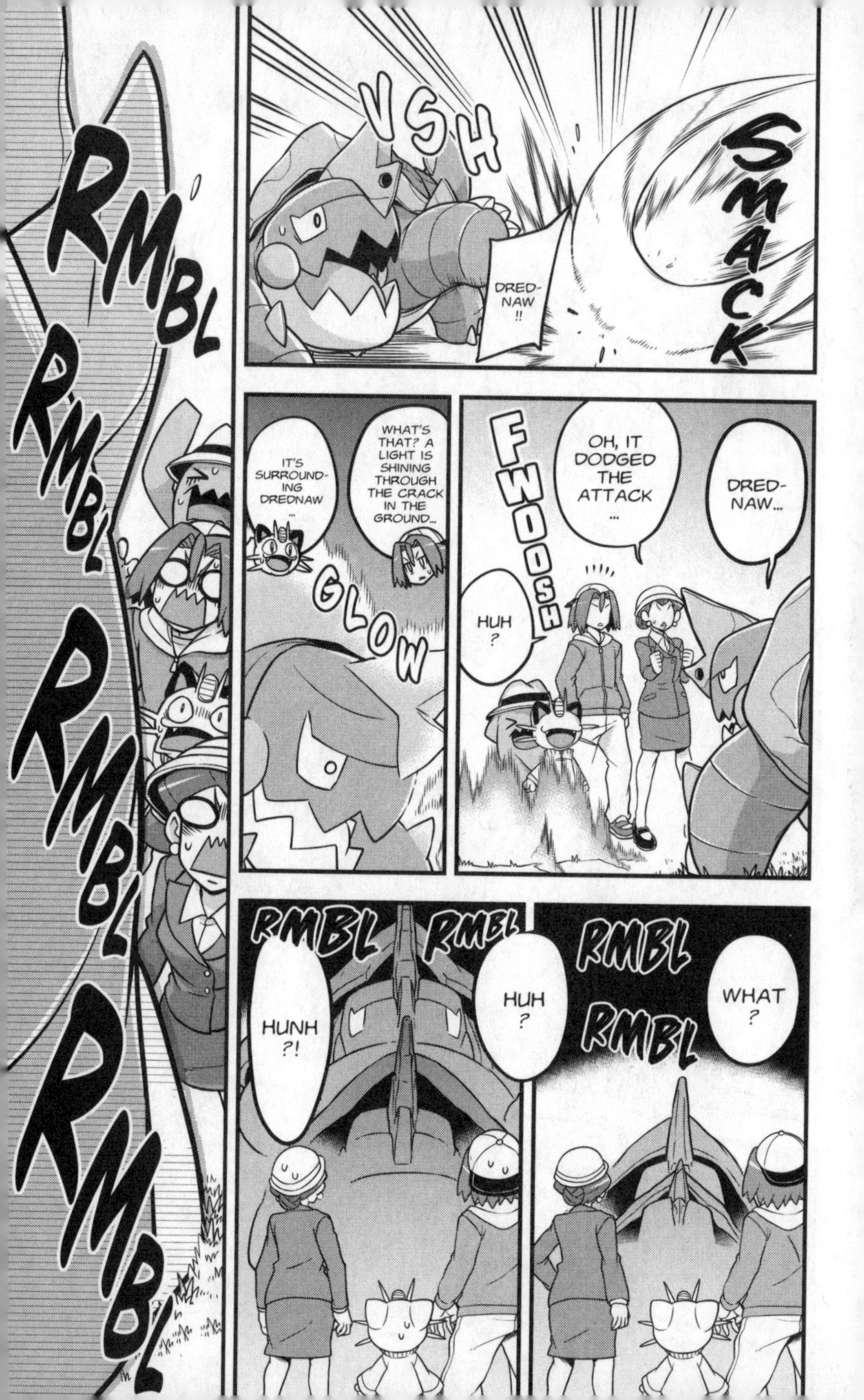
SMACK
VSH
DRED-NAW!!
DRED-NAW...
OH, IT DODGED THE ATTACK...
FWOOSH
HUH?
WHAT'S THAT? A LIGHT IS SHINING THROUGH THE CRACK IN THE GROUND...
IT'S SURROUNDING DREDNAW...
GLOW
WHAT?
RMBL
RMBL
HUH?
RMBL
RMBL
HUNH?!
RMBL
RMBL
RMBL
RMBL
RMBL

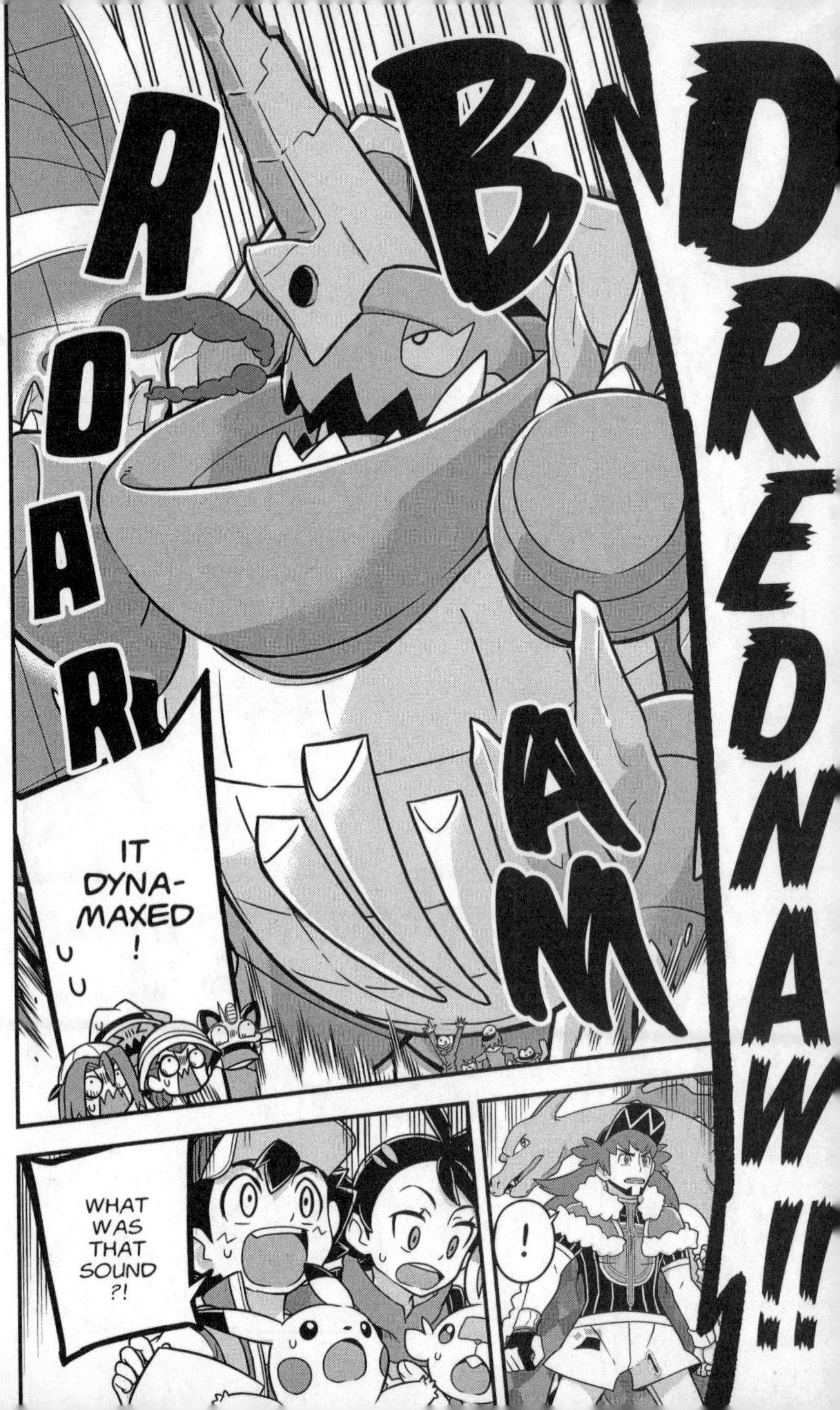
DREDNAW!!
BAM
ROAR
IT DYNA-MAXED!
!
WHAT WAS THAT SOUND?!

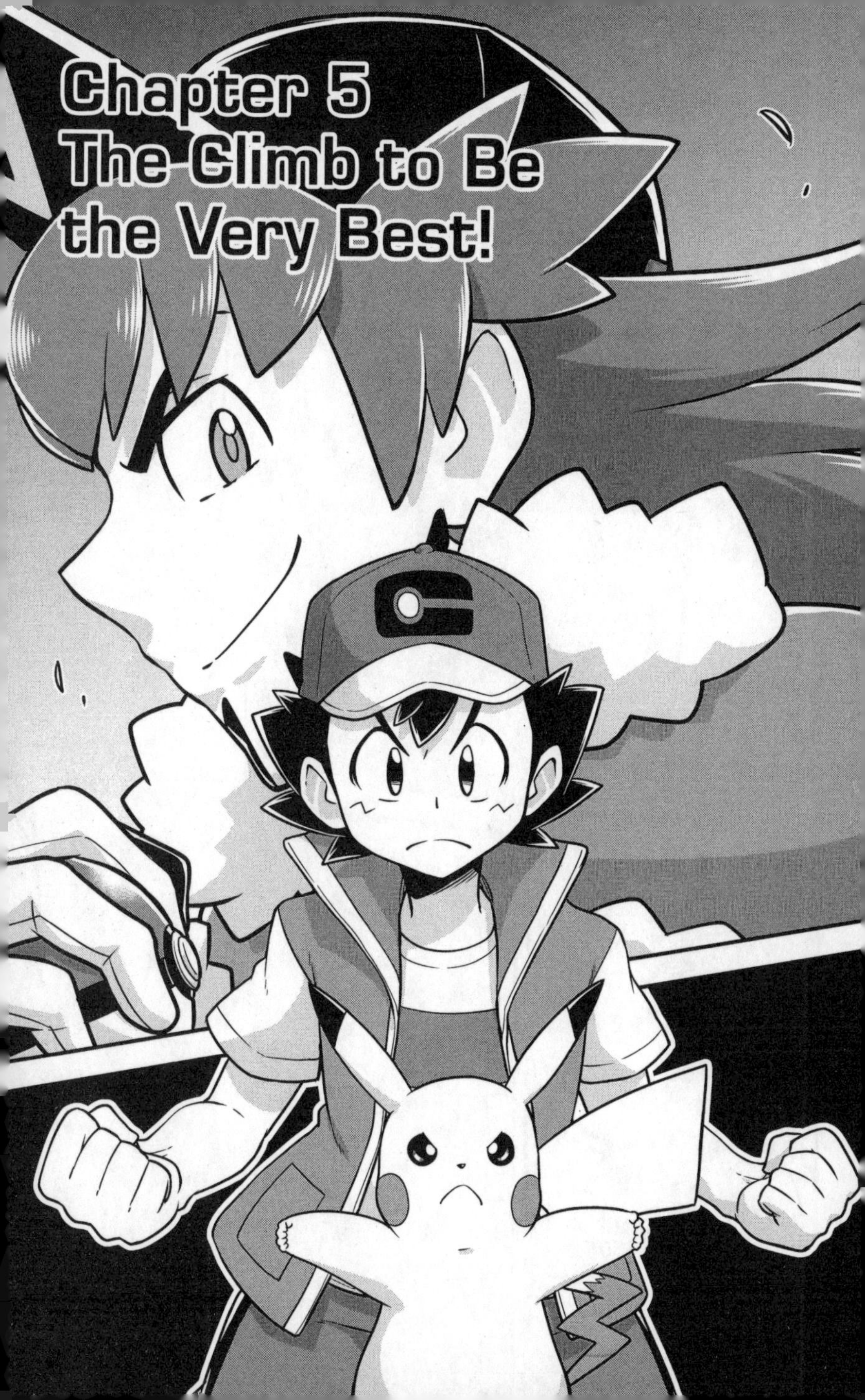
Chapter 5
The Climb to Be the Very Best!

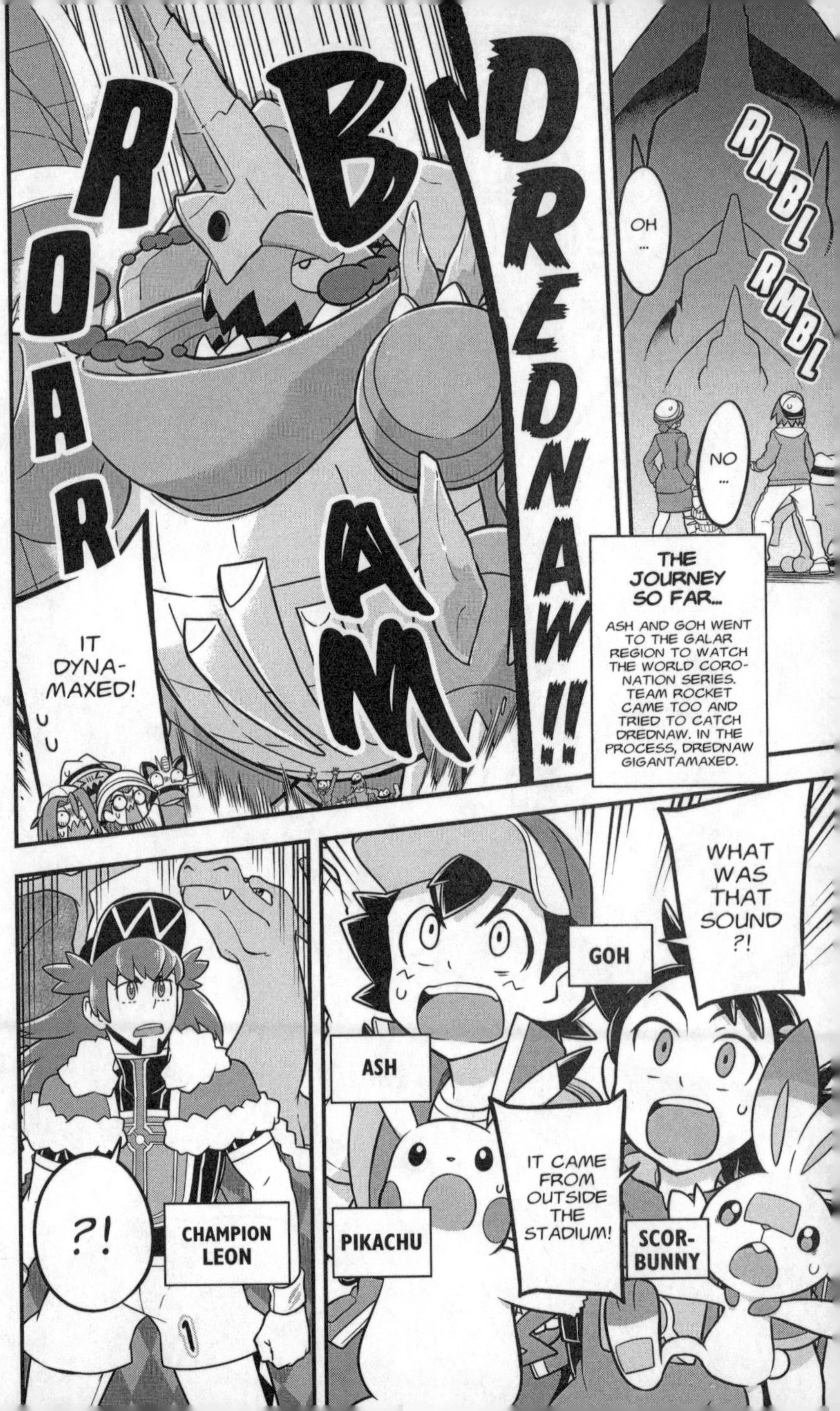
RMBL RMBL
OH...
NO...
THE JOURNEY SO FAR...
ASH AND GOH WENT TO THE GALAR REGION TO WATCH THE WORLD CORONATION SERIES. TEAM ROCKET CAME TOO AND TRIED TO CATCH DREDNAW. IN THE PROCESS, DREDNAW GIGANTAMAXED.
DREDNAW!!
BAM
ROAR
IT DYNA-MAXED!
WHAT WAS THAT SOUND?!
GOH
ASH
IT CAME FROM OUTSIDE THE STADIUM!
SCOR-BUNNY
PIKACHU
?!
CHAMPION LEON

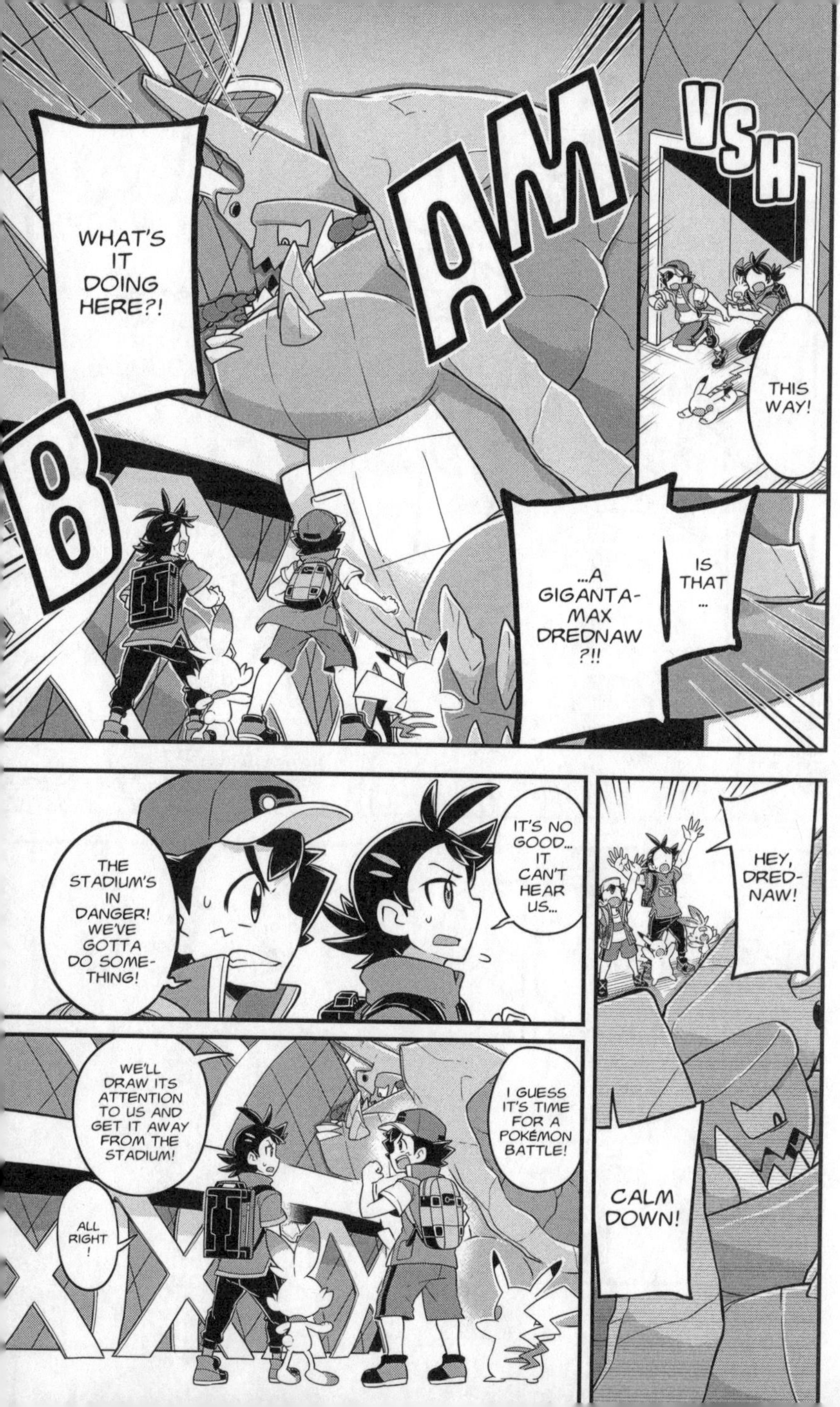
VSH
THIS WAY!
BAM
WHAT'S IT DOING HERE?!
IS THAT...
...A GIGANTA-MAX DREDNAW?!!
HEY, DRED-NAW!
CALM DOWN!
IT'S NO GOOD... IT CAN'T HEAR US...
THE STADIUM'S IN DANGER! WE'VE GOTTA DO SOME-THING!
I GUESS IT'S TIME FOR A POKÉMON BATTLE!
WE'LL DRAW ITS ATTENTION TO US AND GET IT AWAY FROM THE STADIUM!
ALL RIGHT!

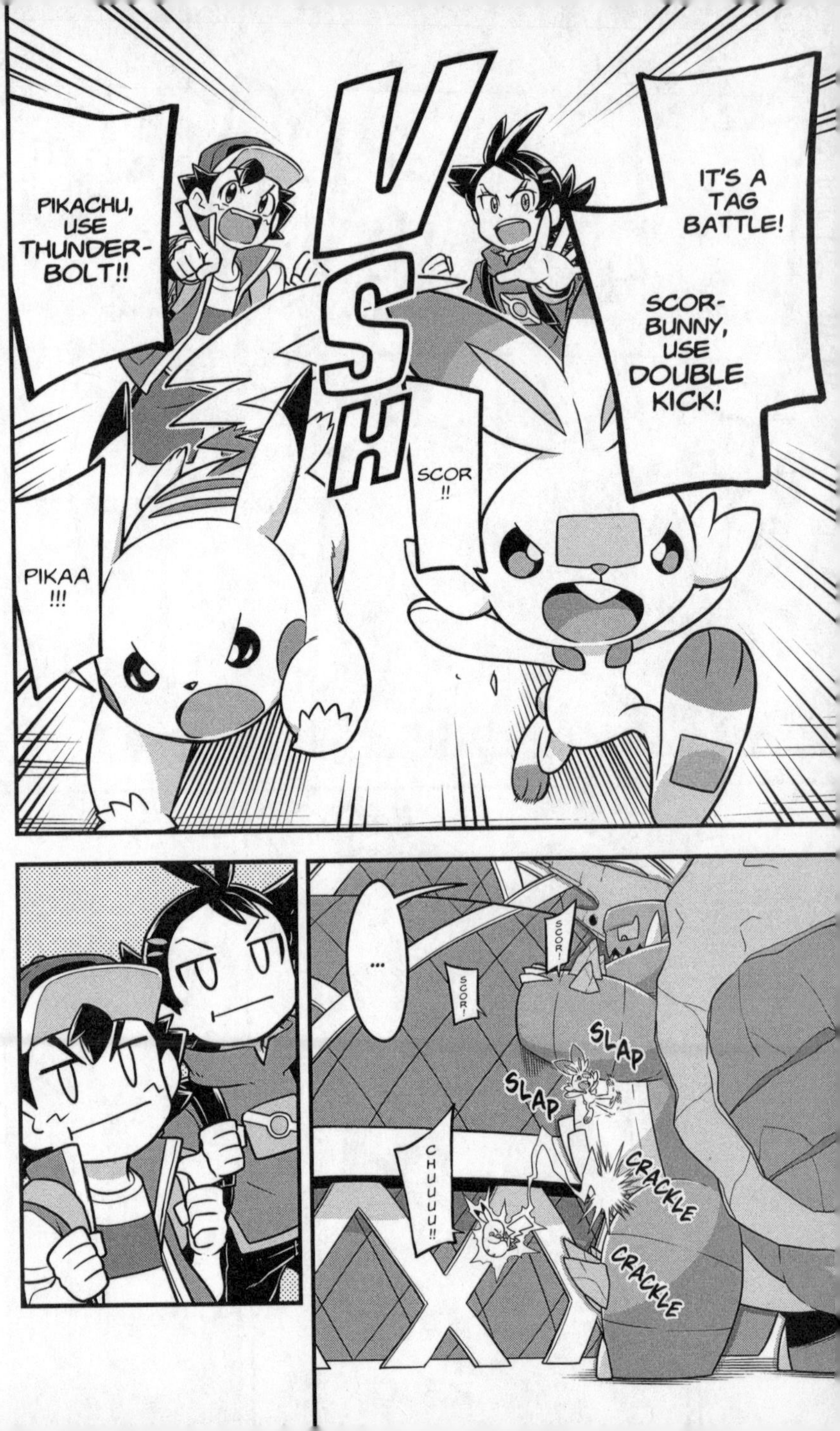
IT'S A TAG BATTLE!
SCOR-BUNNY, USE DOUBLE KICK!
VSH
SCOR!!
PIKACHU, USE THUNDER-BOLT!!
PIKAA!!!
SCOR!
SCOR!
...
SLAP
SLAP
CRACKLE
CRACKLE
CHUUUUU!!

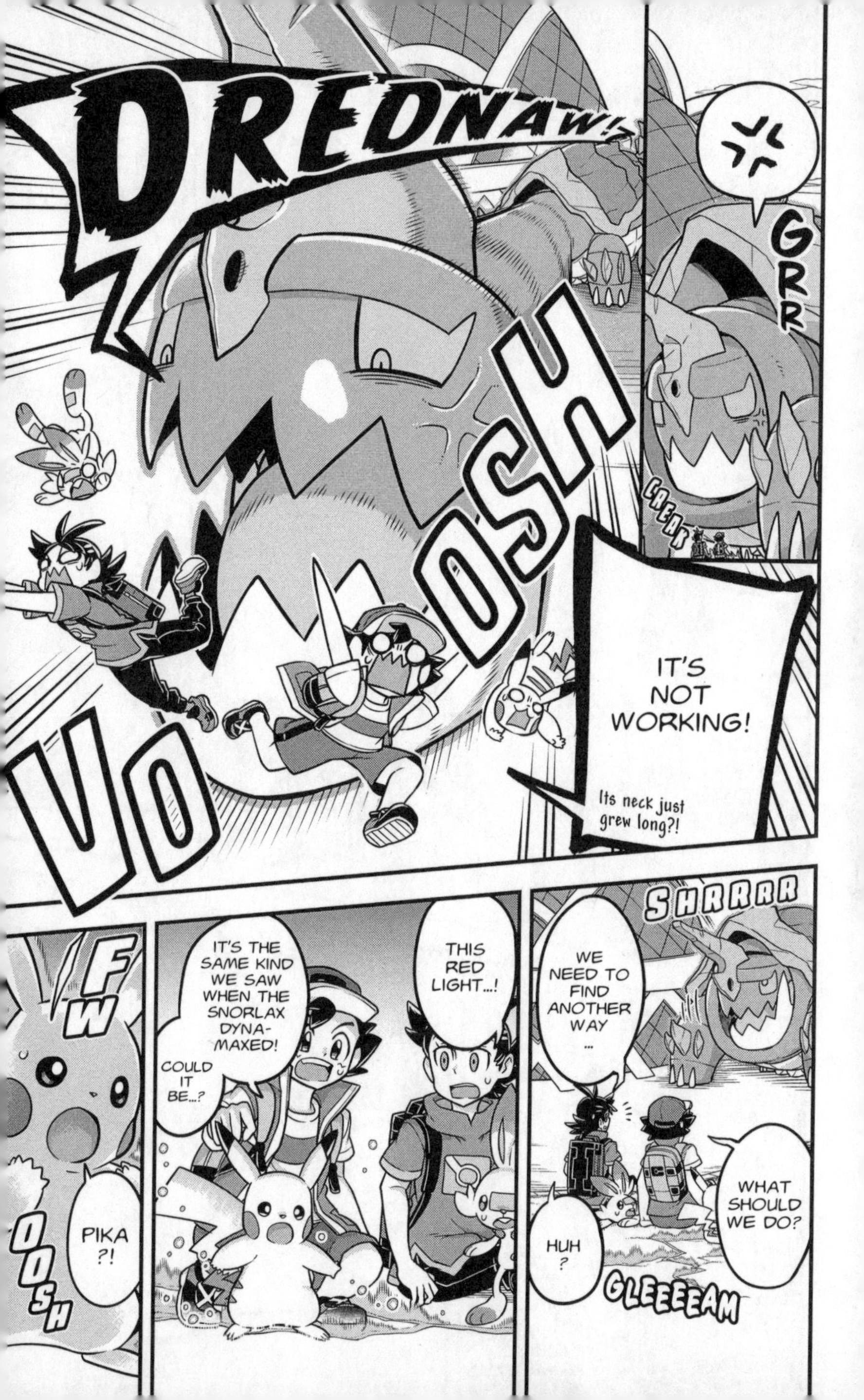
GRR
CREAK
DREDNAW!?
VOOSH
IT'S NOT WORKING!
Its neck just grew long?!
SHRRRR
WE NEED TO FIND ANOTHER WAY...
WHAT SHOULD WE DO?
HUH?
GLEEEEAM
THIS RED LIGHT...!
IT'S THE SAME KIND WE SAW WHEN THE SNORLAX DYNA-MAXED!
COULD IT BE...?
FW
PIKA?!
OOSH

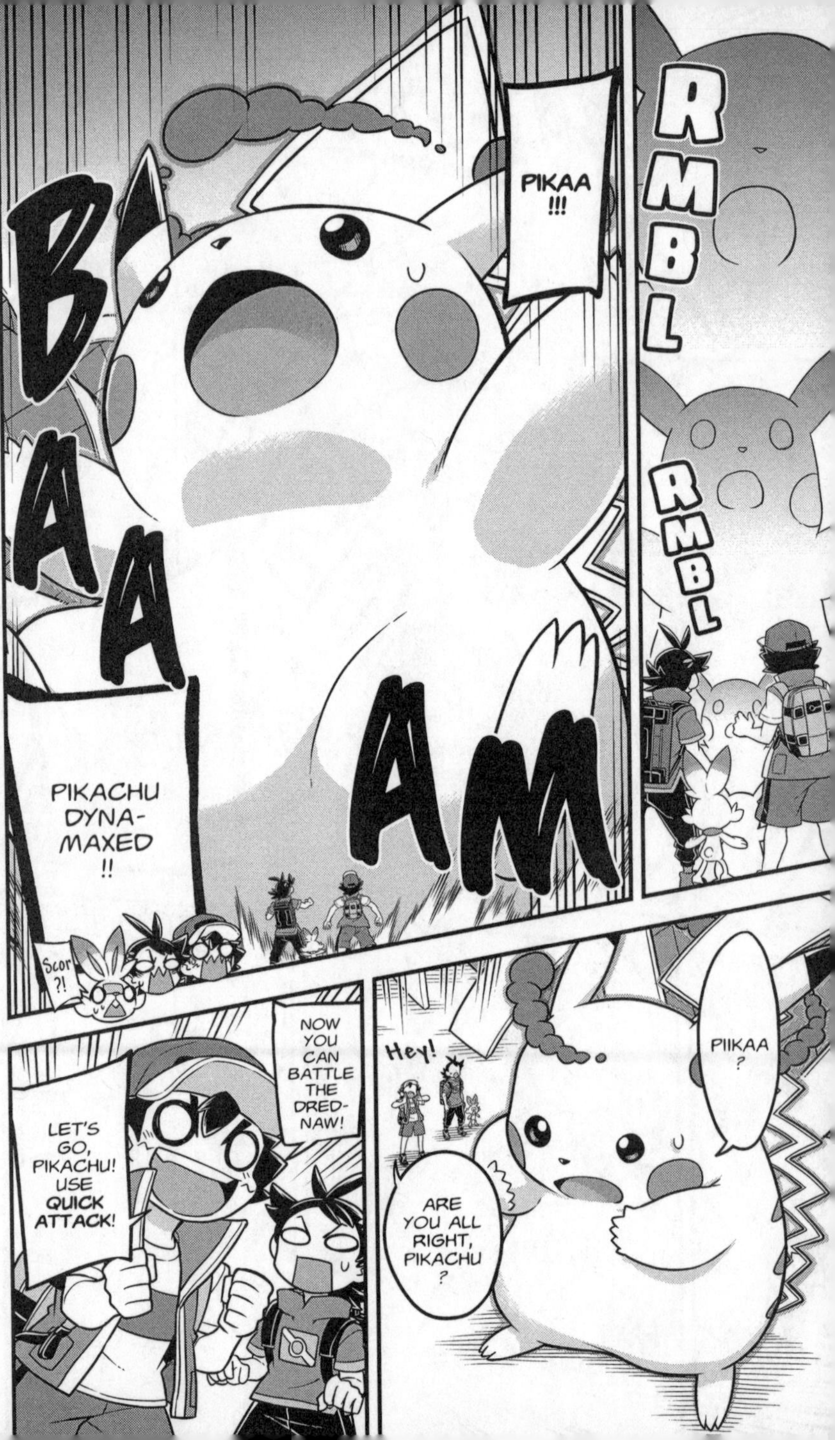
RMBL
RMBL
PIKAA!!!
BAAAM
PIKACHU DYNA-MAXED!!
Scor?!
PIIKAA?
Hey!
ARE YOU ALL RIGHT, PIKACHU?
NOW YOU CAN BATTLE THE DREDNAW!
LET'S GO, PIKACHU! USE **QUICK ATTACK!**

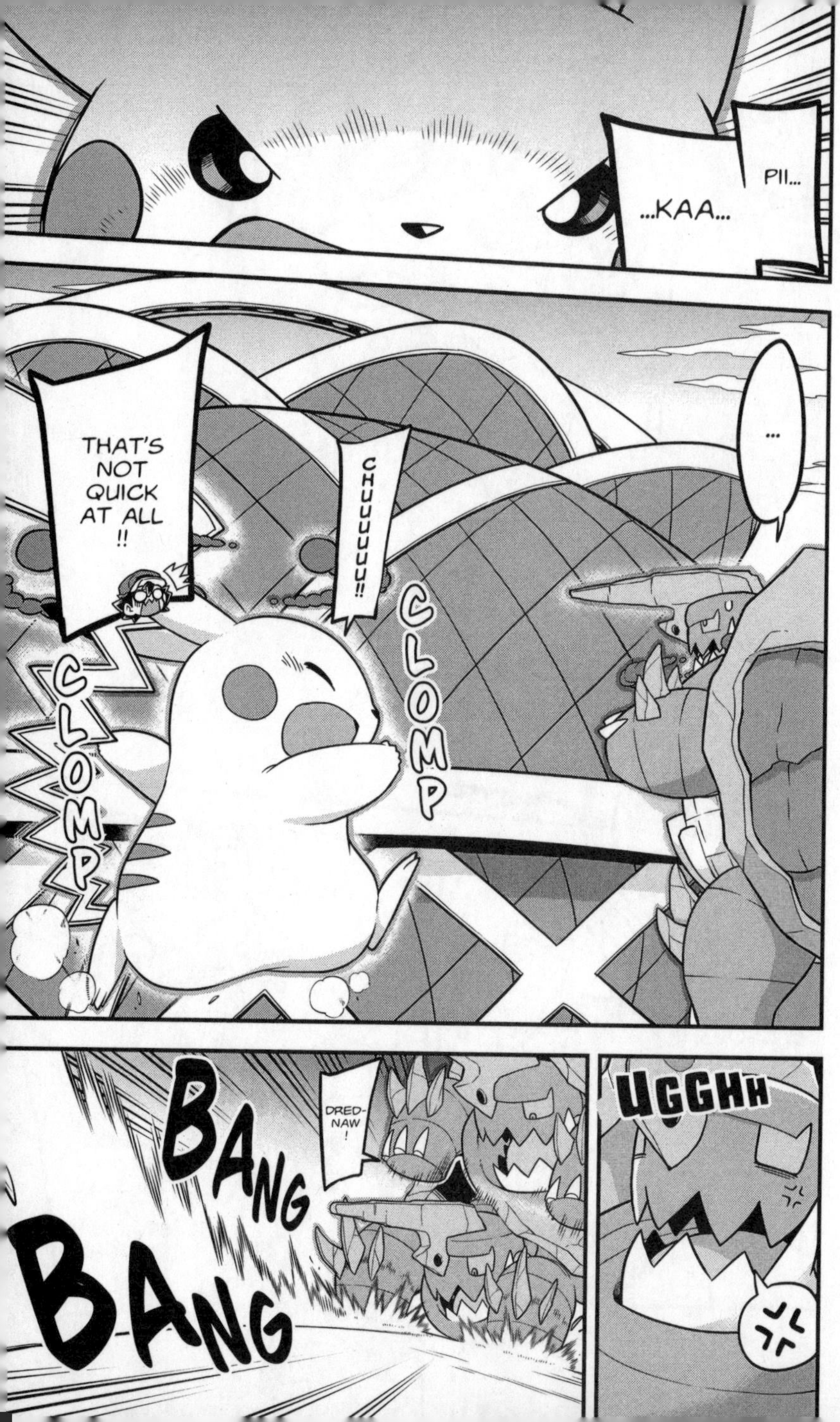
PII...
...KAA...
...
CHUUUUUU!!
CLOMP
THAT'S NOT QUICK AT ALL!!
CLOMP
UGGHH
DRED-NAW!
BANG
BANG

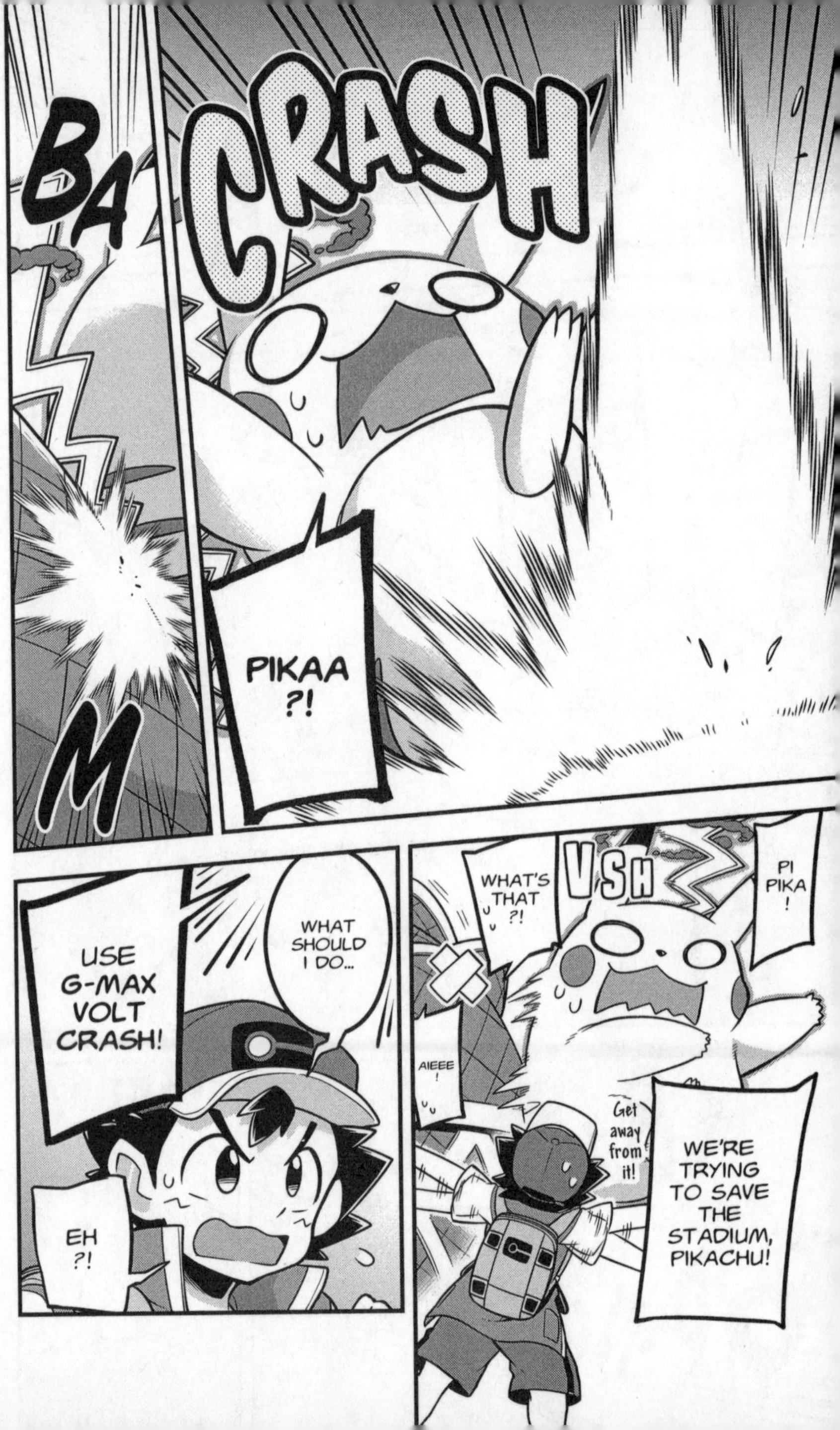
CRASH
PIKAA ?!
BA
M
PI PIKA !
VSH
WHAT'S THAT ?!
AIEEE !
Get away from it!
WE'RE TRYING TO SAVE THE STADIUM, PIKACHU!
WHAT SHOULD I DO...
USE G-MAX VOLT CRASH!
EH ?!

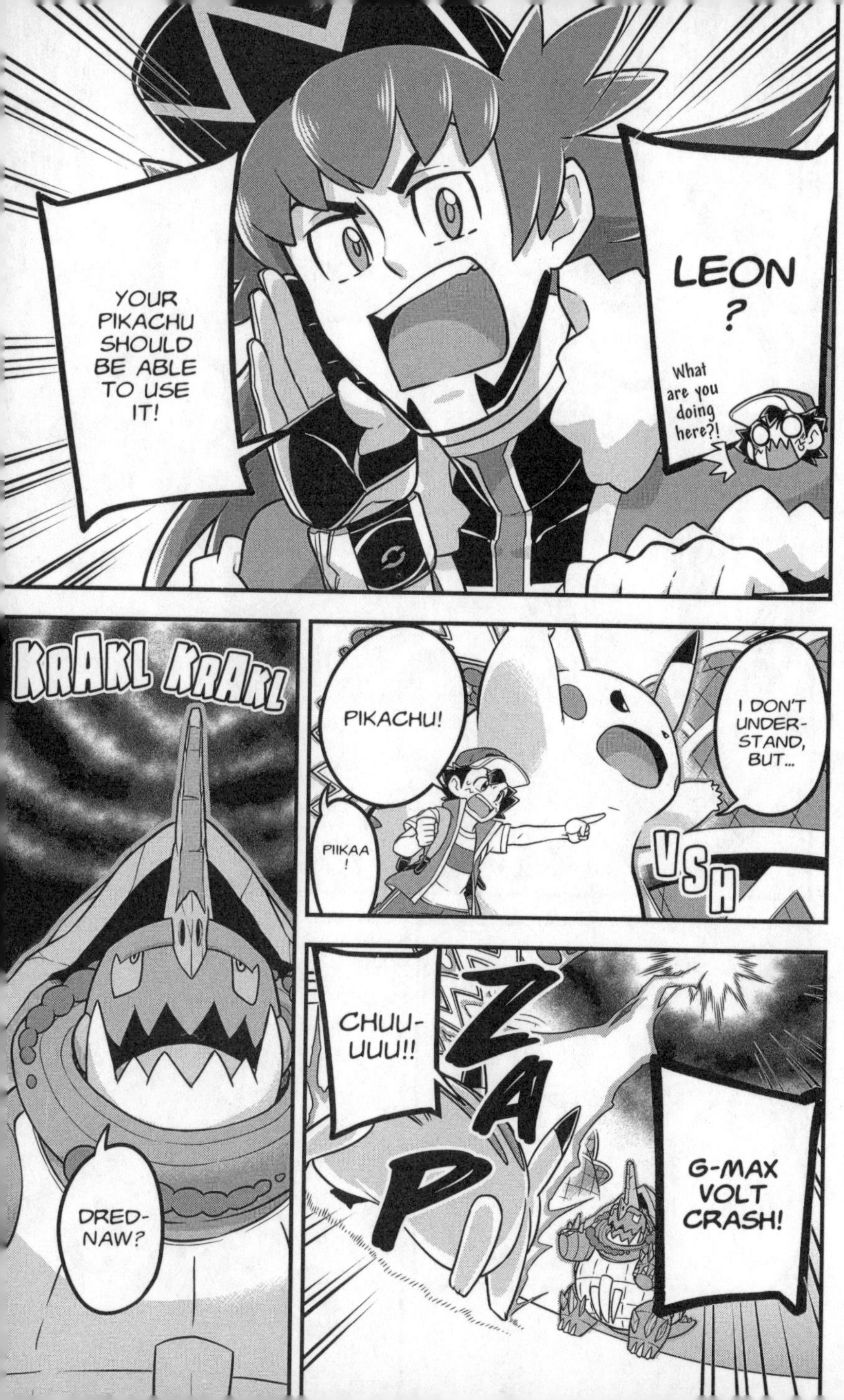
LEON?
What are you doing here?!
YOUR PIKACHU SHOULD BE ABLE TO USE IT!
I DON'T UNDERSTAND, BUT...
VSH
PIKACHU!
PIIKAA!
G-MAX VOLT CRASH!
ZAP
CHUU-UUU!!
KRAKL KRAKL
DRED-NAW?

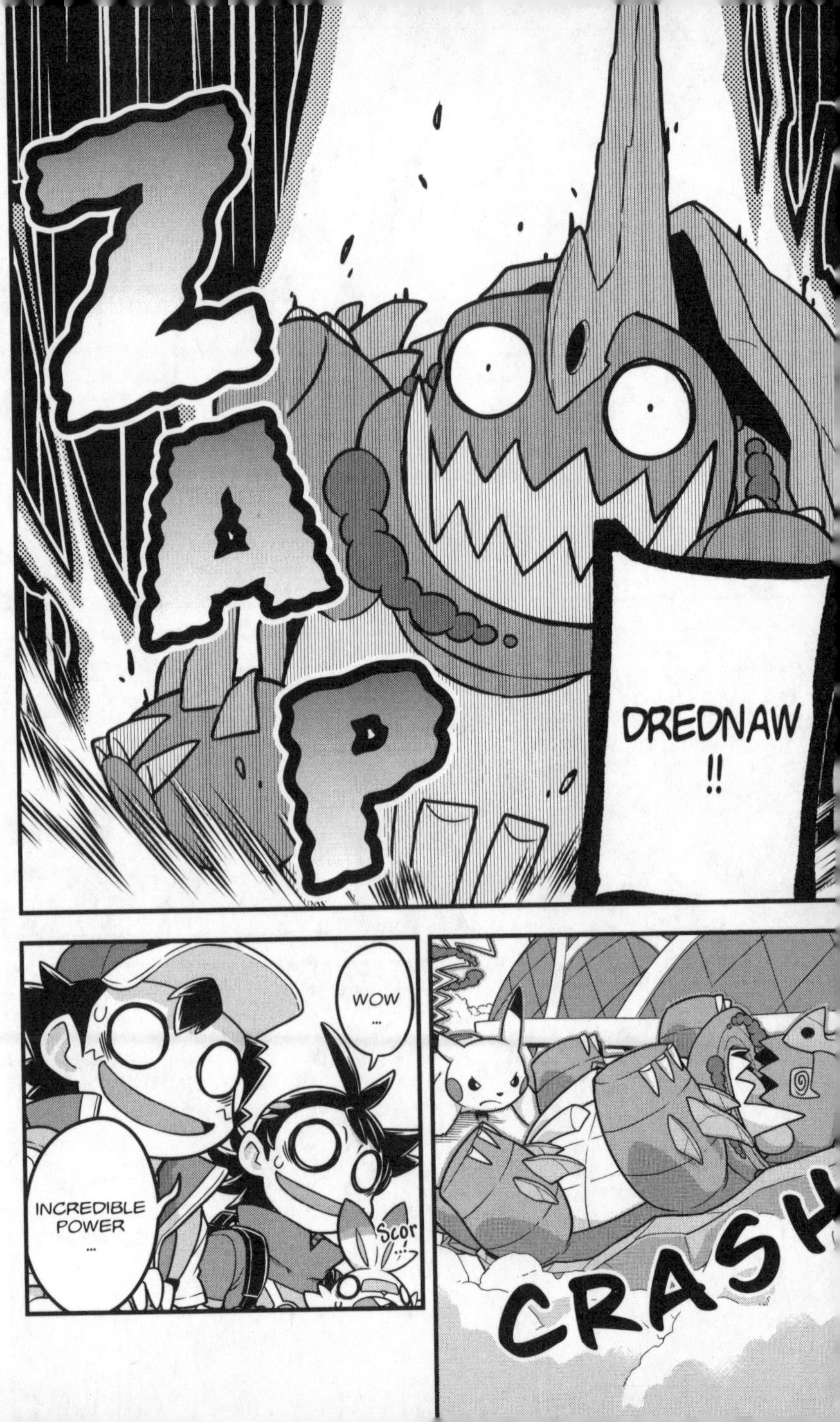
ZAP
DREDNAW !!
CRASH
WOW ...
INCREDIBLE POWER ...
Scor ...!

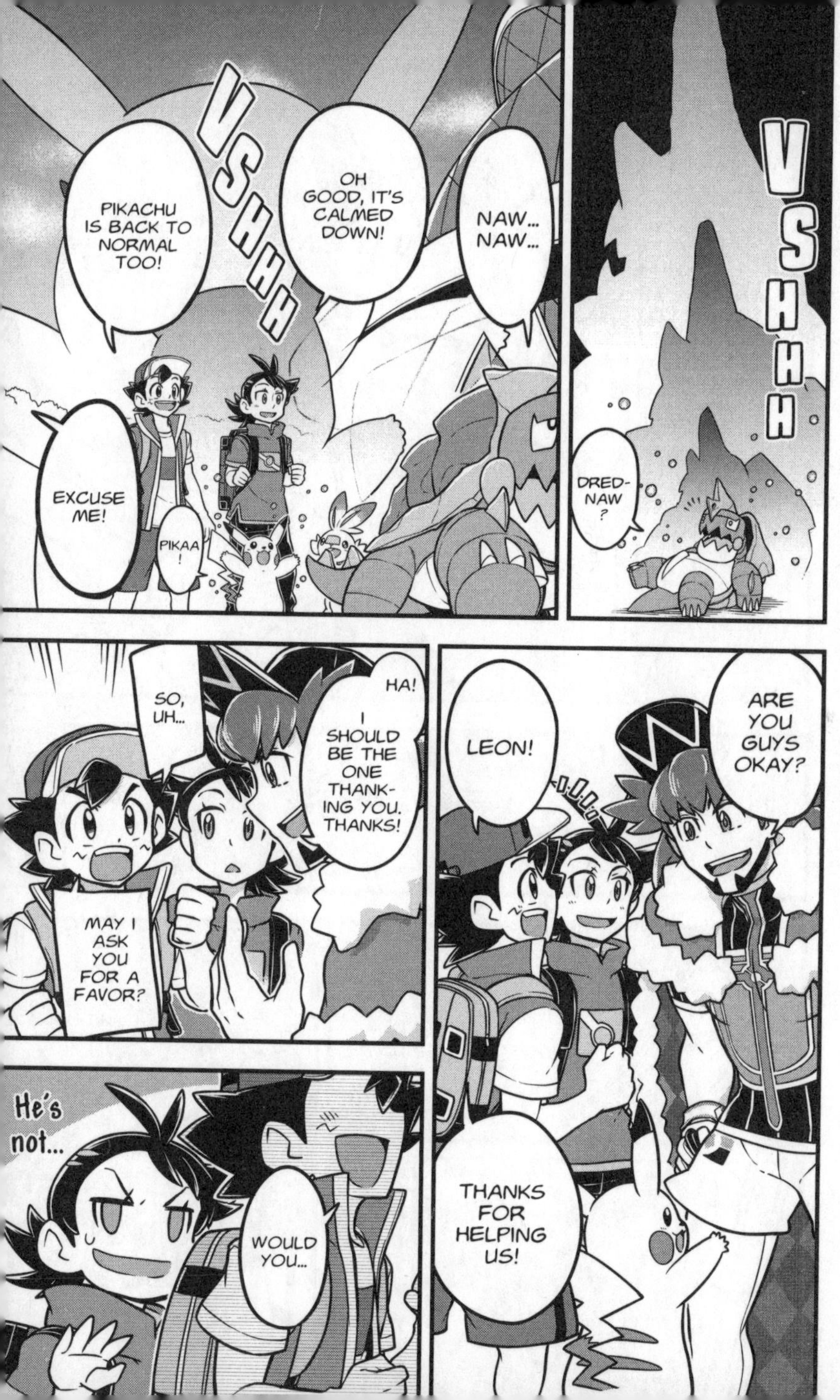
VSHHH
DRED-NAW?
NAW... NAW...
OH GOOD, IT'S CALMED DOWN!
VSHHH
PIKACHU IS BACK TO NORMAL TOO!
PIKAA!
EXCUSE ME!
ARE YOU GUYS OKAY?
LEON!
THANKS FOR HELPING US!
HA! I SHOULD BE THE ONE THANKING YOU. THANKS!
SO, UH...
MAY I ASK YOU FOR A FAVOR?
WOULD YOU...
He's not...

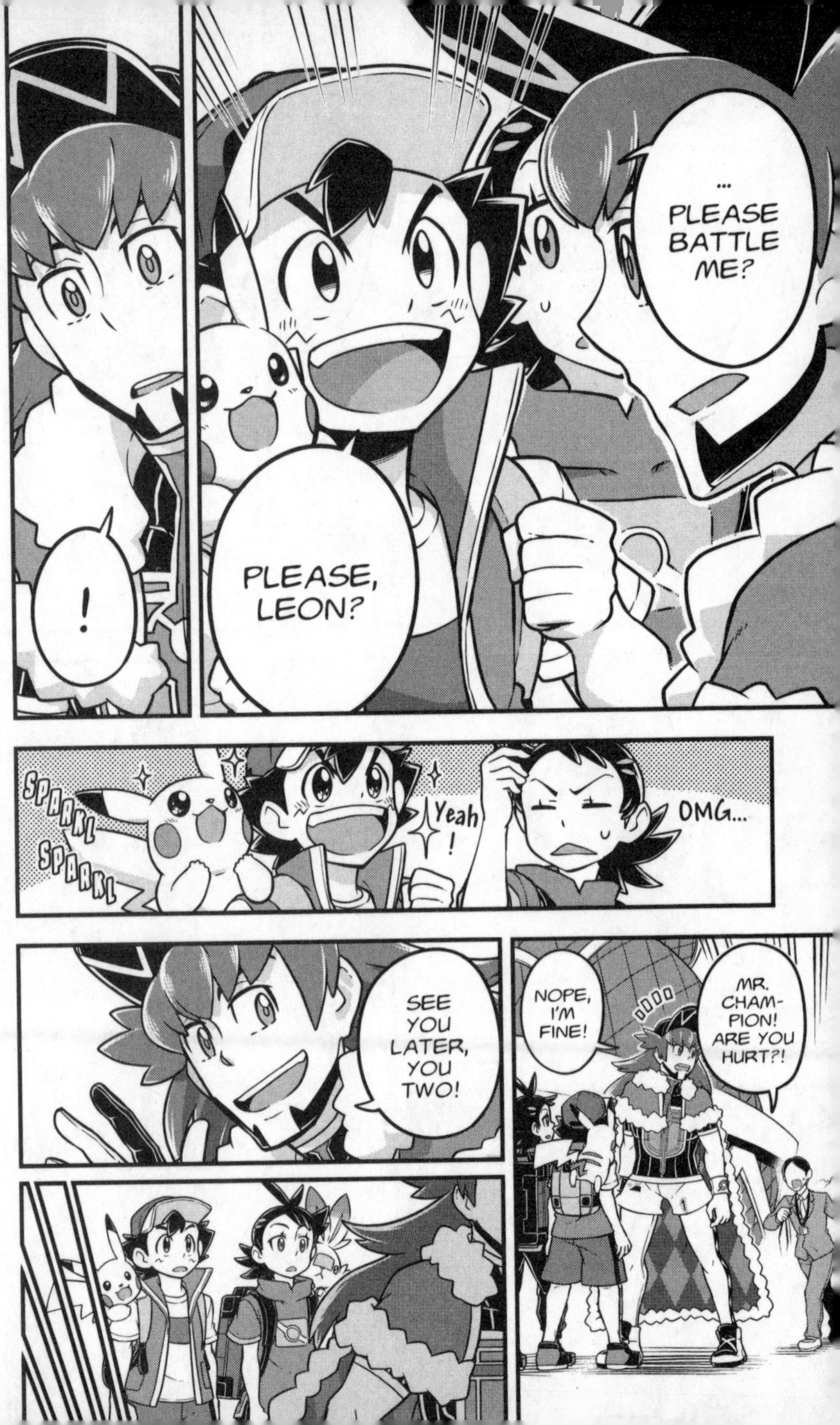
... PLEASE BATTLE ME?
PLEASE, LEON?
!
OMG...
Yeah!
SPARKL SPARKL
MR. CHAMPION! ARE YOU HURT?!
NOPE, I'M FINE!
SEE YOU LATER, YOU TWO!

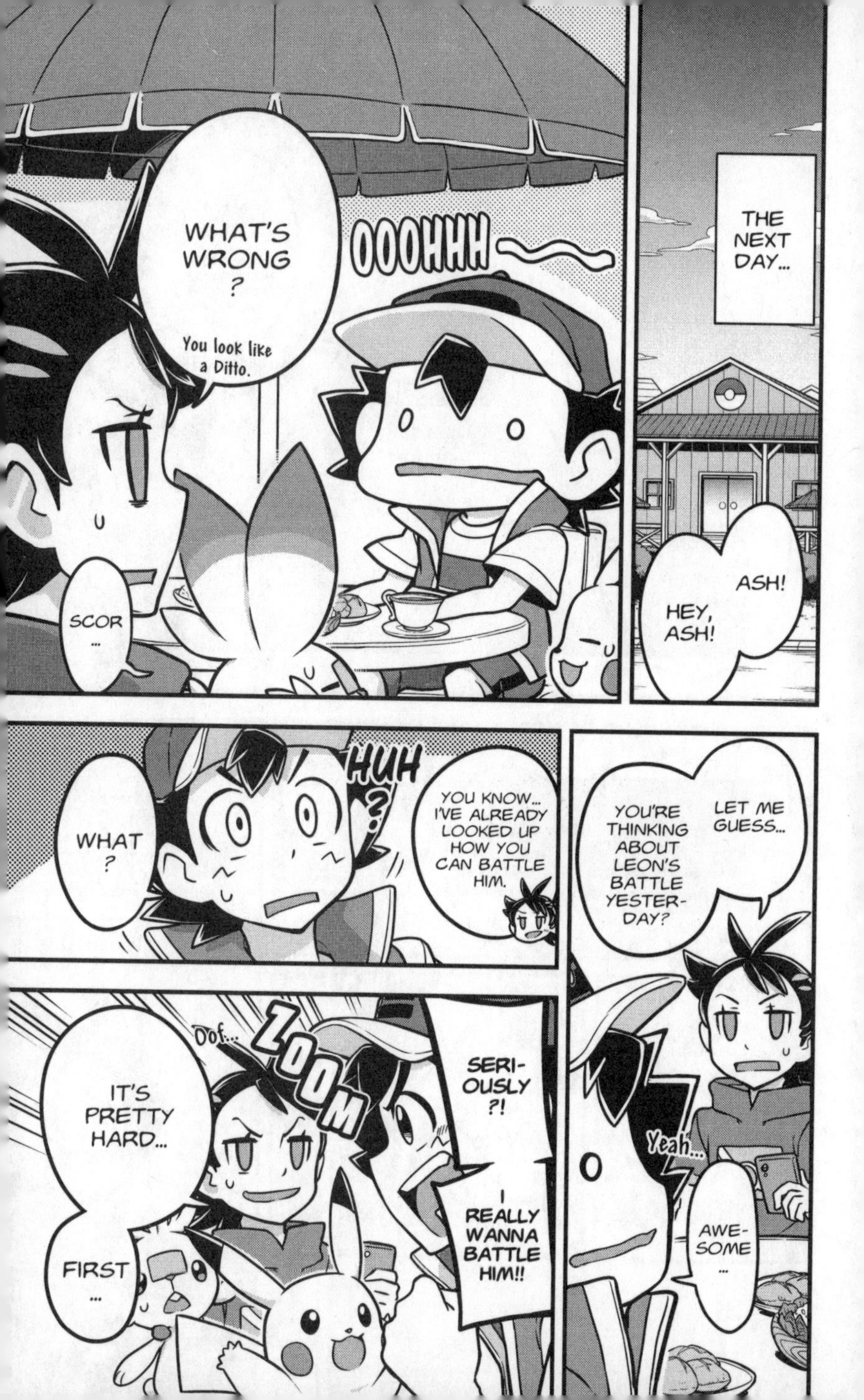
THE NEXT DAY...
HEY, ASH! ASH!
OOOHHH~~
WHAT'S WRONG?
You look like a Ditto.
SCOR...
LET ME GUESS... YOU'RE THINKING ABOUT LEON'S BATTLE YESTERDAY?
Yeah...
AWE-SOME...
HUH?
YOU KNOW... I'VE ALREADY LOOKED UP HOW YOU CAN BATTLE HIM.
WHAT?
SERI-OUSLY?!
I REALLY WANNA BATTLE HIM!!
ZOOM
Oof...
IT'S PRETTY HARD...
FIRST...

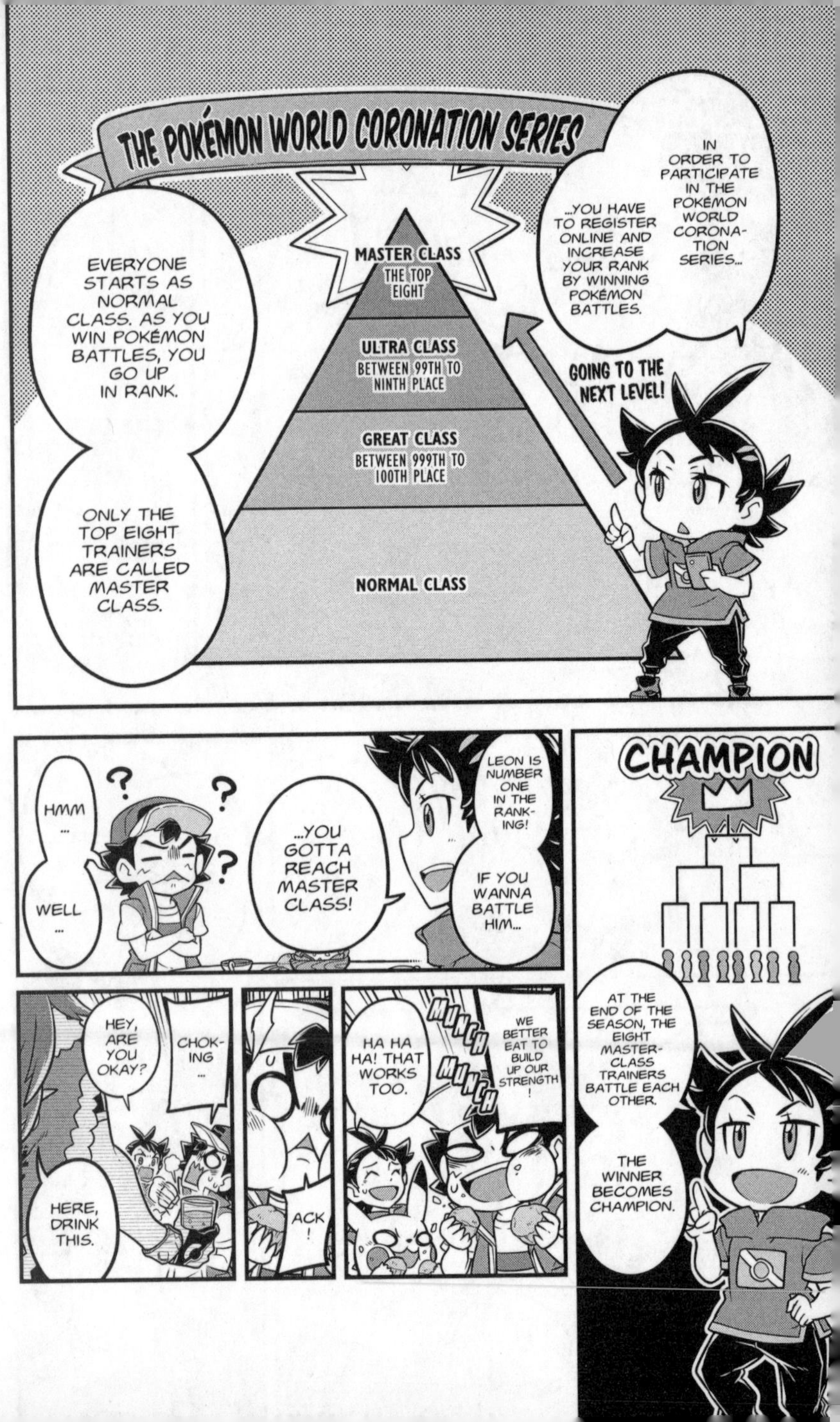
IN ORDER TO PARTICIPATE IN THE POKÉMON WORLD CORONATION SERIES...
...YOU HAVE TO REGISTER ONLINE AND INCREASE YOUR RANK BY WINNING POKÉMON BATTLES.
THE POKÉMON WORLD CORONATION SERIES
MASTER CLASS
THE TOP EIGHT
ULTRA CLASS
BETWEEN 99TH TO NINTH PLACE
GREAT CLASS
BETWEEN 999TH TO 100TH PLACE
NORMAL CLASS
GOING TO THE NEXT LEVEL!
EVERYONE STARTS AS NORMAL CLASS. AS YOU WIN POKÉMON BATTLES, YOU GO UP IN RANK.
ONLY THE TOP EIGHT TRAINERS ARE CALLED MASTER CLASS.
CHAMPION
AT THE END OF THE SEASON, THE EIGHT MASTER-CLASS TRAINERS BATTLE EACH OTHER.
THE WINNER BECOMES CHAMPION.
LEON IS NUMBER ONE IN THE RANK-ING!
IF YOU WANNA BATTLE HIM...
...YOU GOTTA REACH MASTER CLASS!
HMM ...
WELL ...
WE BETTER EAT TO BUILD UP OUR STRENGTH!
MUNCH MUNCH
HA HA HA! THAT WORKS TOO.
ACK!
CHOK-ING ...
HEY, ARE YOU OKAY?
HERE, DRINK THIS.

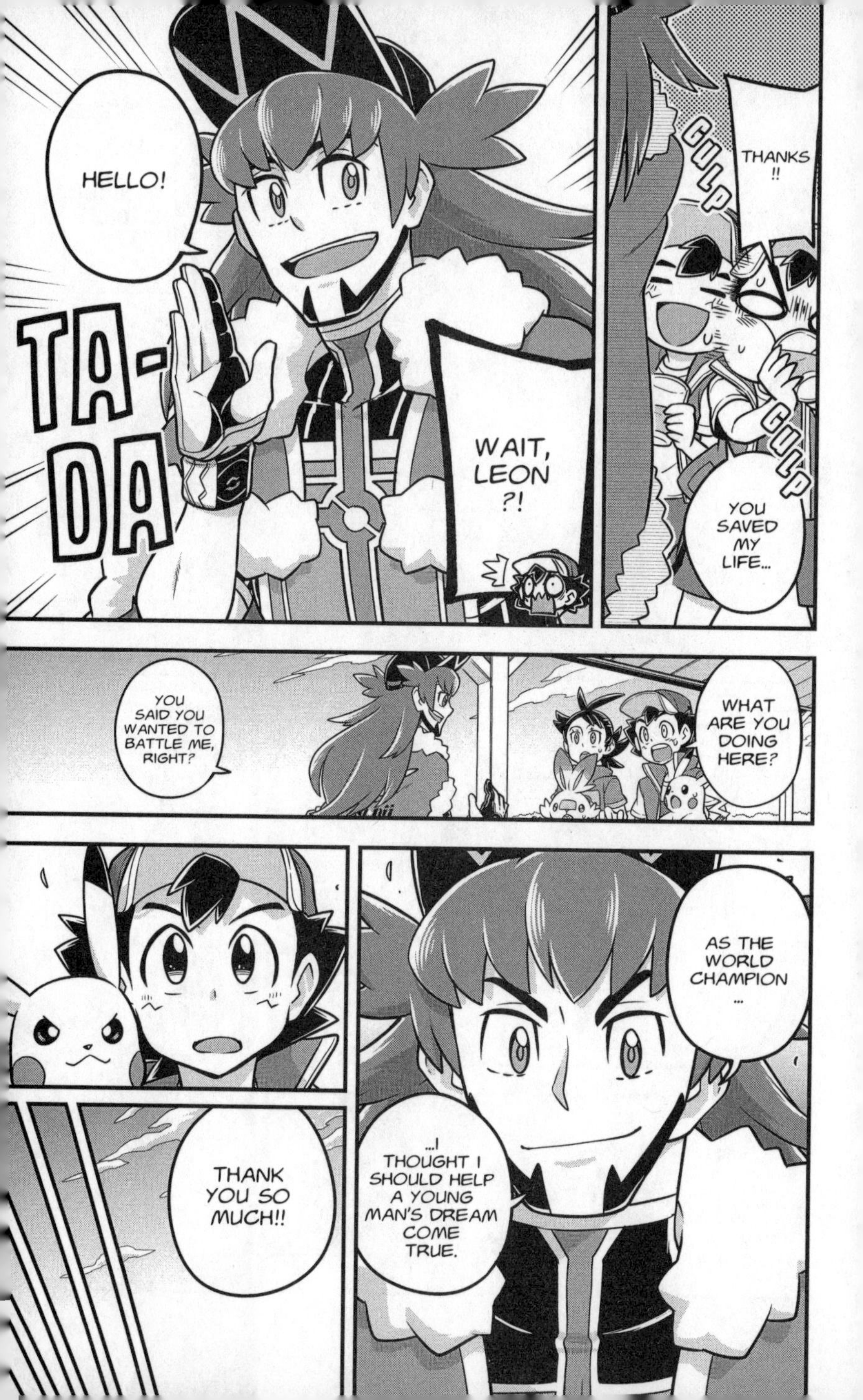
GULP
THANKS !!
GULP GULP
YOU SAVED MY LIFE...
HELLO!
TA-DA
WAIT, LEON ?!
WHAT ARE YOU DOING HERE?
YOU SAID YOU WANTED TO BATTLE ME, RIGHT?
AS THE WORLD CHAMPION ...
...I THOUGHT I SHOULD HELP A YOUNG MAN'S DREAM COME TRUE.
THANK YOU SO MUCH!!

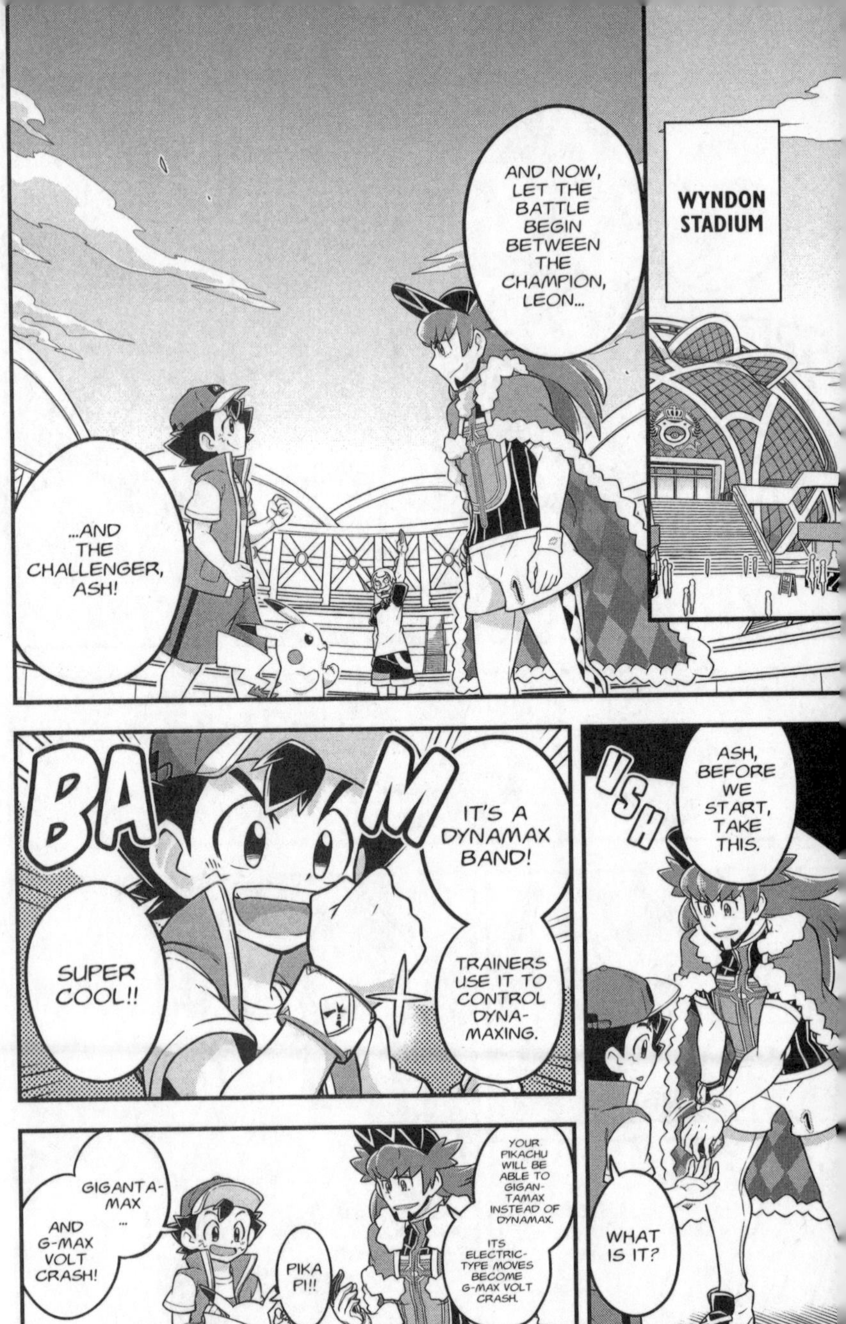
WYNDON STADIUM
AND NOW, LET THE BATTLE BEGIN BETWEEN THE CHAMPION, LEON...
...AND THE CHALLENGER, ASH!
VSH
ASH, BEFORE WE START, TAKE THIS.
WHAT IS IT?
BAM
IT'S A DYNAMAX BAND!
TRAINERS USE IT TO CONTROL DYNA-MAXING.
SUPER COOL!!
YOUR PIKACHU WILL BE ABLE TO GIGAN-TAMAX INSTEAD OF DYNAMAX.
ITS ELECTRIC-TYPE MOVES BECOME G-MAX VOLT CRASH.
PIKA PI!!
GIGANTA-MAX ...
AND G-MAX VOLT CRASH!

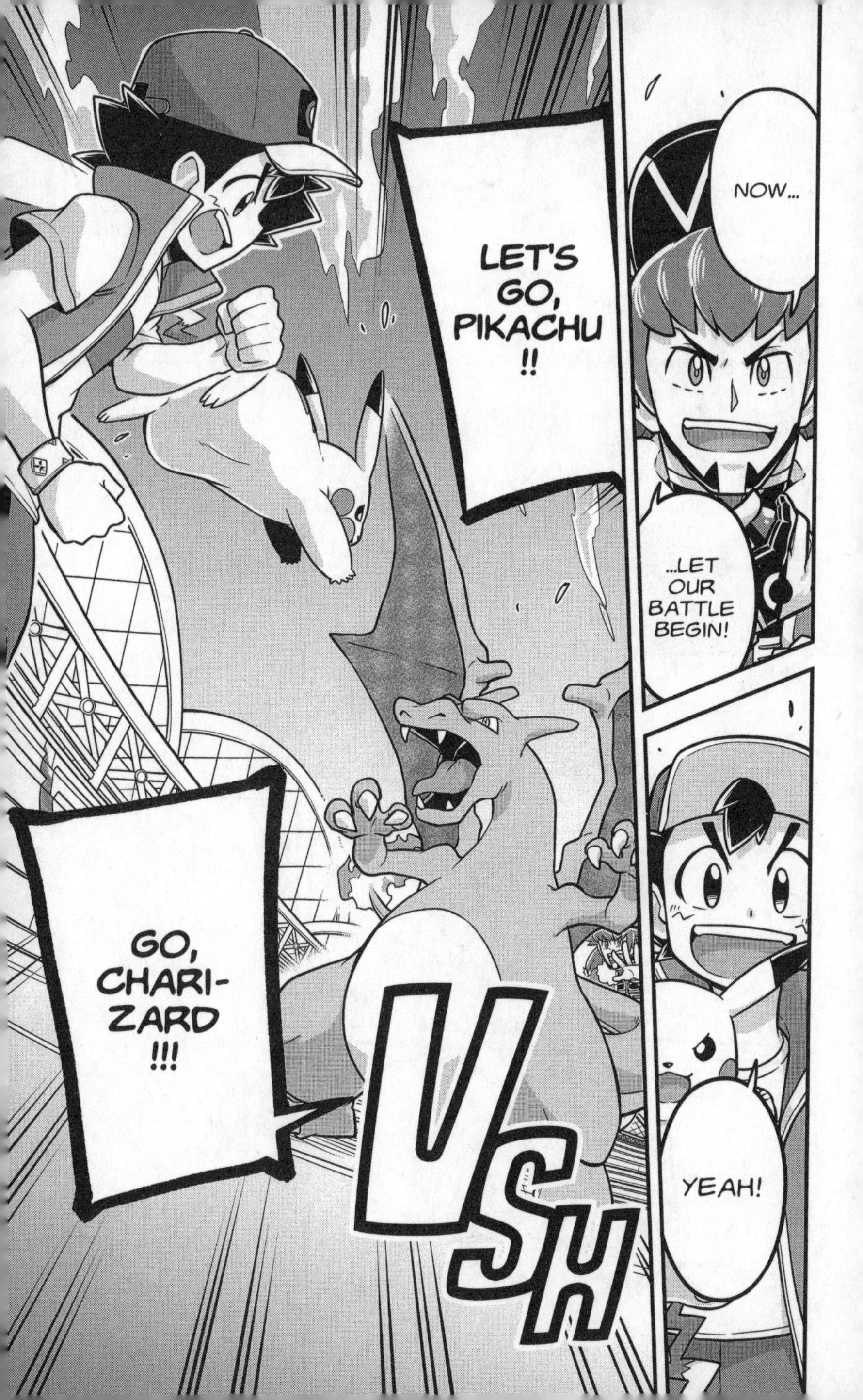
NOW...
...LET OUR BATTLE BEGIN!
YEAH!
LET'S GO, PIKACHU!!
GO, CHARI-ZARD!!!
VSH

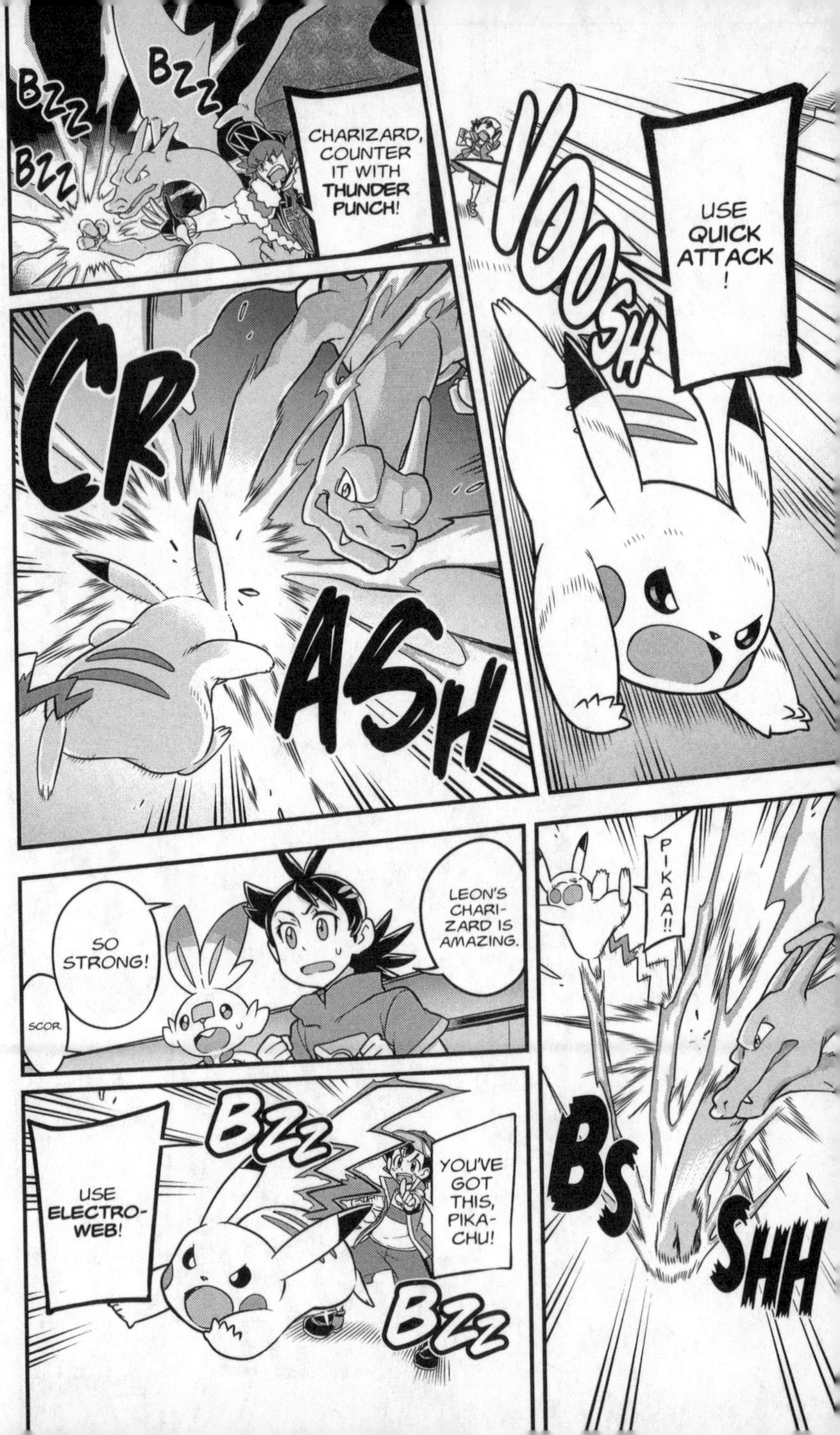
USE QUICK ATTACK!
VOOOSH
CHARIZARD, COUNTER IT WITH THUNDER PUNCH!
BZZ
BZZ
BZZ
CRASH
PIKAAA!!
BSSHH
LEON'S CHARIZARD IS AMAZING.
SO STRONG!
SCOR.
YOU'VE GOT THIS, PIKACHU!
USE ELECTRO-WEB!
BZZ
BZZ

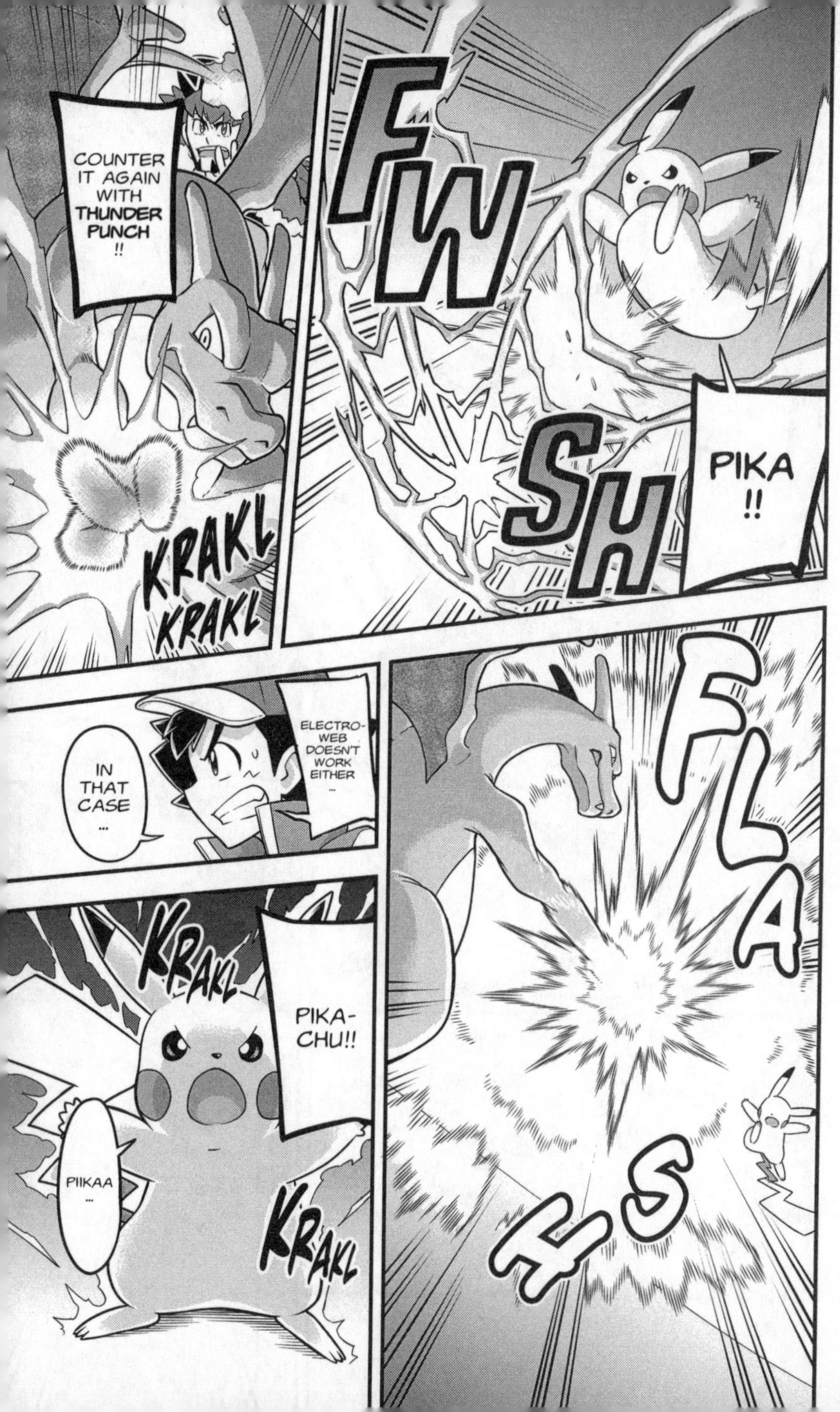
FW
SH
PIKA !!
COUNTER IT AGAIN WITH THUNDER PUNCH !!
KRAKL
KRAKL
FLA
SH
ELECTRO-WEB DOESN'T WORK EITHER ...
IN THAT CASE ...
KRAKL
PIKA-CHU!!
PIIKAA ...
KRAKL

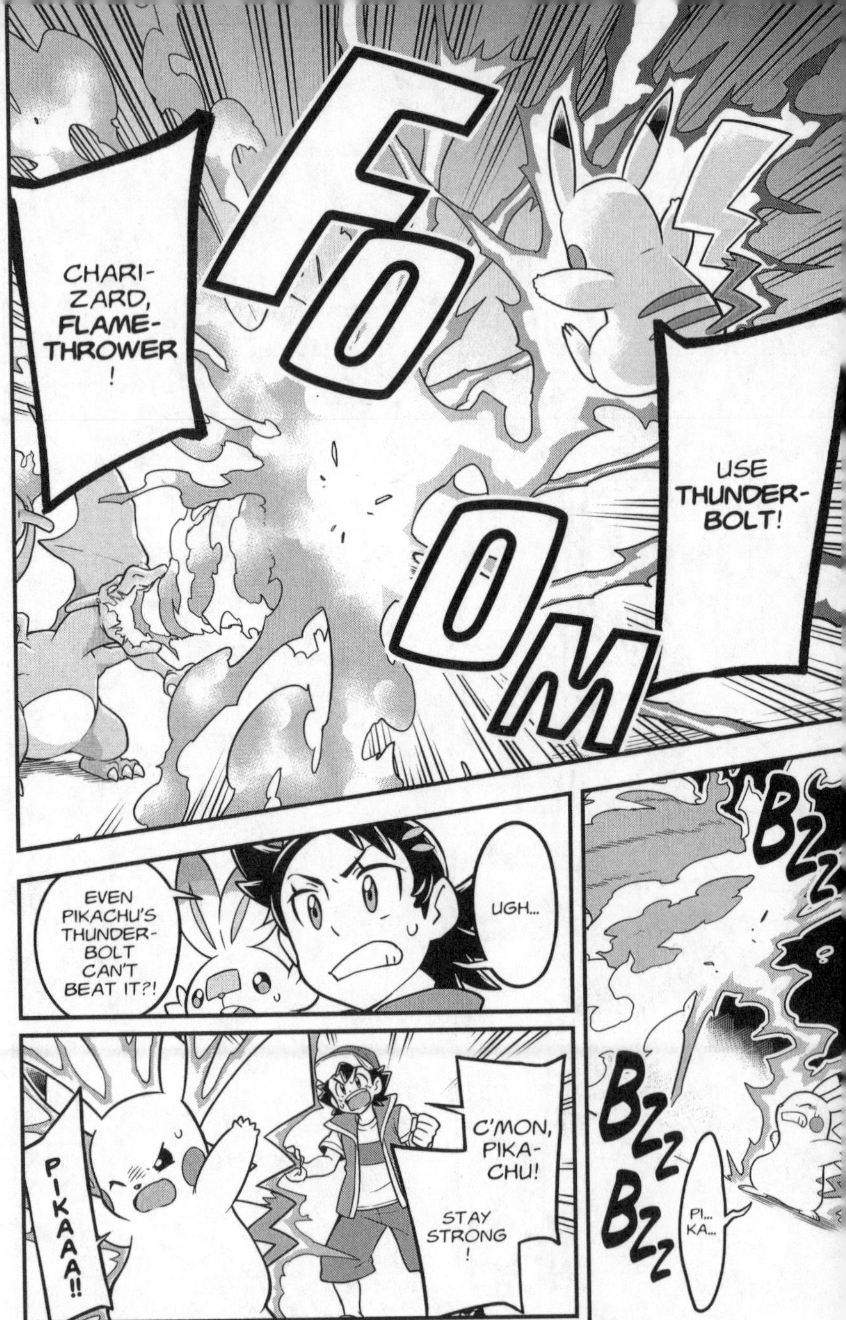
USE THUNDER-BOLT!
FOOM
CHARI-ZARD, FLAME-THROWER!
BZZ
BZZ BZZ
PI... KA...
UGH...
EVEN PIKACHU'S THUNDER-BOLT CAN'T BEAT IT?!
C'MON, PIKA-CHU!
STAY STRONG!
PIKAAA!!

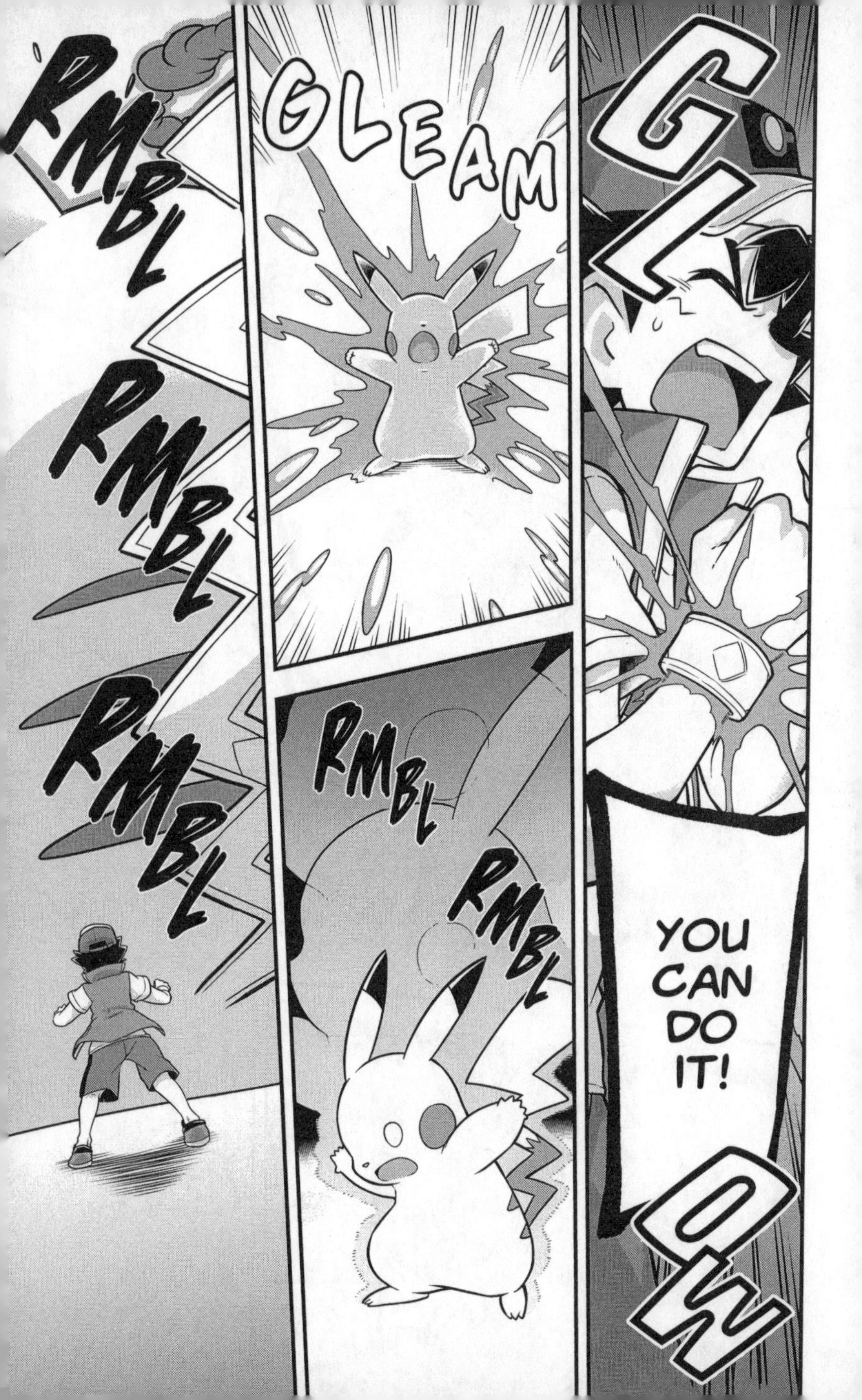
GLOW
YOU CAN DO IT!
GLEAM
RMBL
RMBL
RMBL
RMBL
RMBL

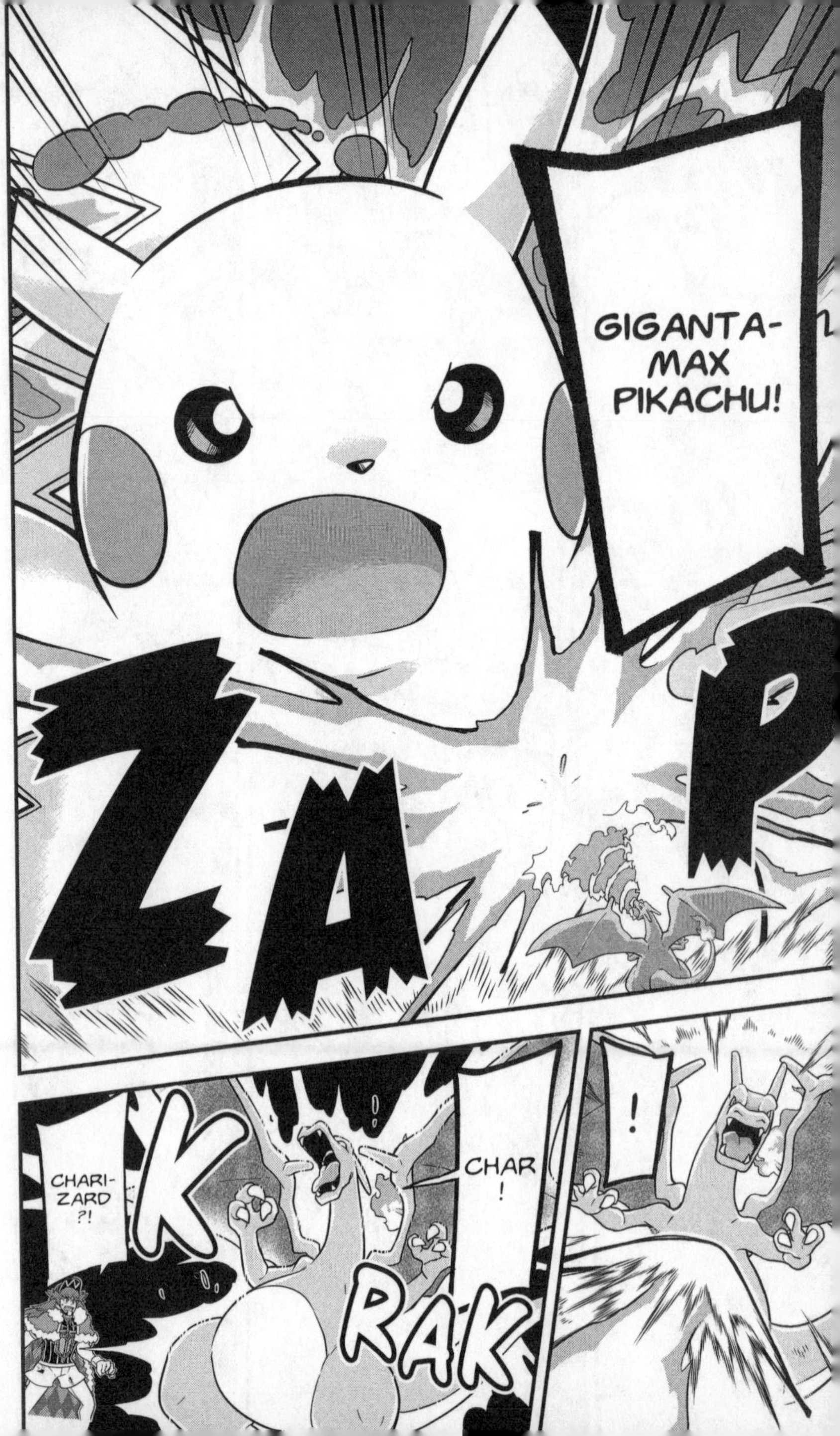
GIGANTA-MAX PIKACHU!
ZAP
!
CHAR !
CHARI-ZARD ?!
K
RAK

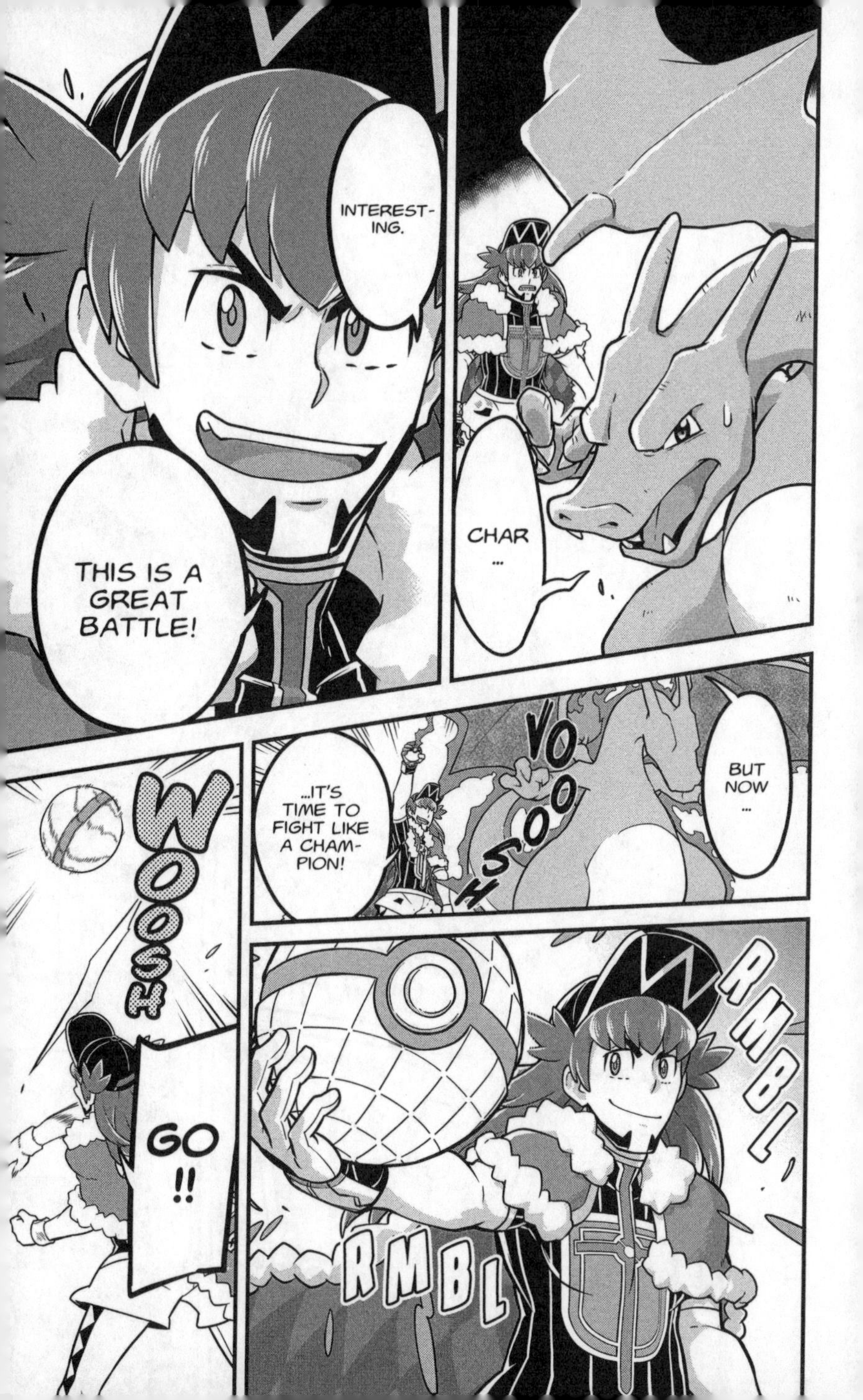
CHAR ...
INTERESTING.
THIS IS A GREAT BATTLE!
BUT NOW ...
VOOOSH
...IT'S TIME TO FIGHT LIKE A CHAMPION!
RMBL
RMBL
WOOOSH
GO !!

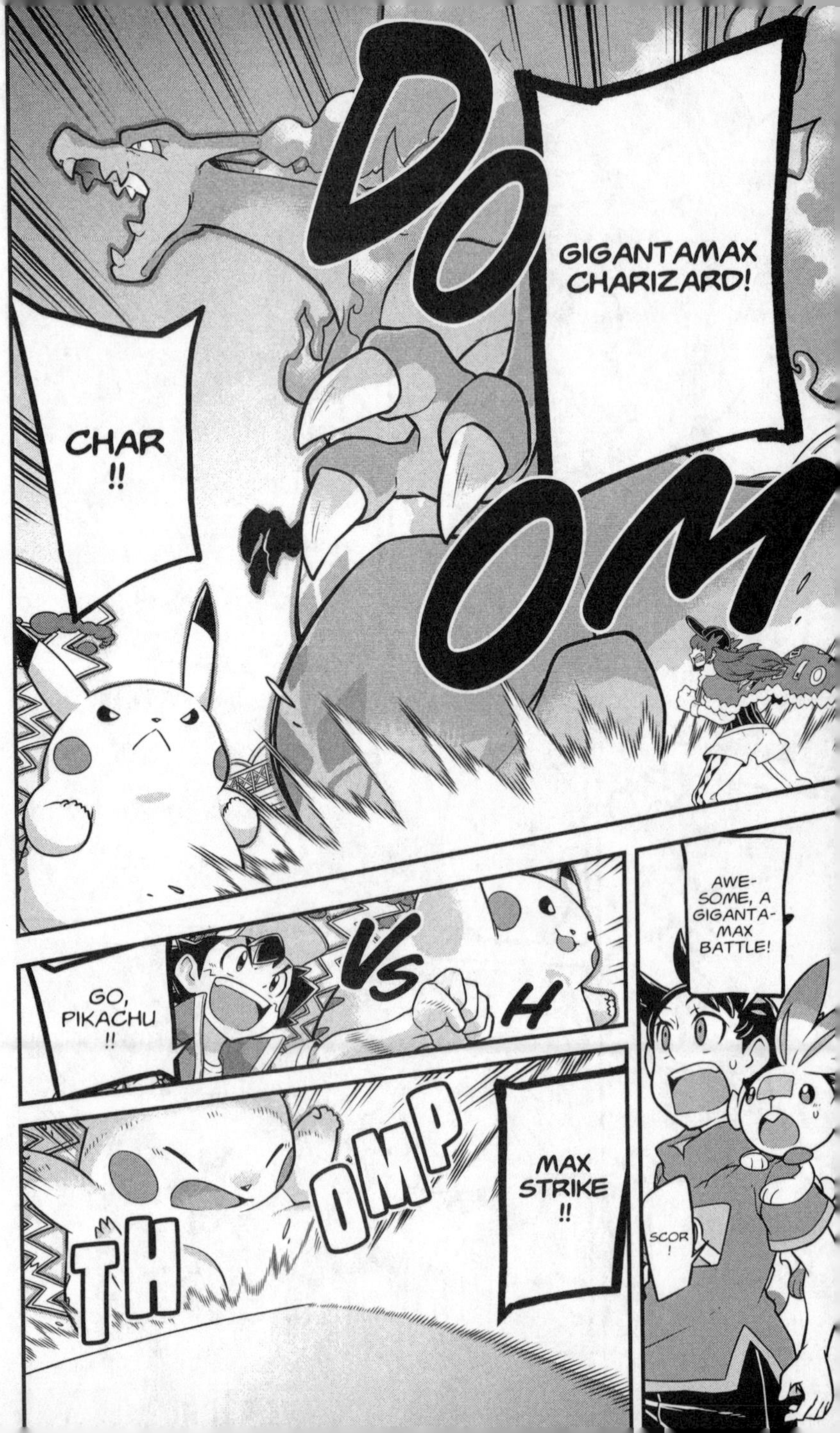
GIGANTAMAX CHARIZARD!
DOOM
CHAR !!
AWESOME, A GIGANTAMAX BATTLE!
SCOR !
GO, PIKACHU !!
VS
H
MAX STRIKE !!
TH
OMP

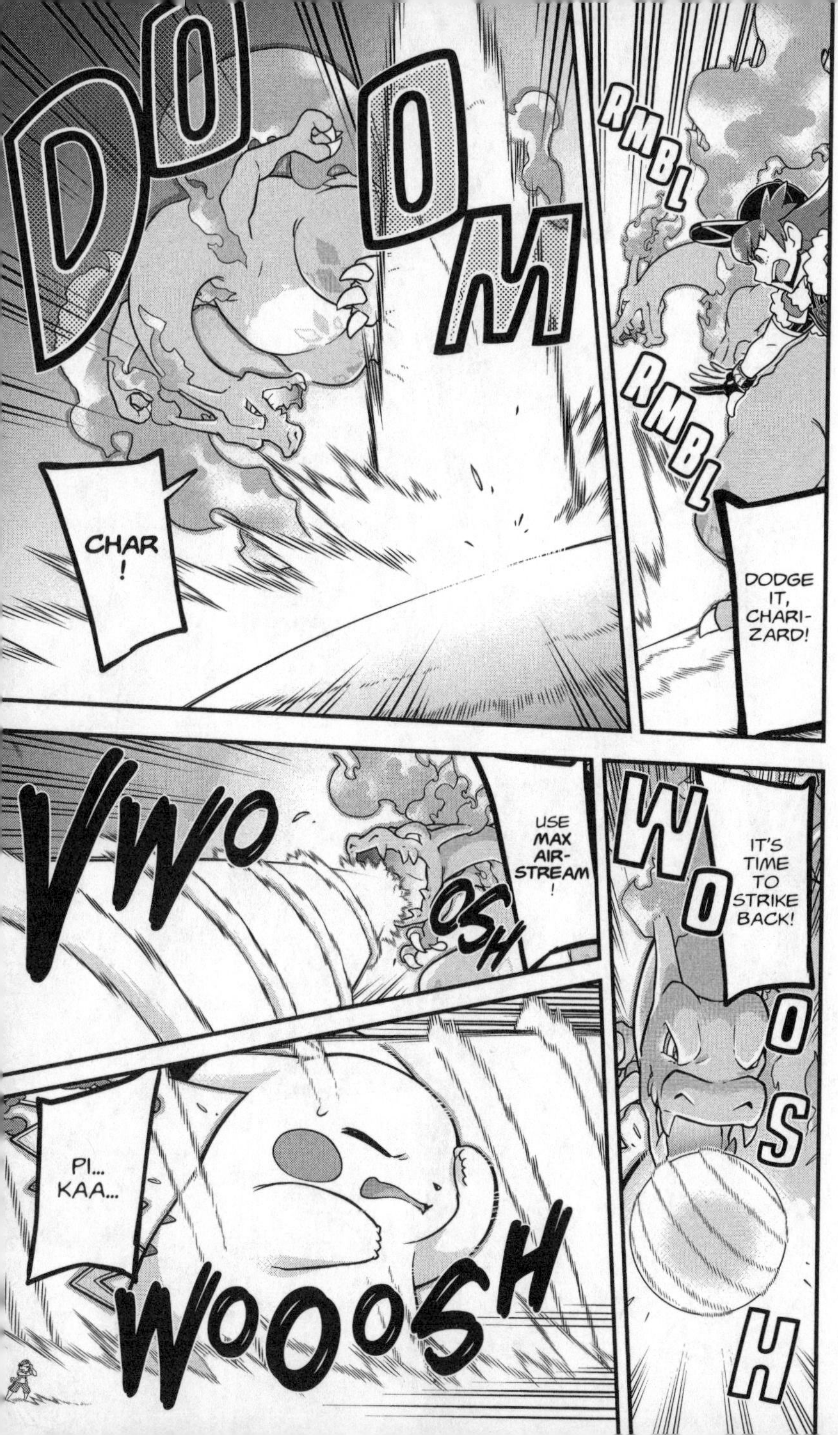
RMBL
RMBL
DODGE IT, CHARIZARD!
DOOM
CHAR!
WOOOSH
IT'S TIME TO STRIKE BACK!
USE MAX AIRSTREAM!
VWOOSH
PI... KAA...
WOOOSH

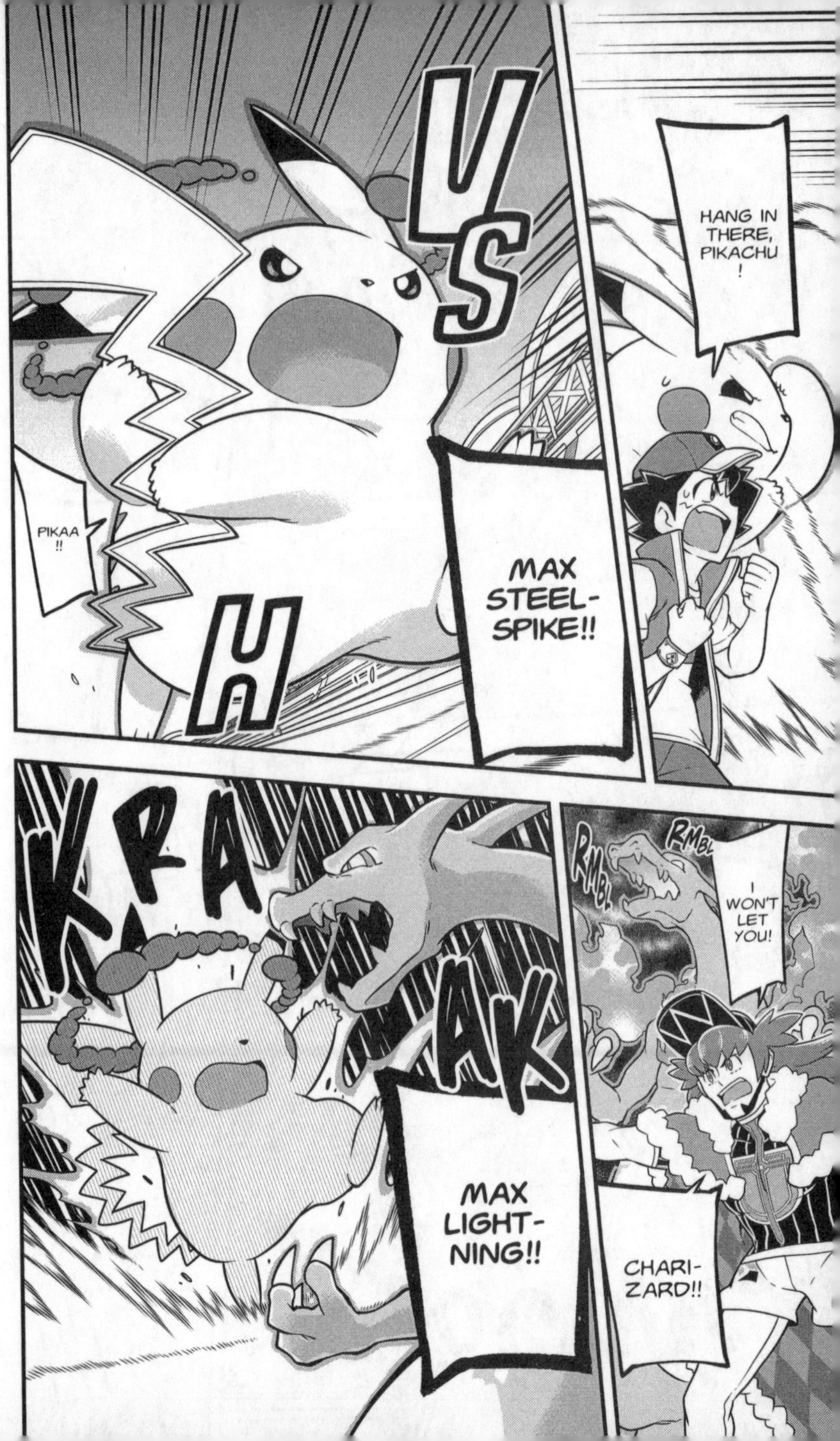
HANG IN THERE, PIKACHU!
MAX STEEL-SPIKE!!
VSH
PIKAA!!
RMBL
RMBL
I WON'T LET YOU!
CHARIZARD!!
KRAAK
MAX LIGHTNING!!

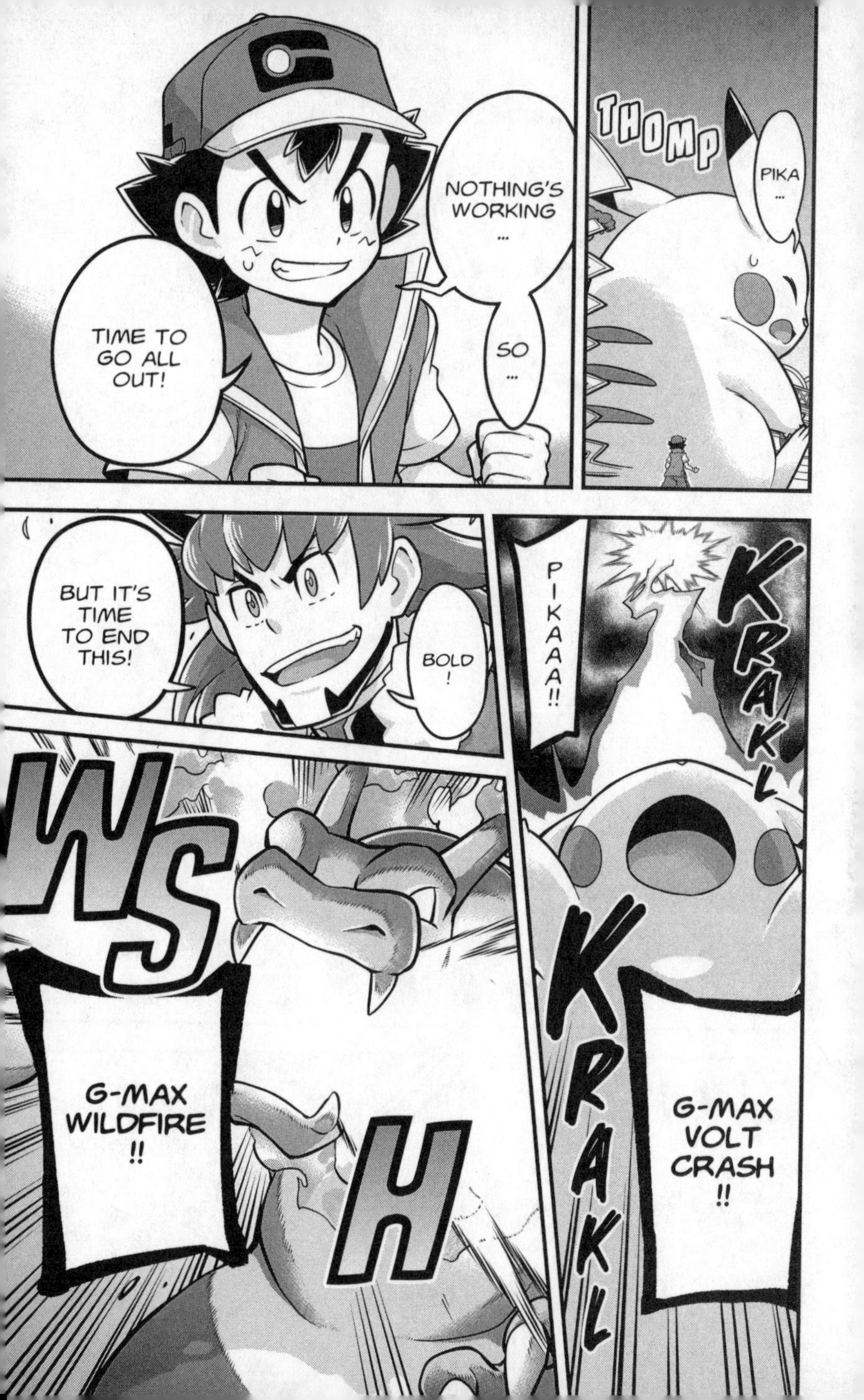
THOMP
PIKA ...
NOTHING'S WORKING ...
SO ...
TIME TO GO ALL OUT!
PIKAAAA!!
KRAKL
KRAKL
G-MAX VOLT CRASH !!
BOLD !
BUT IT'S TIME TO END THIS!
WS
H
G-MAX WILDFIRE !!

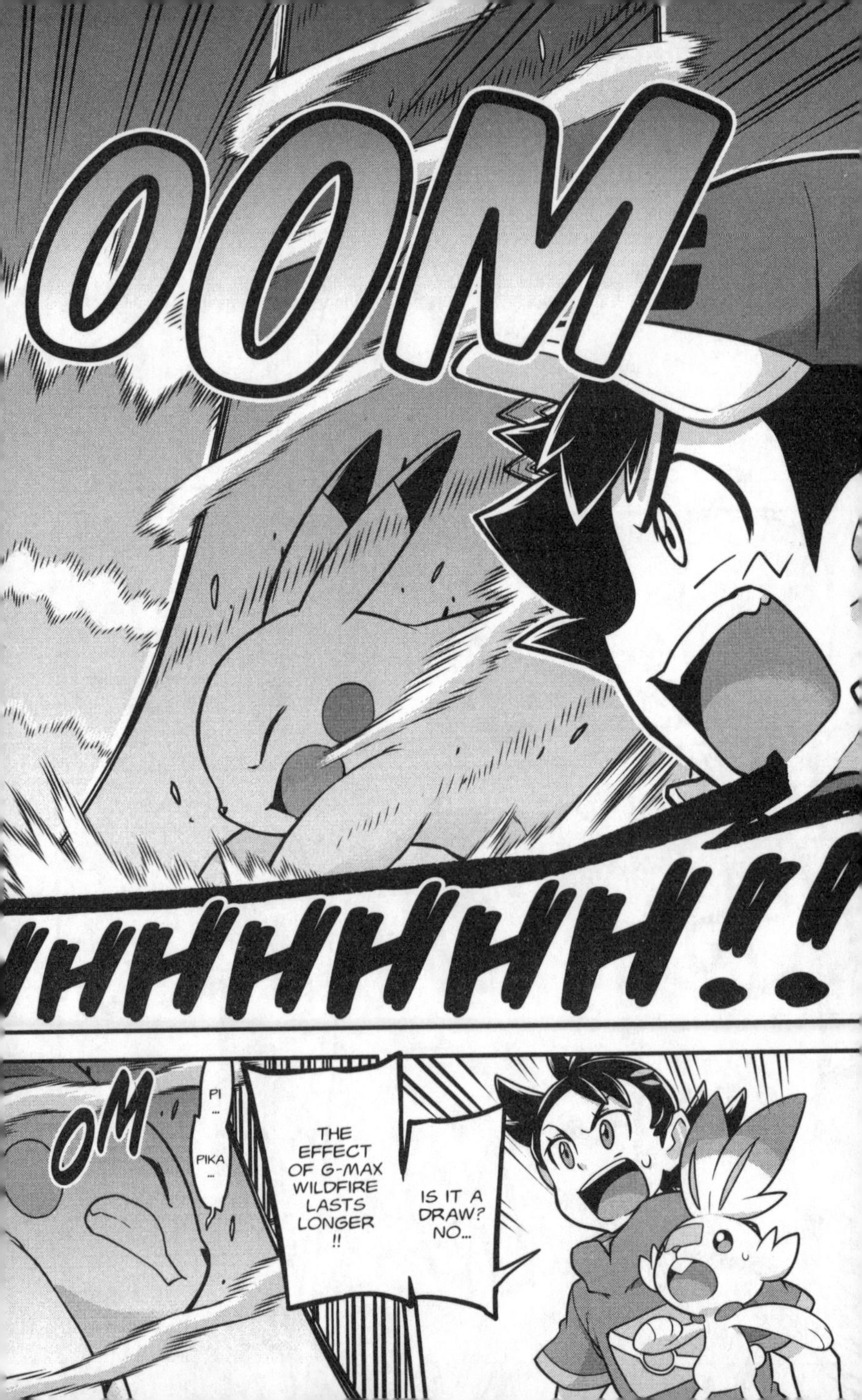
OOM
HHHHHH!!
IS IT A DRAW? NO...
THE EFFECT OF G-MAX WILDFIRE LASTS LONGER!!
PI... PIKA...
OM

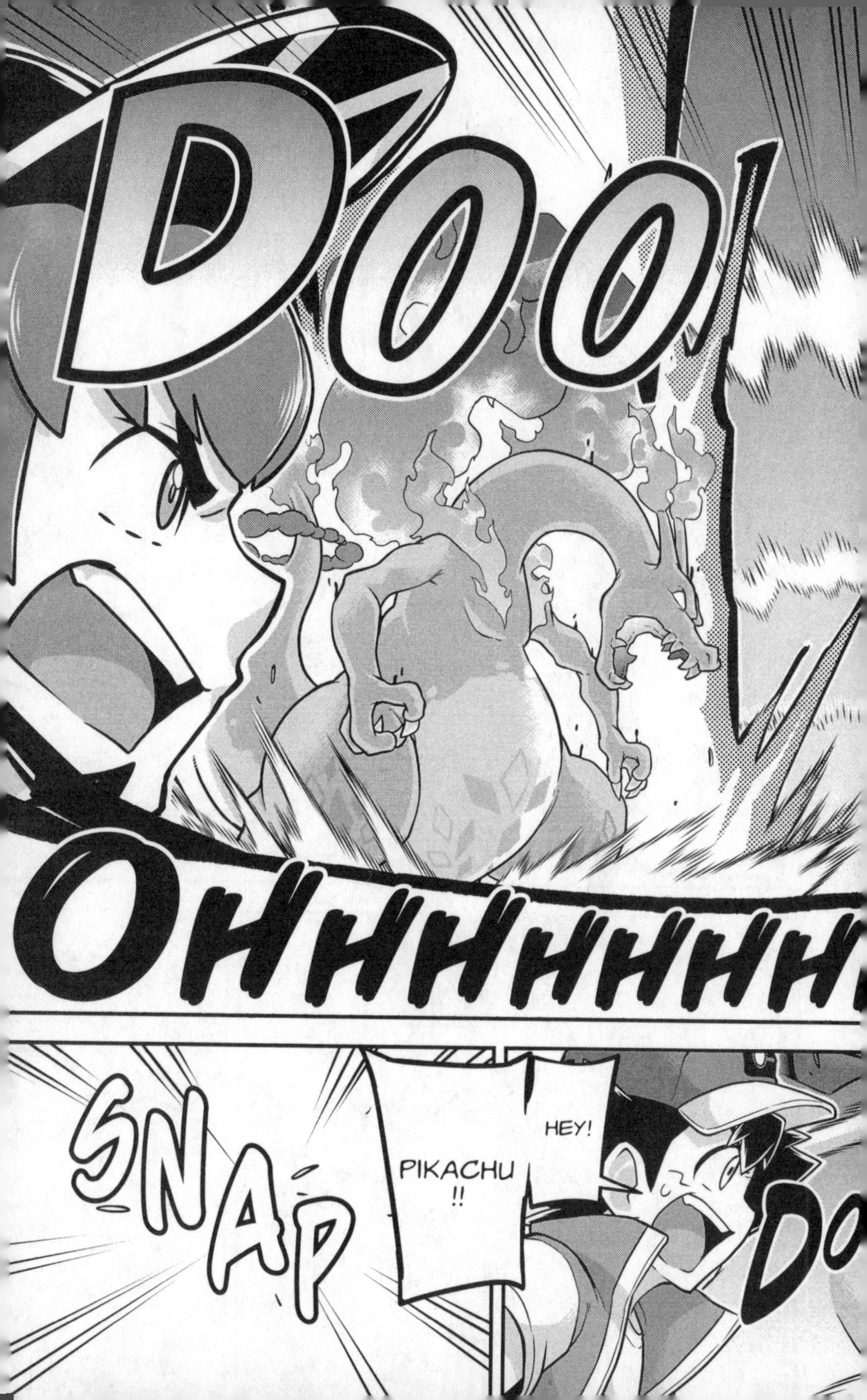
DOOO
OHHHHHHHH
DO
HEY!
PIKACHU !!
SNAP

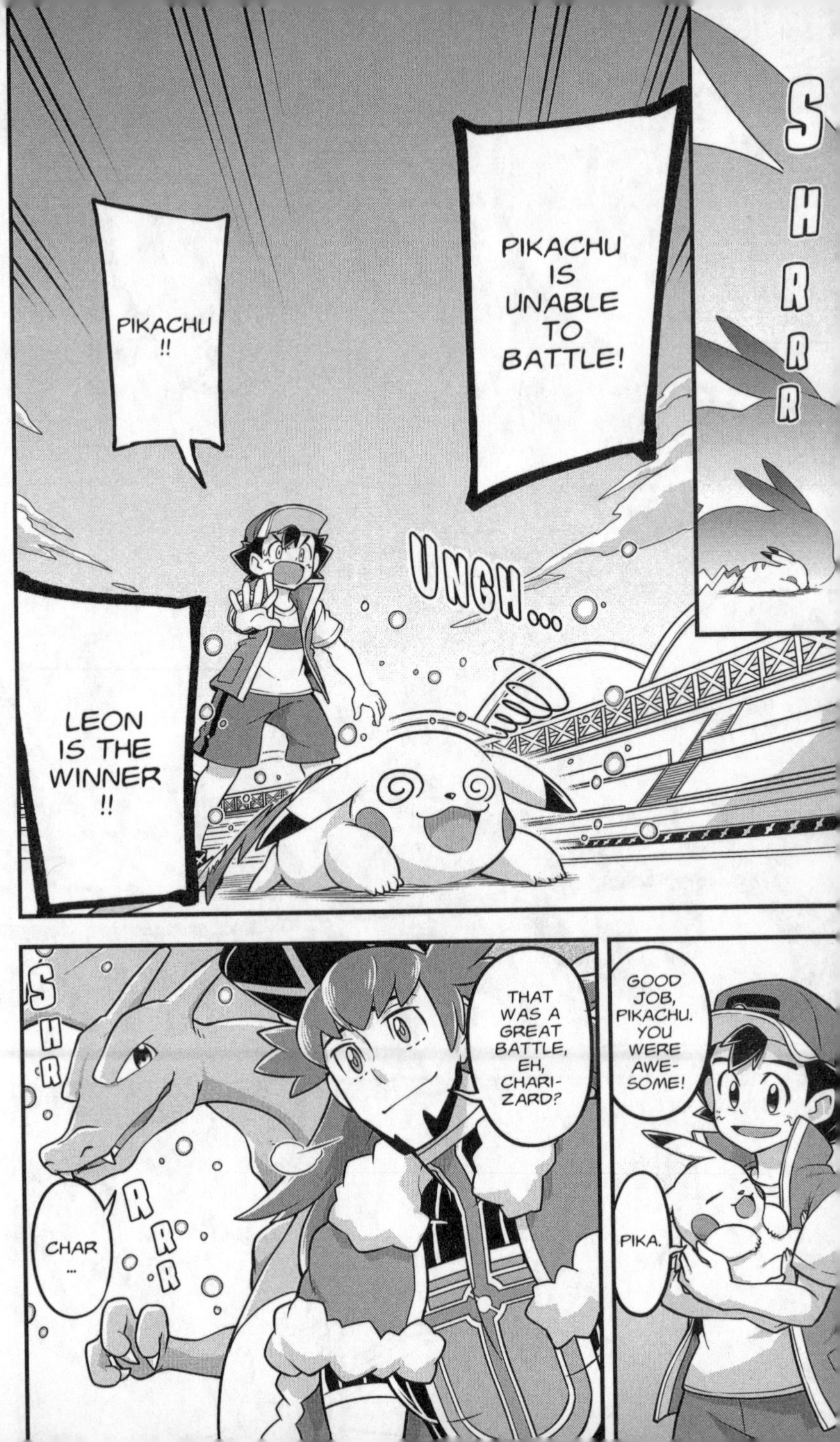
SHRRR
PIKACHU IS UNABLE TO BATTLE!
PIKACHU!!
UNGH...
LEON IS THE WINNER!!
GOOD JOB, PIKACHU. YOU WERE AWESOME!
PIKA.
THAT WAS A GREAT BATTLE, EH, CHARIZARD?
SHRRRR
CHAR...

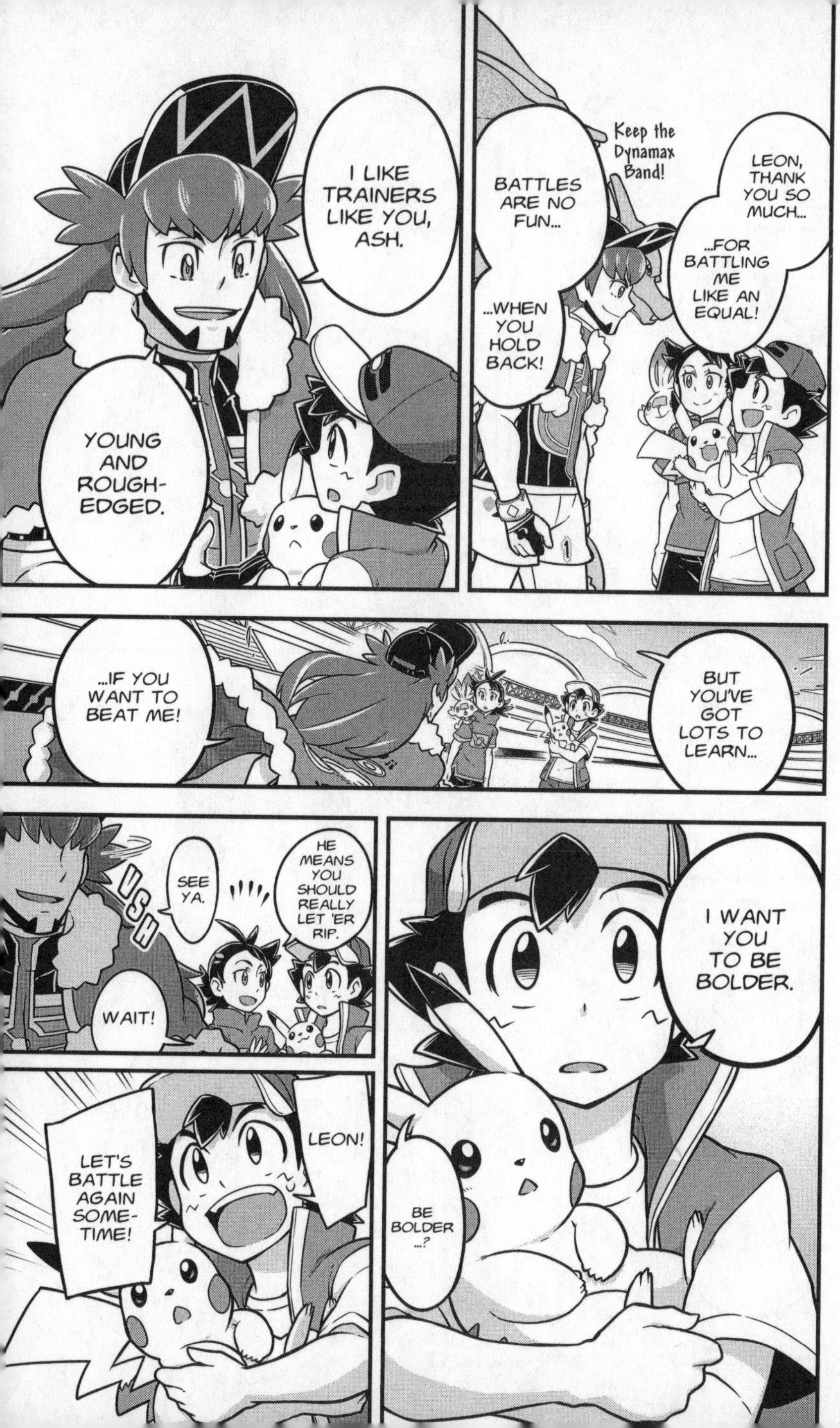
LEON, THANK YOU SO MUCH...
...FOR BATTLING ME LIKE AN EQUAL!
Keep the Dynamax Band!
BATTLES ARE NO FUN...
...WHEN YOU HOLD BACK!
I LIKE TRAINERS LIKE YOU, ASH.
YOUNG AND ROUGH-EDGED.
BUT YOU'VE GOT LOTS TO LEARN...
...IF YOU WANT TO BEAT ME!
I WANT YOU TO BE BOLDER.
BE BOLDER ...?
HE MEANS YOU SHOULD REALLY LET 'ER RIP.
SEE YA.
VSH
WAIT!
LEON!
LET'S BATTLE AGAIN SOME-TIME!

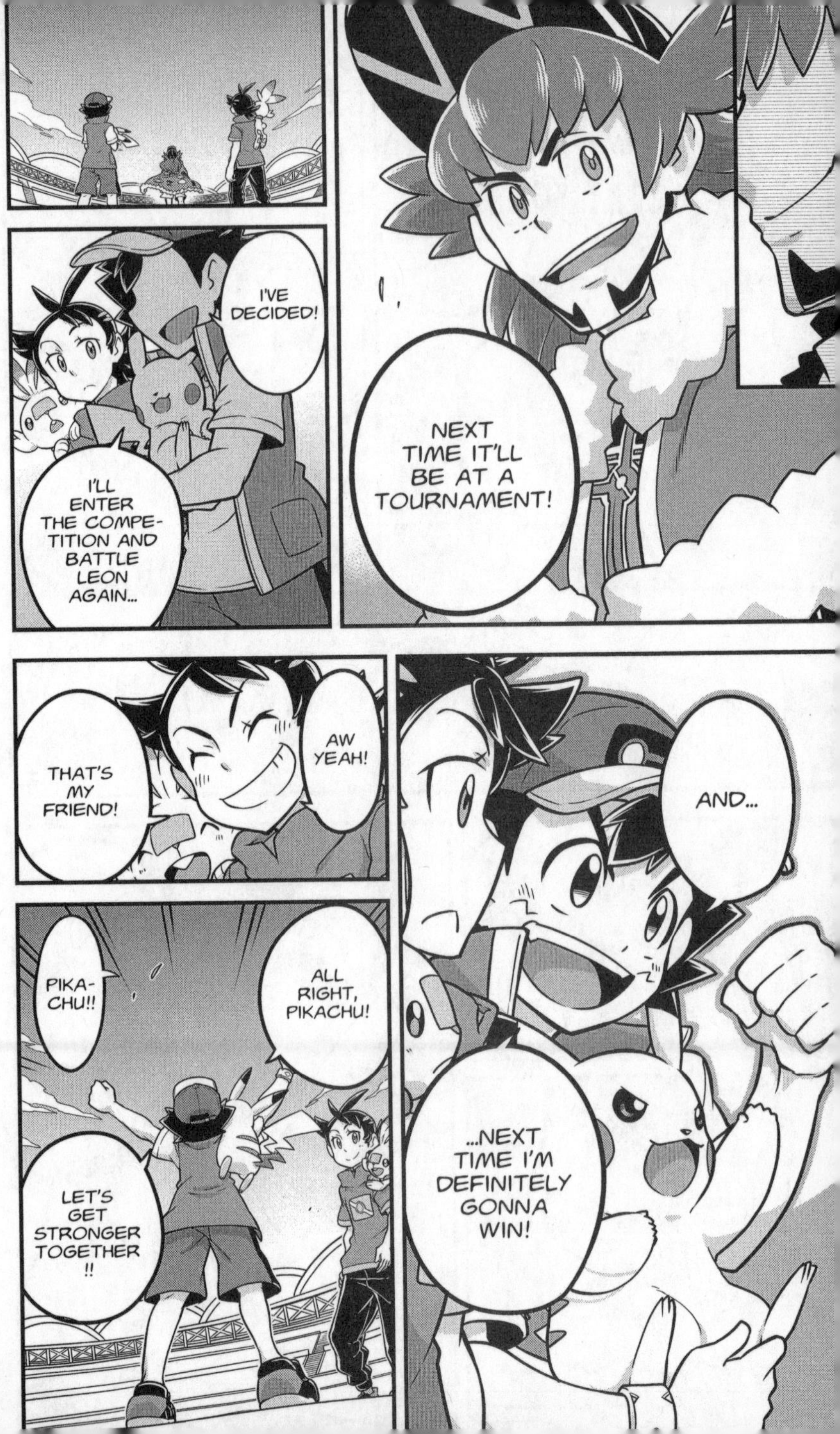
NEXT TIME IT'LL BE AT A TOURNAMENT!
I'VE DECIDED!
I'LL ENTER THE COMPETITION AND BATTLE LEON AGAIN...
AND...
...NEXT TIME I'M DEFINITELY GONNA WIN!
AW YEAH!
THAT'S MY FRIEND!
ALL RIGHT, PIKACHU!
PIKA-CHU!!
LET'S GET STRONGER TOGETHER!!

Chapter 6
Kicking It from Here into Tomorrow!

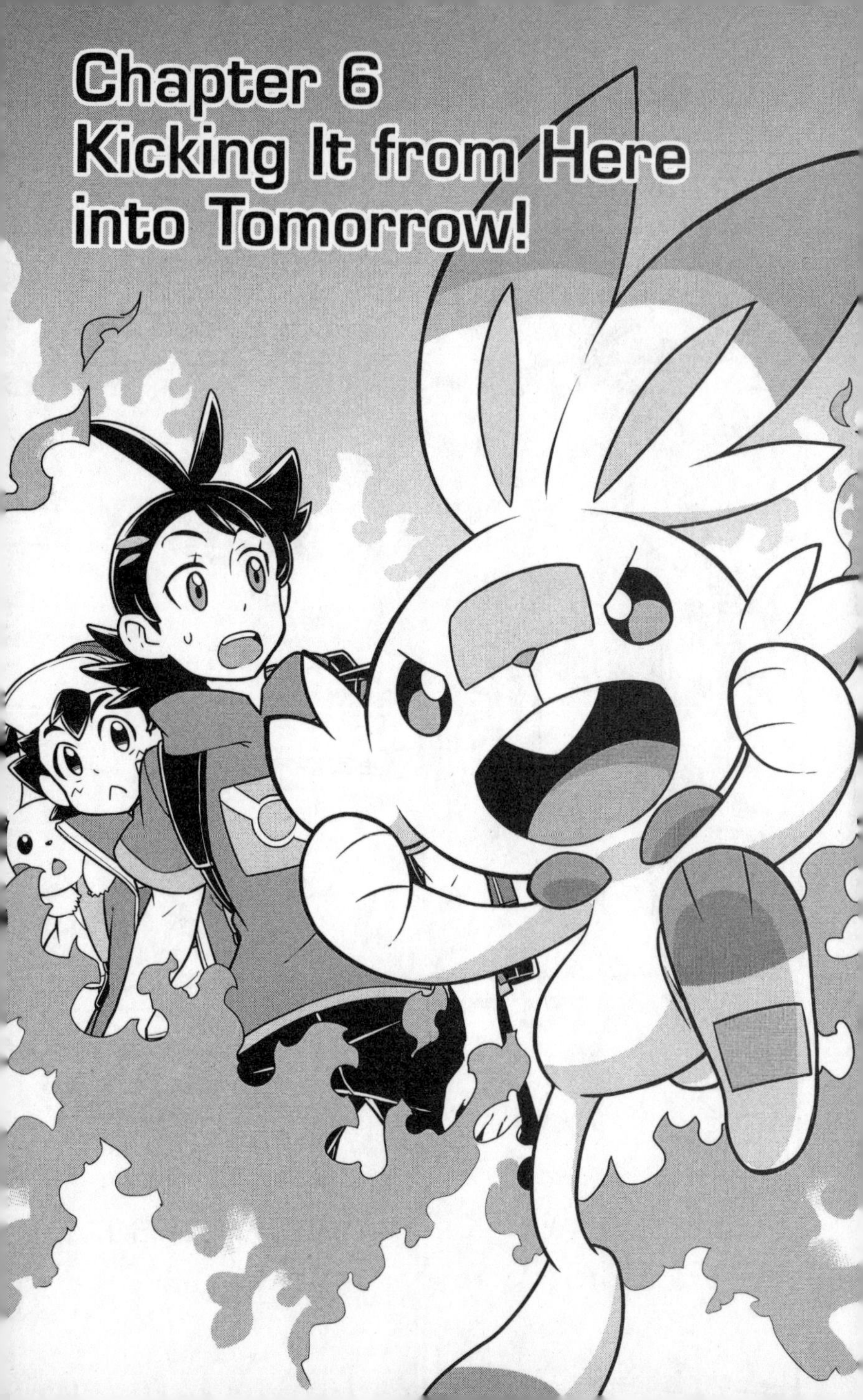

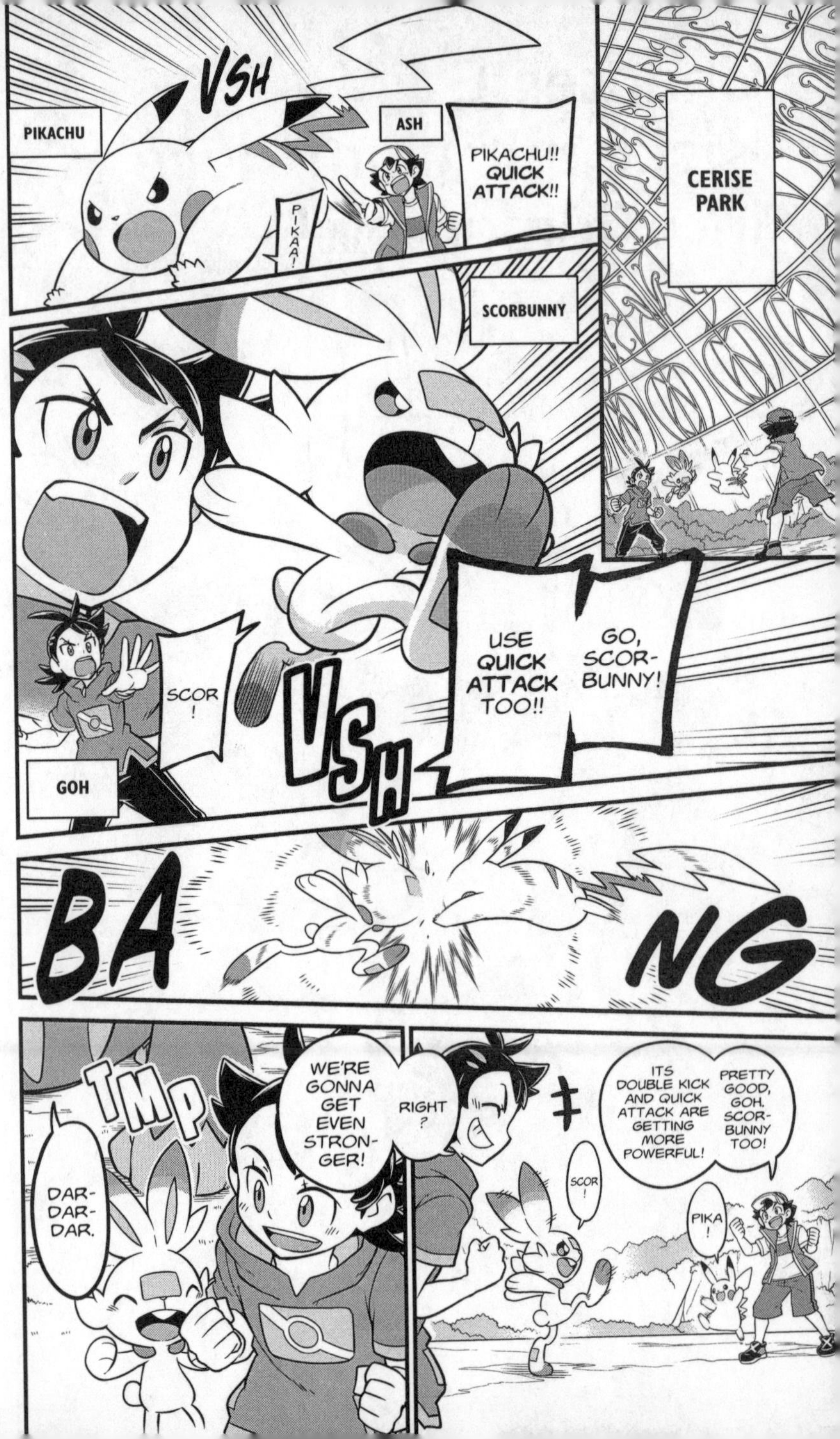
CERISE PARK
PIKACHU!! QUICK ATTACK!!
ASH
PIKAAA!
VSH
PIKACHU
SCORBUNNY
GO, SCOR-BUNNY!
USE QUICK ATTACK TOO!!
VSH
SCOR!
GOH
BANG
PRETTY GOOD, GOH. SCOR-BUNNY TOO!
ITS DOUBLE KICK AND QUICK ATTACK ARE GETTING MORE POWERFUL!
SCOR!
PIKA!
RIGHT?
WE'RE GONNA GET EVEN STRON-GER!
TMP
DAR-DAR-DAR.

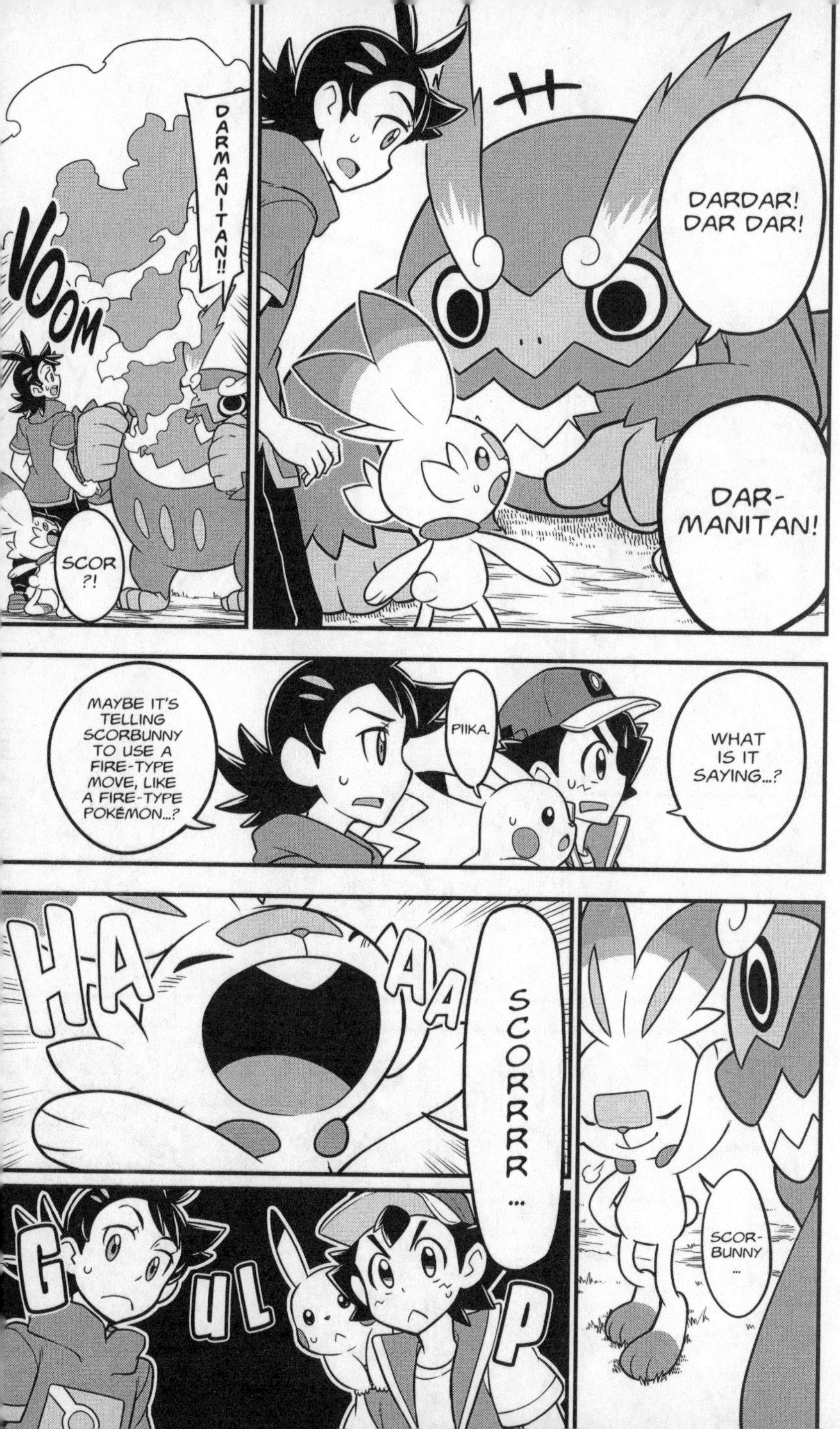
DARDAR! DAR DAR!
DAR-MANITAN!
DARMANITAN!!
VOOM
SCOR ?!
WHAT IS IT SAYING...?
PIIKA.
MAYBE IT'S TELLING SCORBUNNY TO USE A FIRE-TYPE MOVE, LIKE A FIRE-TYPE POKÉMON...?
SCOR-BUNNY ...
HA-AA-
SCORRRR ...
GULP

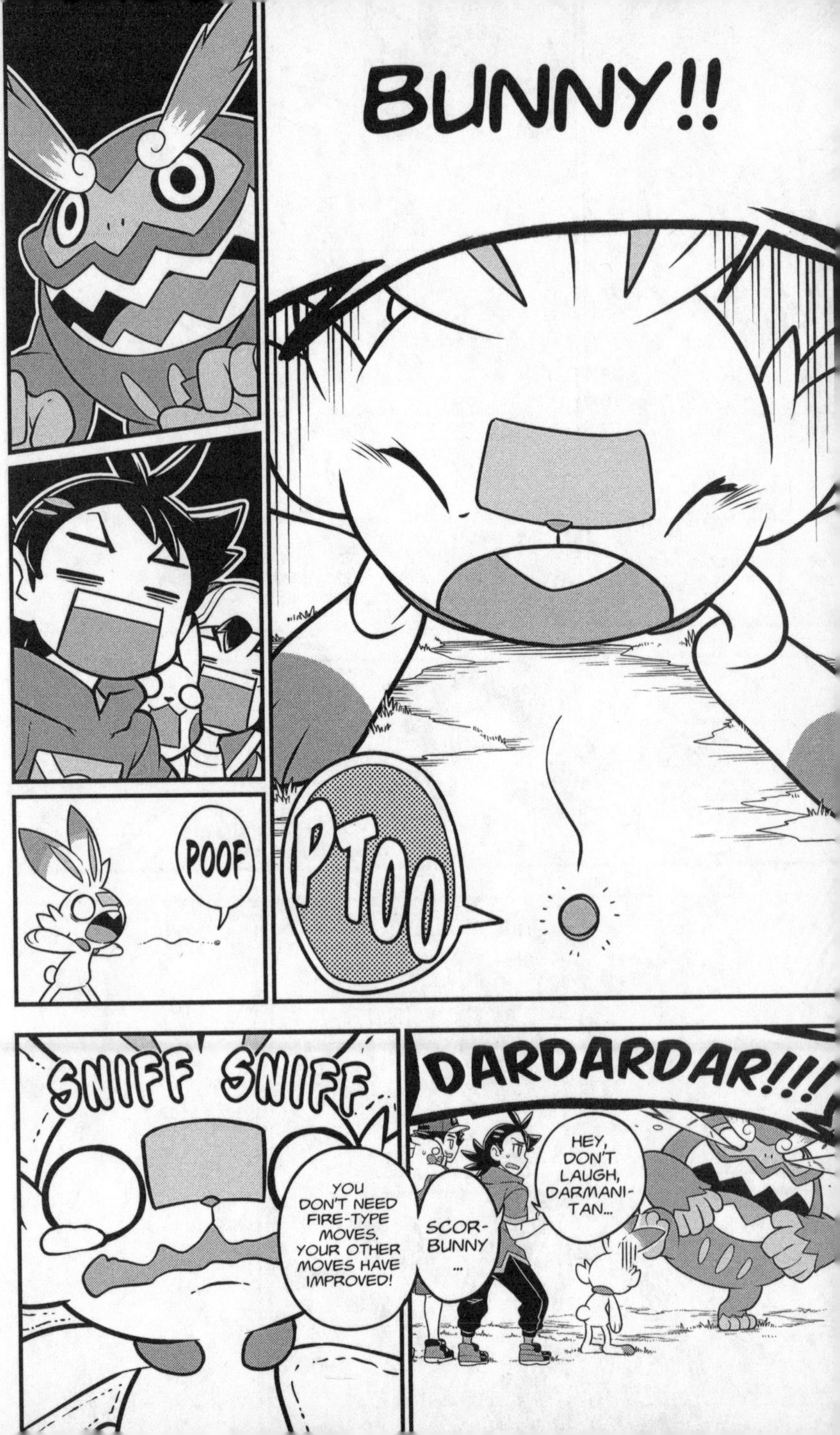

BUNNY!!
PTOO
POOF
DARDARDAR!!!
HEY, DON'T LAUGH, DARMANI-TAN...
SCOR-BUNNY ...
SNIFF SNIFF
YOU DON'T NEED FIRE-TYPE MOVES. YOUR OTHER MOVES HAVE IMPROVED!

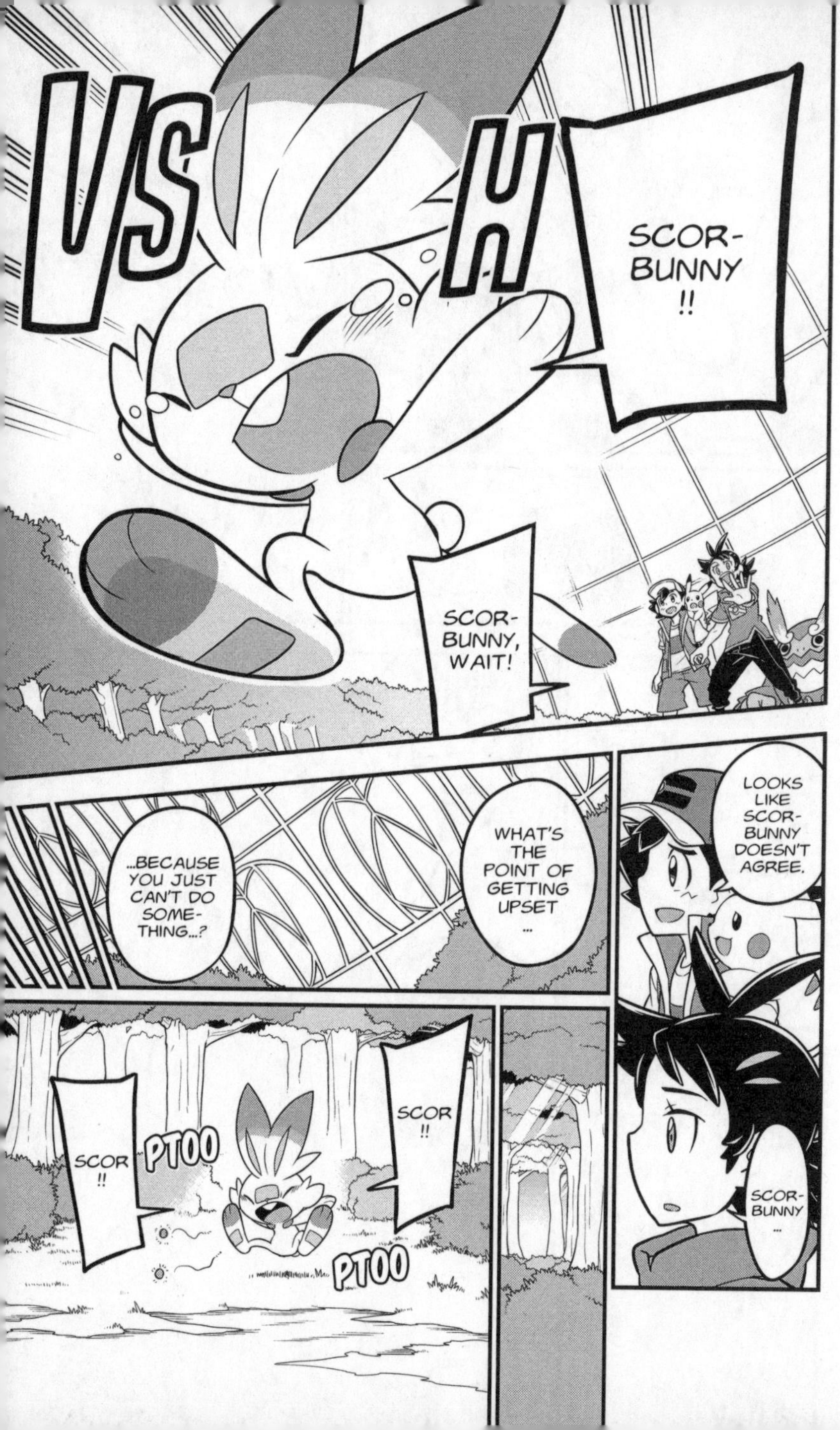
SCOR-BUNNY !!
VSH
SCOR-BUNNY, WAIT!
LOOKS LIKE SCOR-BUNNY DOESN'T AGREE.
SCOR-BUNNY ...
WHAT'S THE POINT OF GETTING UPSET ...
...BECAUSE YOU JUST CAN'T DO SOME-THING...?
SCOR !!
PTOO
SCOR !!
PTOO

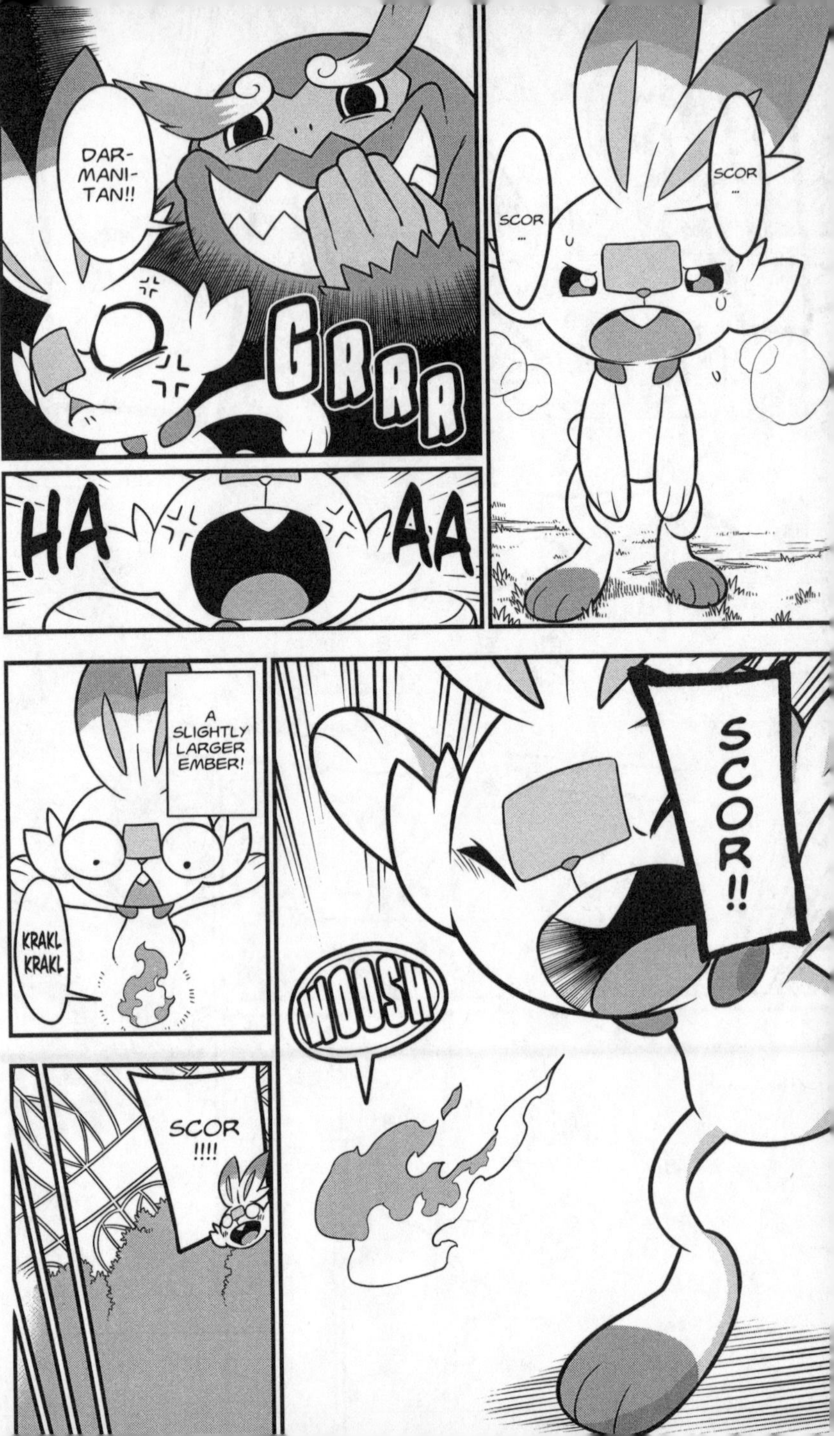
SCOR ...
SCOR ...
DAR-MANI-TAN!!
GRRRR
HAAA
SCOR!!
WOOSH
A SLIGHTLY LARGER EMBER!
KRAKL KRAKL
SCOR !!!!

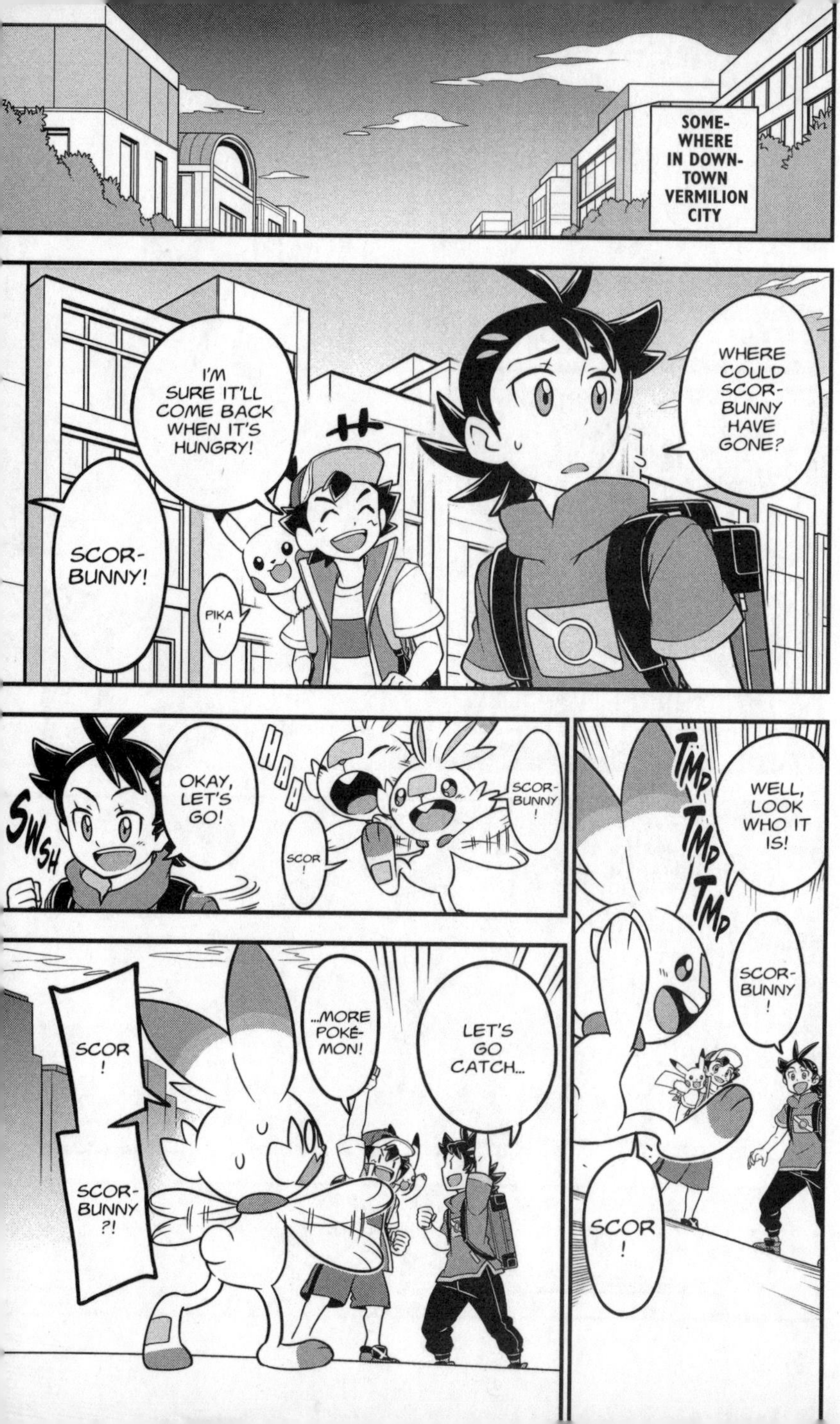
SOME-WHERE IN DOWN-TOWN VERMILION CITY
WHERE COULD SCOR-BUNNY HAVE GONE?
I'M SURE IT'LL COME BACK WHEN IT'S HUNGRY!
SCOR-BUNNY!
PIKA!
TMP TMP TMP TMP
WELL, LOOK WHO IT IS!
SCOR-BUNNY!
SCOR!
SCOR-BUNNY!
HAA
OKAY, LET'S GO!
SCOR!
SWSH
LET'S GO CATCH...
...MORE POKÉ-MON!
SCOR!
SCOR-BUNNY?!

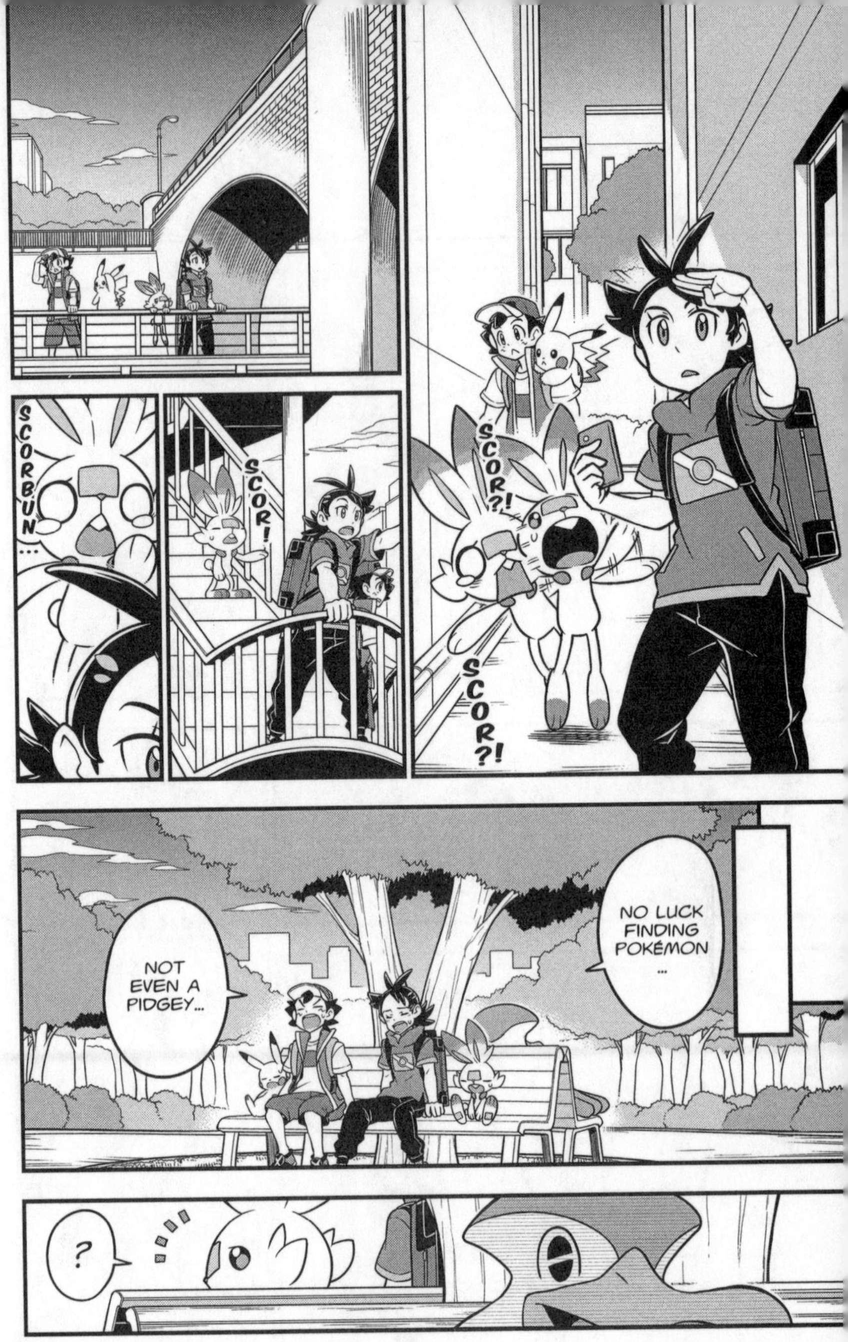
SCOR?!
SCOR?!
SCOR!
SCORBUN...
NO LUCK FINDING POKÉMON...
NOT EVEN A PIDGEY...
?

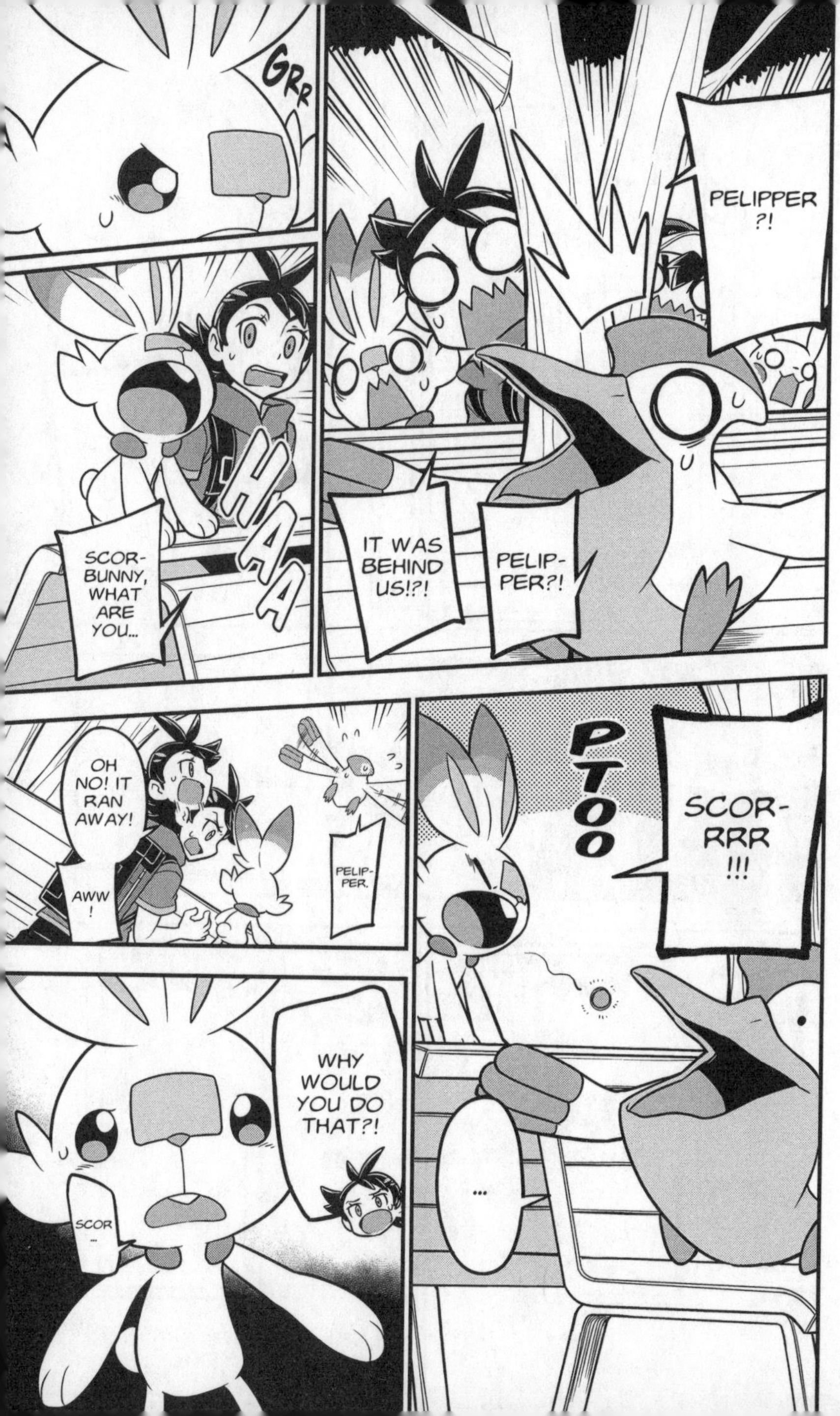

PELIPPER ?!
PELIP-PER?!
IT WAS BEHIND US!?!
GRR
SCOR-BUNNY, WHAT ARE YOU...
HAA
SCOR-RRR !!!
PTOO
...
PELIP-PER.
OH NO! IT RAN AWAY!
AWW !
WHY WOULD YOU DO THAT?!
SCOR ...

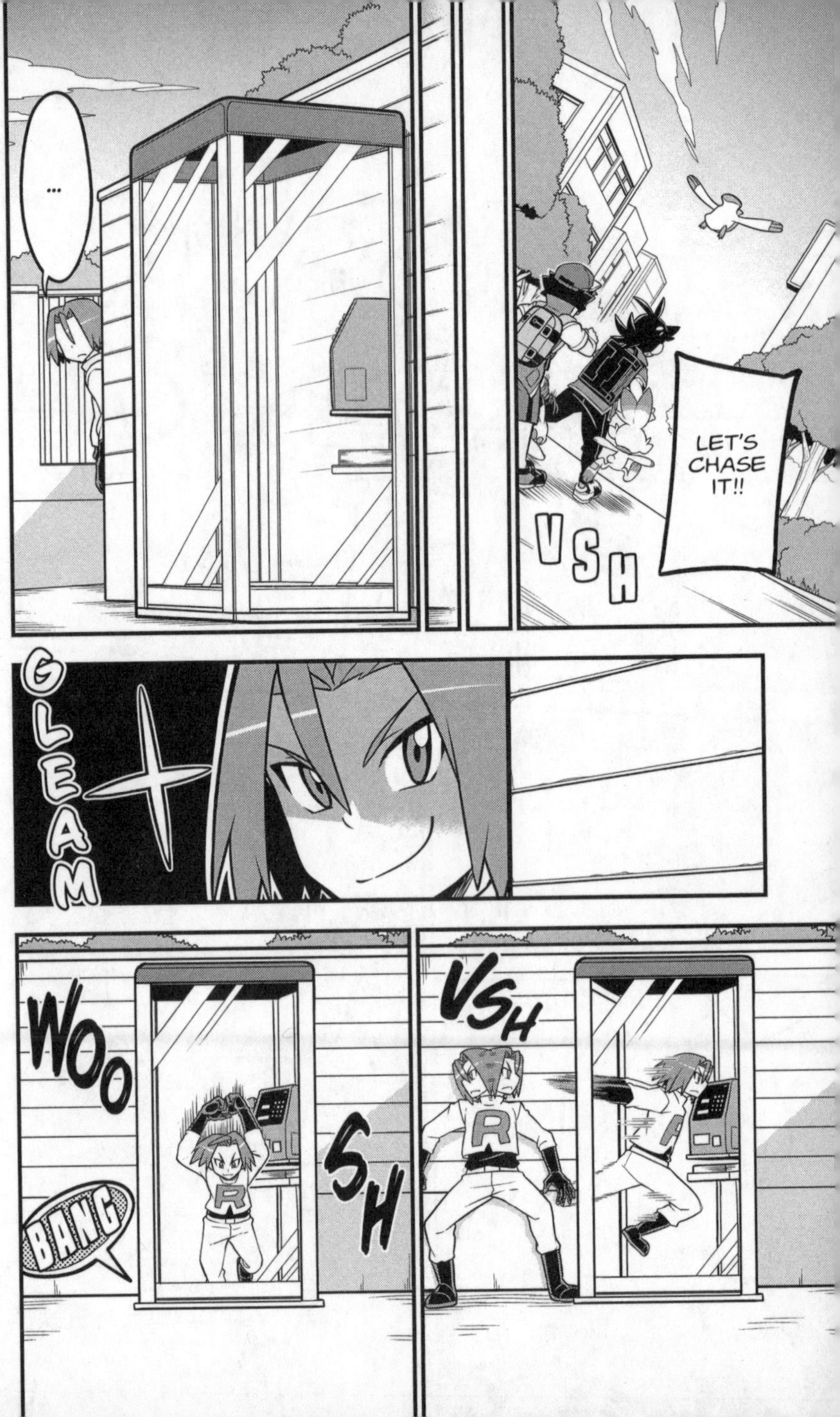

LET'S CHASE IT!!
VSH
...
GLEAM
VSH
WOOSH
BANG

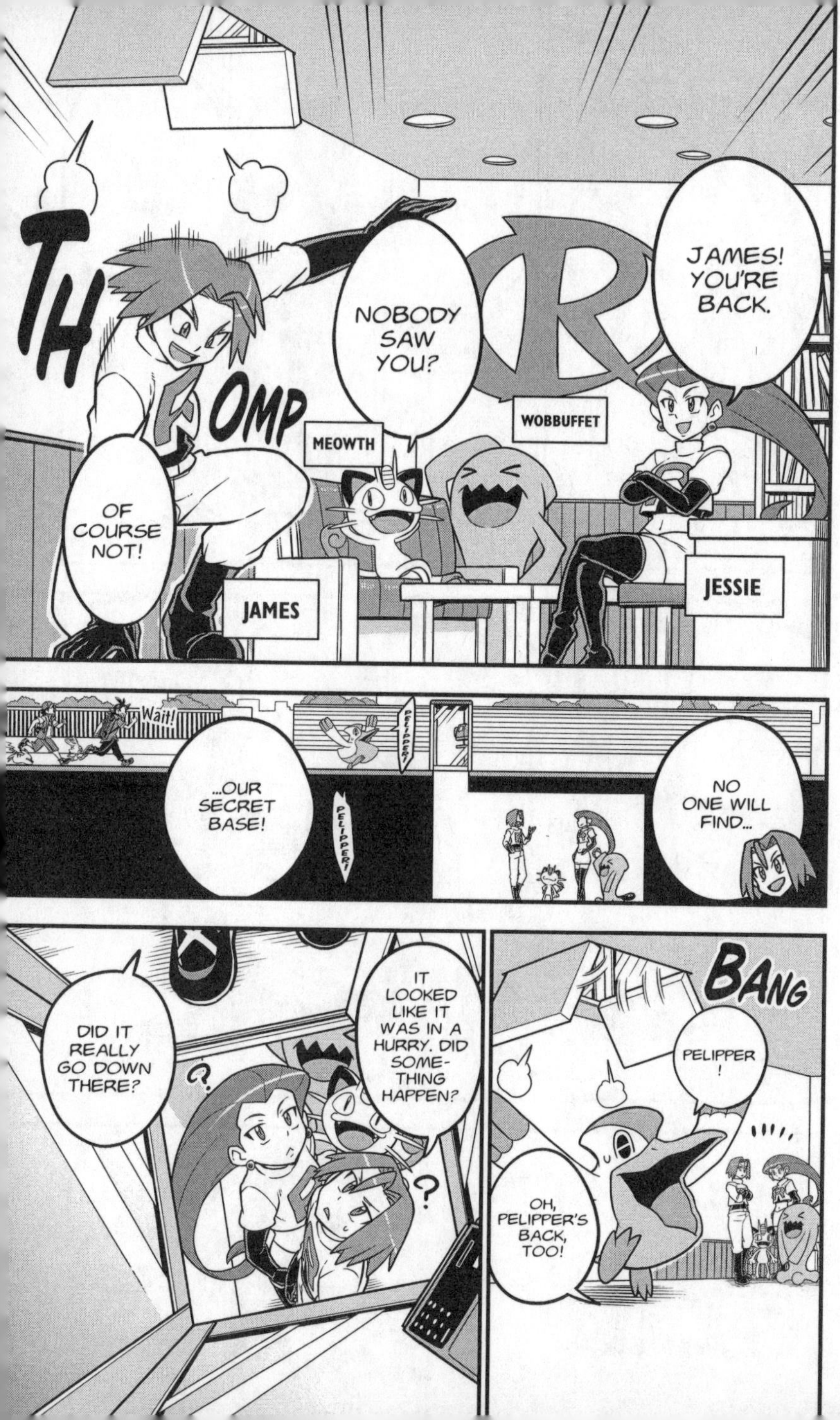
JAMES! YOU'RE BACK.
WOBBUFFET
NOBODY SAW YOU?
MEOWTH
THOMP
OF COURSE NOT!
JESSIE
JAMES
NO ONE WILL FIND...
PELIPPER!
PELIPPER!
...OUR SECRET BASE!
Wait!
BANG
PELIPPER!
OH, PELIPPER'S BACK, TOO!
IT LOOKED LIKE IT WAS IN A HURRY. DID SOME-THING HAPPEN?
DID IT REALLY GO DOWN THERE?

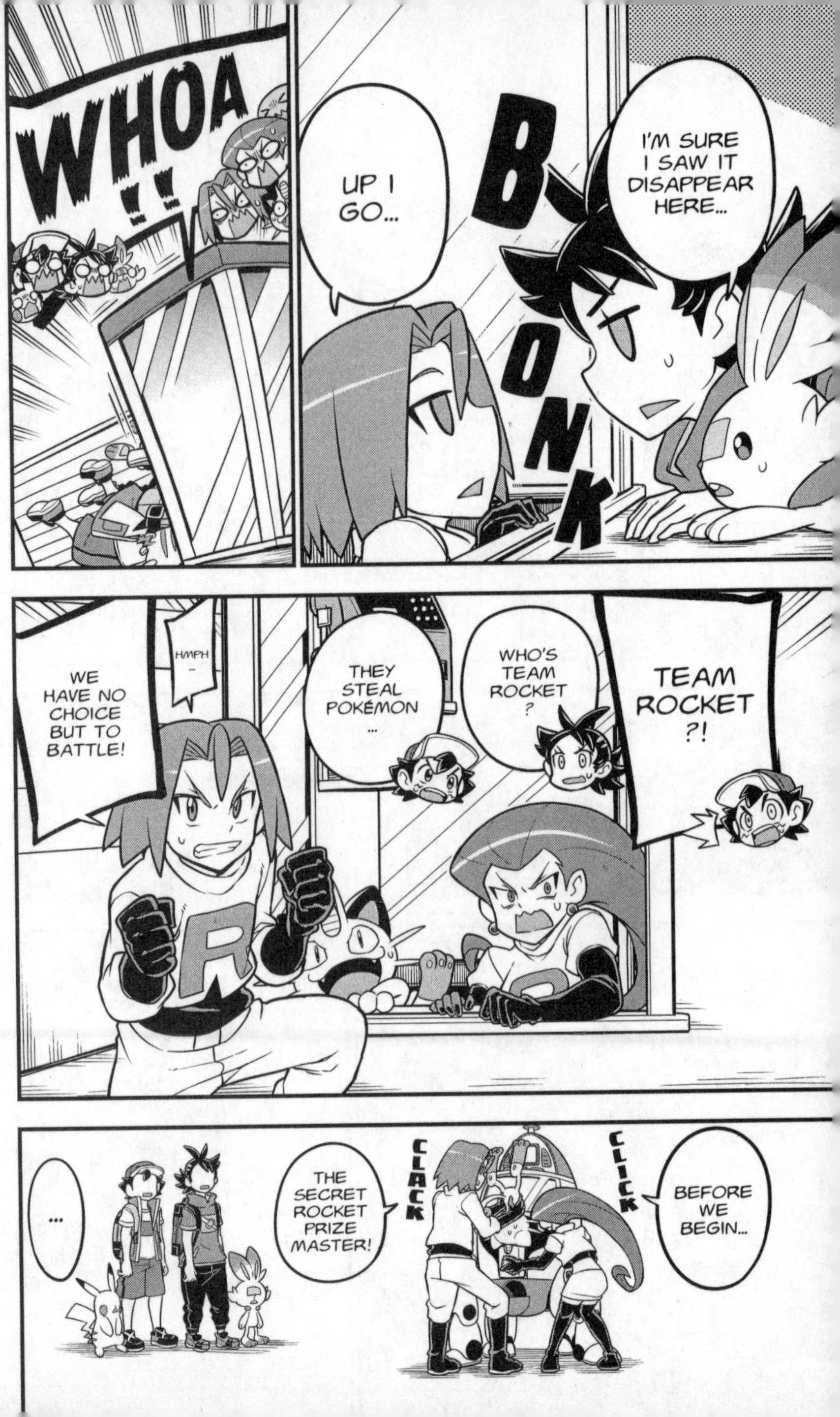
I'M SURE I SAW IT DISAPPEAR HERE...
BONK
UP I GO...
WHOA!!
TEAM ROCKET?!
WHO'S TEAM ROCKET?
THEY STEAL POKÉMON...
HMPH...
WE HAVE NO CHOICE BUT TO BATTLE!
BEFORE WE BEGIN...
CLICK
CLACK
THE SECRET ROCKET PRIZE MASTER!
...

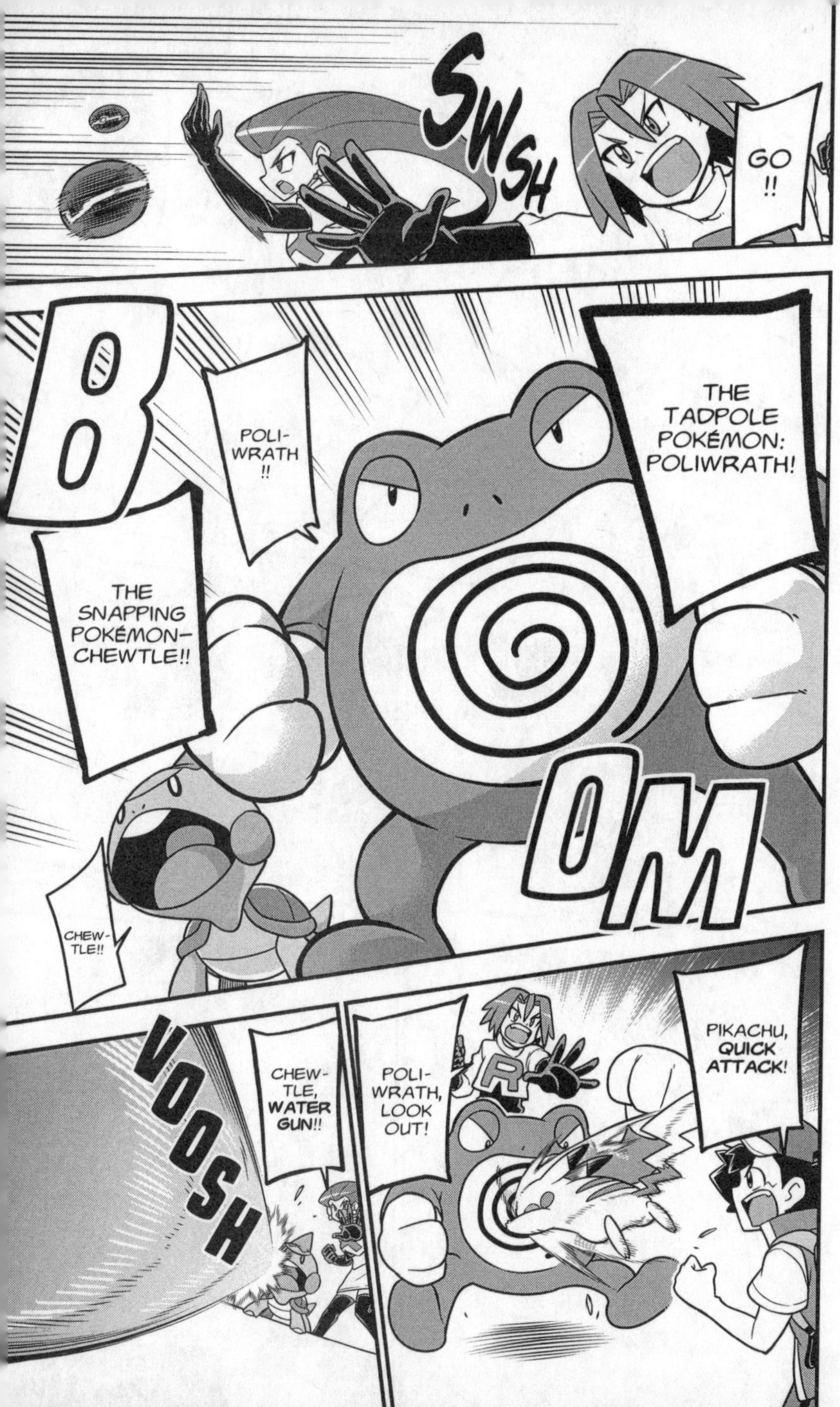
GO!!
SWSH
THE TADPOLE POKÉMON: POLIWRATH!
POLI-WRATH!!
BO
OM
THE SNAPPING POKÉMON— CHEWTLE!!
CHEW-TLE!!
PIKACHU, QUICK ATTACK!
POLI-WRATH, LOOK OUT!
CHEW-TLE, WATER GUN!!
VOOSH

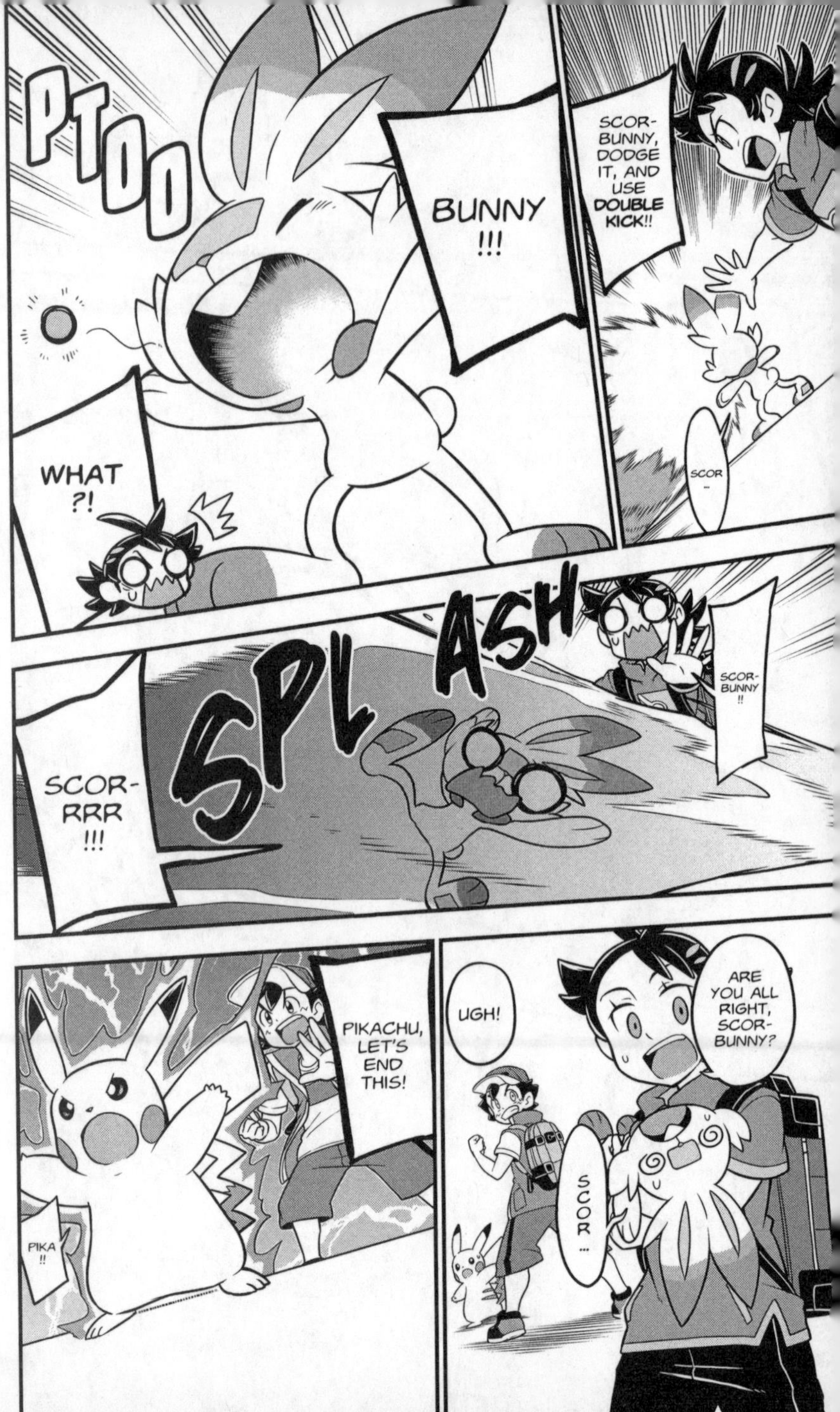

SCOR-BUNNY, DODGE IT, AND USE **DOUBLE KICK**!!
SCOR...
BUNNY!!!
PTOO
WHAT?!
SCOR-BUNNY!!
SPLASH
SCOR-RRR!!!
ARE YOU ALL RIGHT, SCOR-BUNNY?
UGH!
SCOR...
PIKACHU, LET'S END THIS!
PIKA!!

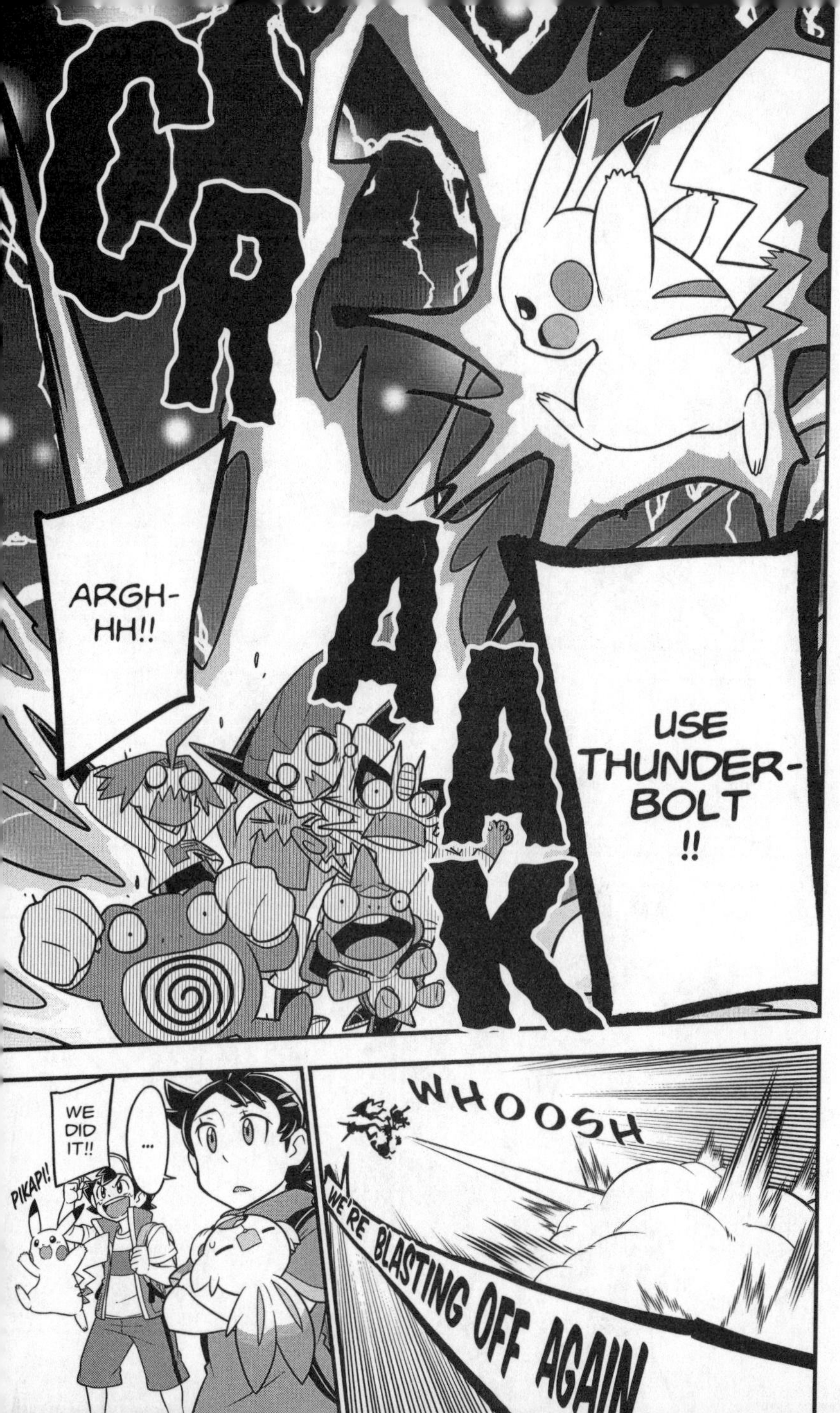
USE THUNDER-BOLT!!
CRAAAK
ARGH-HH!!
WHOOSH
WE'RE BLASTING OFF AGAIN
...
WE DID IT!!
PIKAPI!

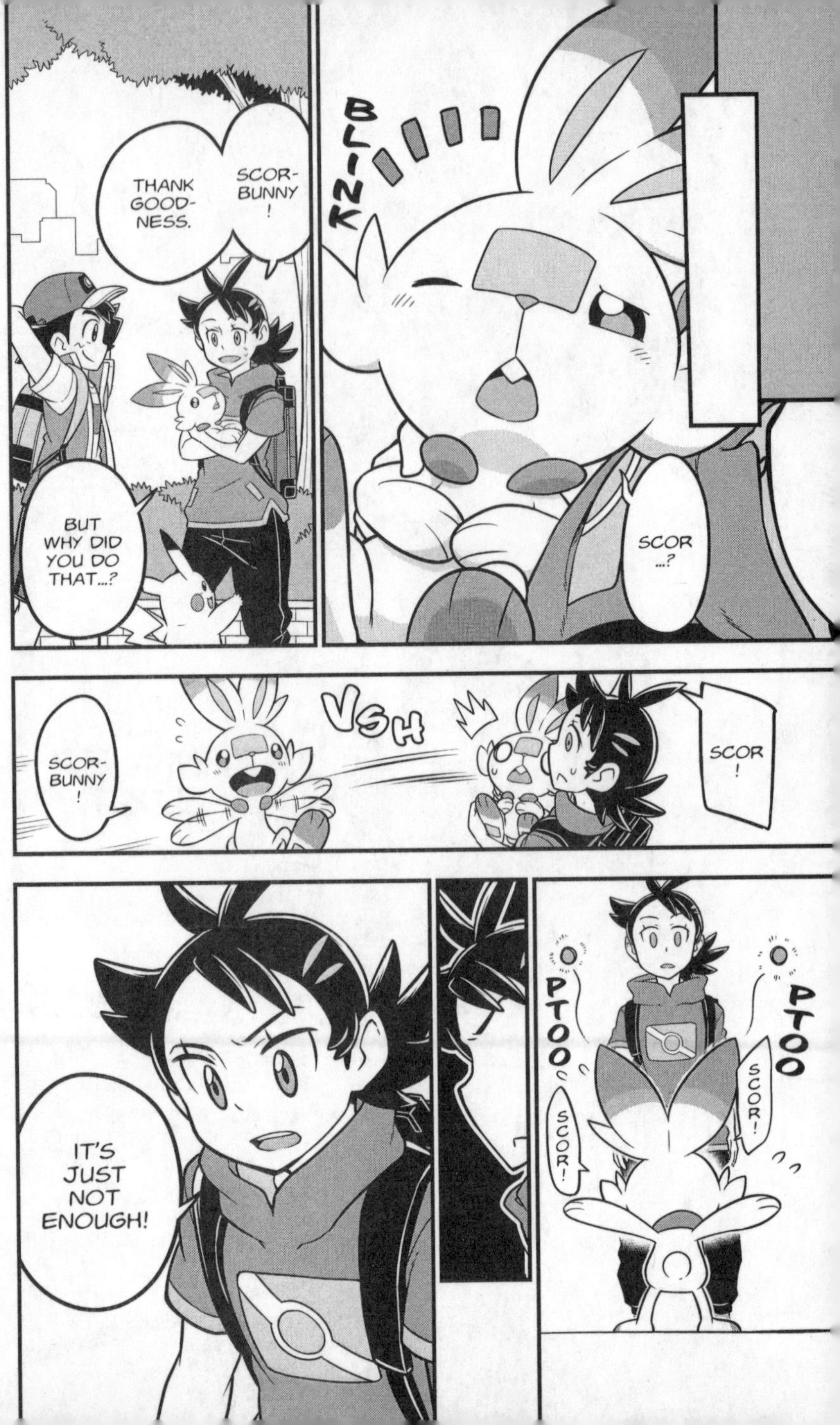
BLINK
SCOR ...?
SCOR-BUNNY!
THANK GOODNESS.
BUT WHY DID YOU DO THAT...?
SCOR!
VSH
SCOR-BUNNY!
PTOO
SCOR!
PTOO
SCOR!
IT'S JUST NOT ENOUGH!

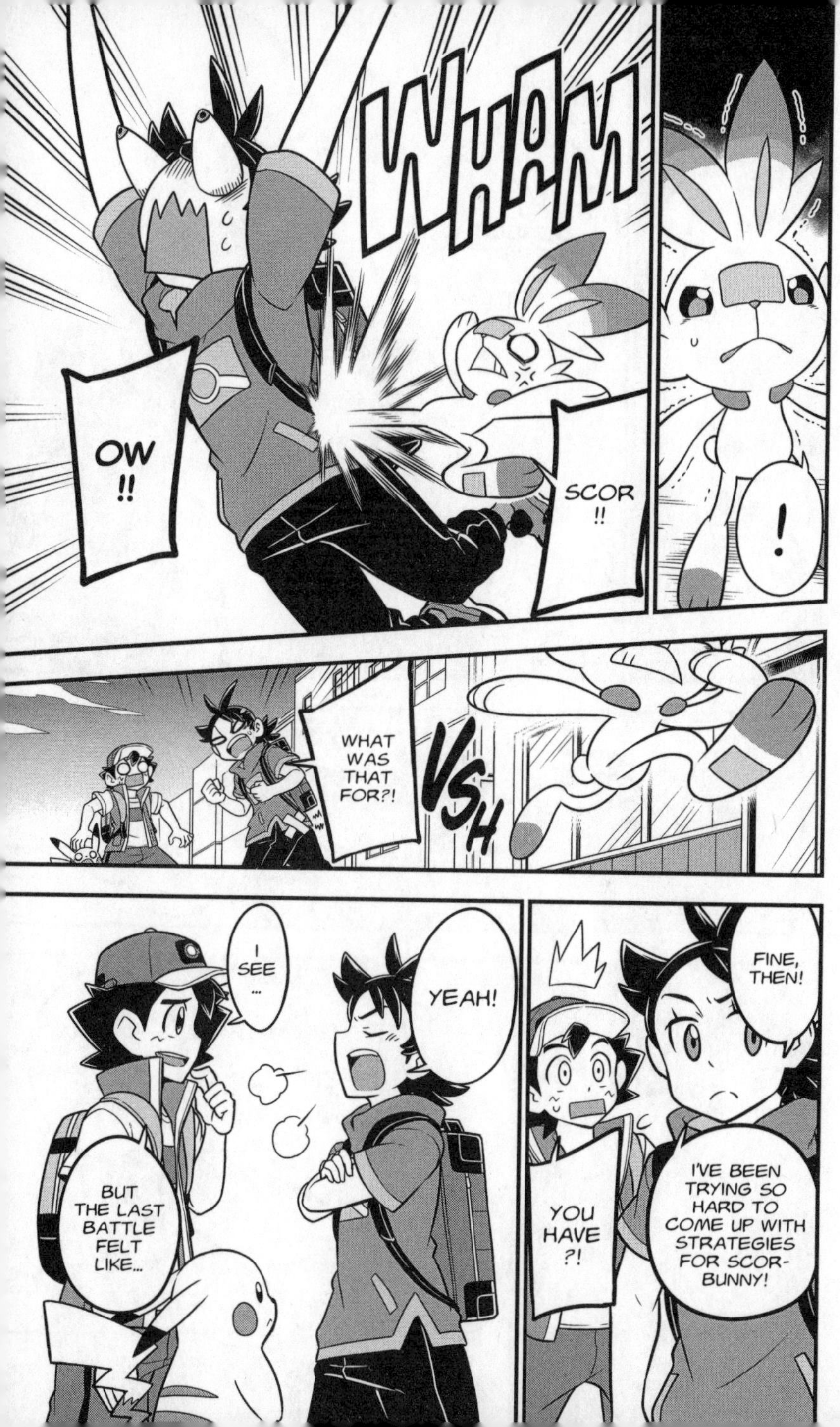
!
WHAM
SCOR !!
OW !!
VSH
WHAT WAS THAT FOR?!
FINE, THEN!
I'VE BEEN TRYING SO HARD TO COME UP WITH STRATEGIES FOR SCOR-BUNNY!
YOU HAVE ?!
YEAH!
I SEE ...
BUT THE LAST BATTLE FELT LIKE...

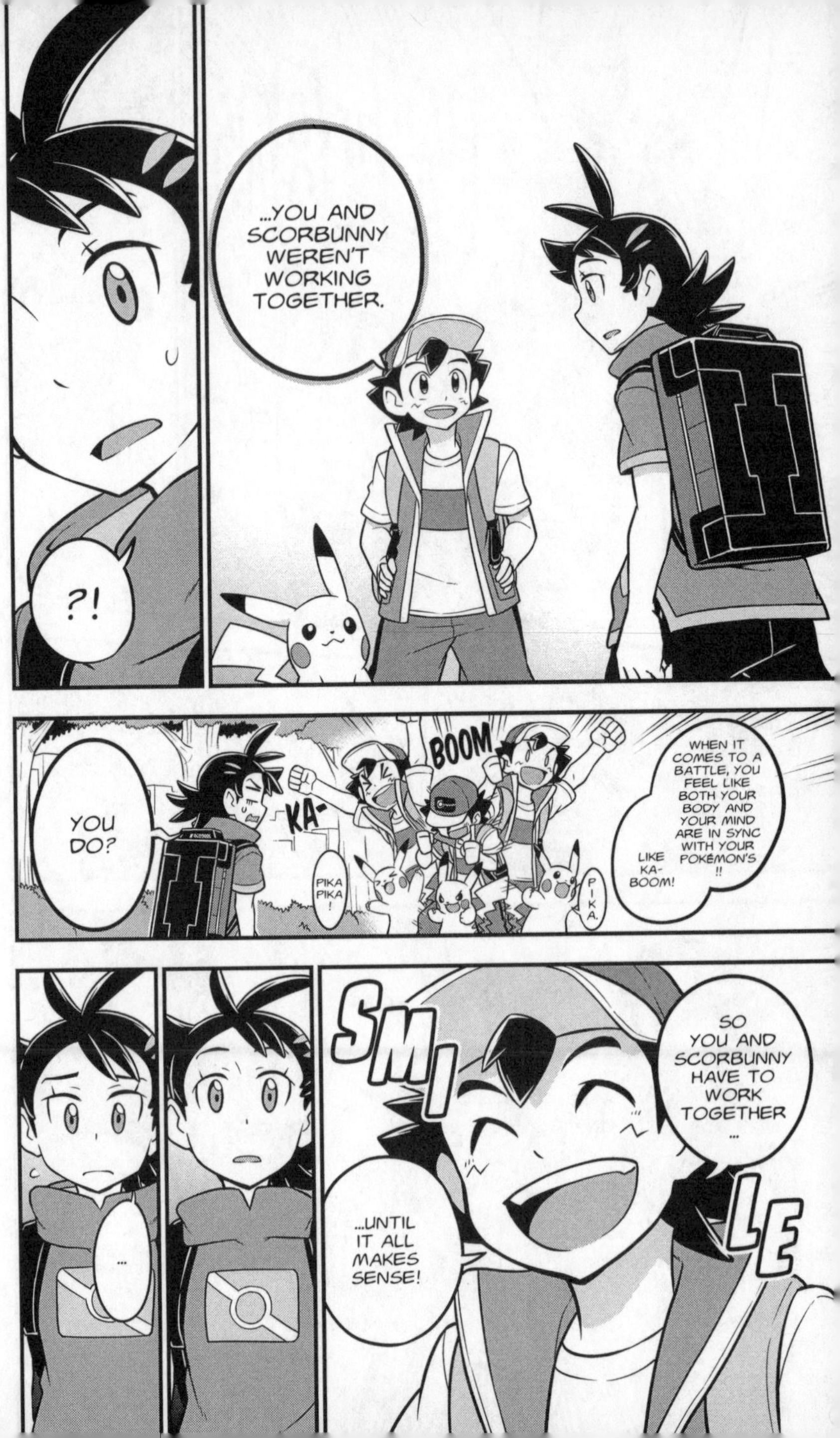
...YOU AND SCORBUNNY WEREN'T WORKING TOGETHER.
?!
WHEN IT COMES TO A BATTLE, YOU FEEL LIKE BOTH YOUR BODY AND YOUR MIND ARE IN SYNC WITH YOUR POKÉMON'S!!
LIKE KA-BOOM!
BOOM
PIKA.
KA-
PIKA PIKA!
YOU DO?
SMILE
SO YOU AND SCORBUNNY HAVE TO WORK TOGETHER...
...UNTIL IT ALL MAKES SENSE!
...

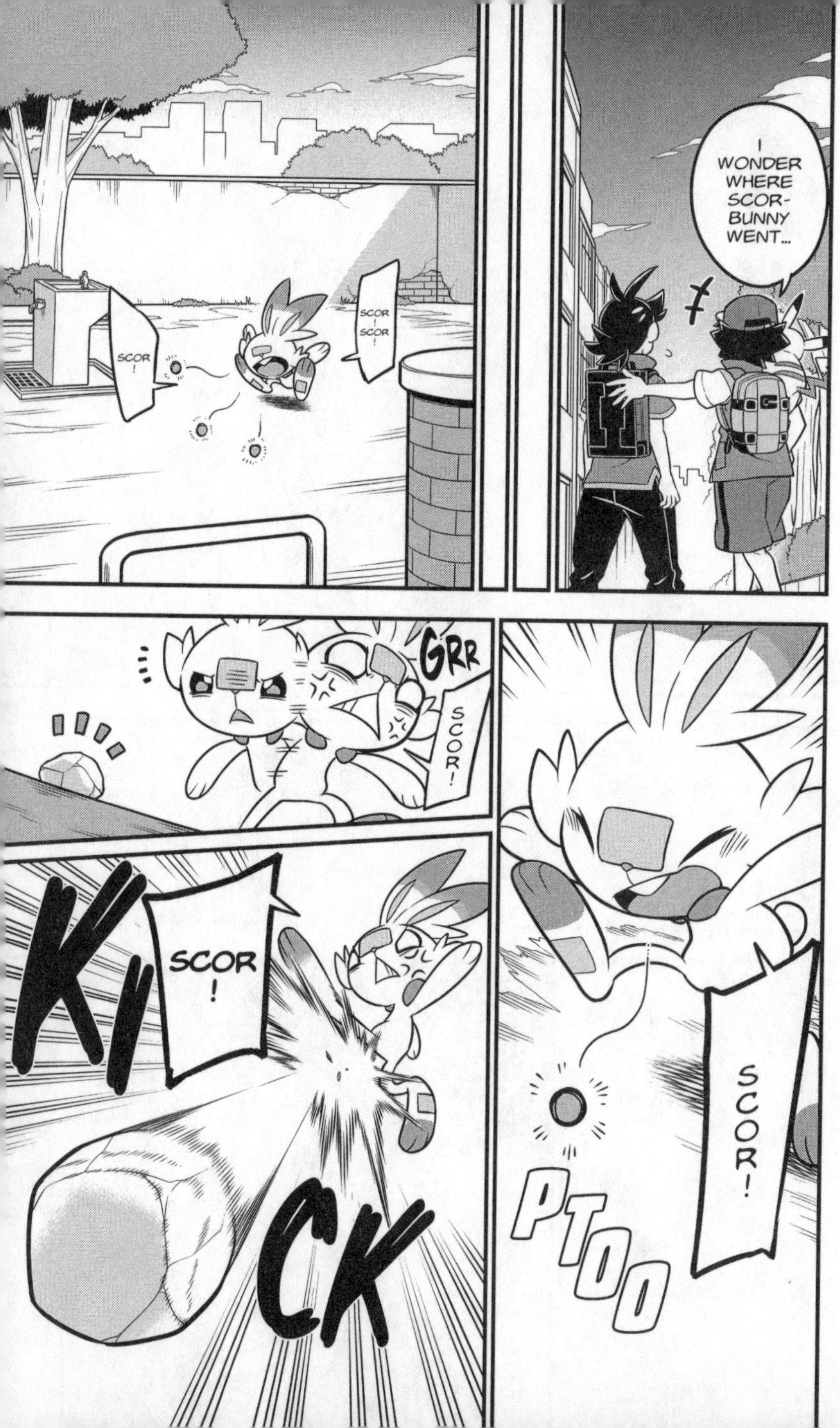
I WONDER WHERE SCORBUNNY WENT...
SCOR! SCOR!
SCOR!
SCOR!
PTOO
GRR
SCOR!
SCOR!
KICK

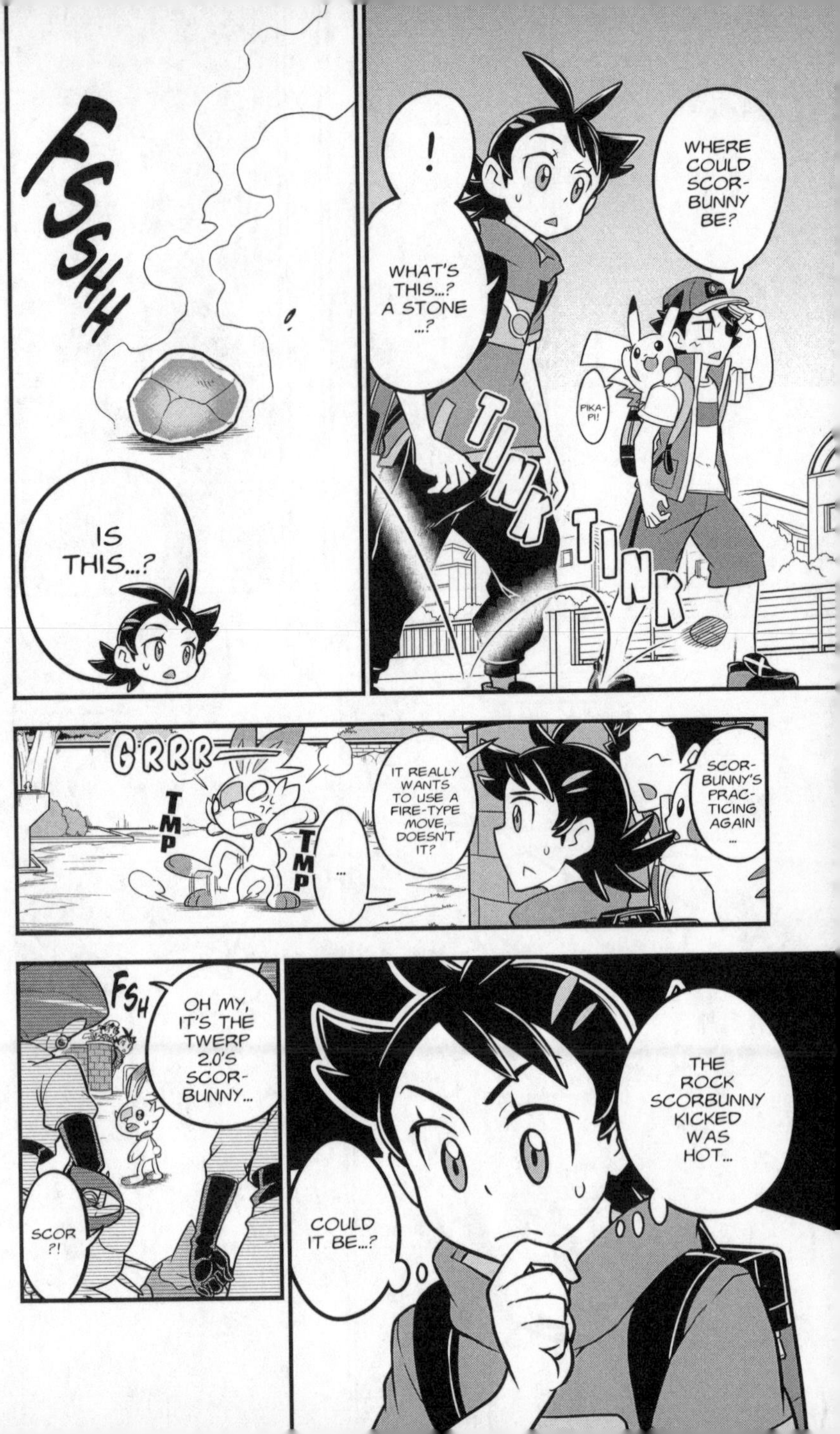
WHERE COULD SCOR-BUNNY BE?
PIKA-PI!
!
WHAT'S THIS...? A STONE ...?
TINK
TINK
FSSHH
IS THIS...?
SCOR-BUNNY'S PRAC-TICING AGAIN ...
IT REALLY WANTS TO USE A FIRE-TYPE MOVE, DOESN'T IT?
...
GRRR
TMP
TMP
THE ROCK SCORBUNNY KICKED WAS HOT...
COULD IT BE...?
FSH
OH MY, IT'S THE TWERP 2.0'S SCOR-BUNNY...
SCOR ?!

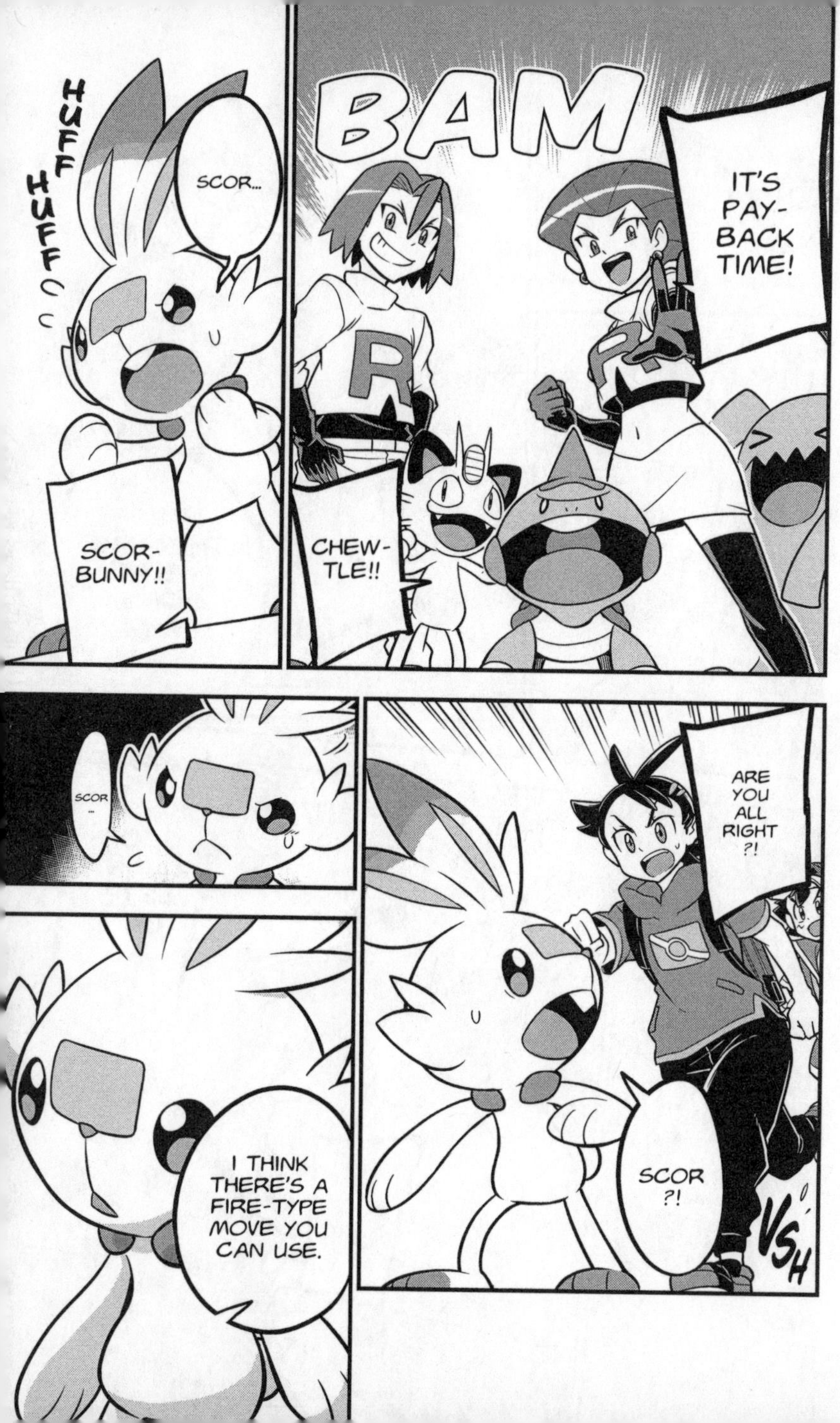

IT'S PAY-BACK TIME!
BAM
CHEW-TLE!!
HUFF HUFF
SCOR...
SCOR-BUNNY!!
ARE YOU ALL RIGHT ?!
SCOR ?!
VSH
SCOR ...
I THINK THERE'S A FIRE-TYPE MOVE YOU CAN USE.

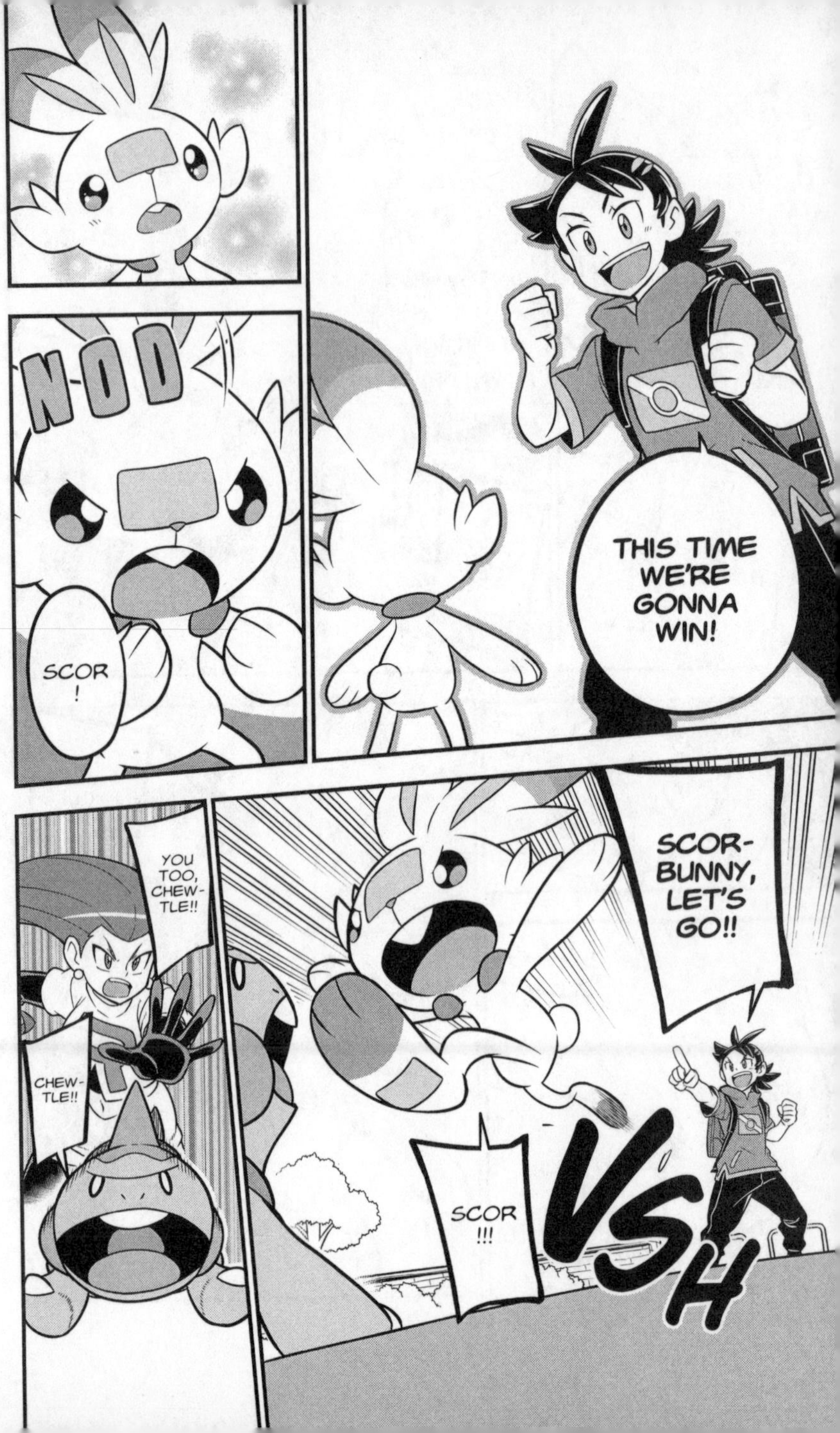
THIS TIME WE'RE GONNA WIN!
NOD
SCOR!
SCOR-BUNNY, LET'S GO!!
SCOR!!!
VSH
YOU TOO, CHEW-TLE!!
CHEW-TLE!!

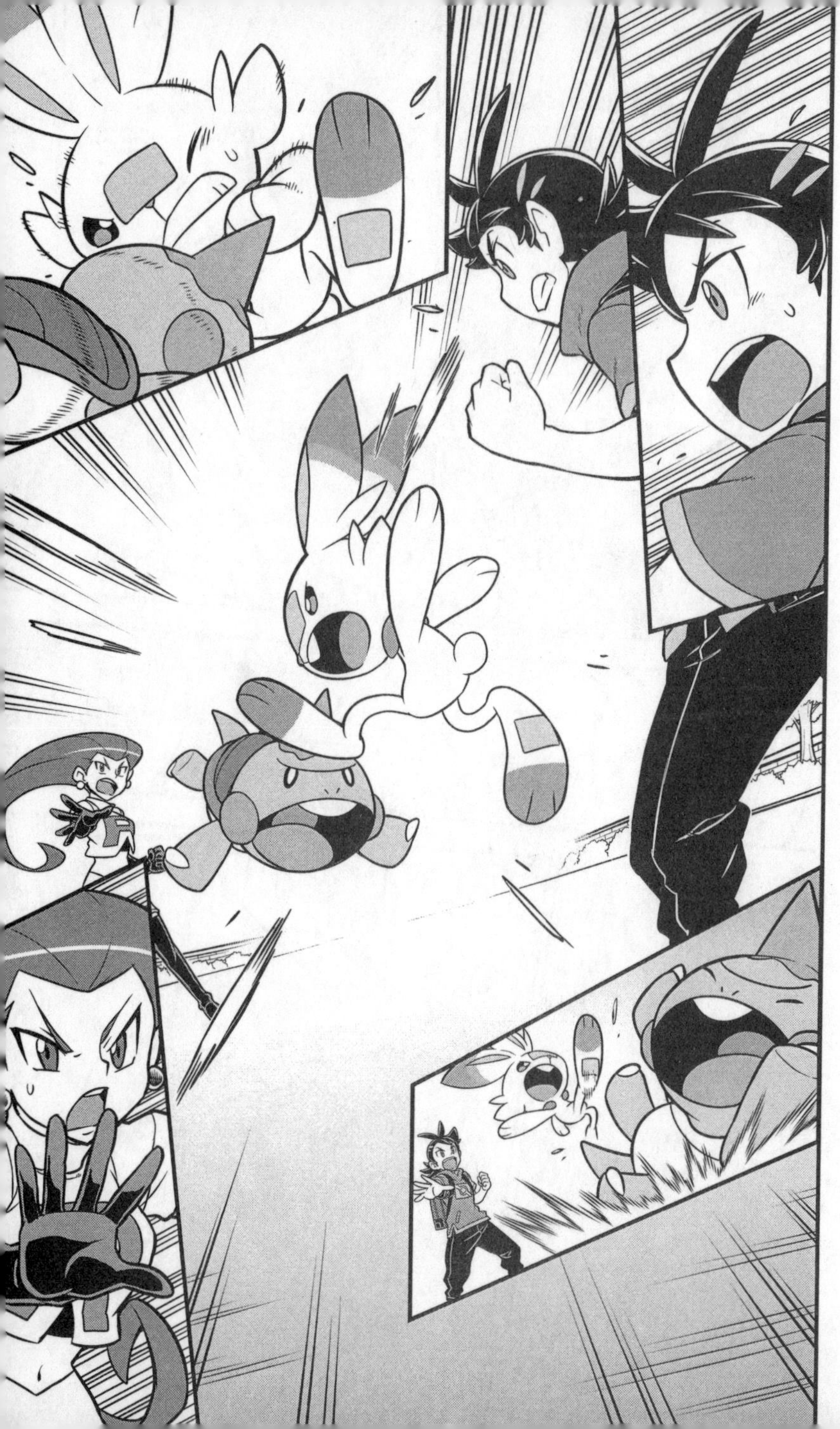

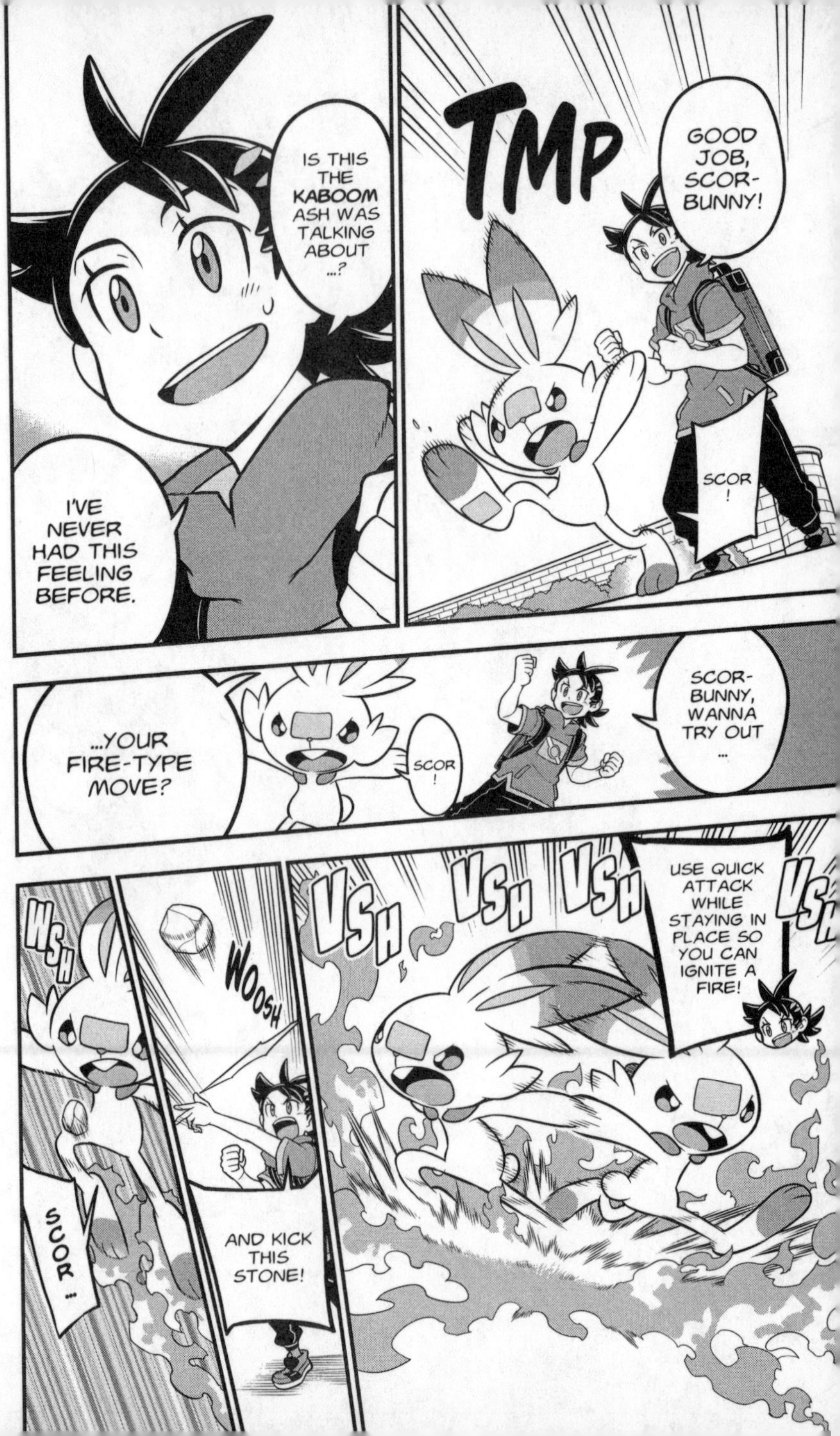
TMP
GOOD JOB, SCOR-BUNNY!
SCOR!
IS THIS THE KABOOM ASH WAS TALKING ABOUT ...?
I'VE NEVER HAD THIS FEELING BEFORE.
SCOR-BUNNY, WANNA TRY OUT ...
SCOR!
...YOUR FIRE-TYPE MOVE?
VSH
VSH
VSH
VSH
USE QUICK ATTACK WHILE STAYING IN PLACE SO YOU CAN IGNITE A FIRE!
WOOSH
AND KICK THIS STONE!
WSH
SCOR ...

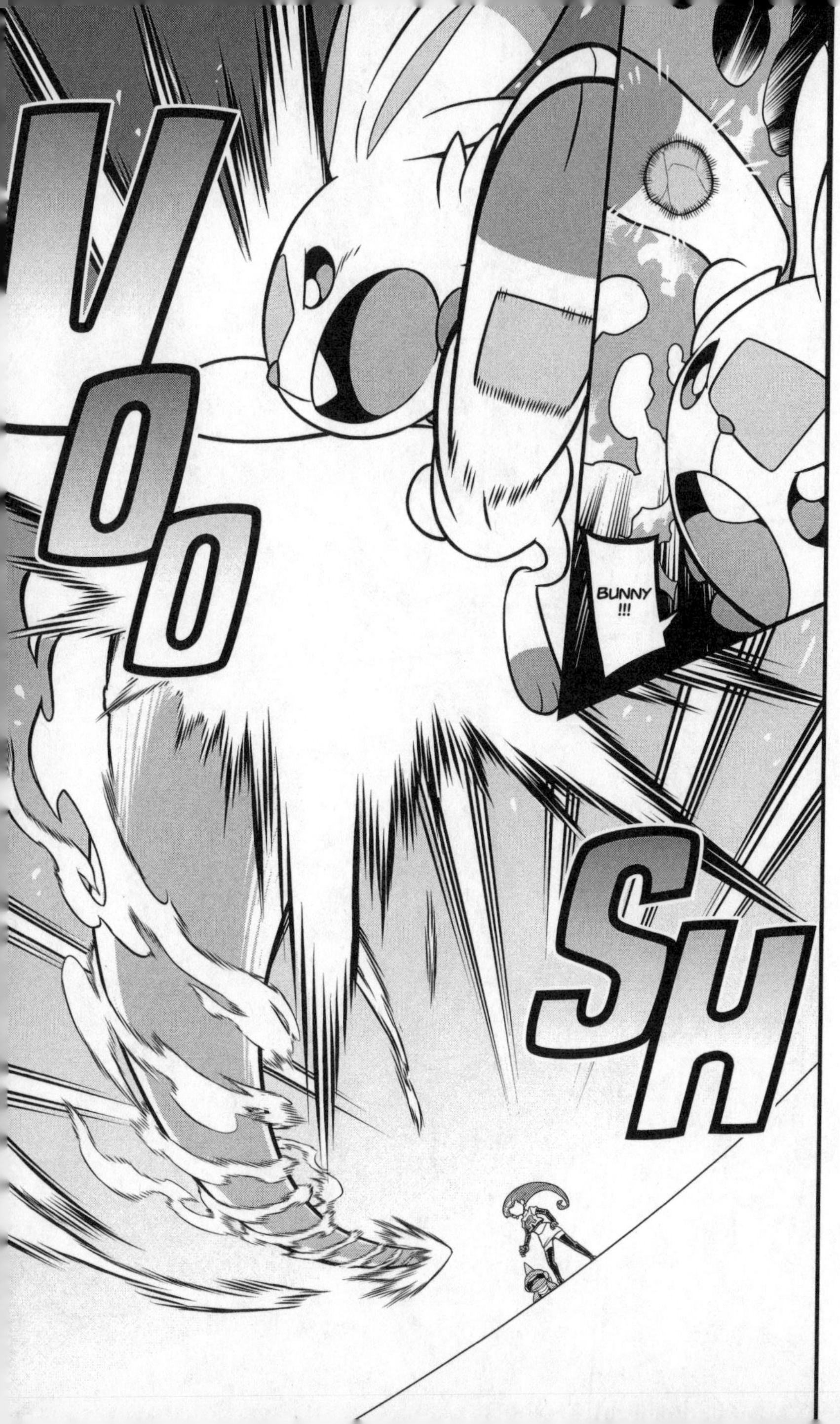
BUNNY
!!!
VOOO
SH

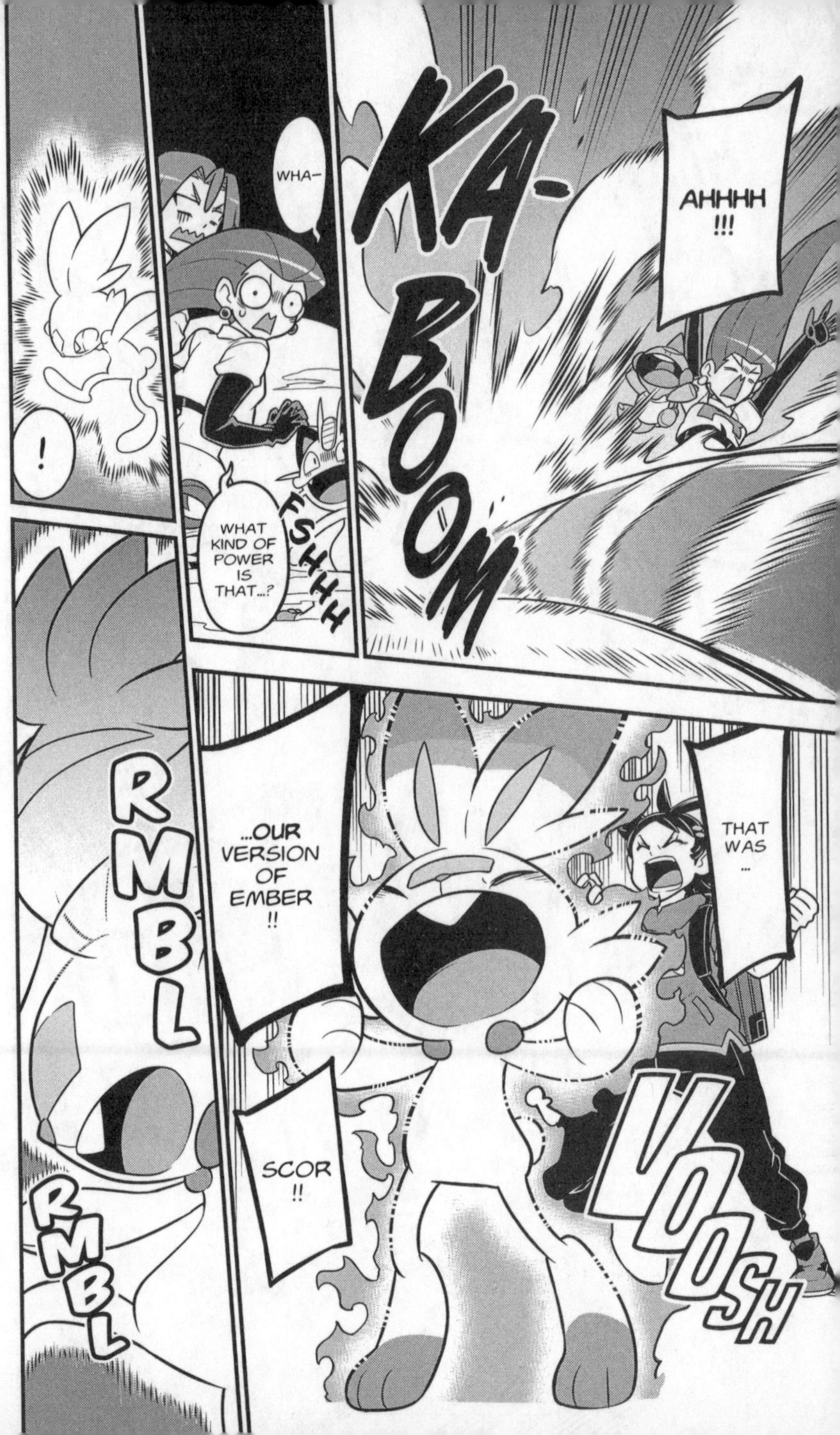
AHHHH!!!
KA-BOOOM
WHA-
WHAT KIND OF POWER IS THAT...?
FSHHH
!
THAT WAS...
...OUR VERSION OF EMBER!!
SCOR!!
VOOSH
RMBL
RMBL

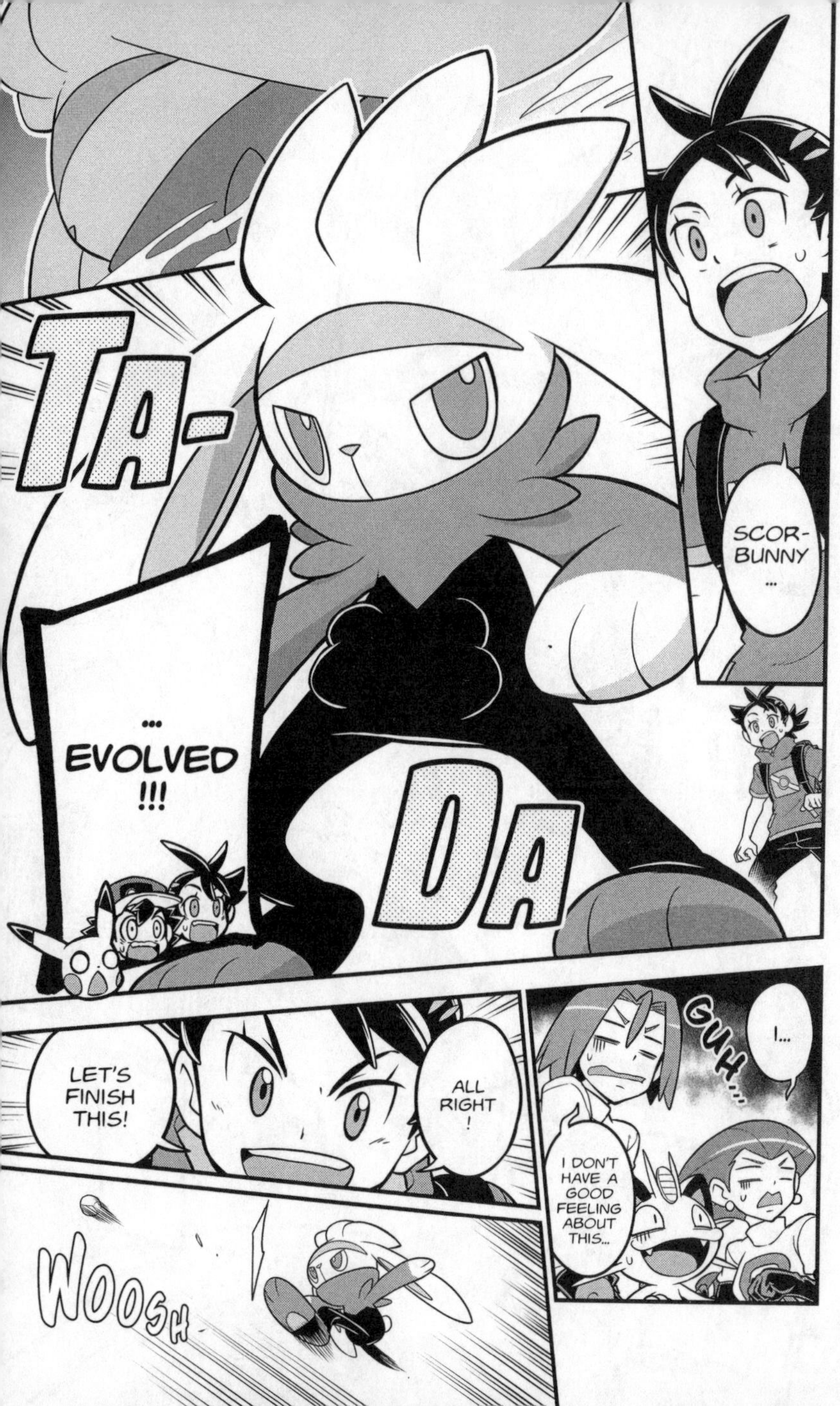
SCOR-BUNNY...
TA-
...EVOLVED!!!
DA
GUH...
I...
I DON'T HAVE A GOOD FEELING ABOUT THIS...
ALL RIGHT!
LET'S FINISH THIS!
WOOSH

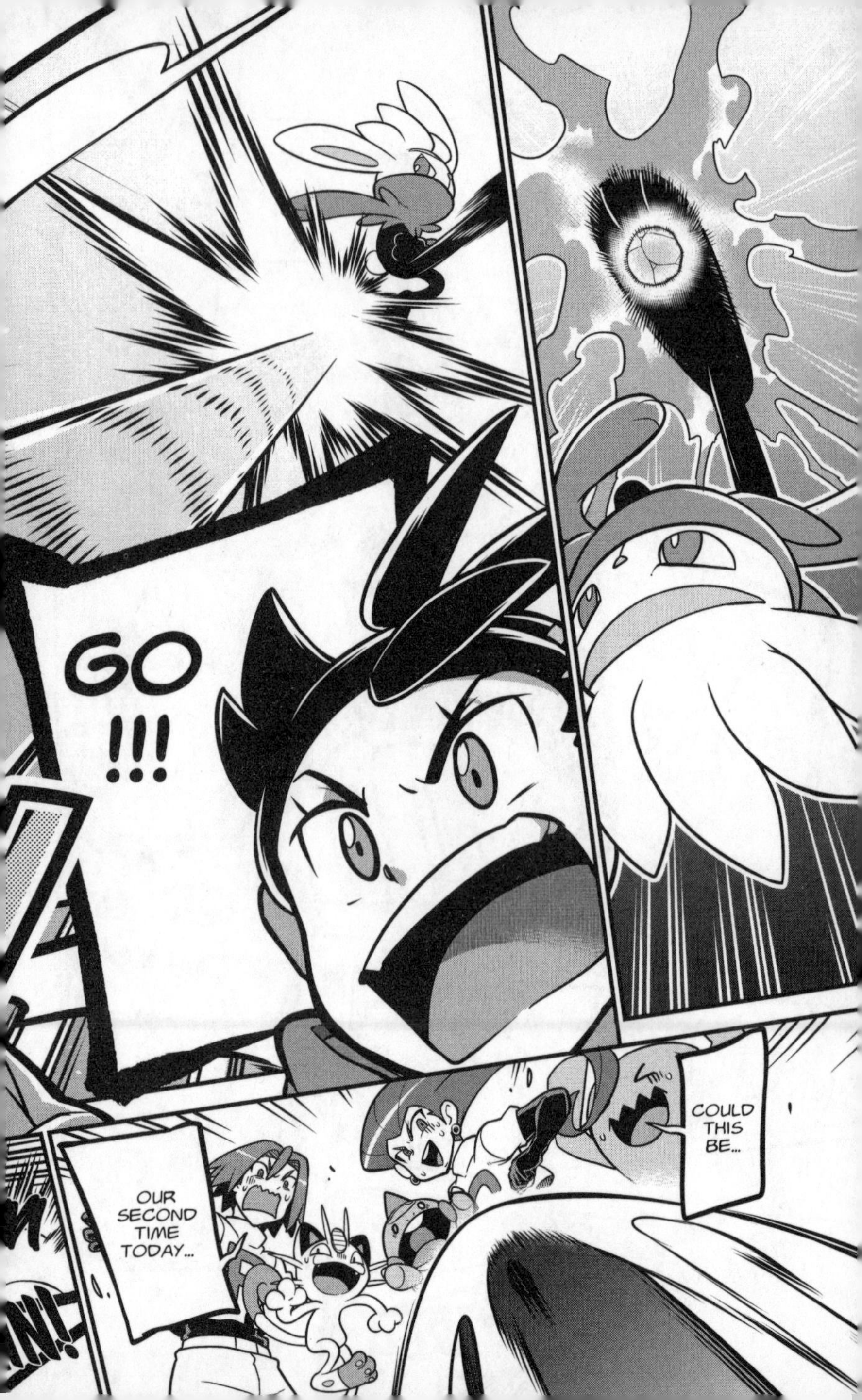
GO !!!
COULD THIS BE...
OUR SECOND TIME TODAY...

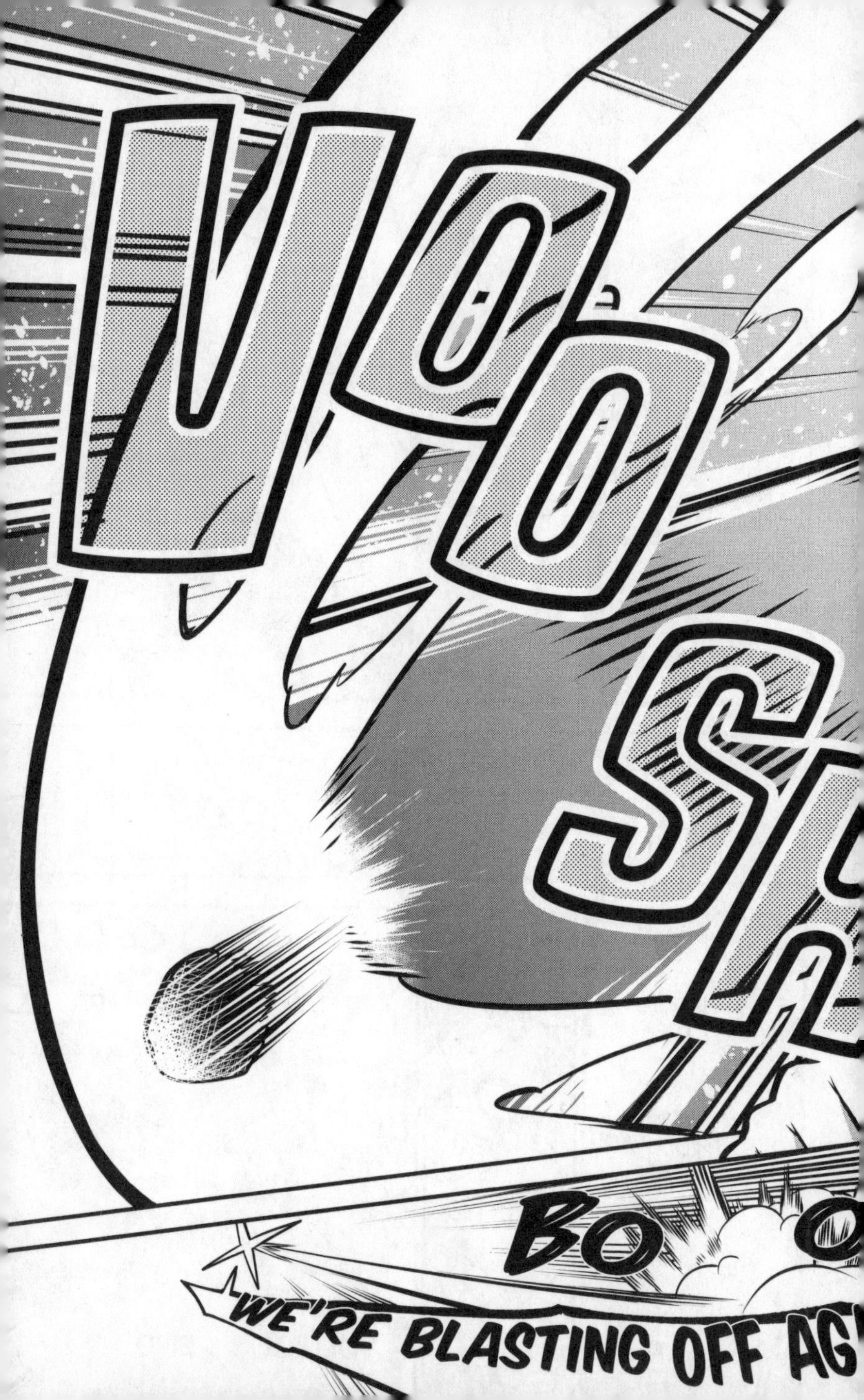
VOOSH
BOO
WE'RE BLASTING OFF AG

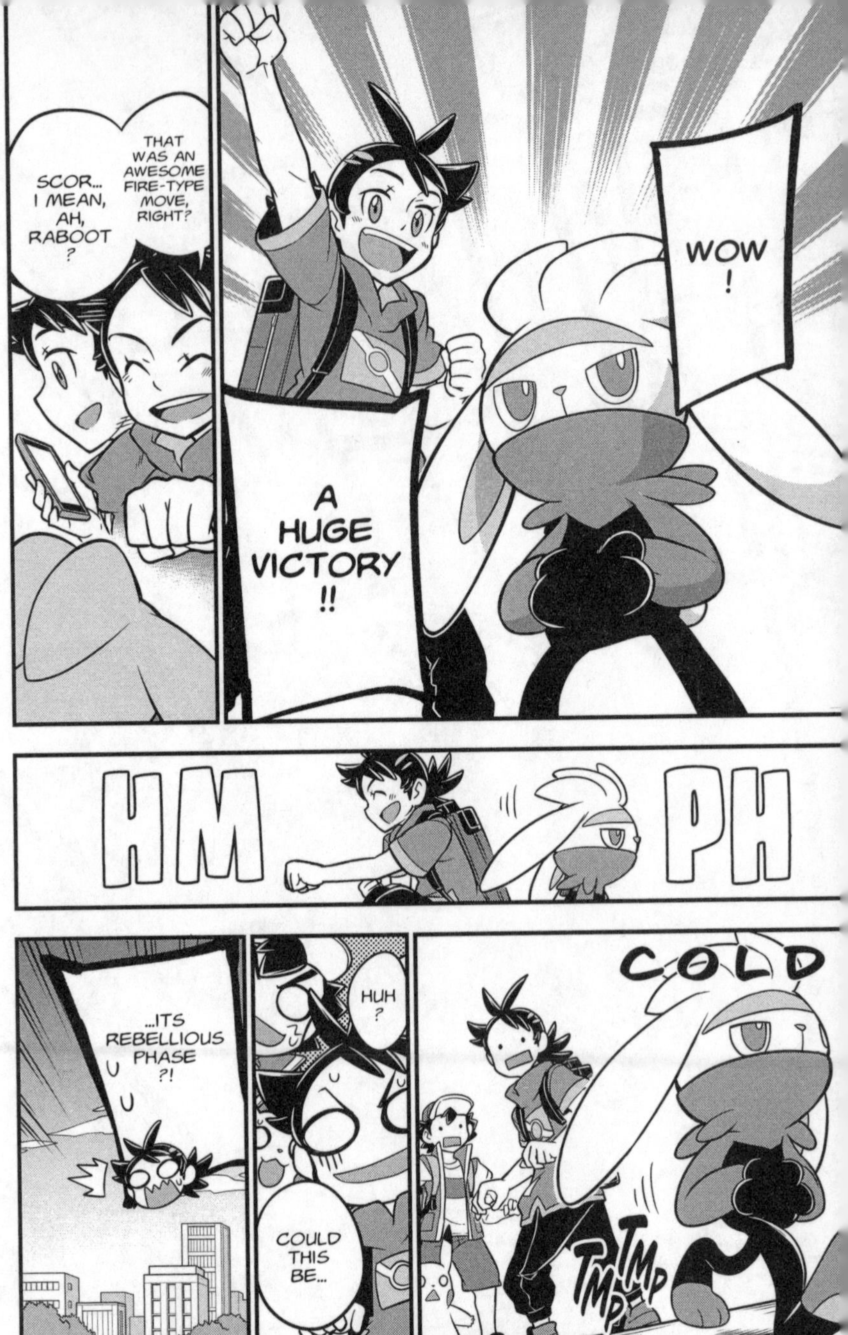
WOW!
A HUGE VICTORY!!
THAT WAS AN AWESOME FIRE-TYPE MOVE, RIGHT?
SCOR... I MEAN, AH, RABOOT?
HMPH
COLD
TMP TMP
HUH?
COULD THIS BE...
...ITS REBELLIOUS PHASE?!

Pokémon Journeys – VOLUME 1 – END

Message From
MACHITO GOMI

Ash wants to become a Pokémon
Master with his partner Pikachu!
Goh and Scorbunny are determined
to catch one of every Pokémon!
New encounters, new challenges...
It's time to explore a new world
of Pokémon!

Machito Gomi was born in Tokyo on March
12, 1992. He won the Effort Award in the
February 2013 Manga College competition.
He is also the creator of *Bakejo! Youkai
Jogakuen e Youkoso* (Bakejo! Welcome to
Yokai Girls' School) and *Pokémon: Mewtwo
Strikes Back—Evolution*.

Volume 1
VIZ Media Edition

STORY AND ART BY
MACHITO GOMI

SCRIPT BY
SHOJI YONEMURA, DEKO AKAO & JUNICHI FUJISAKI

Translation **Misa 'Japanese Ammo'**
English Adaptation **Molly Tanzer**
Touch-Up & Lettering **Joanna Estep**
Design **Kam Li**
Editor **Joel Enos**

©2021 Pokémon.
©1995–2020 Nintendo / Creatures Inc. / GAME FREAK inc.
TM, ®, and character names are trademarks of Nintendo.
POCKET MONSTERS – SATOSHI TO GOH NO MONOGATARI! – Vol. 1
by Machito GOMI
Script by Shoji Yonemura, Deko Akao & Junichi Fujisaki
© 2020 Machito GOMI
All rights reserved.
Original Japanese edition published by SHOGAKUKAN.
English translation rights in the United States of America, Canada, the United
Kingdom, Ireland, Australia and New Zealand arranged with SHOGAKUKAN.

Original Cover Design/Plus One

Printed in the U.S.A.

Published by VIZ Media, LLC
P.O. Box 77010
San Francisco, CA 94107

10 9 8 7 6 5 4 3 2 1
First printing, November 2021

PARENTAL ADVISORY
POKÉMON JOURNEYS is
rated A and is suitable for
readers of all ages.

POCKET COMICS

STORY & ART BY **SANTA HARUKAZE**

BLACK & WHITE

LEGENDARY POKÉMON

X•Y

A Pokémon pocket-sized book chock-full of four-panel gags, Pokémon trivia and fun quizzes based on the characters you know and love!

viz media
www.viz.com

POKÉMON

MEWTWO
STRIKES BACK
E V O L U T I O N

Story and Art by Machito Gomi

Original Concept by Satoshi Tajiri
Supervised by Tsunekazu Ishihara
Script by Takeshi Shudo

A manga adventure inspired by the hit Pokémon movie!

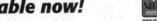

Pokémon
HORIZON
SUN & MOON

Akira's summer vacation in the Alola region heats up when he befriends a Rockruff with a mysterious gemstone. Together, Akira hopes they can achieve his newfound dream of becoming a Pokémon Trainer and master the amazing Z-Move. But first, Akira needs to pass a test to earn a Trainer Passport. This becomes more difficult when Rockruff gets kidnapped! And then Team Kings shows up with—you guessed it—evil plans for world domination!

Story & Art
TENYA YABUNO

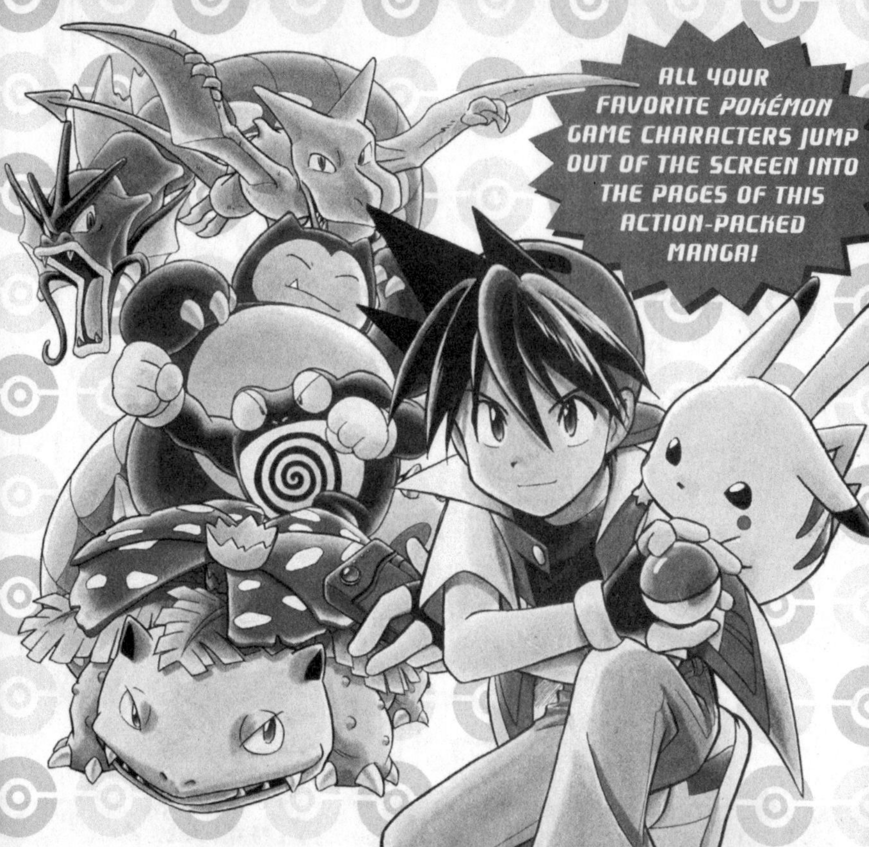
ALL YOUR FAVORITE *POKÉMON* GAME CHARACTERS JUMP OUT OF THE SCREEN INTO THE PAGES OF THIS ACTION-PACKED MANGA!

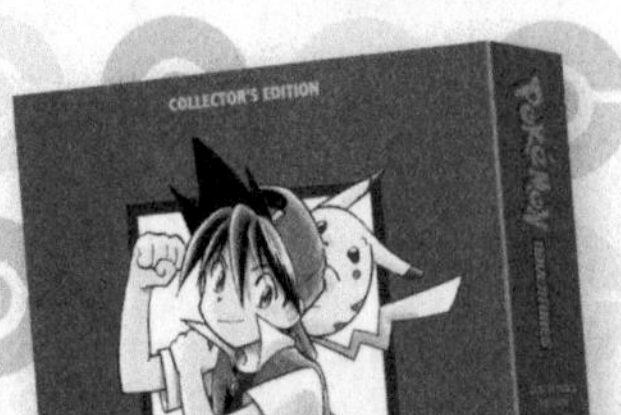
COLLECTOR'S EDITION
POKéMON
ADVENTURES
01
Story by HIDENORI KUSAKA Art by MATO
VIZ

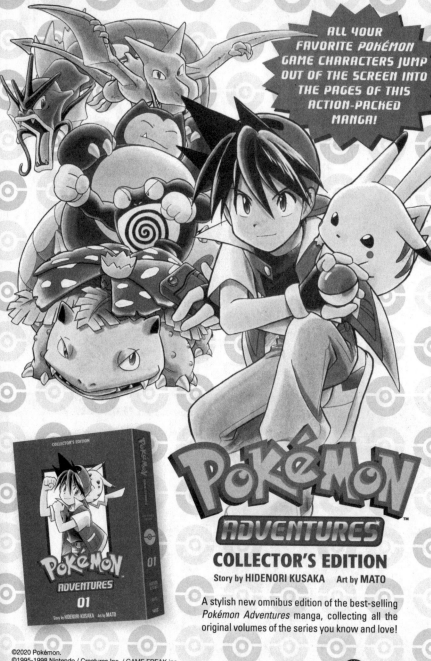

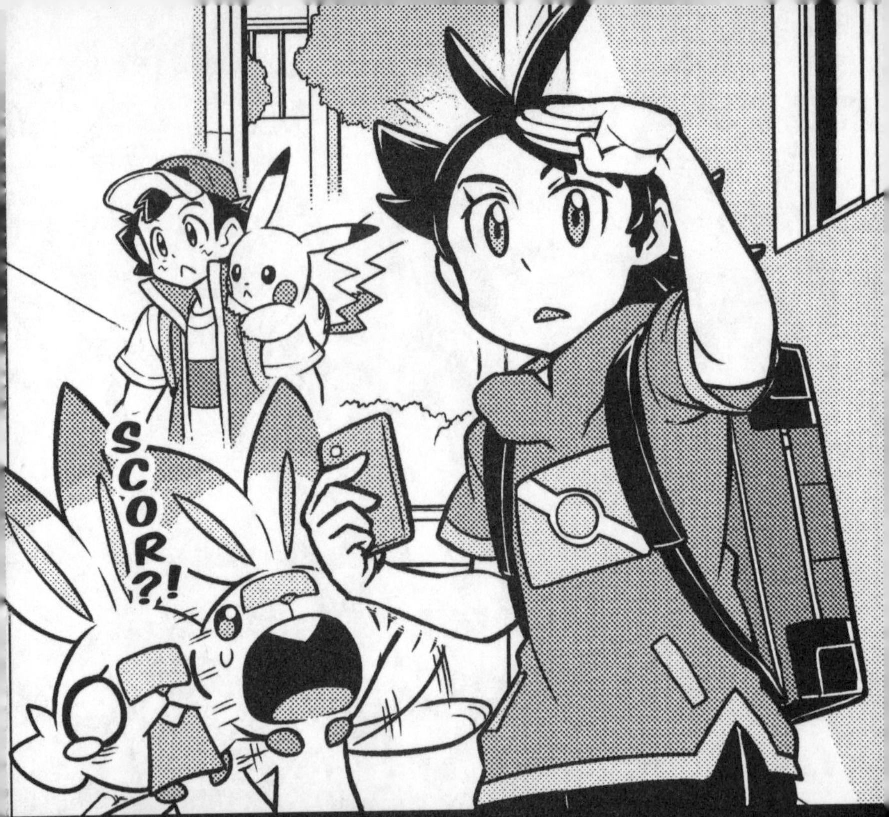
SCOR?!

THIS IS THE END OF THIS GRAPHIC NOVEL!

To properly enjoy this VIZ Media graphic novel, please turn it around and begin reading from right to left.

This book has been printed in the original Japanese format in order to preserve the orientation of the original artwork.

Have fun with it!

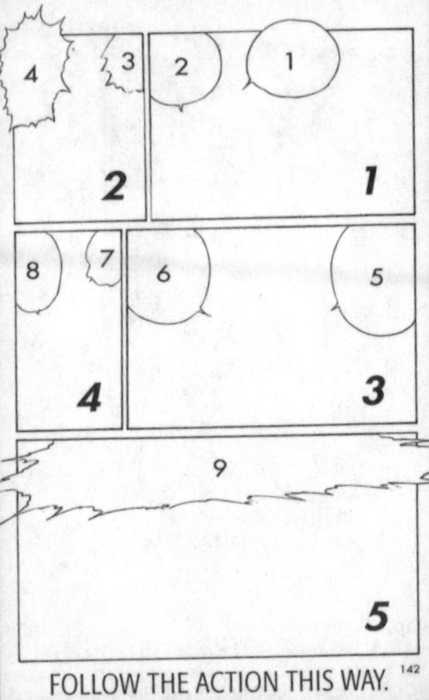
1
2
3
4
5
6
7
8
9

FOLLOW THE ACTION THIS WAY.